Night Shot

Nina DeGraff

First paperback edition June 2024

Cover and interior text design by Nina C. DeGraff
Starry night full moon cover photo: OHishiapply/shutterstock.com
Front cover trees; back cover corn stalks photo: Nina C. DeGraff

ISBN 979-8-9888-3693-3 (paperback)
ISBN 979-8-9888-3694-0 (ebook)

Round Pond Publishing, LLC
54 State Street, Suite 804 #9162
Albany, NY 12207

www.roundpondpublishing.com

For Joe

With special thanks
to Edwin, Nellie,
Isabella, and John

1

"Raymond, if you're up there listening, I could use some help down here," I said, driving through the dark of night, high beams on.

I didn't have anything fancy in mind. I would settle for a convenience store or a gas station, any place where I could ask for directions. By the look of things, everyone except me was either fast asleep or watching TV in Little Edge, Maine at 8:45 p.m. As I crested a hill that overlooked the next few miles, all I saw up ahead was a whole lot more of what lay behind me: dark woods, autumn cornfields, and moonlit ponds.

"Perfect, Alison. Way to follow through on a plan," I said, propping my forehead against my left hand, elbow on the windowsill.

It had taken a half hour to race from my father's farm to the village of Little Edge, and fifteen precious minutes to get lost, backtrack, and then *really* get lost after going through a badly marked fork. How can a person not get lost when the lanes divide and the sign is tipped to one side, suggesting that Miller Road heads off toward the Big Dipper?

At last, my phone rang. I grabbed it from the cupholder, praying that Theodore Lurman was returning my calls. "Hello?"

"How did your interview go today?" my best friend said above the sound of clinking dishes. Arlene was no doubt cleaning up after having a nice, wholesome dinner with her husband and three toddlers in an upscale suburb of Boston, where I would still be living if I had any sense at all. "Did the editor hire you, or—?"

"That's not important right now. I'm lost on a back road."

"God, not again."

"Yes, again, and I can't talk long. I have a crisis to sort out."

"God, not again."

I sighed. "Hang on."

I was already turned around. Who knew what would happen if I tried to talk and drive at the same time. A few birches amidst the gnarled oaks and tall old pines shone in the bright glare of my headlights as I pulled to the shoulder next to a logging trail. The tires crackled over fallen leaves, releasing their sweet scent into the September air.

"Arlene, I've had it with the Bergleys," I said of the cousins who'd been upending my life for seven long, grueling months. "Charlotte and Tyler will never see me as family. No more cutting them slack."

"You realize I've heard this before …"

"While I was in Portland today, Charlotte and a guy named Theodore Lurman dropped by and basically stole two of my lambs," I pressed on. "If I'm too late, it's going to be *really* bad because they won't be Pinkie and Pablo anymore. They'll be cube steaks and kebabs."

The sound of clinking dishes stopped.

"This Lurman guy is a butcher?" Arlene said.

"Yup, he's a butcher, and he's not answering his phone," I said. "My father's map showing local contacts has let me down. I found the place he circled, but it's an old ruin. Burned to the ground. My cell signal keeps dropping out, so I'm left to look for Mr. Lurman's truck. It's big and white, with some sort of dancing pig logo on both sides."

"Ok, maybe he's a good guy," Arlene allowed. "You never know. But what if he *enjoys* his work a little too much? He smiles at you, all agreeable, then he goes nuts and comes at you with a cleaver."

I stared heavenward. "Dire imagery. Just what I need."

"Would it be so bad to get kebabs?" she said meekly.

"Arlene."

"You've eaten a zillion at our house."

"Yes, well, I don't know about any other sheep in the world, but my guys have personalities. You've met them. They're like people."

Arlene sighed, clicked her tongue, and sighed again. I was no stranger to these sounds. When confronted with my problems, which tended to be of the unimaginable variety, people were often at a loss for words.

"By the way," I said. "The editor of *Coast & Candle* magazine loved my rural life photographs. He hinted at hiring me on a freelance basis, possibly this week. It's a game changer. In fact—"

"Great news, but let's stick to tonight," Arlene said. "With Charlotte in the picture, hollering to get her own way, you won't trust the butcher to do the right thing. What then? It's not like you can pop the lambs into your car. They're huge now. A hundred pounds each."

"More like eighty."

Arlene paused. "That *is* your plan?"

"If all else fails. It's not a big deal."

"Sonny, you can't … I mean there's the carpeting to think about, and the upholstery …" More sighs and clicks came over the line.

"I'll deal with it," I assured her. "As for the idea of anyone coming at me with a cleaver, believe me, I'm permanently on guard."

Not long ago, I was happy to approach new connections with assurance and optimism. Then on one awful night, my trust was shredded by the worst of the worst. Liars. Murderers. People who could smile at you one minute, and put you in the ground the next.

Hence, it suited me fine if the butcher wasn't home when I arrived. I owned the lambs. End of story, so I would use oatmeal cookies to coax, trick, or, if necessary, shove Pinkie and Pablo into my car. They would tussle with each other all the way home, and head-butt the back of my seat. At least it would unfold in the dark of night. Nobody would witness the spectacle, and I could be vague on how I'd gotten it done.

I still couldn't believe my father's map showing local contacts had let me down. I glared at the ungainly expanse of paper that I'd unfolded and turned around and tossed aside so many times that it now looked like a huge origami bird. It glared at me in return.

"Describe where you are," Arlene said. "I'll pinpoint you on my app."

"It's dark. There are trees."

"Come on, I want to help."

With a roll of eyes, I ate a cookie while she tossed out random landmarks *near* Little Edge, but nothing *in* Little Edge, which framed my predicament far better than my protests would have done. A tough choice needed to be made. Offering assurances at top speed I indicated my intention to hang up and resume my search.

"You can't leave me hanging!" Arlene hollered.

"I'll call you tomorrow," I promised.

I pulled from the logging trail onto the road. Within a mile the dark fringe of trees on either side of the lane parted, revealing the cloudy, moonlit sky. Once in a while my headlights flashed against the windows of a house or gathered in the eyes of cows grazing in the darkness beyond stone walls, but for the most part, the world had been reduced to gloomy forests and cornfields. Every mile looked the same.

"Charlotte Bergley, you will pay for this," I seethed, picturing her in one of her Sunday dresses. "You want a feud? All right. It's *on.*"

Yes, if you wanted to get technical about it, I'd nodded when she'd said something about taking two lambs at some point, but that was back in February when I was in shock from inheriting a farm out of the blue. If Charlotte had any decency at all, she would have asked the polite questions that were a normal part of a transfer of ownership: "Is today a good day for me to pick up the lambs? Which ones are you willing to part with? And by the way, did you know I'm planning to eat them?"

Admittedly, I'd let a skewed pattern of interaction unfold, starting with the moment my cousins had shown up to gather mementos from the farm. It felt rushed and wrong, but how could I say no? They'd known my biological father, Raymond French, all their lives. Until I'd read his private journals, and grasped the deep bond we might have known if the whims of fate had allowed it, I'd felt like a trespasser in his house.

Charlotte couldn't have agreed more, having hoped to inherit the farm herself, and her notion of what constituted a memento was fairly broad. China, silver, appliances, antiques — anything of significant value had been tossed in boxes and ushered out the kitchen door. If she could have collapsed the buildings into a neat pile and rolled up the fields like a colossal board game, she would have carted them off, too.

4

Closing in on nine o'clock, I had to stop dwelling on anything but getting unlost. The dark lane stretched out in frustrating mystery, and the painted "Darlene's Daycare" sign on my right warned that even if I truly was on Miller Road, Rigg's Brook Farm would not be set off in neon. Hungry and tired, I suppressed a yawn that made my eyes water, liquifying the inky countryside up ahead. I opened the window to let in a current of bracing air, turned on the radio, and pressed the seek button until I landed on a song with a female empowerment theme. A woman wronged. Out for revenge. Playing by her own rules. Perfect.

When I looked up a man was lurching out of the cornfield up ahead on my right, directly into the bright glare of my headlights. With a startled yelp, I hit the brake and skidded to a halt. Some twenty feet away, he squinted against the high beams, hollering and holding up a small black bag. I couldn't hear him above the music. He had an average build but looked big enough to overpower me at five foot four. Talking through his teeth as if in anger, insanity, or both, he moved toward my car.

Clumsy from panic, I wrenched the gear into reverse, and then as my foot missed the gas the car bucked and stalled — a lurching, molar-rattling hop across a yard of pavement. The man quickened his pace, still talking, and now clenching his fist. Whatever he was hollering about, he looked dead set on blaming the whole thing on me.

I fumbled with the keys, unable to tear my gaze from the approaching nut. Should I dive out of my car and run? Scream? I had no breath to do anything as the man dropped to his knees in front of my car. I reached for the gear to reverse away, then pulled hard on the emergency brake instead. The last thing I needed was to make the wrong move and hit him.

"Step away!" I shouted, finally shutting off the music.

I felt the slight movement of the car as he used my front fender to get back on his feet. His head and shoulders appeared. He looked confused and unsteady, squinting against the headlights, then he staggered backwards a yard or two and collapsed out of sight.

"Right in the middle of the road," I said. "Drunken idiot."

"Please," he hoarsely rasped. "Help me …"

I closed my eyes, wishing there was someone to whom I could make the same request. If, say, God happened to be listening, I wouldn't mind encountering one problem at a time, instead of a string of fiascoes.

I called 911 and found the line sketchy.

"My name is Alison Littlefield," I said to the dispatcher. "I'm in my car, and I think I'm on Miller Road—"

"Ma'am?" she interrupted. "Can you repeat the …" The rest of her words were lost.

"I'm on Miller Road either in or just outside of Little Edge," I said. "At least that's where I was heading before—"

"… possible … better location?"

"No, I'm stuck."

She said something, then "… emergency?"

"*Yes*. A drunk is here, asking for help. Like I said, I'm more or less in the village of Little Edge, heading north. Or maybe west."

By the time I hung up, the stranger's efforts to stand had grown weak. As deranged as he'd appeared, I hadn't considered the possibility that he might be ill or injured, desperate to get help, rather than angry. Maybe, like me, he'd had trouble getting through to 911.

I held my breath and listened to the sad scrape of his shoes on the pavement, his quiet groans, and unintelligible rantings. What if his flailing limbs landed in the opposite lane? Another car might come over the rise behind me and not swerve in time to miss him.

"So much for getting my own problems resolved," I muttered, leaving the headlights on and the emergency flashers engaged.

As I stepped out, a breeze swished through the cornfield and rattled a speed limit sign down the road. The moon had slipped behind the passing clouds, brightening their edges, and turning their centers slate blue. Tense and alert as I neared the collapsed stranger, I stopped in my tracks when his hand shot toward me and flapped like a pale bird.

"*Guuhhh*…" He gave a gurgling drawn-out moan as he lay on his back a couple of yards in front of my car. "Uhhh … hi …"

"Yes, hello," I said.

"*Hiiide* …"

"Oh ... hide?" I swung around and searched the darkness for any sign of sudden movement or other indication that I needed to duck back into my car. Sketchy glimpses of the cornfield appeared and disappeared, bathed in red as my emergency lights flashed.

"Keep fr'm," he managed.

"Can you get up by yourself?" I said.

"Don't ... let 'em ... *uhhh* ..."

His weak rantings had me checking the darkness again and again. The wind swished through the cornstalks. Was that a snapping sound I heard? Someone out there, getting closer? Were the stalks parting on my left?

"*Guuhhh* ..."

For a moment the man was silent. I turned back to him.

His eyes were closed, his mouth open. He wore tailored gray slacks and a disheveled pinstriped shirt. Up close, I saw raw bruises on his chin and brow, and blood on his nose. Maybe he'd gone off the road or had been in a fight. But where had he come from? I didn't see porch lights indicating any houses were nearby. The narrow lane some distance behind my car could be a muddy farm road, for all I knew.

I knelt and shook the man's shoulder. "Hello? Sir?"

His face was a ghastly gray. My skin felt electrified as my mind spun back to a man who'd died in front of me a few months ago. The victim on that awful night had looked this same way: an unmistakable, riveting, gut-wrenching, deathly kind of pale. I touched the man's neck, and couldn't find a pulse, or even any warmth. Impossible. He'd just been staggering on the road, hollering things, and trying to get back on his feet. He'd *spoken* less than a minute ago. I checked again. And again. Nothing.

He was dead.

2

"This can't be happening," I said decisively into the night air. "This can *not* be happening."

I was wrong. It was happening.

I gripped my forehead and closed my eyes, trying to remember how to do CPR: mouth to mouth, alternating with chest compressions.

The man's lips were so slack and chilly that I balked at first, and then I forced myself to press on. With my eyes squeezed shut I gripped his nostrils and exhaled into his mouth, startled by the taste of mint. He'd brushed his teeth, stumbled outside across a cornfield, and then died as abruptly as someone turning off a light. How? Why?

Kneeling, I pushed against his chest and counted out a sequence. Air popped and gurgled through his larynx, as if he'd inhaled water, and a dark, oily puddle seeped out from under his back, glistening on the pavement. Alarm prickled through my skin at the same pace: slowly, deliberately. Moths flew in circles around the headlights, making the world surreal and my own hands remote as I struggled to lift his shoulder. There, under his torn shirt, were two round, bloody wounds.

I stared in shock and tried to focus my whirling thoughts. In a yellow necktie that had gone askew, he looked ordinary. Early thirties, average build. A black jewelry bag was beside him. I have no idea why I picked it up. A few items rattled together. Rings? Coins? I tucked it under his hand, following an impulse to reassure him that his possessions were safe, and cringed at the feel of his lifeless fingers.

My gaze took in his neat haircut and striped shirt. His polished shoes and creased trousers. He smelled of a light aftershave, as if his evening had involved a night on the town. I reached toward the sticky puddle and then stopped myself. I wasn't thinking straight. Not at all. So much blood. It was clear the man had either been stabbed, or shot …

I jerked upright and stared into the darkness beyond the stark swath of illumination my car's headlights cast down the road. What was I thinking, sitting there in the open? I lurched to my feet, stumbled to my car, and climbed inside. With the door closed and locked I turned off the lights and stared into the night. The corn plants looked alien, an army of haggard figures. Stirred by breezes, their arms lifted, as if beckoning to me. Beyond the field was a stand of trees, huddled and dark.

I reached for my phone, poised to call 911 with an update, and then I heard the rush of a vehicle coming up behind me. The headlights shone over the crest of the hill, moving fast. Desperate for a helping hand, I was about to open my door when the sedan swept around my car, pulling a gust of wind through the corn stalks and scattering gravel in its wake. I caught a glimpse of the driver's scowl as he blared his horn.

"Hey!" I shouted.

Didn't he see the dead man sprawled out in front of my car?

Of course not. My lights were off.

It was a miracle my car hadn't been rear-ended. Yet headlights might attract the killer. Clutching my phone, I grasped the downside of having another garbled back-and-forth with 911. Walking to another spot was out of the question. I couldn't risk being in the open.

I hesitated as the area around me came alive with ghostly flickers, the cornfield and roadside winking in and out of existence. Blue strobe lights abruptly pulsed in my rear window as a state police cruiser came toward me over the rise. Was the trooper chasing the speeder? No, his siren was off as if he were listening for voices or odd sounds, not sure what to expect. Maybe the 911 dispatcher had heard me after all.

Numb and rattled, I waited while he parked behind me and stepped out with his serious-looking hat in hand. He snugged it on as he walked toward me, instilling a sense of calm. Judging from his silhouette, he had the long, wedge-shaped physique I'd always associated with Superman: strong enough to launch off the ground, yet not so brawny that he'd have trouble with wind shear and turbulence.

He leaned down and held his flashlight at an angle so the edge of the beam illuminated my face. "Sonny? You called 911?"

Squinting, thrown that he knew my nickname, I saw him in split-second glimpses as the strobe lights flashed. First his blue uniform, then his neck, then his face. I held my breath, my heart thudding fast. If the trooper I'd met four months ago had a doppelganger, this guy would be him. The Dan Bolton I'd gotten to know in May had worn plain clothes, with wavy hair and a beard. He'd smelled of cocoa butter when we'd made contact of any kind. We'd made contact quite a lot.

This trooper was clean-shaven but had the same expressive brown eyes and a terrific smile. It wasn't a doppelganger. It was *him*.

Our last interaction was a scorching kiss that nearly convinced him to not head to the Canadian border to complete an undercover assignment. No texts or calls. That was the level of secrecy the case had demanded. We hadn't talked to each other, or seen each other for four months, but judging from the way his gaze reflected intensity and warmth, it took milliseconds for our mutual attraction to flame to life.

The heady, wonderful moment was bound to end.

"What's got you stuck out here?" Dan said.

"You're not going to believe it. There's a man on the road. A stranger. It's not my fault. I tried to help him. But he's dead."

Straightening in surprise, Dan walked around the fender and looked down. "Sonny, turn on your flashers and headlights," he said, reaching for his radio and reporting in without missing a beat.

I did as he instructed, then the night seemed all the more bizarre, the cornfield awash with blue light one second, and red the next, with moths spinning in the swath of illuminated pavement stretching beyond the front hood of my car. Dan's shadow was distorted and long as he walked around the victim and knelt. Now only his hat was visible. Feeling as if I'd been pumped full of helium, I climbed out and joined him.

"Do you know the victim?" Dan said.

"No. He came from over there." I pointed to the roadside shoulder up ahead on the right. "He staggered twenty feet or so and collapsed. He got back up and topped backward. I couldn't find a pulse so I tried to do CPR. I stopped when all that blood came out."

Holding his fingers against the man's neck, Dan blew out a breath and gravely shook his head. "Did he say anything?"

"Just a few garbled words."

For a second, Dan assessed the man's clothes, the pool of blood and the jewelry bag, taking in every detail, and then he unfurled to a little over six feet. His hat, steel blue uniform, and gun belt studded with gadgets made him an imposing sight. If I were a murderer, I would certainly run in the other direction. I wanted to run toward him.

"Wait in your car while I take a look around," he said, gently ushering me away from the body. "I'll be back in a second."

I retreated, sort of. The further away Dan got, the more insecure I felt, so I stepped forward again and stood near the fender where I could follow his progress. His flashlight swept the area in all directions. He followed a blood trail to the point where the man had staggered into view, and then Dan's light illuminated a path of broken stalks in the cornfield and reflected against the windows of a house beyond a line of trees some hundred yards away. Most of what Dan reported in his radio exchange was scattered by night breezes, but I heard, "Gunshot wounds ... K-9 unit."

His voice was a calming influence in the night air, and then my gaze landed on the victim sprawled on the pavement, his eyes blank and lifeless under the stars and lustrous moon. I swayed, tumbling back to the night in May when I'd begged a wounded man to hang on until help arrived. With his hand gripped in mine, I'd hollered, "I'm sorry to be yelling but you need to focus! I mean it. Don't you dare quit on me!"

To no avail.

Staring at the stranger lying face-up on the pavement, I felt the full weight of letting him down in the last moments of his life, his desperate pleas unheard. In the coming days, there would be notifications. Loved ones collapsing in shock. Questions with no answers. Nothing would resolve the heartbreak. The agony of loss would remain.

"Sonny ..."

Dan's hand gripped my elbow, pulling my gaze to his intense brown eyes. "You've had a shock," he said amidst the police codes crackling over his radio. "EMTs are on the way. Do you need to sit down?"

"No, I'm good. I'm ok."

"I know it's tough, but I need to get up to speed fast." He guided me away to his cruiser. "Quick version of why you're out here?"

"I was trying to find Theodore Lurman's farm. My father's old map showed where he lived, but all I found was a burned ruin."

"That's where Theo and his family used to live," Dan said. "Animal activists torched his place if I remember correctly."

As a car approached, Dan stepped away and stopped it with his light. The driver opened his window and stared down at the body.

"Jesus, that's Richard Gartland."

"Are you a neighbor?" Dan asked.

"No, but I know he lives there." The man pointed a grimy finger toward the house Dan's light had illuminated through the trees. "He and his wife moved up from Boston three, four years ago. Bought land from old Mrs. What's Her Name. Caused a huge fuss because Ian McDonnell and his sons wanted to extend their gravel pit. Damn, would you look at that mess. He must've bled out every drop."

"You're the one who passed me," I said, recognizing his car. "You sped by, even though I was stuck in the middle of the road."

"I had to get cash for my card game lickety-split." Nodding toward me, he asked Dan, "She kill the poor bastard? Lover's quarrel?"

"She's a good Samaritan who stopped to help. Pull onto the shoulder, and stay in your vehicle," Dan instructed the sedan driver.

"I'm due back at the poker game," the man complained.

"Park there. Get out your license and registration." Dan crossed back to me with a roll of eyes over the man's priorities. "Sonny, I'll need to see your paperwork, too," he added.

I fetched the documents and handed them over.

"Up to date," Dan said. "That's good."

"I know you need to set up flares, etcetera."

"Before I do, the victim gave out more or less where he is?" Dan said. "Your car wasn't rolling? There was no contact?"

"Not even close. I engaged the hand brake first thing. He used my fender to get back on his feet, then he fell backward."

"I did see your hand brake engaged."

"It's good to see you," I blurted.

"Same here, Sonny."

With a nod, Dan started to step away, then he paused and rubbed his brow with a faced-with-the-unexpected sort of squint that launched the phantom dimples around his mouth. I acknowledged his silent message with a similar twist of eyebrows. A crime scene was not an ideal way for us to meet again. Like other aspects of my life, it was off the charts.

"Back to Mr. Gartland," I said. "He was shot?"

"From what I could see. It's not for sure."

"The wounds were on his back," I said. "That tends to indicate that he was trying to escape. Then what? He waited until the killer was distracted, maybe? It's awful to contemplate."

"It's best to not picture it, Sonny."

"Why I'm out here is kind of a nightmare," I said.

"Your cousins took one of your sheep to Theo's place?" he guessed.

"Two sheep," I said. "I was there when they were born."

"We'll sort it out." Dan gave my arm a bolstering squeeze. "Wait on the shoulder. I'll be back to take your statement in a bit."

He looked calm and deliberate in his actions as he crossed around his cruiser to open the trunk and set up flares around the scene.

I was the opposite in every respect: chilly, distracted, mildly nauseous. Nothing to do but think of the death notification I'd weathered seven months ago on a cold day in February. One minute I was working for a Boston design firm, had some savings, and believed my father was Donald Littlefield III, who'd died when I was ten. The next minute a lawyer called to inform me that I'd inherited a thirty-acre farm in the town of Gracious, Maine, with a strawberry field, a flock of sheep, and a Belgian draft horse.

"You're mistaken in calling me," I'd said with a pang of regret.

Imagine, owning a strawberry farm in rural Maine. It sounded quaint. I'd vacationed in Maine many times in my twenty-eight years.

"Are you the daughter of Evelyn Littlefield, formerly Evelyn Grand of Newton, Massachusetts, daughter of Beverly and Roland Grand?"

My reverie had shriveled into apprehension. "Yes …"

"There are documents indicating Raymond French is your biological father. He and his late wife, Ella, never had children, so aside from two cousins who get items of sentimental value, you're his heir."

I'd known my mother was a sophomore at Wellesley College when she'd married Donald, who was older than her by a decade, but I never imagined the story went beyond hints of an unexpected pregnancy out of wedlock. I had yet to figure out how she'd met Raymond. Local gossips seemed to think it had to do with a basketball tournament.

Maybe it wasn't polite to march into my mother's mini-mansion in Newton and demand an explanation in front of her bridge club.

"We need to talk about Mr. French," I'd said, hands on hips, blowing a stray curl out of my eyes. Only a few weeks before I'd finally found a hairstylist who could tame my unruly mop into manageable layers, and I'd been feeling pretty good about life. "*Raymond* French, who happens to have blue eyes, just like mine?"

She'd paused with her pillar-of-ice, win-at-all-costs bridge club smile intact. "I'm sorry darling, this isn't a good time to break."

"You've heard how she's carried on all this time," I'd babbled to the startled card players after I'd wrenched her secret out of hiding. "'Alison, you have Donald's eye for art! Donald's smile!' Lies! All lies!"

"You were a magnet for turmoil as a child," she'd protested. "What kind of mother would add to that? But go ahead and follow your curiosity. Get all your questions answered. See how you like country life."

Don't try to play reverse psychology with Evelyn Littlefield. Just back away with your eyes squeezed shut and your plans held up as shields.

If there was a bright note to be gleaned from the tumultuous revelation, I'd finally grasped why the man who'd provided my last name had been bent on crushing my dreams and annihilating my self-worth from my earliest days. Either my mother had confessed to Donald that she was carrying another man's child, or he'd figured it out.

I'd attended Raymond's memorial service in a daze, unable to grasp his existence while his friends tried to comprehend his death. His job as a game warden involved conducting rescues, enforcing wildlife laws, and patrolling the deep woods in all manner of foul weather. He was a champion marksman and a Maine Guide. There was scarcely a skill he hadn't mastered or a tool he didn't know how to use, yet even with all his experience and know-how, a mishap during a simple chore had ended his life. A moment of inattention, people said. That's all it took.

After the service, I'd visited Raymond's farm for the first time and stared at his coffee mug on the table where he'd left it half-finished. From his pipe and his boots to his plaid shirts and his tacklebox, every possession in the house had greeted me in impossible silence. A journal he'd left in the kitchen led me to seventeen others on a shelf in his bedroom. In a lively hand, he'd kept track of his cases as a game warden, his progress with the farm, and more than once, he'd written about me.

He'd had no idea that I existed until he'd bumped into my mother and me in Camden, Maine when I was ten.

Seeing Sonny's face turned my legs to sawdust, he'd written. *She was the spitting image of my sister, Olivia, when she was that age.*

Raymond had convinced my mother to admit the truth to him right then and there on the street of quaint shops. Getting her to accept that he wanted a role in my life was another matter entirely.

For a detached moment, the past seven months tumbled through my mind. In the next heartbeat, I was back to the present moment, where I was scraping by on the money I'd raised from the strawberry field, plus freelance work from my Boston ties. Country life was more difficult than I'd expected. Not impossible, or unenjoyable. Just difficult.

In the five minutes since Dan had stepped away, he'd set out flares and was now instructing a group of local firefighters to assemble roadblocks in both directions some distance down the road. One of them was a heavyset man who appeared to have important information to share, based on the way he emphatically used his hands to make a point.

Anxiety had my stomach churning. Pacing with my arms folded against the chilly autumn air, I crossed to a patch of white along the roadside beyond Dan's cruiser. While he was busy conducting the complexities of maintaining law and order, I might as well serve as a boon to society as well and pick up the litter someone had left there.

I reached for what I'd thought was a tattered bag, but as the object winked into view on and off in the strobe lights, I realized it was a cat that must have gotten run over some time ago, its throat reduced to a horror show of bones and matted hair. The eye sockets were empty, the teeth in a grimace, sparking a vivid memory of the human skeleton hand that I'd had the misfortune to pick up and examine back in May.

I would never forget how the strung-together fingers had smelled. Sour and rancid, reeking of death and decay. Tonight, I'd touched Richard Gartland's chilly, lifeless fingers just moments after his blood had pumped straight from his beating heart onto the pavement.

I stumbled away through the swirling lights and doubled over with dry heaves until stars streaked behind my eyes. Dimly, I heard footfalls jogging toward me and then I felt a hand settle onto my back.

"Deep breaths," Dan said. "I'm sorry, Sonny. I know this is a lot." To one side, he called out, "Theo, is there a blanket in your kit?"

Dan's palm was warm, lightly resting between my shoulder blades as a reassurance and stabilizing presence, but no force on earth was up to the task of keeping me aligned as I endeavored to straighten. I swayed, with the cornfield moving in circles around my head.

"Uh oh," I managed, and then the world went dark.

3

Out in the country, if you stand very still, you can hear the rain coming a moment before it arrives. As the drops hit the leaves of trees a hundred or more yards away, the sound is reminiscent of someone inhaling through their teeth. It grows in intensity, often with a breath of wind, rolling toward you in a rush like an ocean wave. For a split second you see the downpour coming — a sheer, glistening wall — then the drumming riff of countless drops hitting the ground sets the world into motion.

A similar sound filled my head as I became aware of the gritty road under my butt, a fixed point in the swirling darkness. In the distance sirens wailed, getting closer, and somewhere nearby a dog barked five times, paused, and then repeated the pattern, nonstop.

A voice floated above me: "That was a good catch, Dan, landing her without harm. I think the dead cat over there is to blame."

"Theo, it's not a good idea for you to be here."

"Miss Littlefield left a half dozen voicemail messages. When I heard her name over the scanner, I couldn't help but worry."

"Why didn't you return her calls?" Dan said.

"Well, Mrs. Bergley left a half dozen messages as well. I figured with a hen fight in the wings, I wanted to wait until morning."

Hearing my cousin's name, I forced my eyelids to open and stirred within the snug warmth of Dan's arms. He'd managed to gently land me in a sitting position, his uniform brightening every other second as the blue strobes on his parked police cruiser pulsed.

"Take it slow," Dan cautioned, helping me sit on my own. His shoes rasped on the pavement as he shifted his knees to give me room.

Still dizzy, I stared at the heavyset man looming over us. "Are you Mr. Lurman? The, umm, butcher? Am I too late?"

"The lambs are fine," he said. "I didn't know there was a dispute."

"They're pets. I want them back."

"Theo," Dan said, "I think you'll find that Miss Littlefield is the rightful owner of the lambs. For now, it's best if you head home. Someone will stop by to take your statement and verify the chain of voicemail messages you received. Don't delete them."

"And please don't harm the lambs," I added.

"They'll be fine," Theo said. "We'll talk tomorrow."

I sagged with relief as the burly, fortyish man stepped away with a slight limp. I looked forward to assuring Arlene that Mr. Lurman wasn't the least bit sinister. In blue overalls speckled with paint, he looked to be a hardworking farmer, willing to handle very tough work.

"Thank you for sorting that out," I said.

"No problem. Hang on."

Dan spoke into his radio as another police cruiser arrived and turned into the lane I'd seen down the road. Flares sputtered nearby, and moths flew in dizzy circles here and there across the eerie scene.

"Mr. Lurman was right," I said. "The dead cat got to me."

Dan nodded. "I figured."

Staring at him, I said, "Sorry, I'm still adjusting to the …" I motioned up and down, indicating Dan's short hair and lack of a beard, his face newly revealed. "And the …" I realized anyone looking on would imagine I was taking it upon myself to bless him because my right hand was now moving sideways to indicate his uniform.

Dan cracked a smile. "You never liked the beard."

"That's not true. I just wondered how you'd look naked. In the *face* area," I added. "Without the beard. When did you get back?"

"A few weeks ago, give or take. I've had to acclimate and adjust," Dan explained while I slowly processed the timing. "From day shift to night, etcetera. It throws a wrench in your circadian rhythms."

"Oh, that's why ... never mind," I managed as I looked away.

His earnestness had a dangerous absorbency, drawing words out of my mouth before they'd been cleared by my head. My heart took over, lurching instead of beating in a normal pattern. What was the *real* reason he hadn't reached out when he'd first gotten back?

"Do you want to talk about it?" Dan said.

"Us?"

"No. Finding the victim. It had to be tough."

"Very." I instructed myself to delay dying inside until I was home, with maybe a shot of tequila in hand. "At first, I didn't know what to think. I started performing CPR, but then—" A vine of alarm curled around my stomach and tightened. "What if he was still alive at that point? Pushing on his chest could have made him bleed faster."

"I would have tried CPR, too," Dan said.

The approaching sirens blared full force and strobe lights crested the rise behind us, all but pushing back the night. Cars and vans peeled away in a mysterious, pre-arranged order, some parking nearby, and others turning down the driveway for the house beyond the trees. Squinting against the glare, I was able to glimpse the swath of broken cornstalks that indicated Richard Gartland's torturous journey to the road — a hundred or more yards of staggering, falling, getting up, pushing on.

"The EMTs will want to take a look at you," Dan said.

Reaching to help as I lurched to my feet, he smelled of soap or a light aftershave. A clean fragrance. Subtle. Once the world stopped whirling, thanks to Dan's steady grip, I found myself at eye level with the top buttons of his uniform. My gaze climbed up to meet his soulful brown eyes, as had happened when we'd kissed back in May.

"I'm sorry," I said. "This is all really ..."

"It's a shock to the system," Dan agreed. "Listen, there was a point in time when the Gartlands lodged a series of complaints about farm-related noise and odors. In the wake of Mr. Lurman's house and barn burning down a few years back, Theo looked to the Gartlands for blame. He threw in the towel on rebuilding. With all that in mind …"

"The *butcher* had a motive to murder Richard?"

"It will be looked into," Dan said. "Given the gravity of the crime, we need to tighten down all the facts. In advance of coming to the scene, the lead detective has asked if you're willing to let us search your vehicle."

I gaped. "Why in the world …?"

"It's not unusual, Sonny. If all goes well, you'll be thankful for it later on. You can exit the situation with less need for follow-up."

"I supposed it makes sense."

"I'll get the search of your car underway and make sure it's done by the book, then I'll loop back to take your statement," Dan said. "You like coffee, as I recall. Black, with sugar, right?"

"Yes. Coffee will help."

He guided me to a fire and rescue van and exchanged a few words with an EMT. Now that I was facing the scene from a distance, it held my gaze. For the officers, confronting a dead body was a routine. As they walked alongside the road, measuring, verifying facts, and talking solemnly, the sight of Richard Gartland lying on the pavement jarred me all over again. I'd let him down during his last moments on Earth. What had he been hollering? What had driven him across the cornfield?

"Miss Littlefield?" the EMT prompted. "Any bumps or sore spots?"

I focused on him. "No, I'm ok."

"Dan says coffee will help," he said, handing me a steaming cup.

I nodded, eager for the heat it brought to my hands. The coffee was strong for my taste, but strong fitted the occasion.

"I'll need a shot of whiskey if Stable Bartlett is about to show up," I said of my father's notoriously irascible best friend.

"He's away on a training stint," the EMT said. "So don't worry, Stable won't be growling at you. Not this week, anyway."

"Thank God."

Our discussion was interrupted by a commotion at the roadblock beyond Richard Gartland's driveway. With the headlights of a car behind them, the gathered onlookers were reduced to silhouettes, but I recognized the voice of the man who was doing the hollering.

"I got information, damn it," Greg McDonnell exclaimed, waving his hands for emphasis. "A guy tore through our field on an ATV earlier. Somebody needs to check out the tracks."

"Settle down," a trooper said, adding a further remark I couldn't hear.

"Yeah, I had a couple of beers, what of it?" Greg hollered, turning to the others who'd gathered nearby. "Do you people see this? I'm a concerned citizen trying to get justice, and they're harassing me!"

The EMT and I exchanged a glance over the irony of Greg complaining about not getting justice. He'd blazed a path of trouble in the area from kindergarten to the present. My father had gone after him for poaching, illegal harvesting, and other crimes. Greg had known better than to retaliate against Raymond, but he'd made up for lost time by harassing me. His brother, Keith, was a bearlike figure looming in the darkness. I'd heard that Greg bullied his sibling mercilessly, and though Keith had a gentle side, he would comply with any order Greg gave.

Most of the people who'd gathered near the roadblock looked ordinary enough, but one man in dark clothes caught my eye, his intense gaze illuminated by the blue strobes. As if seeing me staring his way, he turned and melted into the night, but didn't go far. His cell phone winked on, bathing his hand with light. He was making a call.

"Are you deaf?" Greg was hollering. "There was an ATV!"

I folded my arms and turned away in the hope of not being spotted.

"Do you need a blanket?" the EMT said.

"No thanks, I'm all set." I glanced toward the house beyond the trees as the sharp wail of an ambulance blared to life. "What's going on?"

"Richard's wife got knocked around."

"Oh no …"

The half-dozen officers searching the yard beyond the cornfield and trees were silhouettes, their flashlights combing the ground.

The search for evidence is more absorbing than just about any task I've tackled in law enforcement, my father had written in one of his journals. *It's the only way I know of to wrestle down the despair of arriving too late.*

4

"You and Dan have history, right?" the EMT said.

"History is apparently the way to put it," I said under my breath.

"Now, don't be thinking Dan asked for the look-through," he cautioned, indicating the officers who'd been tasked with inspecting my car's interior. "That's Bricker's doing."

I frowned. "Who is Bricker?"

"You'll find out soon enough," he said. "You were worried about Stable Bartlett's cantankerous attitude? Detective Bricker is worse."

"Great," I said dismally.

"Anyway, I've heard things got dicey up north."

"The story of my life," I murmured.

The paramedic meant well. I only heard half of what he was saying.

As promised, Dan stayed on point as the evidence response team confirmed there was nothing of relevance inside my car. I understood why he directed them to photograph my father's map: it was the reason I'd gotten lost. A colleague joined him as he opened the folds and studied the names, circles, and cryptic notations my father had written on the map. The colleague chuckled, probably wondering why a supposedly vibrant young woman would use a relic to get from point A to point B.

"So, how bad was it?" the EMT said, eyeing me.

"Two gunshot wounds, I think."

"No *shit?*"

I paused. "I figured you'd know."

"It's all locked down. Hush-hush."

"The body is right over there," I said slowly. "In plain view."

"Sorry, our signals got crossed," the EMT said. "I was talking about the business up north. Hang on, I'm being prompted by the team at the primary scene."

I was busy trying to look unreadable whenever Dan glanced at me and our gazes briefly met. He'd thrown together an excuse for not reaching out, a way to avoid confessing that he'd lost interest while he was away on a special undercover assignment. My love life never unfolded as hoped, but this time, I felt trashed and confused. Unable to comprehend how my feelings could have held fast, while his were gone.

"Wow, that's cold," the EMT said, as if reading my thoughts, then seeing my puzzled frown, he added, "The chatter from the primary crime scene. They're saying a couple of knife cuts might've been conversation openers. Whoever is behind Richard's death meant business. Opened the safe. Knocked the wife around."

I wilted internally, wishing I'd heard what Richard had said as he'd staggered toward me, his hand outstretched as he beseeched me to help him carry out a last wish. I decided the way his mouth moved was consistent with him saying, "It's important …" In my mind's eye, I also pictured him saying a word that began with an 'f.' Some mention of his father, maybe? I vowed to figure it out and do right by him, somehow.

"I'm seeing genetics at work," the EMT said, smiling and indicating he was talking about me. "It's true what folks say, how much you're like Raymond. The keen stare and signs of assessing details at a crime scene. You know he was a trooper for a while."

"*What?*" I said. "Nobody told me that."

"It only lasted a year. He was geared for the outdoors, so he ditched the grind and became a game warden. *But*, the penchant for solving crimes had taken hold so he involved himself in cases beyond his duties all the time. Irritated the heck out of cops now and then, but I'll be darned if he didn't come up with clues nobody else saw."

"Thank you for telling me."

"If you're all set, I'll leave you to it."

I shook hands with him, truly grateful for his insights.

I collected myself as Dan approached, determined to deliver a clipped statement, and then wish him well and be on my way.

Dan's smile warmed the night. "Feeling better?"

"Yes. The coffee helped."

As I launched into my account, I didn't delve into theories I couldn't support. I stuck to the facts as I described my night.

"You're doing great," Dan said, writing notes as I talked.

With an effort, I averted my gaze from his excellent penmanship and the way his uniform defined his physique. Dan asked me to confirm that I'd never met the victim before, the time of his death, and specifics on why I was on the road. I sketched out my interview with *Coast & Candle* magazine that afternoon, partly to inform Dan that I had plenty of sway in the world and an exciting life, and also to explain why I was away when Charlotte and Mr. Lurman had taken the lambs.

"You know the rest," I said. "Theo confirmed that I'd called."

"Why come out here, if he didn't appear to be home?" Dan said.

"It was a dire situation. He's a butcher."

Dan studied me, watching and waiting as if he'd guessed that my plan had a few flaws. The urge to fill the silence pulled at me, the way the sight of a sheer drop is at once alluring and alarming. I tried to draw back from the impulse but slipped ever closer to the edge.

"If Mr. Lurman hadn't shown up?" Dan prodded.

"One would want to secure the lambs, of course."

"With a note, or …?"

"A note might have worked. Something heartfelt."

I'd leaned over the precipice. Now I felt giddy.

"Sonny …"

"All right, I planned to bring them straight home. I got three ewes in there once. It's not as hard as it sounds."

Dan looked at me sideways. "By 'in there' you mean …?"

"My car," I said. "A handspinner over in Monmouth bought them. I'd love to have a proper farm vehicle, but my father's truck was sort of …" My hands fluttered. Repossessed was such an ugly word.

"So, you … used your Volvo," Dan said.

"To bring the ewes to Monmouth," I agreed. "They barely obstructed my view while I was driving, if that's what you're thinking."

Judging from Dan's expression, that was the least of what he'd been thinking. I stifled the impulse to say that I'd washed the ewes first. He was smart enough to know how long it had taken for them to dry off, given that the average sheep wears roughly twenty-five pounds of absorbent wool. They were damp when I'd loaded them into my car — *very* damp — but the Volvo was back to normal inside a week.

Dan looked startled as I went from being a backpedaling idiot to the one who was setting the pace. I'd read my father's accounts of investigations and knew what kind of details were important.

"You saw my father's map," I said with a wave toward my car. "Mr. Lurman's name is written next to a circle indicating where he's supposed to live. Trust me, I won't be using the map anymore. This is the umpteenth time Raymond's notations have steered me wrong."

"It's not a map of friends and contacts," Dan said. "Your father's notes appear to indicate crime scenes. He circled the location where Theo's farm used to be, for instance. Before his house burned down."

"The map shows *crime* locations?" I said. "That explains a lot."

Dan hesitated. "Why? Which places have you checked out?"

At one house, a guy had growled "Who sent you?" through a darkened window and I was fairly certain I'd heard a shotgun snapping shut.

"Sonny?" Dan prompted.

"It's not your concern," I said. "Thank you for setting me straight."

Dan studied me with a frown as if it was just sinking in that my demeanor had changed significantly after our initial back-and-forth. With folded arms, I fashioned what I hoped was a neutral expression. I was eager to complete my statement and head home.

"Ok," he said. "Logic says the jewelry bag would have ended up on the road. It was tucked under Mr. Gartland's fingers when I arrived."

"I picked it up in a state of shock."

"Did you open the jewelry bag?" Dan said. "Look inside?"

"No, of course not."

"Why tuck it into his hand?"

"To comfort him. I know that sounds ridiculous."

"No, I understand," Dan said, glancing to his right as an officer in plain clothes arrived to assess Richard's body. "Detective Bricker might have further questions. You know the drill."

"Unfortunately, I do."

"Let's recap," Dan said, holding my gaze. "Earlier today your cousin took two lambs out of a misunderstanding, not a theft. You see them as pets, so you felt it was important to check on their welfare. Make sure they were properly housed, with food and water. You were concerned enough to head straight here. *Very* concerned."

"Yes, and I was—"

Abruptly halted by Dan's pointed gaze and the expressive twist of his eyebrows, I understood that his succinct encapsulation would serve me well. He was saying to keep it tight. Keep it logical.

And just in time.

He'd no sooner closed his notebook when the detective signaled that Dan was needed near my car. In a crewcut, looking to be in his forties, Bricker scowled as Dan updated him, then with an air of impatience, he cut things off and they headed toward me.

After introducing us, Dan said, "He'll be in charge of the case. I've brought him up to speed. He'll take it from here."

I straightened my backbone under the detective's severe gaze. The hand he extended was chilly, his grip unnecessarily hard.

"So," he began. "What's your connection to the Gartlands?"

"I don't have a connection. I didn't know Richard."

"You call him Richard like you do know him."

"Someone mentioned his name."

"You're from Boston. Richard is from Boston."

Hearing the gist of the detective's remarks, Dan frowned and retraced his steps. He stood nearby and looked attentive with folded arms.

"The population of Boston is six hundred and fifty thousand people, give or take," I said. "Obviously, I haven't met them all."

"You know the stats off the top of your head?" Bricker said.

"Apparently I do." I paused and said with irritation, "Maybe you think I'm not capable of rattling off facts because I'm a woman."

Dan lifted his hat and rubbed his head, then set it back down, his gaze saying: *Stick to the facts. Don't let him throw you off.*

"Not at all," Bricker said. "Let's talk about the jewelry bag. I understand you picked it up and looked inside. I know I'd be curious."

Dan hesitated, staring at him. "That's not—"

The detective signaled that he should keep quiet.

"I didn't look inside," I said. "I picked it up, then I put it down."

"Under Mr. Gartland's hand," Bricker pointed out. "You tucked it there, thinking we wouldn't catch onto the fact that you'd handled a critical piece of evidence. I get why you did that."

"I did not open the bag."

"Why tuck it under the victim's hand?"

"Out of shock. I couldn't believe he was dead."

Bricker studied me. "Were you aware that Mr. Gartland hired a PI?"

"How would I know that? I never met him."

"I ran a quick check," he said. "You're unemployed, short on cash."

"Your information is outdated. I had a good strawberry season, and have a steady flow of income from freelance work."

"Bits and pieces."

"Maybe in your eyes. In my rush to help the victim, I left my phone in my car. I'd like to have it in hand before we continue."

"To call an attorney?" Bricker said.

"To record your approach. It's a very effective tool these days."

"All right, settle down."

"Settle *down?*" I demanded.

Having grown up in the Littlefield residence, with a man who'd regretted whatever deal he'd made to accept me as his daughter, and who'd missed no chance to blast me every day, I couldn't hear the two words without bristling to the full extent my temper allowed.

Dan slapped the back of his neck, then apologized when we turned to look at him. "Warm night," he said. "A mosquito bit me."

"How about you help at the primary scene?" Bricker said.

"Yes, Sir." Dan pulled one of the deft moves I'd come to know him for last spring, angling forward in a way that caused Bricker to step back. It wasn't aggressive. Just smooth. This allowed Dan to hover near me.

"We'll catch up later," he said softly.

"There's no need," I said, then not wanting to sound impolite, I added, "Maybe at some point if you have time. I know you're busy."

"What are you doing, Bolton?" the detective said.

"You're new, so you might not know Miss Littlefield played a role in cracking four related murders," Dan said. "She stayed calm while SWAT moved in. Showed courage under fire. She has a lot of fans."

With a scowl, Bricker watched Dan step away. Perhaps it was lost on him that other officers were grumbling about his approach.

"Courage under fire, huh?" Bricker said.

"Do your research. When can I head home?"

The harsh lights of the strobes added stark definition to his frown lines and gray eyes, a portrait I would want to photograph in an alternate reality where his suspicion and severe assessment weren't directed at me.

"When can I head home?" I slowly repeated.

"I find it useful to study folks when their attention is trained elsewhere. From start to finish, you were evasive during your statement, your gaze on the pavement or staring into the night."

"That was from—" I closed my eyes, blushing to my hairline at the prospect of admitting why I'd averted my gaze from Dan. "It was from shock," I said. "I'm sure you understand."

"A half-truth. You think I'm a novice at this?"

"I'm happy to cooperate. What more do you need?"

"I'm glad you asked. I need to have you frisked."

I paused. *"What?"*

"You claim to want to cooperate."

"I called 911, performed CPR, saw that the victim had been *murdered,* but I stayed to be sure his body didn't get run over by a car."

"I've got reasonable grounds," Bricker said. "You interfered with evidence and showed furtive behavior. When asked some standard questions, you demonstrated a combative attitude."

"Because you goaded me."

"Reacting is a choice. Didn't your mama teach you that?"

I clamped down on the impulse to seethe out loud that my mother hadn't taught me one blasted useful thing. "If I refuse?"

"I'll bump a request up the chain."

I glared at his unfeeling gaze, sensing that he grasped my concern over the ubiquitous presence of police scanners in many households in rural Maine. If he put the request over the airwaves, every gossip in town would imagine the worst. Then again, they were already having a field day at my expense. Escaping the scene fast was all I cared about.

"If that's what it takes," I said. "*Not* by you. Pick anyone else. I trust they'll do the job without transferring negative energy."

"No worries in that regard."

He motioned for a female trooper to step forward. For the first time in my life, I was instructed to assume the wide, arms-out stance necessary for a body search. Dan looked on with an expression of outrage and started toward us until two colleagues held him in check.

I waved off his concern, wishing he would stop giving in to sympathy. *Just exit my life and get on with it*, I silently hollered.

"I'm sorry," the female trooper whispered.

"Just proceed. I'm ok with it."

Her hands covered the bases. My shoulders and arms. My chest to be sure my bra was free of hidden objects. I blinked, desperate to keep tears from welling in my eyes. She told me to take off my shoes and stand on the hard, gritty pavement. With Bricker circling us to get an unobstructed view, I clenched my teeth as the trooper patted down my back pockets. My ass, for crying out loud. My thighs. My calves and ankles. I was afraid Bricker would ask me to unzip my jeans in front of a half dozen men to check my underwear, but he stopped short of it.

Shaking, wiping away tears, I didn't look at Dan. Didn't want him to know how crushed and humiliated I felt. This wasn't how I'd expected our first meeting to unfold after a four-month absence. It was tough to stay rational. The notion that Donald Littlefield was coming at me from the grave had been with me since childhood. I'd shoved it from my mind again and again, but at times like this, I lost the fight.

"Can I go now?" I managed.

"If you think of anything else …" Bricker held out a business card.

"No need. I'll remember you without it."

"Suit yourself."

I bit back a harsh final comment.

Given the late hour, I heard Dan appointing a deputy to shadow my car until I got home. I pushed his worried gaze and all else from my mind as I eased my car past the roadblock and onlookers, especially when the sedan driver pointed at me and hollered the words that I'd grown used to hearing ever since I'd moved to Maine: "There she is!"

With a groan, I shielded my face and drove on.

* * *

The deputy helped me find the right roads with signals and flicks of his headlights. I waved when I reached familiar territory, but apparently, Dan had given strict instructions. My escort stayed put and turned behind me into my driveway. Our headlights swept along the pines that bordered the winding, lightless road, and then illuminated the steep hillside, the tires rumbling over loose gravel and stones as we drove past the strawberry field on my right. The long rows that were golden during the day were now silvered by moonlight, curving westward around the slope into the darkness. On my left, a split-rail fence and remnants of a fieldstone wall bordered the driveway. Beyond it, the ground curved downward to the spot where my sheep were grazing. Dodge, my father's Belgian draft horse, was a broad silhouette outlined by the flickering water of Cold Stone Stream, his tail swishing away the last mosquitoes of the season.

You'd think there would be plenty of room to maneuver a car on thirty acres, but between the gray, ramshackle barn looming straight ahead, the dog pen, the house's front porch steps, and the boulders that bordered a flower bed, it was a challenge allowing the deputy enough room to pull in and turn around. I nicked the porch steps backing up, then surged forward and hit a boulder with a horrible grinding sound.

The deputy's headlights regarded me for a moment, the front grill grinning, and then he backed slowly down the driveway.

Still half suspended on the boulder, I shut off the engine and stepped out into the cool, sweet air. A moonlit vista of woods and rolling fields stretched out beyond the smooth curve of my little hill, the sky ablaze with countless stars. The vast dome was where souls were supposed to exist, free of worldly cares. What about Mr. Gartland? I rubbed a chill from my arms as I pictured his spirit scouring the cornfield like an angry wind, begging for help over and over again. And not getting it.

The spooky image had me tumbling back to another night when the sheep had looked the way they did now, with their curly backs aglow on the moonlit slope. I'd grabbed my camera and set up my tripod.

Night shots can be tricky. Darkness calls for a slow shutter speed that turns moving objects into a blur. I'd experimented with using a flash to capture details at the end of each exposure. In one of the photos, I'd found that Paisley had stood her ground while the rest of the sheep had darted away and blurred into a fluid, ghostly specter in front of the glittering stream. On the right was an unexplained illusion — part shadow, part light. It looked like a man clapping his hands together as if herding the sheep along. Thinking of it gave me goosebumps.

I stepped to the split-rail fence as my friendly ewes headed toward me up the slope with a soft peppering of footfalls. Always eager for treats, Magnolia took the lead and looked up at me with a *bah-ah-ah* reminiscent of a machine gun going off. Woolberry added a breathy murmur befitting her sweet face, pink muzzle, and long white eyelashes.

An indignant bark coming from inside the house reminded me that I now owned a dog. As I headed to the porch, yellow feline eyes reflected the moonlight amidst the weeds near the barn.

"Hey, Effie," I said. "Clear the way. I'm letting Luke out."

The wild tabby's intense glare said she hadn't forgiven me for bringing her to the veterinarian to be neutered. One batch of rambunctious kittens over the summer had convinced me to maintain my father's practice of keeping the cat population in check. I shooed Effie away to avoid trouble once I unleashed the newest resident of the farm.

Luke made fast work of completing his business, and then he returned to the porch for love. A year-old cross between a King Shepherd and a Golden Retriever, with an expressive face and a glorious coat of tan, black, and silver fur, he'd sat right down and looked up at me when I'd toured the rows of cages at the animal shelter a few months ago.

I'm the one, his gaze had said. *You'd be crazy to not pick me.*

Now, with the crime scene in mind, I knelt and hugged him.

"Would you bite someone to save me?" I said.

Luke wagged his tail, his dark eyes shining.

"The veterinarian said you need a diet. You're a tank."

Wag.

Brave, polite, and agreeable — good qualities in a man.

Together, we turned and confronted my house.

In the moonlight, Raymond's weathered colonial looked gray, but was a shade that Arlene was fond of calling: "Christmas cookie green."

I had to ignore my mother's snooty voice in the back of my mind saying that green was not an acceptable color for a house. Her voice got louder as I opened the door and stepped into my orange kitchen, with a vivid blue living room on my right. No wall separated the two areas, with polished maple flooring spanning the two rooms. If stared at for any length of time, the colors tended to vibrate in my peripheral vision, especially if I stopped in the doorway with the green siding in view.

Perhaps my father was color blind, or a long winter of deep snow had gotten to him. One of many mysteries to sort out.

I'd come to cherish his humble furnishings: the braided rug made from strips of wool, the pine coffee table, the plaid couch that still held the scent of Raymond's pipe tobacco, and the iron floor lamps with shades that my stepmother, Ella, had punched with flower-shaped holes to let the light shine through. There was a sturdiness in Raymond's furniture, an aura of strength that kept me going during difficult times.

It was impossible to not feel the weight of the night as I put my bag on the kitchen table where Raymond had eaten his last meal.

It was the same table where I'd desperately tried to find shelter when a murderer had burst in with his fists flying, tossing the chairs aside in his frenzy to capture me. Now and then, I'd wondered if fate would ever land me in a reverse dynamic where a man felt so committed and hooked-in that he tossed chairs aside in order to love me. It had crossed my mind that Dan might be a viable candidate at some point.

"Now you know better," I said dismally.

Checking my phone, I felt a pang of guilt for leaving Arlene to think the worst when her requests for an update were met with silence. Her texts had devolved into near madness over the past few hours:

Did you find the butcher's farm?

Hello, it's been an hour!

And so on until she wrote, *?????? !!!!!!!*

I texted, *All is well. Home now.*

I added hearts and apologies for leaving her hanging.

You're getting coal for Christmas, Arlene texted with a scowl emoji.

I sent more hearts.

After a pause, I got one in return.

When I'd first moved to the farm, I'd slept on the couch most nights, plagued by unease over the unknowns outside in the darkness, and a reluctance to get too cozy in my new life before I developed a clear sense of Raymond. Slowly, I'd pushed myself to sleep upstairs, and just then it was no trouble at all to prioritize a good night's rest.

I climbed the stairs to my east-facing room above the kitchen, where I was greeted by soft pink walls and matching blankets. Raymond and Ella had outfitted the room years ago in anticipation of inviting me to stay "once the dust settled." I felt the power of their hopes through the Breyer horses on the shelves, the nature books, the oak bureaus, and the matching vanity with a carved frame of roses and hearts.

As I threw on a T-shirt and crawled under the comforter, Luke curled up on the braided rug beside the bed. Downstairs was the forest green room where Raymond had wondered about me whenever a storm or other distraction kept him awake for hours on end. Now it was my turn to wonder about him as I confronted the dark of night.

5

The forest was a place of hovering darkness where shimmering, tormented ghosts stirred upward from unmarked graves. With a thudding heart, I stumbled through the trees as the spirits clawed at my ankles and gripped my lower legs.

"Why did you pick up the bag?" Richard Gartland hollered, using his weight to drag me down into the leaves. "Why didn't you *listen?*"

"I'm sorry!" I yelped, waking from the nightmare and sitting up in bed in a swift motion that pulled muscles in my stomach and back.

I collapsed forward and closed my eyes.

"That was bad … holy moly …"

I was shaking and my T-shirt was damp from sweat. After my jarring night at yet another crime scene, I should have known my subconscious mind would be primed to revisit the terror I'd experienced last spring with the added twist of Richard Gartland playing a role.

As always, there was a sharp contrast between the peril and violence of the nightmare and the quiet stillness of my pink bedroom, with its lace curtains. The clock on my bedside table said it was five o'clock in the morning. Falling back asleep would be impossible.

I tuned in on the scrambling sounds of Luke playing in the kitchen. Some time ago he'd left the braided rug next to my bed to pad down the stairs, slurp water from his bowl, and reconnect with his toys. I was lucky to have found a self-motivated dog, and I often felt jealous of his ability to work through issues by chewing a rope toy and tossing it from one end of the room to the other. Maybe I should try releasing tension that way. Get a rope toy of my own. Bite it and growl and shake it into oblivion. Even thinking about that kind of activity made my neck hurt. I would have to stick to brooding and agonizing.

Pushing the comforter aside, I crossed to the bathroom and splashed cold water on my face, then I paused with my eyes closed and my hands gripping the edge of the sink. Would a miracle happen today? Or would the bathtub drain mysteriously clog for the third morning, despite my every effort to fix the problem with a plumber's helper?

I shed my clothes, stepped into the shower, and wound the squeaky old knob to the hottest setting I could tolerate to rid myself of the feel of getting frisked. Within a minute, angry bubbles were gurgling from the drain, and the water slowly rose to claim my ankles.

"Dis moi que c'est une baguette!" I hollered, though baguette was not the correct word for "joke." I'd planned to brush up on my vocabulary in the hope of bantering with Dan, who spoke fluent French.

"No point now," I muttered.

I toweled off and turned to the challenge of blow-drying my mop of curls, cast in gloom over failing Richard Gartland. If I'd acted with speed and clarity, I could have held his hand and urged him to hang on until help arrived. I could have conveyed his last wishes to his family and friends. Instead, Richard's loved ones would be left with gnawing questions and uncertainties — a process I'd come to know all too well.

Not paying attention as I dried my hair was a mistake. With curls mounting a full-blown revolt, I gathered them into a ponytail and returned to my bedroom. Once I'd slipped into jeans and a cotton pullover, I paused to assess the long view beyond a window pane that Charlotte's son, Tyler, had broken. On the far side of the driveway, a few maples and an apple tree shaded the pasture fence, where Dodge was dozing in the first rays of dawn. To my right loomed the ancient gray barn that my father had planned to rebuild. To the left of the gravel driveway some twenty yards away down the hill, the long rows of the strawberry field hugged the slope all the way down to a small area cleared for parking.

On weekdays in June, when he was out on patrol, Raymond had used the honor system in the strawberry field, leaving a scale on a table along with a tin where people left money. He was never robbed. His friends said he was one of those quiet, capable men that even criminals knew not to cross. When he wasn't impressing people, he was calmly going about his chores at home with an array of lethal tools.

He'd left me in charge of a daunting void to fill. With half the town predicting that my attempt to keep the farm would fail, I'd taken a secret delight in defying their dire expectations by using Raymond's journals as instruction manuals, which offered detailed timelines.

April 10: put down fresh straw. I got out the wheelbarrow. *May 29: weed the rows.* I got out trowels and shovels. In June, when the strawberries had ripened, Raymond's friends and regular customers began streaming in. At the end of the first day, I'd looked at the bundle of cash in my hands, thinking, "We earned this money, Raymond and I together."

While I was taking in the view, I recalled the EMT's revelation that my father had worked as a trooper for a year. If Raymond's paper map with circled notations indicated the locations of local crimes, I would need to study it closely with his journals within reach. Out of the ashes of last night had come a potentially engrossing new pastime.

At the moment, with the heavy toll of lost life in mind, I reached for my phone and dialed my mother's number.

She answered right away, "Alison?"

"Yup, it's me."

I pictured her natural auburn hair swept into a chignon. She would be wearing a crisp white shirt and a Talbot's jacket — maybe the red one — with navy slacks and designer slingbacks.

"I'm immobilized by shock," Evelyn finally said. "Arlene told me you were planning to hate me until Christmas."

"I was, but last night—" I straightened. Pinkie and Pablo were still in danger. "Gotta go, Mom. I forgot to do something."

"*What?* You don't call me for three entire months—"

I hung up and punched in the butcher's number.

"Miss Littlefield," Theo said. "I've been expecting your call."

"I want to confirm what we agreed to last night," I said. "I want the lambs to be returned to my farm. Whole, I mean. Alive."

"The thing is, Mrs. Bergley has been a customer for years," Theo said. "I'd prefer if you can iron it out between yourselves."

"I'll talk to her. In the meantime, please don't harm the lambs."

"The voicemails Mrs. Bergley left last night were hot-tempered," he said. "She'll be in a pickle if anything happens to you. Here I am regretting the things I said to Richard when our farm burned down."

"That must have been, umm …"

"We've all done it, haven't we?" Theo said. "Threaten somebody in the heat of a bad moment. It wasn't only buildings that went up in flames. We lost heirlooms and mementos that can't be replaced. But it was activists, from what the police pieced together. Folks from away stirring up trouble. Never caught. It stings, but you learn to move on."

"You were on good terms with Richard lately?"

"Oh, yes," Mr. Lurman said. "All it took was a compromise. Less hen manure on the cornfield from my end. Less complaining from their end. Richard came over now and again for a turkey or a nice roast. Liked to set a good table, he and Angela. Not lately, come to think of it. They'd barely raised the framing on their garage when Richard called a halt to construction. It's sat there like a skeleton for months."

"It's easy to get behind," I said.

"That was my thought. I can't see a man like Richard getting too far in the hole. Used to work for a big firm down in Boston, where you're from. Beech and something. Imagine leaving the rat race behind, only to end up with an awful tragedy like this." Mr. Lurman blew out a weary breath. "So, back to Mrs. Bergley's lambs—"

"*My* lambs," I insisted.

"I'm asking if you're up to the challenge of handling them," he said. "Come to find out one of the feisty buggers is still intact."

"The veterinarian lost track during the neutering process," I explained. "Pinkie has top bloodlines, so I'm hoping to sell him as a ram."

"I can put the word out for you."

"That would be great," I said.

Theo promised to return the lambs when he got the chance, with the caveat that he would need to charge me "a bit" if they caused any damage. If I knew Pinkie, I would be buying Mr. Lurman a new barn.

After we ended the call, I picked up a photo of Raymond looking relaxed in his game warden's uniform as he leaned against the railing of a cabin. Beside him loomed a bear he'd rescued when it was a cub. Now "Cookie" was living at a preserve in Northern Maine.

Once again, I wrestled with the need to find some way to make peace with my mother. Her lapses of judgment had inflicted damage. Coming to grips with the toll was a daily exercise. In the end, it came down to the understanding that pain was mixed in with her reasons for not telling me the truth. Right there, in Raymond's face, were factors she'd woken up to every day. Even with the crow's feet around his eyes and the furrows that had carved into his brow from years of weathering, it was clear that my face had been shaped by Raymond's share of my DNA.

He'd certainly known the connection in an instant. After I'd read his journal entry about bumping into my mother and me in Camden when I was ten, I'd honed in on the day he was talking about.

I conjured the memory of quaint shops and blue sky, the cool, salt-smelling harbor. A man recognized my mother and said hello. He held my hand for a second, staring down at me. Afterward, he and my mother had a heated exchange while I peered into shop windows.

I remembered shaking a stranger's hand. Not Raymond's hand.

As a photographer, I'd built my life around the adage that a picture could tell a thousand words. Now, as I studied photos of my father on my bedroom bureau, I found the idea to be thoroughly lacking.

6

On my way down the stairs to the kitchen, my cell phone rang in my hand. I crossed through a warm mote of morning light and opened a cabinet to confront my narrow options. Week-old bread, which would be passable if I toasted it. That morning, toast wouldn't cut it.

I picked up the call. "Hello?"

"What is the matter with you, calling out of the blue and then hanging up with no explanation?" my mother demanded.

The indignant lecture that followed was lost in a hiss of interference as I put a scoop of food in Luke's bowl.

"A local man died last night," I explained, easing her into the news as I pulled a slice of cheesecake from the refrigerator. In between bites, I told my tale, leaving out the cause of Richard's death. Her sighs and murmurs indicated that she'd known my life would come to no good in Maine. She was silent as I wondered what had sparked the crime, and what might have been stolen. It had to be something valuable …

"Good Lord, not again," my mother said.

"I know, it's bizarre after what happened in May."

"I see your flair for understatement is still intact," she said tartly. "You were *kidnapped* by a madman in the dark of night. I couldn't keep track of the story Arlene conveyed. Skeleton parts, shallow graves, a hooker who was teaching you elements of the sex trade—"

"Her name is Nadine, and she's teaching me the very difficult sport of pole dancing," I said. "Think gymnastics."

"You've always had an unnatural curiosity."

"Here we go," I said tiredly.

"I beg your pardon, is this not the daughter who threw away a promising future to live in a stranger's house?"

"We didn't have to be strangers. Raymond wanted to know me."

"When could I have sprung such shocking news on you?" my mother demanded. "During your existentialist phase in high school? The summer you dressed in black and kept quoting Emily Dickinson?"

"Those are excuses, and you know it."

"Hold on darling, I'm watching the television."

I gaped. "This is so typical of how you operate—" Hearing a reporter saying Richard's name in the broadcast, I sat forward in the chair. "They're covering Mr. Gartland's death on the Boston station?"

"Apparently, he used to work for Beech and Grossman in the financial district. You know, the company where a shady accountant was arrested some years ago for … good Lord, you didn't tell me the victim was shot in the back. You found a *murdered* man?"

"The village where it happened is miles away," I assured her. "I have a good network of friends, plus I got a dog a few months ago."

"A dog? You know I'm allergic to dogs."

I rolled my eyes. My mother's definition of an allergy was rather broad. Instead of sneezing and itchy eyes, her symptoms ranged from condemning sniffs to chilly stares.

"Stop rolling your eyes," my mother prompted.

"It's entirely warranted. You'll use any excuse to keep from coming to Maine. You don't want to face the scandal."

"Nonsense."

"Oops, I'm rolling my eyes again."

"You *know* how much I detest displays of emotion," she said. "But you made a gesture in calling me this morning. With that in mind …" She sighed, then softly went on, "You think I regretted my affair with Raymond. When you were born, it was all I could do to not reach out and thank him for giving me such a beautiful child."

I blinked, shocked to hear her say this. A lump that was part cheese-cake, and part emotion kept me silent as she talked about Raymond.

"There was a charming air of decency about your father," she said in a wistful tone. "Don't get me wrong. He was a terrible flirt and *far* too attractive for his own good. How do you think I got into my situation? I had an understanding with Donald at the time."

As always, I found myself biting back the hard truth of how life had unfolded for me under Donald Littlefield's roof. The times I'd heard him ranting in their bedroom: "It's intolerable. I feel cheated. It's her. Where she came from." At six years old, I'd figured it was only a matter of time before his baleful attitude toward me ended with my being cast out. I'd decided I had to be smart and excel in school. I'd focused on building skills that would help me get by once I was on my own.

"I almost told you the truth," my mother said. "You were so much like Raymond. Bold and inquisitive. I was afraid he would steal you away."

"Oh, Mom."

"I was right." She sniffled and blew her nose. "There you are, hundreds of miles from home, with Raymond's awful relatives. They had the nerve to demand that I stop having fresh flowers put on his grave."

"Don't worry, they're mostly harmless."

At least, I'd invested in hoping so. Among the items my father had allotted to Charlotte and the rest of the Bergley clan were vintage firearms. *Nice one, Dad*, I'd thought once my cousins had made their feelings known. *Get the relatives riled at me, and then arm them.*

I told my mother the threadbare positive elements: though Charlotte's benevolence fizzled when it came to me, she donated her energies to local charities when she was not knitting and selling her sweaters, scarves, and hats. Her delicious pies and preserves were legendary.

"I'm sure a certain dentist misses you," my mother said.

"Charles is married with a child on the way."

"Well, I can't say I'm surprised. He was a catch."

After we hung up, I sat and thought about Charles Castle for a mo-ment. Nice guy. Cute. But there was no getting around how I'd felt once we'd settled into a routine. I needed sparks. And I needed someone who wouldn't get high and mighty and accuse me of flinging myself into photography whenever I wanted to avoid deeper issues. *I've got news, Charlie,* I thought. *I'm swimming in deeper issues now.*

"Queue next challenge," I muttered.

I dialed Charlotte's number and paced while the line rang.

"I have *zero* interest in talking with you," she said crisply. "You have the entire town thinking I took those lambs out of spite."

"Charlotte—"

"Having lamb for Christmas is a *family* tradition," she interrupted. "I will not be pressured into changing our holiday plans."

"I didn't want to go this route," I said with a dark tone. "But there's an enlightening story about your son that's under wraps for now."

One of Raymond's journals mentioned a time when Tyler Bergley had filched the toys the town had gathered for low-income families. It hadn't taken my father long to put the pieces together. Pressure was applied. The toys had reappeared, and both Charlotte and her son had "volunteered" to help at a local soup kitchen, red-faced and visibly contrite.

Charlotte said nothing. I heard her breathing.

"I think Raymond was too soft on Tyler," I said after I explained the depth of what I knew. "Stealing from the poor has to be one of the lowest kinds of theft. Let's see if the gossips in town agree."

"You wouldn't dare!"

"The only way around it is to cancel your order with Mr. Lurman. He's expecting your call, so I'd get to it."

I hung up, hoping her maternal instincts were greater than her animosity toward me. During the waiting period, I washed the dishes left over from yesterday. At least, I tried to: the drain glugged and backed up as the shower had done. Instead of emptying this time, the water sat belligerently in the sink as if to say, *I've made it all the way from the bottom of the world. I am not about to leave without a fight.*

Charlotte called a moment later.

"I canceled my order," she said. "Mr. Lurman is expecting a check, and I will be owed an equal amount as well."

"Equal amount meaning …?"

"The lambs are worth two hundred dollars each. That's four hundred dollars for Mr. Lurman, and four hundred dollars for me."

"*What?* That's not even dimly fair—"

Click. Charlotte hung up.

I returned to the sink. The dirty water glared at me.

The receptionist at the plumber's office said slow drains in multiple rooms indicated there might be a clog in the outflow system or a buildup of sludge in the septic tank. All I cared about was that the problem could be solved cheaply, quickly, and by someone other than me. Because of a cancellation, they could send a truck that afternoon.

I refused to mail a check to Charlotte. There had to be more useful dirt in Raymond's journals for applying more pressure. In the meantime, I would put a check in the mail for Mr. Lurman, and stop by the hardware store to finally buy some paint for the kitchen. It was time to take at least that small step toward making the house my own.

7

It was a dewy September morning, with the sun on the horizon to the east across the driveway, warming the air, and causing me to squint. I stepped off the porch and crossed to the welcoming committee that lined up along the fence, come rain or shine. With Pinkie and Pablo at Theo's farm, and three ewe lambs sold to a handspinner, the flock was now twenty-five. They jammed together into a tight knot of curly wool as I scratched their foreheads. Dodge thudded over on his plate-sized hooves, his tail swishing, with festive sprigs of purple clover in his mouth.

I was three feet away. There was no need for hollering, but as he greeted me, he let loose a barrel-chested whinny, a sound so resonant and deep that I could feel it in my bones. I'd taken riding lessons during my youth, but couldn't recall any other horse with that kind of wall-penetrating voice, and a boisterous personality to go with it. Dodge loved to play with toys, especially a giant green ball with a loop that he could grasp with his teeth. He liked fetching it, as a dog would do.

"Big, silly goof," I said, patting his huge neck.

I led Luke to his pen and closed the wire gate. As always, he looked dejected to be left behind at first, and then he rediscovered a favorite bone. Luke circled three times, settled into position, then closed his eyes and gnawed contentedly. Again, I was entirely jealous.

Across the road from my steep gravel driveway, Joan Dumas's yellow Cape and trim, flower-decked yard always beamed encouragement toward my entrance of overgrown weeds on the opposite side of the wooded lane. Joan's two teenagers, Harry and Jess, had played a significant role in bringing me up to speed on the chores that needed to be completed on a daily basis. The family had become great friends.

It was no surprise to see Joan rushing down her porch steps the moment she caught sight of my approaching car. She signaled me over.

I climbed out and crossed the wooded road.

"Tell me the rumors aren't true," she said.

In her thirties, with a freckled face and natural blonde hair, Joan gaped as I sorted fact from idle chitchat: yes, I was there when Richard Gartland staggered out of the cornfield and died in the village of Little Edge; no, I'd never met him before; yes, he'd died of gunshot wounds.

"He must have tried to get away, I suppose," I said. "Or maybe he tried to help his wife, and got shot … you know, in the back."

"Good Lord," Joan said. "A burglary gone wrong is the favored theory, but there's a possible link to your old stomping ground."

"I know. He used to live in Boston."

"Apparently, an old colleague of Richard's went to prison a couple of years ago. An accountant, I think. It's one of the reasons the Gartlands left Massachusetts. His wife, Angela, used to be engaged to the ex-con. You know how these things can go."

"Ex-con? He's out now?"

"As of recently," Joan said. "Frank Winthrop. They showed him on the news. Some hot shot attorney won the appeal on his case."

"Any word on how Angela is doing?"

"She's still in the hospital," Joan said. "A few years ago, Angela and Richard invested in Apogee Antiques to help Carl Woodlee keep it afloat. It's where I got our mantle clock. Plus, you know the Morgan silver dollar your father carried in his pocket for luck? He showed it to Richard to get the history behind the minting, that sort of thing."

I hesitated. "They knew each other?"

45

"Between your father's job and the folks who came to pick strawberries, you'll be hard-pressed to find someone who didn't know him. What happened to that silver dollar? Did you ever find it?"

I rubbed my brow. "It's around somewhere."

If only she'd told me about it *before* I'd frittered away the change in the house. Maybe the lucky coin would turn up. I'd look again.

"Once Brumby finds out you've landed in trouble, you know he'll make a beeline for your farm to offer his version of moral support," Joan said of my father's longtime farrier, whose handsome grin might have swayed me in a weak moment if he wasn't a womanizer who'd left a trail of broken hearts and angry husbands across the state.

"Maybe I'll say yes this time," I said with my stalled love life in mind.

Joan gaped. "You can't be serious?"

"I'm not that desperate yet," I admitted. "Can I hire Harry and Jess for a few hours this afternoon? I'm doing some painting."

"Sure, but remember, Harry is all thumbs."

"He'll do fine," I said.

The teens had helped me in the berry field during peak season when visitors arrived from dawn to dusk, manning the weighing table I'd set up under a yellow canopy. At fourteen, Jess handled the cash box and related transactions with the efficiency of a bank teller.

I paused and studied Joan's frown. "What's wrong?"

"I don't want to cause trouble."

I sighed. "Too late. You just did."

"Ok, you know the furniture and mementos and other items Charlotte took from the farm when you first inherited the place? It's come to light that she's been …"

"What?" I prompted.

"She's selling Raymond's things."

I'm sure I looked as if I'd been stung in the forehead by a pack of killer bees. Joan rushed on during my moment of disbelief.

"You know Raymond hand-tied his own fishing flies, starting in grade school," Joan said. "To surprise him one year Ella took his finest work and made a shadow box display with the name of each fly underneath, like

Painted Lady, Blue Winged Olive, and Wooly Worm. The collection hung in your living room for ages."

"Are you saying …?"

"I've heard the shadow box ended up at Apogee Antiques, Richard Gartland's store. If so, maybe you can buy it back."

"*Buy* it back? I'm supposed to own the collection."

"I know. Hopefully, it's still there."

"Where are his other possessions? In Charlotte's house?"

"Well," Joan said carefully. "Given the fact that her house was already packed with stuff … Raymond's things are in her barn."

"In her *barn?*" I demanded.

"An updated barn. More of an outbuilding."

"Unbelievable."

"Don't do anything rash," Joan said.

Charlotte had filched possessions that I would cherish and was now selling them to the highest bidder. Oh, rash was just for starters.

* * *

Painting the kitchen dropped to a low priority. If Richard Gartland had provided the money to prop up Apogee Antiques during tough economic times, I needed to get there as soon as possible in case Richard's widow decided to put the place up for sale and scatter the inventory to the four winds. Sudden deaths often led to sudden decisions.

Positioned on Main Street, the store looked quaint, with collectibles like serving dishes, a rocking horse, and craftsmen's tools in the windows. "Apogee Antiques" was painted in gold script on the oak door. I cupped my hands against the glass and looked within, seeing shelves with more treasures from bygone days: stacks of lace, vintage dolls, botanical prints, and dinnerware on a mahogany sideboard.

Two men were talking inside near the counter, and based on Joan's description, one of them was Carl Woodlee. In his mid to late fifties, he was dressed in a beige cardigan and matching slacks — not a risk-taker, at least when it came to clothes. He was speaking loudly to a frail man in a wheelchair who looked to be in his nineties.

"Ken, focus," I heard Mr. Woodlee saying. "*Where* would it be?"

I reached for the doorknob and found it was unlocked. The scent of polished wood wafted around me as I stepped into the store. Mr. Woodlee gave up his back-and-forth with the older gentleman. In front of the counter, where a beautiful antique cash register gleamed, he muttered to himself as he flipped through a stack of paperwork.

Nearing him, I said, "Excuse me."

"Merciful heavens!"

As Mr. Woodlee spun a pile of folders flew from his hands, scattering papers across the floor like so many leaves. I knelt to help pick them up and noticed they were an inventory of antiques.

"Are you Carl Woodlee?" I said.

"Yes, but we're closed today. There's been a tragedy."

"I know. I'm so sorry for your loss."

"I just came to collect a few things. Here, give me those." Carl paused and stared at me, his hands trembling so much he nearly dropped the pages again. "You! The detective showed me your photo."

I groaned. "Detective Bricker?"

"Yes. Why would he ...?"

"I was on the road last night. I'm the one who called the police."

"Good heavens."

"It was shocking. I'm very sorry for your loss."

"Who are you, again?" Carl said.

"Sonny Littlefield. My neighbor told me my father's shadow box collection of handmade fishing flies ended up here at the store."

"Littlefield ... it doesn't ring a bell."

"His name was Raymond French."

"Why yes, we do have Raymond's fishing fly collection," Carl said. "The trouble is, I can't focus on sales today."

"I apologize for the timing, but the thing is, my cousin, Charlotte, had no right to take the collection."

"You're saying she *stole* it?"

"Let's say she took it without permission in a bad moment."

"If it's stolen property …" Mr. Woodlee searched through items hanging nearby. He plucked a shadow box from the wall and handed it to me. "Take it. I had no idea the provenance was corrupt."

He was distracted and clearly in a hurry, but under the circumstances, I wanted a proper receipt to prove I'd paid for it.

"I want to buy it," I insisted. "How much?"

Carl checked the tag. "Two hundred dollars."

I paused. "Two hundred? That much?"

"One hundred," he said.

"Umm …"

"Seventy-five?" Carl said. "How about thirty?"

"Perfect." I handed him cash. "Can I have a receipt and a bag?"

"If you insist," Carl said with an exasperated sigh. He stepped behind the counter to complete the transaction.

Thrilled to have secured the shadow box, I smiled at the man in the wheelchair, confirming my first impression that he was quite elderly, possibly in his nineties. In a gray suit that had perhaps fit well in the past, he now looked shrunken and gaunt. His pale, wizened face was where my gaze lingered, the note of tragedy in his eyes.

"I'm Sonny Littlefield," I said, extending my hand.

"Ken Babik," he said.

Mr. Babik couldn't have weighed more than a hundred pounds, but his wide-knuckled hand alluded to past strength as I shook it.

"Don't know any Littlefields," he grumbled, squinting at me from beneath a pair of bushy eyebrows and glasses that needed cleaning.

"She's Raymond French's daughter," Carl said, stepping from behind the counter with the shadow box in a bag and a receipt in hand.

"We had an understanding, Richard and I," Mr. Babik said with glistening eyes. "I couldn't have asked for a better friend."

"It's a terrible loss," Carl said.

Signaling for me to pay attention, Mr. Babik said, "I need you to do something important." His hands wobbled as he searched his pockets and pulled out a plastic sleeve, indicating I should take it. Inside was a gold rectangular coin with a central, embossed character.

"Ken, this young lady is in a hurry," Carl said loudly.

"I'd meant for Richard to inherit my collection," Mr. Babik persisted, peering at the coin as I handed it back. "He loved this one in particular. It's an Imperial Japanese coin from the 1800s."

"It's beautiful," I said.

"I have Greek drachmas and doubloons. Tiger tongues from Laos, and a bullet coin from Siam." Mr. Babik slipped his chilly, trembling fingers around mine, his eyes brimming with tears. "The coin collection is to go to Angela, now. Tell her how sorry I am."

"I don't know Angela," I managed.

"Ken, we'll take care of it later," Carl said. "There'll be plenty of time to visit Angela once she's back home, the poor dear."

"No, it needs to be done now, in case they come after me next."

"Nobody's going to come after you," Carl said.

"It's that blasted business with the letter, all the probing and fiddling I prompted Richard to carry out," Mr. Babik said with anguish. "If I could go back and do it over again—"

"*Ken*," Carl said sharply. "Stop chiding yourself."

"Talk to Richard. He'll know what to do."

"Ken, Richard is why we're here. He's been … never mind, rest easy for a minute, all right?" Carl looked apologetic as he ushered me to the door. "When someone's memory starts slipping, you think they'll be free of worst-case scenarios, but Ken has become obsessed with the notion that robbers are taking over the town."

"There's no denying what happened."

"Don't trust that rascal private eye!" Mr. Babik hollered, desperately signaling to us from his wheelchair. "I'd bet my bottom dollar this mess is his doing! Richard won't listen. He's very stubborn."

"You know, Detective Bricker mentioned a PI," I said. "It's important to share any concerns with the police."

"It'll be sorted out," Carl assured me.

"I really am sorry for your loss."

"You're very sweet. Goodbye."

Carl closed the door and locked it once I'd returned to the sidewalk.

I paused to text Joan that I'd secured the shadow box.

That's great! she texted back.

I was about to head to my car when plaid-clad arms wrapped around me from behind and a rough, cigarette-smelling man rumbled in my ear.

"How's my favorite girl?"

"God …" With a disgusted grimace, I wrenched away and confronted Greg McDonnell's crooked grin. "What is wrong with you?"

"*Shhh*, you don't want to attract attention after making a spectacle of yourself on the road. You're quite the outlaw."

I shook my head. "A man *died* last night."

"That's why we're here, to help with stuff."

Greg indicated his brother, whose beer gut loomed over tight jeans as he studied the sidewalk with an air of awkwardness and gloom. A poster boy for the harmful effects of street drugs, Keith looked out on the world with vacant, watery eyes, and his face had aged beyond his twenty-plus years. People said he used booze and drugs to anesthetize himself against the harsh abuse of his older brother. Every so often, a glimpse of humanity surfaced in Keith's face, but any sympathy I'd ordinarily feel was blotted out by rumors that he would do whatever Greg told him to do. Not to mention that Keith's barrel chest and the width of his arms where he'd rolled up his sleeves were patently intimidating.

"Listen." Abruptly serious, Greg said, "You're one of us, now. I saw you getting frisked. I could tell you didn't like it one bit."

"I wanted to get home. I was fine with it."

"We heard the back-and-forth, so it's pointless to lie." Greg fumed for a second, frustrated that I wasn't letting him get to his point. "We can bury the hatchet from now on. That's all I'm saying."

"Golly, what good news."

"Hey, don't blow me off."

"Fine, let's bury the hatchet. I have other errands, so—"

"Why were you in the store?"

"To buy something that belonged to my father."

"Such as?"

"None of your business."

"Richard was a neighbor, so it is my business. I'm set to figure out how and why he died. Maybe collect a reward." Greg sniffed. "Me and Keith are about the only ones who don't have a motive. Lots of guys are hot for

Angela. She's too high-maintenance for my liking, but other sorts have a whole porn movie situation in their heads over her. Last night could've been set up to *look* like a robbery, you realize."

"Greg—"

"You've got pissed-off guys who lost wages when Richard stopped construction on their garage," he said, listing grievances on his fingers. "You've got pissed-off ATV riders who threatened all kinds of grief over the fences he put up after people barreled through their woods at all hours. I *saw* a guy fleeing last night on an ATV."

"Why, Greg?" I said, unable to stop myself. "Why the sudden interest in getting justice?"

"Because Mr. Gartland was a cool dude," he said vehemently. "When my dad died, Richard helped us sort out overdue taxes and didn't charge a cent. I told him, if you ever need anything, I'm the guy. He gave us work hauling furniture for old Mr. Babik in there." Greg motioned toward the shop. "Ninety plus, but he keeps buying shit. It'll haunt me forever, the fact that I never got to help Richard like he helped us."

I groaned internally, refusing to believe that Greg McDonnell and I had anything in common. I sensed that he was offering bits of stories to entice me into sharing what I might know. There was zero chance that he wasn't working some sort of shady angle.

I was about to be rude when Greg looked over my shoulder and traded his air of swagger for a guarded frown. Turning to follow his gaze, I saw a man waiting next to my car with folded arms. He had dark hair and clean-cut good looks, the kind of man who wore his expensive suit well. My mother would take one look at him and say, *Now, he would be a good prospect for you. Why can't you find a man like that?*

"See you around, Littlefield," Greg said.

He signaled to his brother, and they walked away.

"You're welcome," the man called over, then he stayed in place, blocking my door when I arrived in front of him.

"Why did Greg react that way?" I said.

"I'm an attorney. It's one of the perks."

"If you don't mind, I'm in a hurry," I said.

"Bear with me for a second," he said, holding up his phone to my right and studying a photo of me on the screen. "My impression from a distance was correct. You're Alison Littlefield."

"Why do you have a photo of me?"

"The Maine state police made it a mandatory exercise."

I groaned and closed my eyes.

"You're in their crosshairs," he confirmed, handing me a business card. "Nathan Kitteridge out of Boston, your old stomping ground. The gentleman over there is my client, Frank Winthrop."

He indicated a pale, scowling man slouched next to the brick front of a real estate office on the quiet street. I hesitated, aware that Frank was the ex-con that Angela Gartland had been engaged to before he'd landed in prison. He was also the man in dark clothes I'd seen at the roadblock the previous night. I remembered how he'd melted into the shadows to make a call when he'd seen me looking his way.

"Three questions, if you don't mind," Nathan said. "Why were you on the road last night? What did you do right or wrong to land in the crosshairs? And what brings you to Apogee Antiques?"

I sighed and offered a rough recap of events.

"You're saying the fact that you were on the road can be chalked up to wrong place, wrong time," Nathan concluded. "Your summary of Bricker's attitude is on point. I'm surprised he can find his way home. Can I see the heirloom you bought from the store just now?"

To speed things along, I complied with the request.

"My father died last winter," I said. "He made these fishing flies."

Nathan studied the box, front and back, then he held it up and cast a questioning glance at his client. Frank shook his head.

Nathan handed it back. "I appreciate your candor."

"If that's it, I need to head home."

"Of course." He stepped away from my car, and then he turned back to me with a faint smile. "Sorry if I'm wrong, but I think I saw you checking me out when you first caught sight of me."

"I was assessing you. There's a difference."

Nathan chuckled. "Listen, my first hours in Maine have felt like I've been teleported to one of those living history places. I need a local guide to help me sort out throwbacks like the McDonnells. Let's meet for a drink tonight. Dinner too, if you're up for it."

"Mr. Kitteridge—"

"Call me Nathan, come on."

"I'm off men at the moment."

"Perfect. I'm off women." As his client exhaled and folded his arms, signaling impatience, Nathan dropped the banter. "You're forthright. Eye contact. No signs of guile. The police hassled you last night all the same. My client was the victim of incompetence along those lines. If you end up needing representation, let me know."

Having learned the value of keeping track of people who approached me in the wake of a crime, I stowed his business card in my bag.

"I doubt I could afford you," I said.

"Just saying. Take care."

Nathan's smile indicated he wasn't finished flirting, and I had to admit it was uplifting to land in a man's sights after getting my heart crushed last night. I nodded to Frank Winthrop in parting, but he was not in a friendly frame of mind. His dark mood looked permanent.

8

"It is a sad, sad day when I have to get intel on your life from your mother," Arlene said when I remembered to call her on my drive home.

"I'm so sorry," I said earnestly.

With my phone in a hands-free holder, I tossed out a recap of my night, sparking familiar responses like, "You've got to be *kidding* me!" and "Not again!" I apologized, blew kisses, and signed off.

When I got home there was barely any time to prepare myself for the arrival of the plumbers. At ten minutes 'til one, I topped off Luke's water dish in his dog pen near the barn. As always when he grasped that he was in for more alone time in his designated enclosure, he stared at the beagle-sized house, then gazed up at me, perplexed.

"Tiny houses are in," I said. "You're on the cutting edge."

Minutes later, a black truck lumbered up my driveway, its engine growling from the steep climb. Behind the cab, a partially filled tank of unpleasant substances sloshed as it lurched over gullies and bumps. Luke sniffed the air and barked, inspiring the plumbers to make sure he was restrained before they stepped down from their cab.

"*Bluuhh*," Bubbah, my ancient ram added in a low voice that had been heavily sandpapered by time, his frizzy head appearing as he perched his front hooves on the bottom rail of his small corral. Ever the optimist, he pleaded his case to anyone who stopped by: "Let me out so I can get to the sheep ladies down there! I'm starved for love!"

As I crossed to the truck, I heard the wiry driver saying to his portly partner, "The guy was shot in the head, execution style." Clad in blue work clothes that looked suspiciously unmarred by work of any kind, he pressed his forefinger against his temple.

"Let's be careful to not fuel gossip," I said, "but the police believe the victim was wounded while trying to escape."

"You're thinking of last week's episode," he said.

"You're talking about a TV show?"

"You thought I meant what happened to Rick Gartland," he said with a knowing expression. "Somebody ran *over* the poor bastard."

"No, he was—" I sighed. "How long will the pipe work take?"

"I got an idea what last night was about," he persisted. "The day we pumped the Gartland residence tank, I heard the wife crying."

"Look, my pipes are clogged, so … she was crying?"

The plumber nodded solemnly. "She says to Richard, real upset, 'You don't need to protect me. I want to know what's going on.' Richard was known to advise people in bad financial situations now and then. Maybe he helped a shady sort, and she got nervous about it."

"You heard her say those exact words?"

"Now, don't get stuck in one lane," the wiry plumber cautioned. "After all, it was a woman who lost her mind and ran Richard down in cold blood. A mistress scorned. That's my best guess."

I sighed. "Back to the pipes."

"Right." The plumber frowned as he glanced around. "Where's your tank at? Didn't Brenda tell you to dig up the lid before we got here?"

"No."

He gave the other man a long-suffering look that said, *How many times is Brenda going to forget to relate this critical piece of information?*

"We've got to do that first," he said with irritation. "We need to see if the snake goes all the way through the pipe on that end."

"Here's a shovel," I said, fetching one from the weeds.

"We've got our own equipment," the plumber said. "It's an insurance type thing. And that one's worse for wear."

"Ok, suit yourself."

Consulting blueprints I'd found amongst my father's papers, we determined that the tank was in the narrow strip of grass across the driveway from the kitchen, very close to the pasture fence, and within the dappled shade of the maple tree. With the wiry murder expert looking on and offering instructions, the portly fellow dug up the lid.

"The heck kind of crazy placement is this?" the plumber complained. "This tank is so far down, we'll hit China before we're done."

"Dare I ask what you mean?" I said.

"The lid is usually a foot or two deep. Easy access. What do you think we have going on here, Harve? Three feet or so?"

"Looks that way," the digger said.

I sat nearby, swatting away flies that appeared to have arrived with the truck as I read an online account of the murder.

The article was more of a tribute than a news story, focusing on the presentations Richard had offered from time to time at venues around the state, along with Ken Babik, the elderly man I'd met in Apogee Antiques. Attendees included the governor, who said Richard's descriptions of the history of vintage items were "enthralling."

The plumber picked his teeth as he read over my shoulder. "They're right about those talks. Richard gave the whole history of items, with tips on how to tell the real deal from knock-offs."

"Is there any money to be made with antiques these days?" I said. "I heard the shop was struggling at one point."

The plumber snorted. "I'm not about to buy moldy old stuff. If you're into it, Carl Woodlee is your best bet. Retired teacher, so be prepared to get bored if you ask a question. You know how some people go on and on, no idea you're yawning inside."

"Totally," I murmured.

"Old Mr. Babik is a hoot. The last time we pumped the tank at his house, he came out all excited. I cracked the code!"

I hesitated. "I don't understand."

"That's what Ken hollered to us: 'I cracked the code!'"

"When was this?" I said.

"Six months ago. Before you ask, he didn't say what it was all about. Anyhoo, let's hope they catch the woman behind the awful business before she runs out and … Harve, watch what you're doing!"

Once the lid was unearthed, the two men tromped down the cellar steps to uncap the main pipe. I waited upstairs in the kitchen. When something as fundamentally important as indoor plumbing breaks down, it's a comfort if the repairmen make the proper amount of noise. I therefore perceived all the cursing and banging going on in the basement as a good sign, though it was hard to not worry when the wiry plumber hollered, "Watch out, Harve! That stuff is shooting past the bucket!"

The snake made some progress, causing the kitchen sink to gurgle and finally drain. All looked well, but then the snake encountered resistance of a mysterious and troubling nature. Their operation moved back to the yard across the driveway. The portly worker pulled a thick, very unpleasant hose from the back of the truck, wrestled it into the hole, and flipped on a pump. Once again, progress was made for five minutes, then he frowned as the machine started making a horrible gurgling sound.

"That ain't right," he said and killed the switch.

Taking charge, the wiry plumber pushed his coworker aside and knelt on one knee next to the hole. "Uh-oh, see those roots?" He shined a flashlight into the blackness, and sure enough, there were roots. "I wouldn't want to be you, Miss. They've wrecked the tank."

He theorized that for an indefinite period, the nearby maple tree had essentially been the house's septic tank. The tree had gotten parched, sensed a reliable source of water nearby, and had at it.

"These old steel tanks rust," he explained. "Nowadays, people use concrete. I bet the actual clog is in the pipe under where we're standing, but you've got the whole works gone. The biggest cost'll be a new leach field. That could run seven, eight grand."

"*What?*" I said. "Good Lord."

"Oh, yeah," he said. "It's got to be done according to code. Job one for the plumbing inspector is approving the leach field."

"Why can't I let the tree handle things?"

The plumber snorted and slapped his knee. "You think you've got a clog now. Wait'll the ground freezes come winter."

I paced in a circle. If I emptied my savings on this disaster, I would be out of luck if an even bigger problem came along later on.

"The inspector you mentioned," I said carefully. "Would he necessarily have to be involved if it was a low-key kind of job?"

The plumber stepped back and looked me up and down. "What, you're not thinking of handling the situation yourself?"

"Of course not. I'm just curious."

"Let us know if you give it a whirl. We'd pay to see a woman messing around with a septic tank, right Harve?"

I sighed. "Thank you for spelling things out."

"I'll check the basement," he said. "Make sure we got everything. And I'll make sure your pipe is free draining for now."

His wink said he needed to use the facilities.

Truth be told, this dovetailed with my sudden plan of seeing if I could coax Harve into doing a bit more digging. Sure, I felt guilty about it. He would probably welcome a break, but with his bossy co-worker out of the picture, he brightened and seemed more than willing to help a poor woman who'd been handed a bad piece of luck.

"Excellent," I said as he made quick work of deepening the hole where one would find the pipe. "You work fast. Your wife is lucky."

"Tell her that," he said. "She's put me on a diet."

"Because she cares."

I glanced toward the house. No sign of the other guy yet.

"I'd say that pipe is over four feet down," Harve said.

"Golly. You're getting there fast."

"You are going to dig it yourself," he guessed. "You'll need to go deeper than the pipe so you can complete any repairs. It's not a permanent fix, mind you. The roots will grow back."

"Thank you so much for your help."

"It's nothing. Like I said—"

"What the heck is going on here?" the wiry plumber said, hoisting his beltline into place as he arrived. "Harve, have you lost your mind?"

"It's my fault," I said. "Tell Brenda to bill me."

After they packed up their equipment and left, I stood in the driveway and glared at my Christmas cookie green house. The tank was still intact

59

for the most part, even if it had been invaded by roots. That meant the plumber was right: the real problem lay in the route leading *out* there. Maybe if I fought the roots into submission, I could buy some time until I could afford to hire a contractor to do the job properly.

I picked up the shovel and started digging with grim determination. Nothing would ease the pain of never meeting my father, but for the past seven months, living on his farm had kindled the sense that we were working together — Raymond starting the journey, and me finishing it. After twenty-eight years of missed birthdays, the farm was his only gift to me, and by God, I wasn't going to give it up easily.

As I dug into the chore, blistering my hands, a familiar phenomenon occurred: LuAnne Cutler, Mariana Dobnia, and Kirsty Fenemore, the reigning princesses of my old neighborhood in Newton, leaned into the back of my mind. When I'd first heard from Raymond's attorney, I'd rashly elaborated on what little I knew about my father's "estate." Now I had a burning dread that LuAnne and her snobs-in-waiting would show up with their wealthy husbands and say, "*This* is the place you inherited?"

As always, they wore pretty cocktail dresses and designer pumps.

"What a novel idea, keeping in shape through ditch digging," Kirsty said. "The rampant weeds are a classy touch, don't you think?"

"Sonny must have meant she'd inherited a *mistake*," Mariana said.

"This farm has a lot of potential," I muttered. "One day, you'll all be green with envy."

"The very color of your house," LuAnne cooed.

As I fell into a steady rhythm, my thoughts returned to Richard, and the way he'd looked as he'd staggered toward me. His last sensory perceptions on earth involved falling onto an unforgiving road, the headlights of my car so intense he'd had to squint. That bright light had seared his image into my head. "It's important," he'd hollered if my guess was correct. Then, what? I frowned in concentration. He'd spoken with urgency. "Can't," I ventured. "Can't what? Let me down? Let me die?"

I abruptly stopped shoveling.

If I were mortally wounded, God forbid, I would want to stop the bleeding. Richard had done the opposite, his heart pounding from his effort to push on across the cornfield, which had drained his life away all the faster. When my car had approached, he didn't show his wounds. He held up the black jewelry bag. What message could be so urgent that it would blot out the most elemental instinct of all: to survive? Surely it had to be more than a precious *thing* that had driven him on.

I shivered, recalling the empty, lifeless feel of his neck as I'd checked for a pulse. By the time I'd reached him, the mysterious, vibrant energy that had brightened his eyes and governed his whims was gone. From his body, at least. How could the sum of his whirling thoughts and pooled emotions simply vanish? Souls had to exist beyond the moment of death, in heaven, or in the living world. A part of the wind and the rain.

I marveled that my father had taken an oath that included a pledge to put his own safety aside in the performance of his duty.

Dan had taken a similar oath. It still brought gooseflesh to my arms when I recalled how he'd run through a hail of gunfire in the hope of saving me. Brave to a fault, except when it came to leveling with a woman from his past. Then he couldn't find the right words.

The rattle of bicycles pulled my gaze toward the Dumas's house across the road at the bottom of the hill. Fair-haired and freckled, my neighbors, Harry and Jess, grinned as they leaned into the work of peddling up the hill. Harry tripped over nothing as he stepped off of his bike. He'd just turned sixteen and was endearingly uncoordinated.

"I thought you were going to paint," he said.

"Well, something else came up."

The five words that best described my life.

9

"You know what?" I said. "I need to put on serious work clothes."

"Maybe we should, too," Jess said.

"No need. I'll be doing the hard part."

While my helpers raked the dirt around the hole into a neat pile, I changed into jeans, boots, and one of my father's flannel shirts, tying the tails so they wouldn't hang down to my knees.

When I returned to the work site, Harry shook his head as I picked up the short, flat shovel I'd been using.

"That's a roofing shovel, Sonny. It's for removing shingles."

"That explains the tar on the handle."

Though Harry was appalled that I was using an improper implement for the job at hand, I did not fetch a replacement. It made sense to use an old, beat-up shovel on what promised to be a tough job.

Within an hour, a tangled network of roots told me I'd reached the source of the problem. I climbed into the trench with one of my father's pruning saws, the soil damp under my knees and gritty on my hands as I set the blade in place and leaned into the work. My mother had never let me play in the dirt as a child. I was making up for lost time.

My co-workers sat on the edge, looking down at me.

"I bet Raymond would solve that murder in two seconds," Harry said. "He had a way of getting to the bottom of things."

"Raymond was a smart, talented man," I agreed.

"He had an important case on his mind around this time last year," Harry said. "I could tell 'cause he'd fall into bouts of frowning. Like maybe he'd heard something that fit something else."

"Harry bugged him about it," Jess reported.

"How did that go?" I asked.

"He'd smile and ruffle Harry's hair."

"Like I was still a kid," Harry grumbled.

In last year's journal, my father mentioned an old case he was looking into. The lack of further entries suggested he'd resolved it.

"Mom says Mr. Lurman is in hot water," Jess said. "It wasn't until the police asked to see his ATV that he claimed it was stolen. As in *after* the murder. The police aren't buying his story."

I paused, recalling Greg McDonnell saying he'd seen an ATV fleeing the scene, though I wouldn't take his word as fact.

"We need to give people the benefit of the doubt," I said, pulling a huge tap root free, sending dirt everywhere.

"Not when it comes to Charlotte," Harry said.

Puffing, I sat on my heels. "You're right about that. From now on, if you see her come up here when I'm not home—"

"Sonny?"

"What?"

"There's a police car coming up your driveway."

All sensation left me. "A police car? What color is it?"

"Blue. It's a state trooper."

Oh my God. It was probably Dan, and there I was in a ditch, sweating, and covered with dirt. While my mind spun in helpless circles, I heard tires crunching on the driveway twenty feet away.

Harry and Jess waved. "Hi!"

"I'm not home," I hissed. "*Psst.* Do you hear me?"

A car door opened. "Is Sonny around?"

"Right here in the hole," Harry said, pointing down at me.

I closed my eyes and wished for an instant death. When that didn't happen, I told myself it shouldn't matter. Dan had delayed reaching out, a shock with crushing effects. Policemen were known to be complicated. I did not need a complicated man in my life at that point in time. The best thing, the *only* thing to do was to pretend it was perfectly normal for a woman to be digging a giant trench on her side lawn.

I climbed to my feet and squinted against the sun. Dan did a double take, then he slowly grinned as he walked over, his blue uniform defining his sexy, quarterback physique with every move. His shadow arrived first, adding to the dwarfing effect of standing four feet below sea level. It was like looking up at some sort of Titan roaming the earth.

"Afternoon," Dan said.

"Hello." Floundering for an intelligent, witty response, I indicated the crater engulfing me. "Roots invaded my pipe."

"The trials of owning an old house are many," Dan said, and then he just loomed there above me, admiring the scene for all it was worth. Memorizing it so he could paint a vivid picture for his friends and colleagues: *You should've seen Sonny Littlefield today …*

"You didn't have to come," I said. "I got the message."

Dan's eyebrows twisted. "What message is that?"

"*You* know." I rolled one hand.

"I kind of don't. If you're talking about Bricker—"

"No, I meant— never mind."

"Sorry to hear you have plumbing issues." Assessing my array of tools, Dan pointed to my shovel. "That's for removing shingles."

"I told her it was a roofing shovel," Harry said.

"Are you here about last night?" Jess asked him.

"Just checking in. Seeing if all is well."

"Did you know Raymond?" she said.

"I think we met a time or two."

"He died during that blizzard back in February," Harry said. "Went up the ladder in the middle of the night to clear ice dams from the roof. Nobody can figure out why he didn't wait until morning. He was always smart about stuff like that. The best man ever."

"I bet he was," Dan said softly. "I've heard you two are a big help for Sonny. Indispensable is the word she used."

"We're glad to help," Jess said, as always looking youthful and wide-eyed and earnest as her pale hair stirred in the breeze. "You'll solve the murder over in Little Edge, won't you? Back in the spring, Sonny got dragged into a terrible mess. We almost lost her. She's never been the same since. It's had us worried for months."

"Honey, I keep telling you I'm fine," I said.

"We're working nonstop to get answers," Dan assured the teens.

Indicating I needed help climbing out, I said, "Harry, can you …?"

"Here, let me," Dan said, extending a very clean hand.

"Never mind," I grumbled. "Clear the way."

"Are you sure?"

"I am *absolutely* sure."

With a groan, I heaved myself out of the ditch and swatted ineffectively at the dirt on my clothes, feeling like a grubby rodent as I squinted at Dan. His grin lit up his entire face. I knew that smiling would do nothing to enhance my own appearance. A smiling, grubby rodent would either look pathetic, or downright horrifying.

"All set?" Dan said.

"I'm great. Just dandy."

"Can I see inside your cruiser?" Harry said. "The computer and stuff?"

"That's a good idea," I interjected before Dan could respond. "Show them your 'stuff' while I step inside for a minute, ok?"

I glared at Luke as I crossed to the house. If he'd forewarned Dan's arrival by barking, I might be in the middle of an entirely different situation right now, though there truly hadn't been time to escape. Seeing me look over, Luke thumped his tail on the ground, as if he expected to be congratulated for being so well-behaved.

Even after instructing myself to be strong, I moaned when I saw myself in the bathroom mirror. My blue eyes were like luminous orbs within a frame of dirt, and a thicket of bedraggled curls poked out from under my baseball cap. Holy hell, had any woman at any point in time — including the entire course of prehistory and the filthy Middle Ages — ever looked so horrible? And what was the greasy glob on my forehead? I scraped some off and sniffed it. Tar from the roofing shovel.

"Sonny?" Dan called out as he opened the kitchen door. "I promised to show Harry the cruiser next time."

"Is it imperative that we talk today?"

"I'm here. Let's catch up."

I gripped the sink and closed my eyes, thinking maybe it was best to get the fiasco ending of our relationship over with now.

I traded my filthy top for a button-up shirt I pulled from the hamper and set about scrubbing my face, but it was hopeless. I was not coming out of the bathroom looking clean unless I had the fire department spray me down with a pressure hose. I pulled my hair into a gritty ponytail, gave the open window a longing glance, and went back to my kitchen, where Dan was leaning against the sink with his thumbs looped on his gun belt. His brown eyes conveyed concern the way a lamp cast light.

"I sent a text," he said. "Alerting you that I planned to stop in."

I glanced at my phone on the table. "I didn't see it."

"I figured. Listen, I know last night was tough."

"Why is Detective Dicker showing my photo around?"

"Detective *Bricker* has a stick up his keester," Dan said, not quite able to suppress a smile. "I'm sorry he had you frisked."

"Don't worry, I know how to move on."

The kitchen light was off, thank heaven, adding shadows to the room instead of harsh light as I crossed to the refrigerator.

"Iced tea?" I said. "Soda?"

"Iced tea would be nice."

Now that I'd offered, I realized I only had one bottle left. I handed it to him and poured myself a glass of the iced tea I'd brewed a few days ago.

Setting his tea aside, Dan took the glass from my hand, snagged my jeans, and pulled me toward him before I could turn away.

"What are you *doing?*" I demanded.

"I want to hug you. It drove me nuts to not be able to last night."

"I'm covered with dirt."

"This fabric is NASA-engineered," Dan said, plucking off my hat. "I hose myself off at night, then I'm good to go at dawn."

I dipped my shoulders and slipped away to escape the up-close-and-personal reminder of his muscles and freshly washed awesomeness. Was he out of his mind, imagining a hug was the right move?

"What's going on?" he said. "Talk to me."

66

Arriving at a framed photo of Raymond on a bookcase, I picked it up and studied his weathered features for the umpteenth time. The new story of my life included men deciding to not reach out to me. I knew the facts. But seriously, how nice would it have been for fate to have nudged Raymond in the right direction years ago?

"Sonny," Dan said softly. "I'm worried about what Jess said."

"You never told me you knew Raymond," I said.

"We met in passing. I didn't really know him."

"I never asked if you were here in February when …"

"The night Raymond died? No, I was up north."

"Right." I retrieved my tea and sat down at the table. "I'm still not clear on how ice dams happen. I suppose I should look it up."

"Ice forms on the cold outer edge, forcing meltwater to seep under the shingles. When my parents had a leak at their house, it took three coats of primer to cover the stains. How bad was the damage here?"

"No damage, thank heaven."

"There must be stains on the ceiling tiles," Dan said.

"No."

I'd memorized my father's last journal entry: *Sleet, snow, wind — it's quite a mess out there tonight. No surprise the power is out. Just before I cranked up the generator, I heard a snowmobile whining on one of my trails. Whoever it is has to be crazy to be out in this kind of weather.*

Somehow, the awful conditions hadn't kept Raymond from heading outside himself. If only he'd put off clearing the roof until daylight, when the wind wasn't blowing and sleet wasn't icing up the ladder, he would still be alive. People said the fall must have knocked him unconscious, and that he didn't suffer. I wasn't so sure. The thought of him shivering in the snow, unable to move, had kept me up many nights.

"What led people to think he was trying to fix a leak?" Dan said.

"The first responders found a pan he'd put upstairs to catch the water. It was still there the first time I came to the farm."

"Did the roof leak during subsequent storms?"

"No. Why are you obsessing over this?"

"Sorry." Dan held up his hands. "Just curious."

Unfurling from his relaxed pose, he joined me at the table. Or rather, he took command of the table, flexing his muscles until his uniform and array of gear settled into place. Seriously, did the fabric need to be that tight? It was a wonder all the furniture in the room didn't snap to his shoulders like iron filings gathering on a magnet.

"I noticed your upstairs window has a broken pane," Dan said. "Harry thinks Charlotte's son did it. If you want me to step in—"

"I don't. It's being handled."

"Your cousins are still a problem."

"It's not a police matter. Let it go."

Dan rested his hand on the table in front of me. "I know last night was upsetting. Bricker made it worse. I'm really sorry."

"I told you I'm fine." Frowning, I turned the glass of tea in my hands. "Imagine if Richard had stayed put until help arrived. Does his obsession with the jewelry bag make sense to you?"

"Sonny, I can't talk about the case."

I rolled my eyes. "Here we go. I'm not allowed to ask."

"It's more than that," Dan said. "I had to choose—"

"Ok, let's get the rude awakening out of the way," I said with sudden irritation. "I got the message that things have changed. Frankly, I'm in the same mindset because it's so typical of how guys operate, letting silence do the talking. So, here's how things will unfold from now on. Bricker is a giant pain, but he's in charge of the case. Let him come and follow up if there are any ... will you *please* stop that," I said, indicating the winces and eyebrow gyrations Dan's face kept taking on as I spoke.

"I was trying to tell you I had to choose. Work on the Gartland case or pick up where you and I left off. It's clear how I landed."

"Totally clear. You delayed reaching out."

"I told you why. You nodded like you understood."

"You didn't buy that. Your laser vision was going full tilt." I wiggled my fingers in front of my face to indicate how the process worked. "Bricker honed right in on my feelings. It's why he had me frisked."

Dan hesitated, clearly appalled. "No, your demeanor had to do with your plan for the sheep, and—" With a wide gaze, he devolved into a fast recalibration of the night, which had a crumpling effect that took me off guard. "No, no, no," Dan moaned, rubbing his face. "You're right, you shut down *after* we first talked. I didn't connect the dots."

"Wait, stop," I said. "If you weren't on the scene, the same thing would have happened. My plan was iffy. I picked up evidence, and reacted when Bricker baited me. Don't take what I said to heart."

"It was a factor, clearly."

"Look, you're out there every day risking your neck. The truth is, you were an ace last night. Even so," I carefully went on, "Insomnia seems a little thready as an excuse for a multi-week delay."

"Sonny, wrapping up the border gig was involved," Dan said. "I had to create a buffer zone. Make sure it didn't follow me home. Plus, Aaron's parents delayed scattering his ashes until I got back. The ceremony was last week in Vermont. It didn't feel right to reach out to you with turmoil in the wings. I had to get clear of it."

Seeing Dan's sorrowful eyes, I felt my anger slip away. Aaron Pierce was a colleague and childhood friend who'd taken his own life. Dan had coped with the shock by agreeing to an undercover assignment up north. He'd figured his pain would be easier to handle if he left town, though isolation was not a healthy path for healing grief.

"I'm sorry," I said softly. "That must have been hard."

"Listen." Dan reached across the table again. "Taking on the border role was a mistake. I did it for all the wrong reasons."

"I was just thinking that."

"Sonny, we didn't have a normal arc in May. We both had trauma to sort out, so we figured it was best for me to finish my assignment up north. The problem is, I couldn't focus. That kind of work is intense. There's no time clock." Dan shook his head. "In terms of processing events and getting to a stabilized zone, it didn't happen."

"You were worried I would be upset about that?"

"Not upset, exactly. I just …"

"Got stuck in your head about it."

Dan spread his hands. "Perfect wording."

"I can relate. You heard Jess out there. All my friends are driving me nuts about—" I paused and stared at a two-inch scar under Dan's hairline.

As I leaned closer to study it, he looked wary and leaned back. "That wasn't there in the spring," I said. "It looks recent."

"I cut myself shaving," he said wryly.

"Then you have really bad aim."

"Sonny." Dan closed his eyes as if attempting to formulate an answer that stopped my questions. "It's the sort of case that needs to stay locked down. It's over. Everything worked out."

I tumbled back to the EMT using the same wording last night. *How bad was it? It's all locked down.* I'd misread what he'd been talking about, but his inference was putting awful ideas in my head now.

"Stand up," I said.

"What …?"

I pushed my chair back and motioned for Dan to obey my order, and then I hugged him the way I should have done the moment I'd climbed out of the ditch. As much as I wanted to sink into Dan's warmth and the way he relaxed into a relieved exploration of my shoulders and back, I spent a moment sliding my fingers over his torso to test for any signs of injury under his uniform. Reaching around to draw my arms forward, Dan held my hands close to his chest and looked me in the eyes.

"Stop that," he said. "I'm not injured."

"Not injured *anymore* is what I'm hearing."

"It's the same concept."

"What happened?"

"Let's agree there's a lot to catch up on," Dan said. "I'm sorry to stop in on short notice. It's the only free slot I have today."

"You'll tell me eventually?"

"Of course. Now, take my hand. We're going to make a pact."

I hesitated. "Not until I hear the terms."

"We cut each other slack," Dan said.

"That's it? No complicated bylaws?"

He pondered the request. "Ok, if I say anything dumb, you'll tell me right away. If you say anything dumb, I'll pretend I didn't hear it."

"*You'll* stay silent? That's a hard sell."

"Stop stalling." Dan motioned for me to take hold of his hand. "You don't want to make me late for work."

With a slow smile, I allowed him to interlace our fingers and snug our palms together. So much for resisting his magnetic pull.

"Are we in agreement?" Dan said.

"I guess so."

"Oh my God, I've missed hearing you say that," he said, reacquainting himself with my face, the same way I was studying his phantom dimples, clean-shaved jawline, and worrisome new scar. "Please don't misread the delay," he went on. "There's an adjustment period after undercover work. I'm embracing a reset mentality. Structure and routine."

"Hence, you're in uniform. Back to basics."

"Exactly," Dan said. "You're aware it's harder than ever to do police work. Detective rank might be my next move."

"If not that direction, then what?"

He shrugged. "I have a side hustle. At least I had one before I took the gig up north. If I can get it in gear again, I'll fill you in."

"How do you feel about sheep farming?" I said.

"Is that a lucrative field?"

"There's definitely a field involved."

Dan started leaning in for a kiss, then he paused with a worried frown. "You're tensing up. Is it the uniform?"

"You're armed. Are there rules to be aware of?"

"Well, here's option A." Dan kissed my forehead, and then studied my dismayed reaction. "Not the right vibe?"

"I feel like a waif in a Dickens novel," I said.

"I'm carrying almost thirty pounds of gear," Dan explained. "Cuffs, a sidearm, ammunition, this nifty whistle on my shirt. If you start coming at me, all heated up and out of control ..."

"I'll be very well behaved."

Dan cracked up. "You fell for all that?"

I gaped. "Here I am, trying to be respectful ... *mmm* ..."

My protest melted away as our lips connected and blended into instant warmth and soulful chemistry. Even with the crime-fighting tools on his belt, he took me on a sexy ride, kissing me gently at first, then playfully, his hands snugging me close until there was zero space between us. I'd come to enjoy the feel of his soft beard when we'd kissed in May. Now, reveling in the sensation of his shaved jawline and upper lip, I started making happy sounds in the back of my throat.

With a frustrated growl, Dan ended the kiss. "How did you get more delicious?" he murmured. "It defies logic and science."

"The sidearm wasn't the only issue," I said, torn between how cozy I felt in his arms and the sense that I'd dreamed the past half hour. "Somehow, feeling good about anything doesn't seem right. We're fresh out of a murder scene. Richard is in the morgue."

"Last night was an ordeal," Dan agreed. "Another tragedy. A senseless death. We can't let it kick the stuffing out of us. We're up to the challenge of sorting it out. Square one. If you're free this weekend, I'll bring you to the coast for dinner, maybe a walk on the beach."

I smiled. "That sounds nice."

Dan led the way outside. In the sunshine, at the bottom of the porch steps, he looked up at the roof above my bedroom window.

"That's where the ice dam formed?" he said.

I nodded. "The first time I came here the ladder was frozen in place where Raymond set it up. It was stuck to the ground."

"Storms with ice are the worst," Dan murmured.

"Joan asked about a silver dollar Raymond liked to carry in his pocket. I've looked for it in the house, but not out here."

"Let's see." Dan brushed the grass aside with his boots, combing the area by degrees. Just when my hope started to fade, he knelt and reached down. "Here it is, a Morgan silver dollar, 1888."

"I should have known," I said, staring at the precious find as Dan put it in my palm. "Raymond always carried it for luck ..." My voice trailed off. His lucky token hadn't worked the night he'd died.

"I'm sorry, Sonny," Dan said softly.

"This is great. Thank you for finding it."

"I like the look of your dog," he said as we continued down the driveway past the pile of dirt. "Part shepherd?"

"A King Shepherd, according to the folks at the pound."

"Excellent choice. Smart, loyal, likes to work."

Arriving at his cruiser, Dan frowned at the roofline again, confirming what I'd come to know of him: a sense of humor balanced by depth and complexities. I couldn't help but want to know more.

"I can't thank you enough," I said.

Dan focused on me. "For what?"

"Last night. The tight-narrative approach."

"Did you reach Theo today?" he said.

"We're all set. Charlotte has backed off."

Once he was in his cruiser, Dan checked a computer screen on the dashboard. "I need to head out. Let me know if Bricker gets in touch. And no more digging, ok? I'll make a few calls."

"I'm *almost* done."

Dan cracked up.

As he pulled away, I turned and found my sheep lined up along the fence, shoulder-to-shoulder, like a team of scientists who'd been appointed to observe my life and arrive at important conclusions.

"It's a crazy development," I said. "You remember what he's like. One minute I'm mad, the next minute he's got me kissing him."

Dodge tossed his mane and split the air with a resonant whinny, and Luke added an annoyed bark indicating he hadn't appreciated being side-lined in his pen during the exciting activity of the past few hours. I let him out, and then knelt and petted his soft head and ears.

"I don't suppose you made dinner for us," I said.

Luke wiggled and grinned.

Hopefully, a nourishing option could be dug out of my freezer. I had a clandestine mission to tackle that night before Dan took any more steps toward setting up a foothold of law and order in my life.

10

From behind a bank of feathery passing clouds, the moon offered just enough light for me to move with the right mix of speed and stealth. I felt a flutter of nerves as I pressed my way through a thicket, mindful of stepping on grass and firm ground so I didn't leave any footprints.

As predicted by my sources, nobody was out and about in the rustic village of Gracious, Maine at 9:05 p.m. I'd been told where to park so my car wouldn't be seen and how far Charlotte Bergley's barn was from the lane. All I lacked was an accurate sense of how much undergrowth I would need to plow through before I got there.

Finally, the dark hulk of a building was visible up ahead. I pressed on, determined to know if what Joan had told me was true.

Pulling a flashlight from my jeans, I reached out to lift a branch to one side as I stepped forward, and then my eyes jerked open from the searing agony of a thousand hooked thorns puncturing my thighs.

"*Crrraap*," I growled between my teeth. "*Oww* ..."

Looking down, I saw that the long arms of a bristling rose hedge had consumed my legs all the way up to my front pockets.

With my eyes squeezed shut, I unhooked the vicious pinpoints ten at a time, suffering horrifying backlashes and repeat puncture stabs, as if I'd encountered some sort of alien guard shrubs come to life.

Even my cousin's rose bushes hated me.

Breathless, my hands bleeding and sporting a fringe of thorns that refused to let go, I broke free of the roses and staggered the last few yards to the back windows of Charlotte Bergley's outbuilding.

I glanced at her house beyond the manicured yard to be sure a light hadn't sprung on. All was quiet. To avoid unnecessary glare, I cupped my hand around the flashlight as I held it against the glass. Amidst boxes here and there, some items appeared to be old toys that Charlotte's son had outgrown, but I saw beautiful cabinets that matched the empty spaces in Raymond's house. They were covered with dust. I could tell each one was made of either solid oak, maple, or pine.

In an open box, I saw dinnerware with the same pattern as stray pieces the Bergleys had left behind during their pilfering. There was a velvet case with an emblem indicating it contained a set of fine silverware. Dozens of other items must have belonged to Raymond. Fishing poles. Tackle boxes. Photo collections. I saw patchwork quilts that I suspected had been sewn by Ella: precious, handcrafted heirlooms left in the open, gathering dust, susceptible to insects, damp conditions, and mold.

Fuming, I retreated along the path I'd come in on, this time finding a spot beyond the roses so I didn't lose any more pints of blood. Somehow, I had to shame my cousins into returning the precious items they'd taken from Raymond's house. They'd called the shots for long enough.

* * *

A part of me knew that if I spoke out loud or thought too hard, I would return to a realm where my father was out of my reach. But if I didn't say something, he would finish his coffee and toast, pull on his parka, walk out the door into the stormy night, and never come back. I had to warn him that the ladder would be slippery with ice …

"Rrroof!"

Blinking awake, I squinted at the bedside clock. It was 10 p.m. Without a warm male body within arm's reach, there was absolutely no use for waking up at that time of the night. Luke disagreed. He was downstairs jumping around and barking at the top of his lungs.

"Rrrrr!"

"Luke," I moaned. "Please stop."

"Rrroof! Rrroof!"

"This is why my mother is allergic to dogs," I said, pushing the covers aside and dragging myself out of bed. My T-shirt hung down to my knees, and so did my hands as I slogged down the stairs and crossed the dark kitchen. Hours of ditch digging had done a number on my shoulders and back. I would never walk upright again.

Luke pawed at the door and looked up at me.

"You have to pee?" I said.

"Rrroof!"

"Thank you for not using the floor," I said, opening the door to let him out. "From now on, no water after eight p.m."

As he bounded off the porch, I followed after him and paused next to the railing with my arms folded against the cool September air. Behind a bank of clouds, the moon added a spell of silver light over my darkened fields. Crickets chirped here and there, and the air smelled of grass and loam. I jerked out of a yawn as I heard hooves drumming in the darkness. Beyond the fence across the driveway, Dodge wheeled to a halt and stared toward me, stock still, with the sheep behind him.

Luke was below me on the right, sniffing the latticework door of Cat Town, the storage space under the porch.

"Luke, no chasing kitties," I said.

He yipped and clawed at the wood.

"*Hey.*" I rushed down the steps, then winced my way across a stretch of gravel. "You're scratching the paint."

I grabbed his collar and pulled, to no effect. As he barked, nearly bursting my eardrums, I let go and clapped my hands.

"Luke, no. Bad boy."

With an excited gleam in his eyes, he lunged at the latticework door and furiously pawed the wood at top speed. I heard the snap of wood, then Luke shoved his head into the opening he'd created.

"Oh, you are in big trouble now," I said, grabbing a length of twine lying on the grass to use as a leash.

He yipped and lurched into me as if a cat had scratched him on the snout, allowing me a chance to secure the twine around his collar and pull him away. I tied the makeshift leash to the railing that flanked the porch steps. Luke whined and rubbed his face on the grass, clearly unhappy about getting scratched on his busybody nose.

"Stay put," I said. "Just look at what you did."

As I leaned down to inspect the damage, something reached out from under the porch, grabbed my T-shirt, and pulled.

My face hit the latticework so hard I couldn't yell, or even breathe, my sight beset by shooting stars. Childhood terrors rushed through my head. Visions of monsters hiding under the bed, lurking in the closet. The creature was using me as leverage for its birth from beneath the porch, pulling on me and emerging at the same time.

Desperate to get away, I felt my T-shirt stretch and tear, and then I was gripped by the shoulders and spun to face the night sky. A tentacle wrapped around my neck, with another one gripping the top of my head and pressing downward extremely hard.

Choking, wide-eyed and struggling, I clawed at the creature's muscular hold, desperate to inhale. My fingernails caught at confusing seams and folds as if the monster's skin was thick as heavyweight fabric. The pressure on my neck was horrible.

"*Shh*," the monster soothed in my ear. "Relax."

A rushing noise eclipsed the night, sucking me down, and down, and down into blackness. My hands weakened. They fell to my sides.

Awash in spinning stars, I inhaled a gulp of cool air as the constricting force released, and then a bitter liquid hit the back of my tongue. Gagging, miserable, I swallowed, feebly pushing at whatever was oddly rubbing my throat, and then I swallowed again.

"Perfect." A hand tapped my face. "I'll be right back."

My eyes rolled. "*Uhh …*"

11

With a spinning head, wide eyes, a slamming heart, and a high-pitched ringing in my ears, I squinted against the fluorescent lights and assessed my surroundings. Curtained enclosure. Flimsy gown. ER nurse bustling past the bed I'd woken up on ten seconds ago. If I had been faxed to the surface of Mars and discovered that I could breathe in the lightless vacuum of space, I couldn't have been more astonished.

"What's going on?" I demanded.

"Thank your stars you're in one piece," the nurse said. "Think twice next time. Don't take pills when you're feeling down."

"When I'm *what* …?"

"There's no shame in it. What matters is taking the right dose."

I gripped my aching skull. "This is insane. Why am I here?"

"Your neighbor found you on your driveway. You were out of it, and got scraped up from being knocked down by your dog."

"Luke? I don't …"

I paused, mid-protest.

Most of the night was locked in haze, but I *did* recall letting Luke out to pee, falling against the door of Cat Town, and my head hurting, beset by whirling stars. Past that point, all I could remember were disjointed nightmares, from a monster grilling me with questions about Richard to Joan shaking my shoulder in an effort to wake me. I recalled a dizzying car ride to the hospital. Nurses. Doctors. Detective Bricker. Dan. Their roles in the nightmare spun through my mind like split-second glimpses of scenes flashing outside the windows of a subway car.

"Still foggy?" the nurse said.

Massaging my aching brow, I felt a bandage over a bump that hurt. "Do I have a concussion? Is that why I'm here?"

"That, and concern over the medications you took."

"This is—did you say medications, *plural?*"

"You took a very big risk."

"I did *not* take anything …"

I held my breath, desperate to convince myself that she was wrong, but it was almost as if I could hear myself saying, *I took pills.*

"It's six thirty," she said. "Breakfast will be in an hour."

"I'm not hungry. I need to leave."

"It's best to wait and see what the doctor has to say. It might be mid-morning before he's available to check in."

"That's *hours* from now." I summoned a firm tone and straightened my spine. "I would not have agreed to come here. Who do I speak to about clearing this up in a faster time frame?"

"I don't make the rules." The nurse offered a glass of water. "The best thing you can do for yourself right now is hydrate."

I closed my eyes and drank the water down, then motioned for more. I couldn't recall ever being so thirsty in my life.

"Get some rest," the nurse said on her way out.

How could I possibly rest?

Instead of a clear idea of how I'd ended up in the ER, I was left with feelings that had detached themselves from related events. Shock. Terror. Disbelief. The sense that I'd been duped and robbed. Maybe that was from earlier in the night when I'd gone to Charlotte's property. I pushed the hospital gown from my legs and confirmed there were puncture wounds and scratches from running into the rose hedge.

I couldn't focus amidst the antiseptic smells of the hospital: rubbing alcohol, medicinal odors, and harsh cleaning products. Panic was threatening to take hold. I had to get out of there.

With the hospital gown flowing around me, I lurched out of the curtained area and collided with Dan — a blurred impression of aftershave and strong hands and a gray Hawaiian shirt that somehow managed to be expressive and understated at the same time.

As I tottered backward, he reached out to steady me, his hands sliding down my bare back, quite low down, until he was gripping my butt. Eyes wide, I felt adrenaline and other chemicals surge through me, completing the task of bringing me into the present moment.

"Sorry." Dan steadied my shoulders. "Are you ok?"

"I'm just … what are you doing here?"

"I'm your ride home."

"The nurse said—"

"Let's catch up in here, where there's less activity."

Dan gently steered me into the curtained enclosure and offered to "help" me onto the edge of the bed, which involved his warm hands finding temporary purchase on my bare thighs, retreating, then landing home again until we were more or less at eye level.

"Ok, wow," I managed. "Umm—"

"All set?"

"Dan, I have no idea—"

"It's being sorted out. Just listen, ok?"

He explained that Detective Bricker's wife worked the night shift in the ER. When Joan had brought me in just after one a.m., Mrs. Bricker had connected my name to the Gartland case and indulged the poor judgment of alerting her husband. He'd shown even worse judgment by heading straight there and questioning me while I was high.

"Wait," I said. "This business of me being high—" I closed my eyes. "Start from the beginning. *How* did I get here, point by point?"

"Luke came to Joan's house and whined at the kitchen door," Dan said. "She drove up the hill and found you outside. You were groggy, your eyes dilated. She brought you to the ER to have the bruise on your forehead checked. Concussions can be tricky, so—" Dan paused to address the nurse as she came in. "Give us a minute, please."

"This isn't the right time for a visit," she said with impatience.

"I'm a state trooper and a close friend." Dan handed her a business card. "I don't have time to explain, but from a legal standpoint, you'll want to comply with my request. Now please, give us a minute."

Assessing his stern demeanor with a wide-eyed gaze, the nurse cast a glance at me, and then she retreated without further delay.

"This is getting worse and worse," I said.

"Let's not delve into specifics right now," Dan said, kneeling to pick up the shopping bag he'd dropped when we'd collided. "I figured a fresh change of clothes would be a good thing."

"Sure, but ..."

"Your mother told me your size, etcetera," he said.

"You talked to my *mother?*"

"And your friend, Arlene."

"Oh my God ..."

"We can go over everything in detail later on," Dan said, then with an uncertain, puppylike twist of his eyebrows, he added, "I'm acting on information that you have a phobia of hospitals. It's fine if you prefer staying here a bit longer."

"I want to leave. This is a nightmare."

"Go ahead and change," Dan said softly. "I'm sorry if you feel rushed. I know it's confusing. We can talk when you get out."

"Can you ... maybe ..."

"Can I what, Sonny?" Dan said.

"H-hold me? I'm really scared."

"Of course."

Enveloped in his warm arms, I closed my eyes and burrowed against his chest, trembling and torn apart inside, beset by horror show glimpses of the night that made no sense. A swirling monster face, with blue neon markings, and the sight of my fingers dripping like candles held too close to a fire. It felt real one second, and impossible the next.

"Poor Joan," I managed. "I've wanted to be a role model for Harry and Jess. Now I'm the opposite."

"Joan worried you'd feel that way. She left you a note." When I refused to release my grip on his shirt, Dan reached to one side and said, "Here, I'll read it. She says you were wet from dew. She got you into warm clothes.

Saw the bruise, brought you here. Joan apologized for having to get home to Harry and Jess, and signed the note with hugs and kisses."

"She's the best neighbor ever."

"Sonny, I'm sorry I wasn't there for you after what happened in May," Dan said, his voice a comforting rumble against my ear. "Whatever is going on, whatever you need, we'll sort it out, ok?"

I nodded.

"Let's get you out of here," he said. "I think that'll help."

I peeled away and secured the bag he handed me. In the bathroom, I took one look at myself in the mirror, and stuck my head under the faucet. A bruised forehead was bad enough. I was not going to spend another minute looking as if an eagle had nested in my hair.

Step by step, I would task my way through the challenge of getting home. I would push the questions to the background. Thank Dan for the ride. Smile to let him know I was okay on the inside, even if I didn't look that way from the outside. Then I would drink a gallon of coffee and piece together what in the heck had happened to me.

Like an iffy meal that didn't quite want to settle, the crazy bits and pieces in my mind churned to the surface. *Lies won't work with me. You know what I'm here for. Focus. Say—it—again!*

I closed my eyes and gripped the sink, no idea I was uttering a frightened moan until Dan startled me by tapping on the door.

"Sonny? Are you ok?"

"Yeah," I managed. "I'm fine."

"If you have nausea, they need to know."

"No ... I'm fine."

Confronted by my ashen face and wide eyes staring back at me from the mirror, I realized that all the friends who'd prompted me to see a counselor over the summer had been right after all. Coping on my own had limits. At some point, a mind could throw a tantrum until a past trauma was brought to the surface and dealt with. There had to be a therapist who was up to the kind of challenges my story would present.

"Sonny," Dan prompted.

"I'm *fine*."

Thank you for being annoying, I silently added. There was nothing like a flash of irritation to help clear the fog.

I liked the silken feel of the outfit Dan had bought — a step above regular sweatpants, with a matching shirt. I pulled it on, saw my breasts saying hello quite friskily in the mirror, and closed my eyes. Reaching into the bag, I confirmed with dismay that he hadn't brought a bra, though he had included a package of underwear in my size. Boy short style, 100% cotton. My mother must have volunteered the particulars: *Don't buy anything with lace. Alison is allergic to lace. It makes her itch.*

When I emerged, Dan was standing next to the bed with a pair of sneakers. "Forgot socks, damn it," he said.

"It's ok. Thank you for …"

My voice trailed off as a doctor stepped in with a brisk smile. I had a feeling he'd waited nearby until I'd returned.

"Miss Littlefield. You look chipper today."

"I have a lot of questions. For one thing—" I stopped short, catching onto Dan's subtle signals that it might be best to let the doctor speak first. "But please continue," I managed.

"Certainly," the doctor said. "Excellent."

What followed was a confusing instance of experiencing only the "forth" part of a back-and-forth, with the doctor checking my pupils and stating aspects of my health history. With increasing alarm, I started to ask how he'd gained access to details about events that had happened years ago in Massachusetts, but my every response was cut short by Dan's signals to let the moment unfold. As I was prompted to confirm my history of experiencing nausea, headaches, and memory issues in reaction to certain medications, Dan steered my nod into more of a sideways motion, indicating to the doctor, *Maybe, but let's move on.*

"Your vitals are in the normal range at this point," the doctor said. "Do you have any questions before I give the all clear?"

"Actually, I—no," I managed. "I'm good to go."

"You'll be sure to keep an eye out for symptoms of a concussion for a few days, just in case?" the doctor said. "Excellent." He briskly shook my hand. "Please accept our apology for any confusion overnight. Tell Terence I'll be seeing him on the golf course."

"I ... will do that," I said. "Totally."

Warmth sank into my skin and relief calmed my heart as Dan and I stepped from the shadow of the hospital into the September sunshine at 7:30 a.m. He held up a remote on his key ring, and an answering chirp came from a red, extended-cab pickup truck.

Dan helped me into the cab, then reached past me for a second, which had his awesome shoulders and clean-shaven face just inches from my stunned eyes as he slipped a familiar leather jacket over my shoulders. I'd worn it on our motorcycle ride back in May.

He climbed in, set the key into the ignition, turned to me with a wide-eyed expression, and blew out a breath.

"I guess it's good to have connections," he said.

"Ok, let's go ahead and start with that mystery element. Who is this Terence the doctor mentioned?"

"No idea. Your mom will fill you in." Dan placed a call on his phone, and then my mother's voice was coming over the speaker.

"What is taking so long?" she demanded.

"Evelyn, we're good," Dan said. "She's out."

"Thank heaven. Alison?"

As Dan held his phone closer to me, I leaned away. With his eyebrows adding emphasis, he signaled that I should speak.

"Hello?" my mother said crossly. "*Helllooooo?*"

I closed my eyes and took Dan's phone. "Hi, Mom."

"What is the matter with you, leaving me to holler like that?" she said.

"I can't talk long. I'm on my way home."

"Come to Boston. Let me take care of you."

This insupportable notion helped clear the fog a bit more.

"I'm fine, just a little bruised."

"You were found in an intoxicated state on your driveway. I'm sending Stanley. I insist you leave that dreadful place at once."

Stanley was a twice-divorced next-door neighbor in Newton that my mother had pressed into service at every available turn for many years, all but making the poor man — a respectable podiatrist — her chauffeur, caddy, and all-around lackey. The same thing would happen to me if I returned to Newton and fell into her clutches again.

"I'm not leaving Maine, but Dan indicated that you pulled strings to get me released. Some guy named Terence?"

So began a dramatic tale of her outrage in hearing that I'd been interrogated by a detective in the ER, thanks to his unprincipled wife. High-level contacts in Boston's banking, golfing, and political spheres were woken up and cajoled into action in the dark of night. I waved off Dan's attempt to keep track of all the names, indicating there would be no logical thread to follow, and the exact timing was out the window.

"I didn't rest until I had assurances that lawsuits and other measures would follow any further wrongdoing or delays," my mother said.

"Well, it worked," I said. "Thank you."

"As to the tangled web of your life, what is your involvement with that young man? He took on a tone with me."

Dan gaped, whispering, "I didn't take on a tone."

"What kind of a tone?" I prompted.

"First, he said, 'Are you aware that your daughter is digging up her septic system all by herself?' Then I said, 'Of course not, my daughter never tells me anything.' Then he said—"

"Dan is sitting right here, you realize."

"Regardless of his tone, I agree, you need to hire an expert. I've sent money to your account."

"You didn't have to send money."

"Alison, you're taking the money," she said firmly. "You can't sell that ramshackle eyesore with a faulty septic system."

"I'm not selling my father's farm."

"Daniel?" my mother prompted.

He hesitated. "Yeah?"

"You'll talk sense into her, surely?"

"There's no need. Your daughter is very capable."

"I hope to heaven you're using protection. The last thing we need—"

"Bye Mom, thank-you-for-helping," I said so fast the words blended together. "I'll-call-you-in-a-couple-of-days."

I hung up. "Sorry about all that."

Dan cracked up. "I'm tough. I can handle it."

Keenly aware of Dan's brown eyes and manly presence in the confined space, I knew that looking pale and wide-eyed with shock was not an issue anymore. I was blushing up to the roots of my hair.

"I'm sorry for steering things in the hospital," Dan said. "Once your mother threatened legal action, we entered a situation where what you said could be taken out of context, or twisted around."

"Joan told you I was here?"

"Once she got home," Dan agreed. "I wish she'd called me first thing. By the time I arrived Bricker was questioning you in the ER."

I groaned. "I'm sorry I ruined your night."

"I don't see helping you in negative terms, so don't be hard on yourself," Dan said. "Let's walk through what happened."

"It's a little blurry. I remember Luke barking at 10. He needed to pee. I came downstairs and let him out. Then …"

Glimpses jerked through my skull, the awful monster face with neon markings hovering nearby, swirling. Panic seized me. I felt winded. Dazed. Pinned down. I cringed, unable to orient myself.

"*Sonny.*" Dan gently grasped my shoulder, pulling me from the crazy fragments, his brown eyes full of concern. "It's ok."

"I don't remember. It's all chopped up."

"That can happen with certain medications. The doctor on call made some mention of Swiss cheese amnesia."

"*What?* Oh my God …"

I hovered in disbelief, hearing three words I'd learned for the first time when I was six. I knew very well how two of my fingers had gotten broken. I had good reason to not say, so I'd pretended to not know. My mother's back and forth with the doctor was alarming. *What are you implying?* she'd demanded. *We're not that sort of family.*

"Sonny?" Dan said.

"Can I ask a dumb question?"

"No question is dumb. Ask away."

"Did I … did I tell anyone that I took pills?"

Dan looked sympathetic. "You told Joan and the ER staff. Bricker as well, unfortunately. And you told me."

I stared blankly. "I told *you* that I took pills?"

"It was as if you felt compelled, which fits who you are, when you think about it. Your drive to dispel confusion."

"I need to get out of here."

And by "here," I meant the entire current version of my life. Nothing had felt normal for days. For months, I admitted.

"I have an idea that might help clear the fog," Dan said. "Do you mind if we make a stop on the way to your farm?"

"Will it involve food? And is Luke ok?"

"He's fine. He's at Joan's house."

Dan started the engine and swung out.

The truck purred around corners, eased to stops, and surged forward with a low growl, a study of power held back. After we crossed a bridge, the rolling motion of the truck carried us through forests and past lush meadows. I closed my eyes, warmed by the jacket around my shoulders, and the sunlight flickering on my face.

"So sleepy," I murmured.

Dan's hand slipped around mine. "Get some rest."

* * *

Dimly, I was aware of the gentle rocking motion of the truck coming to a halt. I drifted back into a restless doze.

"Sonny?"

The world exploded with noise, and I knew what would happen next. Jerking awake, I hollered, "I didn't open the bag!"

"*Sonny.*" Dan gently gripped my shoulder. "I'm sorry. You were dozing. I didn't mean to startle you."

I squinted. "It's bright and loud here."

"It's the ocean." Dan indicated the dramatic scene of upturned rock ledges and churning waves beyond the sand parking lot and grassy lawn. "I figured with all that's happened in the past few days, why wait for the weekend? I hope you don't mind."

I focused on the sixty-foot pines shading a picnic area, and rugosa rose bushes studded with pink blossoms and crimson fruit. On our left was a lighthouse and a small museum perched near a cliff that sharply dropped away, with the blue Atlantic continuously in motion beyond. An offshore storm added a bank of slate-colored clouds to the distant horizon and pushed the surf into explosive waves against the rocks.

"I know this place," I said. "I came here as a child."

"All the better. I've got breakfast."

"Where did you …?"

"I had somebody meet us." Dan indicated the two large take-out bags he was holding. "I love delivery apps."

"This is a surprise. I love the ocean."

Squinting in the bright light, I nodded in thanks as he snugged sunglasses over my eyes, and then I followed him to a picnic table.

For ten minutes, all I could focus on was the egg and Canadian bacon sandwich he handed me, then the second sandwich he handed me, along with crispy fries and a chocolate shake that was so thick, it was tough to pull through a straw. All the while, I absorbed the warmth of the sun on my shoulders, inhaled the misty salt air, and sank into the rhythmic tumult of the waves exploding against the rocks thirty yards away.

Gulls added their shrill calls to the morning scene, eyeing our food with bright yellow eyes as they glided past us overhead. Dan tossed a scrap upward, then smiled as one of the gulls caught it.

Now and then I addressed his worried glances by smiling and leaning against him, and then I returned to the question I couldn't answer after telling Dan and others that I'd taken pills. *What* pills? The only ones in my medicine cabinet were probably long expired.

"Sonny, it's natural to feel anguish over not getting to a victim in time," Dan said. "If you're feeling burdened by Richard's death, you need to stop. You stepped up beyond what others would do."

"I have been plagued by regrets," I said.

"It's a form of survivor's guilt, which makes Bricker's approach all the worse. The baiting and harsh tone, then having you frisked in front of a crowd of gawkers. A colleague held me in check but I wanted to go over there, and—" Dan's scowl said it was a good thing he'd been stopped. "Add that to the shock of seeing me. In hindsight, I get how you interpreted my delay in reaching out. If at all possible, please understand that it was a sign of caring. I wanted to set the stage. See? That's not the right wording. I wanted to be clear of any hurdles."

"You explained why you delayed."

"Bottom line, I understand why you had a rough night."

"It's my own fault."

"That's crazy," Dan said. "Nothing is your fault."

"You'll catch on one day. I've learned to not hope too much, or expect my life to smooth out. Ever since I can remember ..."

Donald has been coming after me. He'll never quit.

To my horror, I burst into tears.

"Why do you do this to me?" I managed. "I never cry in front of people. I *hate* it. But here you are again, acting all supportive."

"It's ok, Sonny. Let it out."

With Dan's arm around me, holding me close, I sobbed into a napkin from our breakfast, drenching it within seconds, tossing it to the side, then drenching another one. Every ache I'd held at bay for weeks welled up and poured out. Arguments with my cousins and other foes in town. Feeling alone. Seeing Richard's blood on the road. Getting frisked. Worst of all, the new clenched place in my mind. A monster was in there, clawing to get out. I locked it down. Enough was enough.

"I guess that was overdue," I managed, wiping the last of the tears and willing myself to get a grip as a group of vacationers arrived and gawked our way. "Why is crying so painful?"

"I'm told it's healthy," Dan said. "But I never cry, either."

"There's a lot to talk about, but I need to get home. Not before sitting by the water for a while, if you have time."

"Absolutely."

Dan offered a hand as we navigated the massive, angled metamorphic ledges on our way to the thundering waves.

The sea breeze was delicious, drawing my gaze to the rugged coastline extending into the shimmering distance. White foam gathered on incoming waves for miles, creating a current of lulling, rhythmic sounds, from the booms and splashes of the nearer waves to the thuds and hisses of the surf a hundred yards away. I didn't mind in the least what the wild mist might be doing to my hair. With the wind buffeting our shirts, we sat close enough to the surf to catch occasional splashes of water. We had to holler to hear each other amidst the roar of the hypnotic, tide-driven waves lifting in a succession of five-foot arcs, then booming downward against massive stone ledges that were slick with seaweed.

"See there?" Dan pointed to three small black birds bobbing perilously close to the dangerous surf. "Black Guillemots."

I watched in amazement as one of the birds dove straight down and disappeared beneath the foam, not more than ten feet from the boulders. The force of the ocean water had to be wild and unpredictable in that spot, a churning menace to navigate.

"What are they catching down there?" I said.

"Fish and invertebrates."

"How do they not get crushed?"

"It's what they do, how they roll." Dan's arm hugged me. "Remind you of anyone? Maybe you were a Guillemot in a past life."

"Bricker predicted you'll get fed up with me."

Dan frowned. "He said what?"

"You heard him last night. You came to the ER."

Like a firecracker going off in my mind, specific words blazed through the chaos of outlandish elements. *Your boyfriend will rethink his options and see you as a problem. Trust me, you're better off on your own.*

"I didn't hear the back-and-forth before I arrived," Dan said. "Bricker mentioned me specifically?"

"The confusing thing is … did he come to my farm?"

"Not that I know of. Why?"

"That's where I picture him demanding to know what I took from Richard's jewelry bag. He was angry, really awful about it." Seeing the level of Dan's scowl, I said, "I think I'm mixing things up. What I'm talking about feels more like a nightmare than a real event."

"Bricker did question you in the ER. If you want to take action—"

"No need, let's leave it alone." I gripped Dan's arm. "If you had tried to go after him for having me frisked, I would have put you in an armlock. Don't compromise your job on my behalf."

"I won't, Sonny."

"I don't suppose you've ever had amnesia."

"No, but in college a guy in my dorm sleepwalked, which is kind of similar. He'd get out of bed, even leave his room. When someone made a video of him, he thought he was being punked."

"He woke up like me, with a giant blank?"

"It was always around final exams," Dan said. "Low-level stuff, compared to murder scenes. I know you'll confront the issue head-on. It's clear that you want answers. I'll help any way I can."

His faith in me would have to suffice until I regained faith in myself.

"Did I see ice hockey gear in your truck?" I said.

"I'm hoping to get back to it this winter," Dan said. "Downhill skiing, too. Any sports in your wheelhouse?"

"Softball. Bet I could strike you out."

Dan smiled. "Bring it on."

We turned our faces to the sea mist, with gulls gliding by overhead. In the wake of an explosive wave, a divot of water formed against the rocks, streaked with churning eddies as it sank downward, exposing barnacles and glistening seaweed on the boulders. Above it, an incoming wave rose up, curling at the top from the momentum of the tide pushing behind it, and then gravity started winning out, creating a ponderous forward lean just as the outgoing trough reached its lowest point.

Boom.

Spray reached us, and then the impact dissolved into a delicious fizz of churned-up water sliding downward to rejoin the sea.

"Awesome," Dan said.

"Thank you for bringing me."

"It's good for me, too. A chance to rest the mind."

I nodded. "Hallelujah to that."

12

Dan was relaxed behind the wheel, all that truck putty in his hands as he steered down wooded lanes and sent a couple of calls directly to voicemail without missing a beat. One of the calls warranted a frown and a response. With his phone to his ear, Dan engaged in a subtle back-and-forth that suggested the person being discussed was within hearing distance.

"Not yet," he said. "Understood. Got it." Seeing me watching him as he hung up, he stowed his phone in his pocket. "Sorry."

"Was that about me? You're getting flack for helping me?"

"Not at all. It's a work thing."

"I saw Roy Allen's name on the caller ID," I said of the detective who'd led the murder investigation in May. "I wouldn't mind getting his take on things. Bricker had no right to grill me while I was out of it," I added, frowning as the detective's awful rant spun out of the confusing murk. "I remember him talking about somebody getting double-crossed."

Dan studied me. "If this is a sharp recollection, I'll loop Roy in straight away. Was a nurse nearby? Someone who can corroborate it?"

"Not that I can recall."

"Sonny, until you can offer specific details …"

I signaled surrender with my hands. "I know I shouldn't raise alarms about him without proof. I'll sort it out. I promise."

I paused as Arlene sent a photo of herself, her husband, Lance, and their three children smiling with their hands framing heart shapes. Caleb, their nine-month-old, added his happy grin to the effort.

As Dan looked over, I showed him the photo. "Given the late hour, I assume your conversation with Arlene was brief?"

"Don't worry, if she divulged any secrets, I didn't hear because her daughter kept hollering, 'chicharrones de pollo!'" Dan said.

I cracked up. "Sounds like Sarah, her four-year-old. Chicharrones de pollo is a crunchy fried chicken with Latin spices. It's a family favorite from Puerto Rico. Arlene's mother grew up there."

"You mentioned her father one time. A big influence, if I recall."

I nodded. "Byron March. History professor. He's developed a detailed timeline of his black and brown ancestors. Hardships. Milestones. He feels connected to them through shared abilities and strengths. It's a powerful thing for him. Spiritual. So, when I found out about Raymond, Byron urged me to come here and build a sense of ..." I paused, still fixated on my earlier point. "If what I heard Bricker say is true, that someone got double-crossed, maybe it explains why Richard hired a PI. Then again, it could indicate marital troubles. My plumber saw Angela in a moment when she was really upset. Crying. Maybe it had to do with a secret. A threat. You can't imagine how desperate Richard looked."

"Sonny ..."

"His death can't be about a *thing* he was trying to protect. He spent his last moments on a mission. I'm certain of it."

"We're getting answers every moment the case unfolds," Dan assured me. "It's not your burden to carry. You need to let it go."

"This is frustrating beyond words."

"Show me some photos from your travels," Dan prompted.

I sighed. "Ok, this is from a trip to Costa Rica."

Dan nearly swerved off the road as he leaned over and grimaced at the image on my phone. "What's that thing on your arm?"

"It's Galleta, a pet tarantula I saw at a nature center. Look at this close-up of her feet. They're fuzzy, and have tiny claws."

"I think I might throw up," Dan said, then he narrowed his eyes and faintly smiled. "Of all the shots in your library, you picked one that would spark a reaction. A classic passive-aggressive move."

"Not even close," I said feebly, and then I grinned.

"Game on," Dan said. "Wait until it's your turn."

"Thank you for making me laugh," I said. "And for the excellent job of putting on a normal front, even if—" I closed my eyes. "That came out wrong. You're always as you seem. Zero artifice."

"You can trust that in me, Sonny. No matter what."

"You can trust what's in front of you right now as well. If there's one thing I've perfected in life, it's how to bounce back after a shock. Last night is like a party in the next building. I can mostly tune it out. It's not denial," I quickly added. "I will address it when I'm ready."

Dan nodded. "Listen, it's been on my mind that your father left you a number of firearms. Are they properly stored?"

"In a locked cabinet," I agreed.

"How about we visit the practice range this week?"

"You're making it sound urgent."

"With the case in the wings, I can't help but revisit what happened in May," Dan admitted. "In a moment of panic, you tossed the perpetrator's weapon into the leaves instead of disarming it."

"I've had nightmares about the gun going off as it landed." With that awful night in mind, I said, "Yesterday, you talked about having to create a buffer zone to be sure the border work didn't follow you home. It seems impossible. Crimes spill in all directions."

"Don't let it worry you, Sonny." Dan reached over and squeezed my hand. "Prosecutions are in progress. That's part of the reason for maintaining a tight lid. Things will relax over time."

As Dan turned into my driveway and climbed past the lofty pines that bordered the road, my sheep looked up from grazing with sprigs of clover in their muzzles. Hearing the growl of an engine, I sat forward, shocked to see a man on a backhoe digging up my side lawn.

Dan groaned. "It's my father. He gets carried away."

"I can't afford a whole new septic system!"

"Don't worry, he won't charge a dime."

Once Dan parked and we stepped out, he used every symbol known to man for halting work in progress—a cutting motion under his chin, a time-out, and then both hands motioning at once. In response, his father gave quick waves indicating he was *almost* done. Maybe it was wrong to enjoy seeing that Dan had his own issues with an out-of-control parent. As he glanced at me with a look of apology, I smiled to convey my take on the scene. Dan cracked up and shook his head.

Seeing that Joan had dropped off Luke on her way to work, I crossed to his pen. Once the wire door was open, he tumbled out to greet me with an extra measure of excitement, softly whining and sniffing my clothes.

"I'm fine," I assured him. "On the mend."

As the backhoe finally growled to a halt, Dodge delivered a thunderous whinny into the sudden quiet, the best welcome home nature had ever devised. I patted his neck on my way back to Dan.

The delay helped calm my nerves as I faced meeting his father. Given my off-the-charts history of getting dragged into crimes, logic suggested the introductions would be tense. *Seriously, fate?* I silently demanded. *You haven't thrown enough at me in twenty-four hours?*

With silver hair and a big smile, Mr. Bolton senior defied my grim expectations. He had the look of an absent-minded professor as he walked over, his pressed chinos, blue cardigan, and white shirt at odds with the business of digging a hole. I couldn't help but wonder if he'd stopped in to complete the task on his way home from playing golf.

"Norris Bolton." His hand enveloped mine. "Pleased to meet you, Sonny. Looks like you've landed on your feet again."

"Dad, what are you doing?" Dan said. "I told you to wait."

"What for? I bet her first taste of digging was enough."

"Dan told you about it?" I said with raised eyebrows.

"Lord, yes. He said you were covered in dirt."

"I said you looked good *despite* the dirt," Dan insisted.

Norris nodded. "That's right. He said—"

"Dad, we talked about this, remember?"

"Now, don't be embarrassed." Norris clapped his son's back. "I can see her resemblance to that actress you've always had a crush on."

"It's not just that—"

"Of course it's more," Norris agreed. "She's smart and plucky. Patient with your layers of nonsense. That makes her a saint."

Dan looked helpless, as people do when a parent blunders around in their plans, but overall, he was holding up well.

"Don't worry, your mother is footing the bill for a new tank," Norris went on. "Parents don't see helping their kids as an expense. It's a way for her to share in your experience up here away from home."

"I thought Uncle Shelby would do the work," Dan said.

"Sprained his back," Norris reported. "Truth be told, I'm happy to have an excuse to get on the old bird." He gestured toward the backhoe. "Mind your step over there until the new tank arrives. Hopefully, the murder will be wrapped up by then as well."

Judging from Dan's wide gaze, he appeared to be picturing his father mowing down my house with the yellow scoop.

I used his distraction to press Norris for insights. "Has anyone mentioned what was in Richard's jewelry bag?"

"Tie clips and such," Norris confided. "Not *one* valuable item. That's why Bricker has mistrust where you're concerned."

"It takes two seconds to come up with theories," I said, listing a few on my fingers. "Richard grabbed the wrong bag in a moment of confusion. Maybe an item was *missing*, and he wanted to tell someone. If the item was a slip of paper and blew away, it could be anywhere."

"Exactly," Norris agreed. "An open mind is what's needed."

"Are there any solid leads?"

"Well, Richard was liquidating assets and seemed to be preparing for trouble," Norris whispered as if he imagined members of the press in the weeds. "He was backing out of business deals, and he had a plane ticket to the Cape Verde Islands. *One* ticket, if you catch my drift. Not the first place I'd think of to visit, but to each his own."

"Ok, this needs to stop," Dan said, abruptly catching on.

"Whatever was up for grabs in the Gartland household had to be pretty big," Norris persisted. "I've heard mention of a precise, military approach in what went on, and Richard getting tortured. Forget about a garden variety murderer. It has to be a psychopath."

"Dad, for the love of God," Dan said. "I mean, *why?*"

"Sorry," Norris murmured, then in a brighter tone, he returned to the business at hand. "Didn't take but a minute to get the trench in shape. I just need to load the backhoe onto the flatbed."

"Let's get to it," Dan said, "So we're out of Sonny's hair."

"Hang on, there's the other thing," Norris said pointedly. "You wanted to check that issue of *concern*. Remember?"

"What issue of concern?" I said.

"The broken window pane," Dan said, casting his father a severe look. "I wanted to take measurements. Help with the fix."

"It can wait. I covered the broken pane with cardboard."

"That won't hold if it rains," Norris insisted. "Let Danny assess the damage. Meanwhile, you can help me load the bird."

Once he secured my keys, Dan gently steered Norris away a few steps and conveyed a message I couldn't overhear, but could easily guess at: *I'm begging you, don't rock the boat with difficult subjects.*

His father professed full agreement, his hands and demeanor indicating he would be a perfect angel from that moment on.

Once his son stepped away, Norris widened his eyes, which I took to mean, *He's intense at times. You just have to go with it.*

"I sure love seeing an old barn," he said, smiling as he gazed up at the weathered peak. "Think of the history in there."

"I'm worried it might collapse."

"Let's check." Norris led me to the double door and peered upward into the hay-smelling interior. "The timbers are in great shape."

"What about the roof?"

"Well, there's a touch of sunlight here and there. Minor holes."

Norris and I arranged half bales of straw in the trench so tightly that I could walk across them without missing a step. With the backhoe loaded on the trailer, I looked toward my house and was surprised to see a flash indicating Dan was taking photos of my bedroom ceiling.

"What is he doing?" I said.

"He's a stickler for details. Likes to get all the facts."

"A leak in the ceiling is the reason Raymond went out during a storm in February," I said. "Dan asked if it left any stains."

"Sometimes, damage can be hidden," Norris said.

"Should I pry the tiles loose to check?"

"I'm sure there's no need," Norris said with an unconvincing level of drama. "Leave it be. Dan will handle it."

"I don't expect him to. He's helped me out enough."

"Nonsense."

"I'm serious. I want you to know I'm miserable about dragging Dan into another mess. To be honest, I'm surprised you're being generous with me. He's a model citizen. Steady and calm …"

"Except for the ill-advised undercover job," Norris pointed out. "You take tribulations in stride and keep a level head on what's right and wrong. That's why I'm on team Sonny. And just so you know, I'm acting out of gratitude. Back in the spring, you helped Dan part with the motorcycle he inherited from Aaron. I can't thank you enough."

"Dan did that on his own."

Norris chuckled. "You won't let people be grateful, will you?"

"Maybe this once," I said with a smile.

Norris started to climb into his truck, and then paused.

"You're a champion of the downtrodden, but don't extend sympathy to that Frank character just yet. I don't trust a man who's got an attorney by his side 24/7. And while I'm at it, Bricker was unfaithful to his wife not long ago. The guys say he stops being an ass when it comes to Angela Gartland. In her company, he blushes to his roots."

I gaped. "Isn't she still in the hospital?"

"I'm not saying she's reciprocating," Norris said. "I'm offering intel to keep in mind in case it helps navigate your way along."

"I appreciate it. I really do."

Norris studied me. "I'm worried you've got sorrows tucked deep down. Was it insomnia that led to taking pills?"

"I *didn't*—" I closed my eyes and regrouped so I wouldn't sound harsh. "Please don't worry. It's an isolated instance."

Norris nodded. "If you ever need fatherly advice …"

"Thank you," I managed, blinking back tears and suppressing the impulse to hug him. "For helping out as well."

I waved as Norris pulled away.

Dan appeared to have completed his measurements inside the house and now stood at the bottom of my porch steps, studying the ground. Luke raced toward him as if to reaffirm that he was a friend. I'd never seen my dog so keyed up. It had been a rough night for him as well.

"Hey, big guy," Dan said, kneeling to scratch his neck.

A split second too late, a flick of motion amongst the weeds caught my eye the same instant that Luke saw Effie the wild tabby looking toward him with her tail twitching. With an angry yowl, she sped past his excited effort to befriend her and disappeared into Cat Town.

"Luke, no chasing kitties!" I hollered.

My pace slowed. I touched my brow, dizzy as I recalled yelling the same thing last night. *Luke, no chasing kitties. Bad boy!*

"He didn't harm her," Dan assured me.

"I know, I just … had a weird moment."

"It's par for the course with cats and dogs, and explains how the slats got broken," Dan said, indicating the latticework door. "I bet either the tabby or some other animal was down here last night."

In the shadow of the house, gooseflesh claimed my arms as I stared at the broken door. When I'd first moved to the farm, Cat Town was one of the places I'd had to check with a flashlight before I could fall asleep, fully aware it was irrational to think that something awful might be living there. Now it felt as if my worries had led to consequences in the real world: a glimpse of tripping forward and hitting the latticework, the world dissolving into stars, and tentacles reaching out from the darkness and grabbing me. Then what? It was as if my mind had switched off.

However nutty it seemed, I checked for teeth marks on my arms. Of course, there were none. Just a sore neck and minor bruises.

"Sonny?" Dan prompted.

I focused on him. "Sorry, what were you saying?"

"The door is fixable."

"Good. Excellent."

"Did you rake here after we found Raymond's silver dollar?"

I looked down at the area he indicated. Instead of growing every which way around the steps where it was tough to mow, the grass was neat and tamed as if a magic spell had caused the blades to point north. Nothing on my farm was obedient, certainly not grass.

"Sonny?" Dan prompted. "Were you trying to find something?"

"No, I didn't rake."

"What's this?" Dan knelt and plucked a glass vial from the crevice next to the latticework. "From a soil test kit, maybe?"

I took it and held it to the light. The vial was a few inches in height, with a rubber stopper. Beads of moisture were inside.

"Raymond wanted the pH in the berry field just right," I said. "To be honest, I've dropped the ball on it."

"Maybe Harry took over. Did he come back after I stopped by?"

"I can't imagine when. After you left …"

I'd waited until dark to conduct a clandestine inspection of Charlotte's outbuilding. If she found out about it at some point, she wouldn't hesitate to demand that I be charged with trespassing.

Dan straightened with a look of regret. "You're spent. I should have brought you straight home from the ER."

"No, the coast was wonderful. It was perfect."

Studying me with a worried frown, Dan said, "My father doesn't think before he talks. He didn't say anything that upset you?"

"Norris was great. In that regard, you're the luckiest man alive. Now, I've worked out the math," I said, steering him toward his truck. "You got less sleep than I did last night."

"Yeah, I need to head out if you're all set." Looking distracted again, Dan paused and added, "I want to borrow the map you used the other night. The one with Theo's old address."

"You're sure Raymond circled crime scenes?"

"That's why I want to study it," Dan said. "To be sure."

"It's still in my car, I think."

When his departure was further delayed by a call, I grabbed a wooden basket I'd left near the porch and followed the path that led to the orchard behind the house, determined to thank Dan with a gift that was unique to my farm. Working quickly, I put Seckel pears in the basket, then crisp, red Empire apples that were at their peak. Finally, I added a bonanza of white nectarines, which had a sweet flavor reminiscent of honey.

I lugged the basket uphill through the orchard. Emerging from the path, I saw Dan pacing with the map in one hand and a bottle of antacid in the other. He took a long swig as if it were a soda pop.

"What are you *doing?*" I snatched the bottle from his grip. "You can't drink this without measuring it out. You'll get messed up."

"A colleague just updated me." Dan indicated his phone, looking as if he wanted to pitch it into the weeds. "Greg McDonnell is telling people you got high because you were celebrating a windfall."

"Greg is a jerk. Nobody will listen to him."

"What if the killer gets wind of it?" Dan paced and rubbed his head. "It's happening again. Complexities. Odd elements left and right. Circles upon circles, with you right in the middle of it."

"Dan. *Dan.*" I gripped his arm to stop his pacing. "You were calm two minutes ago. It's not like you to lose it."

"My mind is on switchbacks," he admitted. "It's a challenge I've faced after the border gig. To not jump at shadows. I don't mean to upset you, but my gut is screaming that things are off."

"Maybe it'll help to know I've been building my skills all summer," I said. "Brumby taught me some self-defense moves, plus Nadine Gilbert helps me train when she's in town."

Dan rolled his eyes. "Sonny …"

"Don't give me that look. Nadine is a *former* hooker, and pole dancing takes crazy strength. As for the ungluing I just witnessed, how about if I hang onto that map? You have enough on your plate."

"Uh-uh." Dan held it out of my reach. "You'll go straight in and cross reference crime locations with entries in Raymond's journals."

"It's *my* map. Hand it over."

"Tell me I'm wrong."

"Look, you're an alpha, but I'm a version of alpha too," I said crossly. "Don't imagine you can run my life."

"I'm not trying to, Sonny."

"The heck you aren't. You scoop me up from the ER and drag me to the coast without asking. You press me for answers when I don't have any." Breathing hard, I stopped abruptly and covered my eyes. "I'm sorry. You haven't pressed for answers, and you're right about the map. I'd head straight in and cross-check the crime locations with Raymond's journals. Keep the map for now, but I'll want it back."

"Of course," Dan said.

"I don't know what's wrong with me."

"You're in one of those cycles where new challenges hit the fan before you're finished resolving old ones. It starts to feel like that weightlifting move, the 'clean and jerk,'" he added with air quotes.

I paused. "Umm ... the *what?*"

"You've never seen it on the Olympics? Here's the 'clean.'" Flexing as if holding barbells, Dan wrenched his fists to shoulder height. "You hold this racked position," he went on, "balancing the ungodly weight but aware you're only halfway there. Then the *'jerk.'*" With a growl, Dan hoisted the imaginary weight over his head. "I'm not doing the stance right. It takes a step forward, but you get the reference, I think."

"One, that is totally my life. I've never seen a better analogy. Two, it was nice to watch. Can you do it again?"

Dan smiled. "That's all it took to get out of the doghouse? I can't repeat it right now. I think I pulled something."

I cracked up. "You weren't lifting an actual weight."

"I went through the motions," he protested.

In hopes of erasing my burst of irritation and conveying gratitude for his help and support that morning, I snagged his gray Hawaiian shirt and planted a quick, but hopefully stirring kiss on his lips.

"Hang on, not so fast," he murmured as I pulled back.

"I need to explain why I lashed out," I said. "Support from friends is wonderful, but to recover from bouts of chaos ..."

"You need space," Dan said. "I get it."

"Just a day or two."

"No worries. While we're here ..." Dan pointed toward the stream. "The low area down there is where Raymond wanted to re-dig the beaver pond that got overgrown. With a few tweaks to redirect the flow of water, you could encourage beavers to set up shop again. Amphibians, insects, and all kinds of birds benefit from their efforts."

"Redirect the flow, huh? You sound like an engineer."

Dan shrugged. "On paper, I am an engineer."

"That's what your degree is in? It makes total sense."

"Yeah, I'm big on building stuff, making sure I know how all the parts work." Dan brushed a curl from my face. "That part of me wants to take charge and address your memory loss with ... honestly, I don't have a clue. The rest of me knows how strong you are. Direct and focused. You need to find your own way, at your own pace."

"That version of you is optimistic? Maybe even flexible?"

Dan raised an eyebrow. "Define flexible."

I didn't dare.

"These are for you," I said, indicating the basket.

"Awesome, Sonny. Thank you."

As he slipped into his truck and tossed me a wave, I smiled to convince him that I wouldn't fall apart the moment he left me alone.

Now all I had to do was convince myself.

13

With my phone in hand, I sat on the edge of my bed in a mote of afternoon sunlight, shocked by what I'd found on my nightstand, and utterly trashed by the knowledge that Dan must have seen it, too.

"Sonny?" Arlene prompted. "Was it there?"

I regarded the bottle of muscle relaxants that I'd had for two years, ever since I'd sprained my back during a climbing mishap.

"Yes, the bottle was here," I said. "The more confusing thing is the glass of water on the nightstand. It's crazy. I don't remember going downstairs to get water, let alone taking these pills."

"Check the bottle. How many are left?"

I dumped the pills onto my hand, and counted them twice.

"Sonny?" Arlene prompted.

"I took three in the past. I know it for a fact because I put tick marks on the label. Now three more are missing."

Arlene heaved a sigh. "I'm sorry. I know it's a hard moment."

"Why would I have taken *three?*" I demanded.

"You're under stress. Exhausted and sleep deprived."

"They didn't give me amnesia in the past."

"To be on the safe side, keep the pills out of reach from now on."

"Already on it," I said, retreating down the stairs.

I slipped the pill bottle into a plastic sandwich bag and stowed it in a drawer, then I frowned and sniffed the air. For seven months, the scent of cinnamon had wafted through the kitchen from an unknown source. The stove? The cabinets? I could never decide. It always brought Raymond to mind. Cinnamon toast was the last meal he'd ever eaten. Now, I picked up on a sharp odor that I couldn't quite place.

My skin prickled and my heart thudded as I looked past the kitchen table to the living room. I was alone. My mind was playing tricks, conjuring unknown perils lurking in the shadows. I shook it off and hovered over the kitchen sink. Maybe Norris had put a product in the septic tank to stabilize it, and the odor was strong enough to travel up to the house through the pipes. That sort of made sense.

"Sonny?" Arlene prompted.

"The pills are tucked away in a kitchen drawer," I reported. "Now, I've delayed the big question long enough. What did you say to Dan?"

"In a nutshell, I think you're both overanalyzing things," Arlene said. "You're afraid of getting burned. He's worried you've been traumatized. I advised him to not waste time dithering. You need to go on an official date, release the pressure, and just talk."

"Don't call him again," I said. "I forbid you."

"Don't give me a reason to call him."

"Arlene—" I paused, wincing, conflicted, with my eyes closed. "Ok, I need to say this. There was another time when I felt this way. In grade school. I flunked tests. Couldn't focus. Fell asleep at my desk."

"I remember it," Arlene said softly.

"Donald convinced a doctor that I had ADD," I said in a hoarse whisper. "He put drugs in my food for two months. He did it behind my mother's back. To this day, she has no idea he stooped that low to minimize my presence. It's a miracle I figured it out."

"It wasn't a miracle. You outsmarted Donald."

"I know this time is different," I said. "Apparently, I told everyone that I took pills last night. I just … I can't believe it."

"Here's the plan," Arlene said. "First thing tomorrow, go to the hospital and ask for a record of your blood work. If the tests show that you did take the pills, don't waste time by bashing yourself to pieces."

"Ok," I said glumly. "I suppose that'll work."

Pacing after we hung up, I caught sight of Raymond's lucky silver dollar on the countertop where I'd put it, and a ray of hope blazed through the fog. On the living room bookshelf was an index that my stepmother, Ella, had created years ago to help Raymond keep track of his journal entries. He'd kept up with the index after Ella had died. With my pulse racing, I checked index entries starting with recent years, and all but broke down with emotion when I came across a line with the names Ken Babik and Richard Gartland next to Apogee Antiques.

I grabbed the journal Raymond's index cited, plus two earlier volumes, and burst out of the house. Luke bounded out after me, wagging his tail, then he looked disappointed when I plunged into one of the rocking chairs instead of charging out to play with him on the lawn.

Soon, I found the right entry.

Finally got around to visiting Apogee Antiques when Mr. Gartland was scheduled to man the cash register, Raymond had written. *Brought out my lucky coin as a conversation opener, then asked if I'd heard correctly that he was interested in handcrafted furniture from the late 1800s. Certain makers, specific styles. He said the pieces he finds along those lines are purely for his private collection. Smiling. Affable. No sign of shifty motives.*

Truth be told, the folks I overheard in the diner seemed to be thrilled to have gotten a good price for an old cabinet they'd inherited from an aunt. What struck me as odd was that Mr. Gartland and Ken Babik had approached the couple out of the blue, rather than the other way around. I suppose it makes sense that they'd heard about the item through a customer who'd stopped by the store. I shook his hand and left. Told Joan it's a shop she should visit.

I'd hoped to find a clue that helped put the case in overdrive, but the lack of a "smoking gun" scarcely mattered. In picturing the scene, it was as if I was the one reaching out to shake Mr. Gartland's hand. It wasn't closure, exactly. Just a link that bridged time and space.

I picked up the other volume that I'd flagged with broken hearts and flipped the pages until I found the entries that resonated with my turmoil. Until that point, Raymond had written down his thoughts and plans in an easygoing scrawl. After a span of missing days, it looked as if he couldn't hold the pen steady. He'd been shaking as he wrote.

March 11: The results came in today. I had questions, but it was like someone had a grip on my throat. Ella murmured that she was okay and rubbed my arm as the doctor explained the disease. She was the strong one. Worried about me, of all things. I can't endure watching her fade. I can't picture her gone.

Raymond's chronicle of Ella's battle with leukemia started on a tight rein. Short sentences. Clipped bursts of emotion.

He'd felt to blame for the unfavorable prognosis, having never pressed too hard about Ella getting regular checkups. She was a shy woman, not apt to complain, even toward the end. Especially then. The free-flowing passages ended on November 2 in a later journal:

Ella passed today. The sky was clear. She looked peaceful.

"Why didn't you reach out to me?" I said, touching the ridges and loops of Raymond's handwriting, the same way I often picked up his shirts, his badge, and his pipe. "I wouldn't have rejected you."

My father had made no further entries for weeks on end, though an occasional worn page suggested that he'd opened the journal, sat with it at the table for a while, and then shoved the journal aside. Later, he'd written of the period when he'd tried to drink his sorrow away.

Colleagues hauled me out of bars by the scruff of the neck more than once. Joan turned away crying when I barked at her to stop fussing. Harry and Jess stopped coming up the hill to pet Dodge. I was going down hard, and that's how I wanted it to be. I asked the good Lord to take me.

I lost nights. Couldn't remember what I'd done. I'd find things where they shouldn't be. The blackouts were alarming. I woke up in my truck one night. I'd driven five miles dead drunk. I picked up the bottle and stared at it in horror. The taste was in my mouth. I couldn't remember drinking it.

I groaned as Joan's car headed toward me up the driveway with a rumble of tires and a plume of gravel dust. I loved my supportive friends, but on that confusing day my energies would be drained by the need to make apologies and offer assurances that felt hollow.

"I'm glad to see the color back in your cheeks," Joan said, arriving with a casserole in hand, and praise for Luke for alerting her to trouble shortly after midnight. "It was confusing," she admitted when I apologized for the jarring moment. "I've never known you to …"

"Take pills? I never have. I get side effects."

"Maybe that's why it hit you so hard," Joan said softly.

"Yeah, umm …" I closed my eyes. "Yeah."

Following her through the door into the kitchen, I only vaguely heard her tips on how best to reheat the casserole.

"Do you detect an unusual odor in here?" I said.

"That's your T-shirt from last night. It smelled of bug repellent. Plus, it was dirty and a little torn, so I figured it was best to toss it in the trash. If you want it as a cleaning rag, I'll fish it out of the bin."

"Bug repellent?" I said, mystified all over again. "No, it was an old shirt to begin with. I'm sorry for all the bother."

"It's not a bother to help a friend," she assured me.

Joan was elated when she saw Raymond's fishing fly collection where I'd left it on a shelf. A nail remained on the living room wall where the shadow box had hung until Charlotte had filched it. Joan returned it to its rightful place and then stepped back to admire the collection.

"Can you show me where you found me?" I said.

"Sure, if it'll help."

I followed her out the door and down the porch steps, then looked on as she attempted to show me how she'd found me curled and shivering on the bottom step as if I'd stopped in mid-crawl.

Joan rubbed my arm. "Hence, the bump on your head."

"That happened outside Cat Town," I murmured.

Squinting in the sunlight with her arms folded and her blonde hair stirring in the breeze, Joan looked distracted as she gazed toward the view of clouds drifting eastward over distant forests and fields.

"You're bound to be concerned about the impact on Harry and Jess," I said. "If you want, I'll tell them I'm an idiot."

"Nonsense. Forget it."

"No, really—"

"Ok, it's time I came clean," she blurted. "I was in love with Raymond. We never got up to anything. But I *wanted* to. My husband and I drifted apart," she added. "You know he's a merchant mariner. The last time he came home—" Joan closed her eyes. "After ten days or so I figured out he'd cheated on me. He left a situation. Down *there*."

I paused, wide-eyed. "You mean …"

"It's fine, all cleared up, but as you can imagine I was boiling mad. I'd hung in thinking it was best for Harry and Jess to have their father in the picture. After the incident, he's been too ashamed to face me. Doesn't write or call. Anyway, I'm sorry I've left you to think things are perfect across the road. Far from it, so don't kick yourself, ok?"

"Umm … Joan, I'm so sorry."

"I know, it's a lot to process. Please don't tell anyone."

"Of course not."

Red in the face, and spent from the sudden download, Joan gave me a heartfelt hug, and then she climbed into her car and reversed with speed down the hill. I felt like a gong someone had pounded with a mallet, vibrating from a whole new picture to sort out.

I found that washing dishes and putting pans into cupboards helped my mind disengage and rest. The noisy pieces from the missing night kept nagging at me. If they resolved into solid memories that were free of nightmare elements, I would invest my attention to them with a sense of relief, even if it meant admitting that I'd taken pills.

I flipped my hands in frustration as another visitor pulled up the driveway, this time an unfamiliar man in an old truck. Jeans. Tattered sweater. Thirties. Not a threat, according to Luke's wagging tail. All the same, my guard was up as I stepped onto the porch.

"Ed Emery." He brushed sawdust from his clothes before shaking my hand. "My mother wanted to come, but her knee is acting up."

"I appreciate the thought."

"Guys who knew Raymond, we make plans to help with chores and whatever," he said. "Then I don't know, months go by."

"I don't expect anything."

"I'm sorry for staring," Ed said in an apparent reference to his bashful glances. "But you escaped a *murderer*. Heck, given the timing, the culprit must've been near at hand, don't you think?"

"I prefer picturing 'the culprit' long gone." I studied him. "Didn't I see you at the roadblock? The McDonnell brothers, too."

"Don't lump me in with those sorry characters," he said with emphasis. "Greg spent the whole time insisting where he was earlier. The more guilty you are, the more you need an alibi."

"We shouldn't direct blame at this point."

"Of course not," Ed said. "I would *never*."

His awkwardness and attempts to look nonchalant had me wondering if his mother with the bad knee or someone else had prodded him into approaching me so they could get the inside scoop without sullying their reputation. Several local gossips worked that way.

"I didn't know Richard," I said. "I have no clue what led to his death. If you hear anyone say otherwise, please set them straight."

"Well, sure, I'd be glad to. I noticed you've got a situation over there," Ed said, indicating the dirt pile. "Need any help on that?"

"Dan Bolton is my go-to guy for help," I said pointedly.

"The trooper? I didn't know you two were …"

"Listen, I have some calls to make. Thanks for stopping by."

"Got it. Take care, Miss Littlefield."

While Ed Emery tramped away to his truck, the sunset was starting to burnish the trees with fiery light, as if nature wanted me to have one last good look around before night fell with a thud.

I felt a flash of irritation at myself for handling the surprise visit with a focus on being polite. Not long ago, I'd trusted people who'd come across as obliging and friendly, only to find out that they'd committed murder and other crimes. Next time a stranger stopped by unannounced, and I wasn't in the mood for visits, I would be cold.

"Cold is a bit much," I said. "I'll be direct and plain spoken, with a mind toward—" I closed my eyes. "Not feeling ridiculous."

Luke crossed the porch to join me, toenails clicking, eyes shining, as if to say, *I'm here for you, even if you are a mess.*

I pulled out my phone and refreshed my knowledge of "Swiss cheese amnesia," which led to entries on transient global amnesia, or TGA. The triggers included strenuous activity, sex, head trauma, emotional upset, and shock. The only outlier in my case was sex. It was a miracle I didn't have TGA every day of my life. The website conveyed the good news that a person could recover their memories. It just took time.

My hope flickered all the brighter when my phone rang and the caller ID indicated it was the editor of *Coast & Candle* magazine.

"Sonny Littlefield," I said, summoning a businesslike tone.

"I'm glad you picked up," Hugh English said. "I know this is short notice, but the Meeting Fair starts in a couple of days. I need photos to go with a feature article and online gallery, and I think your style would be a perfect fit. Are you available to tackle it?"

"Yes," I managed. "I believe I can fit it in."

"Excellent." Mr. English listed the events and people he wanted me to photograph at the eight-day event just a half hour from my house, adding, "Don't miss the modified chainsaw contest. The machines they come up with can cut a house in half in two seconds."

"Any other tips?"

"Plan for traffic and crowds," Hugh said. "Last year the fair had record attendance. On certain days, the place is packed."

"I'll do some advance work to get my bearings."

I sat in a state of wonder after we hung up. This was my life's pattern through and through: in the wake of finding a murdered stranger and a second jarring night that had yet to be explained, I had a new assignment that involved the kind of photos I loved to take.

I would use any extra images to continue defining myself as a Maine artist in the months to come. There was hope for a normal life.

14

A ringing note pulled at me multiple times.

My eyelids scraped open. I stared at my clock glowing in the darkness. It was 8:15 p.m. I dimly recalled eating leftovers and chugging a glass of iced tea that must have gone bad, given its odd aftertaste. Dropped into a stupor, I'd dragged myself upstairs and collapsed into bed with a spinning head and a churning stomach. In the midst of pulling off my hoodie, I'd passed out with one arm stuck in the sleeve hole.

My cell phone was ringing. I reached for it, misjudged the distance, and with the phone in hand, I dropped limply to the floor.

"*Uuuf...*"

Stars swirled through my head. I saw an animal with big teeth and terrible breath. It was Luke. His tail thumped on the floor.

"Sonny? Are you all right?"

Oh my God. I had a talking dog.

"Sonny!"

"Don' shout," I mumbled, face pressed against the braided rug.

Luke paused. "Did I wake you?"

"Bad, smelly dog."

"I know you asked for space, but you're not past the need to check for signs of a concussion. I assume all is well."

We regarded each other for a long, drowsy moment.

"Sonny?"

"Huh …?"

"You're all right, is that correct?"

Luke sounded a lot like Dan.

"Oh," I said. "It's Dan."

"Are you on the floor? I thought I heard you fall."

"Uh huh."

"Dizziness is a classic sign."

"What w's the q'sshin?"

"You're slurring. Is Joan home tonight?"

"S's got a pr'blm down *there* …"

"Repeat that? You're muffled."

"Nnnn …"

"Sonny, focus. Try to stand, ok?"

I lifted my head and squinted at my bed. It looked very far away. I pulled the comforter down to cover myself. With Luke's muzzle resting on my shoulder, I closed my eyes and drifted.

There was a dream of a hummingbird darting in and out of view, shimmering with radiant light, and two kindly figures whispering as they leaned over me in the dark room. While the woman looked on, the man gathered me in his arms and settled me onto my bed.

It was Dan! I loved Dan. He was a wonderful person.

"Sonny," the woman whispered.

I cracked an eye open. "Huh …?"

It was Joan! I loved Joan. She was a wonderful neighbor.

"Her pupils are dilated," Joan said, resting a hand on my brow. "Sonny, are you dizzy from the bump, or did you take pills again?"

"Drag'n s'ys … I t'k pills …"

"Good Lord," Joan said. "Is there a pill bottle anywhere?"

"I saw one earlier when I was checking the ceiling. It's gone now. Has there been any sign of her taking drugs before?"

"Never. Why were you checking the ceiling?"

"I meant the window. The broken pane."

"Charlotte's son did that."

I pawed the air to make them stop talking. Dan sat beside me on the edge of the bed and smoothed my hair. I reached for his warm hand and tucked it under my chin as I closed my eyes. Happy, sleepy.

"This is a shock," Joan said. "She called me earlier. *Coast & Candle* magazine hired her to cover the Meeting Fair."

"We need to get a handle on the pill situation. It can't continue."

"I know. Listen, I need to head home."

"I'll stay and keep an eye out," Dan said.

I drifted, then jerked out of a nightmare of a dragon saying, *You want this over with, right? Answer my questions, and you'll be fine.*

On my stomach, I squinted in the darkness, feeling lethargic, engulfed in glue. Less tummy ache, but still unable to keep the world from spinning. Luke was snoring, and someone else was breathing deeply on the floor next to my bed. I had an idea it was Dan.

I reached for the nightstand to help myself up, misjudged the distance, and dropped limply onto his warm, sleeping body.

"*Aruhh,*" he groaned in my ear. "Jesus! Holy crap."

I blinked. "What the …?"

"You landed on top of me." Dan rolled me to one side. "Sharp elbows, and your knee …" He groaned again. "I was asleep."

"Oops …"

"It's fine, I stayed to make sure you didn't wander around again." Dan sat up and assumed a kneeling position, reached his arms under me, and then growled as he heaved me onto my bed.

"Sorry," I murmured.

"No problem." Dan rubbed my shoulder. "Just sleep."

I drifted, my head swirling. Hearing Dan's voice, I cracked one eye open, so thirsty that my lips and tongue felt crispy.

"You know Frank Winthrop went to prison for check laundering and embezzlement," Dan was saying in front of the moonlit window with his phone in hand. "Now that he's been exonerated, his lawyer is suing the District Attorney and everyone else down in Boston."

"Heyyy," I murmured, kicking out to silence all the talking.

Dan crossed to me. "I didn't mean to wake you," he said. "I'm catching up with my father. Do you need anything?"

"Nnnn …"

"Ok. Just sleep."

His footsteps receded. "Dad? You won't believe it. Sonny's lambs are in the care of one of the suspects, Theo Lurman. Turns out it's not just his ATV that's missing. A knife from his toolkit disappeared, too. It might be a match for Richard's non-lethal wounds."

"Huh?" I murmured.

"Anyway, back to Angela's ex," Dan said. "Frank's mother lived like a pauper, but she was sitting on a fortune when she died. For whatever reason Richard is the one who handled the estate work. The minute Frank got out of prison he and his attorney started checking the chain of actions Richard took. Heirlooms are missing. Jewels and other valuables. I know, it's shady as heck, but here's the kicker. Angela told Bricker that Richard had been secretive lately. She thought he was having an affair starting six or eight months ago. Where do you think Bricker took that? He figures Sonny is the other woman. It's unbelievable. He's obsessed. I'm about to rip his head off and shove it up his ass." Dan paused. "How am I expected to sound? Don't worry, I won't lose my cool."

Fed up with all the talking, I decided to sleep downstairs. I reached for the bedside table, missed, and flopped to the floor.

"*Ooofff.*" I blinked. "*Uhh …*"

"Dad, I have to go. Sonny fell off the bed again."

"W's going on …?" I murmured.

"I've got you," Dan said, kneeling beside me and lifting me in his arms. He swung me around and settled me onto my bed.

I pawed my right hand in space. "Water …"

"I'll bring some." Dan pressed my shoulders against the sheets as if I were covered with sticky tape. "I'll be right back. *Stay.*"

"Ooooo kkk …"

After a moment, I wondered if I'd dreamed that Dan was there. Crazy things were happening. I sat up and slid my legs off the bed. Stood and swayed, and then tripped over Luke and staggered a few steps.

"Sonny, this is dangerous," Dan said, arriving with a cup of water. He sat me down on the edge of the bed. "Here you go."

After a first reviving sip, I pawed for the cup and gripped it with both hands, noisily gulping the water as if I'd staggered out of the desert after days of baking in the unwinking sun. That's how I felt. Scorched from head to toe, my tongue and throat raw.

"All set?" Dan said. "Ok, new plan of action."

He stretched out next to me with my head resting on his shoulder and his arm wrapped around me, holding me in place.

With an excited yelp, Luke jumped onto the bed.

"All right," Dan said. "But stay on this side. Don't bother Sonny. And don't lick my face. *Luke*," he growled. "Settle down."

Snuggling close, enjoying Dan's warmth, I sighed with contentment and stretched my leg over his upper thighs.

"Sonny, that's not cool when you're high."

"Yummy ..."

"We need some ground rules. Keep your leg down here in this range." Dan's hand secured my knee and pushed it off a bit. "All right—*hey*, what did I just say? Leg down. Focus on sleeping."

At one point, as I woke briefly in the darkness, I smoothed my hand over Dan's chest and dimly discovered that his left hand wasn't a hand at all. It was a dog paw. This threw me for a moment. I squeezed it. Definitely a dog paw. This was a problem.

Luke stirred and slurped my hand.

"Oh," I murmured. "That's good."

"What?" Dan said, his voice rumbling against my ear.

"You're not a dog ..."

"I'm trying my best. You're not making it easy."

Snuggling closer, I sniffed his neck, which smelled of coconuts and palm trees and tropical paradise from shampoo his parents had sent him. I liked how he reacted at first because he seemed to enjoy my snuggling, based on the way he shivered. Then he was less happy.

"Come on, Sonny. That is not cool."

"Sleepy ..."

"Then get to it. Show some mercy."

What put me in a deep sleep was Dan's steady breathing. All the lifting and cursing had taken its toll. He dropped into a doze.

I did too, except for those moments when a dragon in the back of my mind was growling instructions: *Repeat after me. I took pills.*

"I ... took ... pills," I murmured.

"It's ok," Dan said softly. "We'll sort it out."

* * *

The scents of coffee and banana bread stirred around me. I yawned and stretched, then squinted at the time on my clock. It was 5 a.m. Dan had slipped from my bed and stepped out of the room a moment ago. I heard his voice downstairs. He was talking to Joan.

Shock propelled me into a sitting position. My dreams had been vivid. This had to be another one. I grabbed a pillow and pulled it to my face, inhaling a wonderful scent that had nothing to do with any of my own hair products. In the same way that the cab of Dan's truck smelled of cocoa butter, my pillow gave off wafts of tropical paradise.

Dan had spent the night.

In my *bed*.

Unlike the solid wall of amnesia that I'd experienced the previous morning in the hospital, there were glimpses of the night, but mostly, they were frustrating, disconnected, out-of-focus snapshots. What was real, and what was a dream? The new story of my life.

My head throbbed and I felt wrung out as I stripped off my clothes and took a hot shower. I'd tramped through the jungles of Costa Rica on minimal sleep, and I'd camped amidst Hawaii's steam vents and volcanic rumblings a time or two. In Europe, I'd eaten bad grapes and ended up in an awful situation I called "The London Cleanse." At no point in my life had sickness or exhaustion collapsed me into a zombie who couldn't piece together details of the past eight or twelve hours. I hadn't just felt tired when I'd woken from the odd dreams. I'd felt drugged.

I paused with a washcloth in hand as a whisper of terror swept through me. For the second morning in a row, I had zero recollection of taking pills. At Arlene's urging, I'd secured the bottle of muscle relaxants in a plastic bag in a kitchen drawer. I *hadn't* taken it out.

I dressed with record speed, trying to reconstruct what I'd done the evening before. I'd looked up a map of the fairgrounds. I'd eaten a snack. That was the last thing I clearly remembered. I stopped abruptly, snapping back to the pitcher of iced tea I'd made earlier in the week. It left an odd aftertaste in my mouth after I'd chugged a glass with my dinner.

Had someone laced it with a drug?

At first, it seemed an outlandish notion. Then I stared at the broken window pane and pictured Charlotte's son hearing that I was in the ER and coming up with a way to step up his evil game.

"Sonny?" Joan called up to me.

"I'll be right there," I said.

I summoned calm on my way down the stairs. No surprise Joan and Dan looked worried as I joined them in the kitchen. Rather than evading the questions in their eyes, I crossed to the drawer where I'd put the pills, pulled them out, and handed the bag to Dan.

"I can't apologize enough for last night," I said. "If you told me I was abducted by aliens, it would be easier for me to accept than what I'm starting to piece together. I apparently told you I took pills the other night. I still don't remember it, but let's say I did that one time. Last night I did not take these pills. You know it's not like me to get high."

Dan read the label, then he dumped the contents of the bottle into his palm. He counted them quickly. "Six are missing."

"I took three in the past. Three more were missing yesterday. Look at the prescription date. They're expired. That's how long I've had the pills without taking them. They were in the drawer until now."

"Unless there's another stash," Dan said.

"There isn't. I'm telling the truth."

Dan set the bottle aside, swiveled one of the chairs, then turned two others to face it. Holy crap, he was instituting an intervention.

"This is awful and unfair," I said.

"Don't see it in a negative light." Dan gently steered me to one of the chairs and sat me down. "Our concern is around how easily you could get injured. It's a miracle you only bumped your head the other night when you ended up outside. It could've been a lot worse."

"You did end up in the ER," Joan said.

"Trust me, I remember."

Sitting in the chair in front of me, Dan leaned forward with his elbows on his knees and his hands clasped. Confronted by the earnest look in his eyes I groaned, having no idea how to convey that this was the absolute worst way to get me to focus. He looked so appealing, so handsome, his arm and chest muscles flexed. I had to avert my gaze.

"Sonny," Dan prompted.

"Great. You think I'm looking away out of guilt."

"How can we help?" he said. "What do you need from us?"

"I need you to trust me. I have a plan for sorting out what happened. It might take a couple of days to get answers."

"We can't afford to wait," Dan said gently. "I'm sorry, but last night when you woke up briefly, you said you took pills."

"I was having a nightmare," I said. "There was this awful, badgering dragon telling me to *say* I took pills. In fact, it's starting to feel so real, the sense of threat, and being questioned … never mind."

"Talking will help. You're with friends."

"I don't want to sound nuts."

"What does your plan involve?" Joan asked.

"Here's my promise. There is an explanation that doesn't involve a hidden drug habit. You're going to need to trust me."

"You're saying you got high by accident," Dan said.

"It happened to me in the past."

I saw that this was not a path for reassuring him. His eyes took on a level of alarm befitting a range of awful possibilities.

"A date gone wrong sort of thing?" he said.

"No."

"How else could you have—?"

"Joan knows some of my history. Donald knew I wasn't his daughter, and spent his life trying to minimize my presence."

"Your *father* drugged you?" Dan demanded.

"He wasn't my father," I pointed out. "It didn't last long and it got resolved. Fast forward to today. My cousins have been trying to drive me out of town, so it's not out of the question for someone to have slipped something into my food while I was in the ER."

119

"Good Lord," Joan said. "Did anything you eat taste off?"

"The iced tea in the refrigerator had an odd aftertaste. I chided myself for drinking it when my stomach bothered me."

"Hang on, I remember you drinking a glass of it when I stopped in the other day," Dan said. "You were fine."

"Exactly. It was plain tea up to that point."

"Is there any more?" Joan said.

"Another glass full, I think."

Joan pulled the pitcher from the refrigerator and held it to the light as if imagining it might shrug and say, *Oops, you caught me!*

"I was fine one minute, looking up maps of the fairgrounds," I said. "Then I drank the tea and barely made it up the stairs. I never changed the lock on the door, so it's possible someone came in and laced the tea while I was in the hospital. Joan brought Luke to her house, so he wasn't on guard here. Like I said, I will sort it out."

Dan stared at the pitcher of iced tea for a moment. With a disgusted growl, he clapped his fist to his forehead.

"Your cousins," he said. "Of course."

"It's just a theory," I cautioned. "Until we know more—"

"*Sonny.*"

With a quick motion, Dan grabbed my chair by the seat on either side of my thighs and pulled me forward so swiftly that it was like being on the Space Mountain ride at Disneyland. I retracted my arms inward accordingly. My knees now touched the front edge of the chair Dan was sitting on, with his legs encompassing mine on either side. This had his intense, fierce gaze about a foot away from my startled face.

"It's time to stop cutting them slack," he said. "The Bergleys walked away with valuables and vandalized your farm. If one of them put a drug in your food, that's a serious criminal matter."

"It's just a theory," I managed.

"I'll send a sample to a friend who's a chemist. If it comes back positive, I'll act on it. Trust me, I will not tip them off."

"But—"

"No buts," Dan said. "We're done letting them take what they want and making your life miserable. I won't stand for it anymore. From now on, if anyone comes at you, they need to answer to me."

Dan was radiating intensity, his brown eyes bright with outrage, and his biceps flexed from gripping my chair. From what little I remembered of the night, he'd been gallant beyond words, soothing me when I woke from nightmares, and holding me close until I fell asleep. Now he was putting faith in my explanation with very little evidence to go on. How could I repay him for all the help and comfort he'd extended to me since the night we'd met on my front porch?

One option would land me in a state of bliss as well. With the same swift move that he'd made a minute ago, he could use those sexy muscles to reach for my butt and pull me onto his lap. It would be an amazing position. Hopefully, the chair wouldn't break.

It wouldn't take long for me to get out of my clothes. He could unbutton his shirt. That would be sexy. He'd unhook my bra and explore a little. His morning stubble would be oh-so stimulating. He hadn't had time to shave. I focused on his lips. We'd tipped toward each other, and his gaze said the same heated-up scenario was playing out in his mind. I closed my eyes. A few more inches, and we were going to kiss.

"Umm, I'm still here," Joan said.

Dan and I pulled back in a confused rush, a little flustered, and then he did a superb job of putting the chairs back where they belonged and taking command of the task of sampling the tea. Finding a small bottle in the cupboard, he measured out an eighth of a cup, then taped the pitcher shut, sealed it in a bag, and returned it to the refrigerator.

"Why not take all of it?" Joan said.

"We'll need a sample if we open a case," he said. "Sonny, it's best to change the kitchen door lock. I think my father can help with that in the next day or two if you don't mind him stopping by."

"Sure, whatever works."

I gave Dan one of my spare keys.

With his hand on the doorknob he said, "With Raymond's weapons in the house, we should prioritize the trip to the practice range. I'm not encouraging you to use one, of course."

"I get it. I should know how to handle them."

"I'll text you with some times."

"Thank you, Dan. Again, I'm so sorry …"

"It's fine, Sonny. We'll get through this."

With a final quick smile, he was off to ship the sample.

Joan and I stared at each other once he stepped out, leaving the kitchen oddly silent after Dan's force field exited the building.

"I guess he wants answers fast," she said.

I nodded.

He was right. There was no time to waste.

15

I suspected there would be trouble when I announced to Luke that he would be left behind to guard the house while I was in town for a couple of hours. Sure enough, Luke's furry brow gathered over his glistening eyes, and his tail and ears drooped pathetically. Without uttering a single word, he let me know that I'd wounded his pride, stripped him of his sense of self-worth, and triggered his fear of abandonment.

"You would be dangerous if you were a man," I said, holding the door open to let him bound through.

On the drive to the hospital to get a record of my blood work, I kept getting spellbound by the shifts of light as I drove past trees. The same could be said of my fractured memories: rushing glimpses I couldn't quite catch, then sudden bursts of darkness, with a new twist that put my heart in a vice. Why did the swirling nightmare elements seem to be revolving around a persistent, repeating voice that felt more and more vivid, more and more real? More and more like it wasn't a dream.

The temperature was fifty degrees when I reached the hospital at 8:30. Passing clouds and a light breeze were forecasted for the day. For Luke's comfort, I parked in the deep shade of a maple tree, opened the windows four inches, and filled his water dish on the floor. Luke wagged his tail as if his past life before I'd adopted him had included guarding the car while quick indoor business was being conducted.

There's plenty to look at, Luke's gaze assured me.

I paused, allowing an elderly couple to precede me through the entrance, and then I stepped in and instructed myself to ignore the bright lighting and antiseptic smells that triggered memories of the time I'd held back from telling my mother that two of my fingers were broken. An infection had set in. I was lucky to have healed completely.

I exchanged smiles with a passing nurse. A baby wailed, and a doctor was paged. Unnerving whirring sounds came from a doorway.

I found the business office, showed my ID, and drummed my fingers while I waited. Getting my record took all of five minutes.

In the hallway, I braced myself to see metaxalone, the muscle relaxant I'd found next to my bed, but the record listed benzodiazepine, zolpidem, THC, and psilocybin, which I recognized from news reports about people using "magic mushrooms" to cope with stress.

"Good God," I murmured. "This can't be right."

"Miss Littlefield?"

Mired in confusion, I looked up and studied the woman who'd said my name. In her fifties, she was dressed in navy slacks and a pink sweater. The smudges under her gray eyes said she had led a disappointing life and had suffered the worst of it recently.

"You are Miss Littlefield?" She slipped on a pair of glasses and leaned in to examine me as if I were a painting in a gallery.

"Have we met?" I said. "I don't seem to recall …"

"I do apologize. I'm Rose Matthews. I recognized you from the picture they showed me. I assume you're one of my daughter's friends."

"Who is your daughter?"

"Angela, of course."

"Listen, I need to see if the clerk gave me the wrong—" I paused and held my breath. "You mean Angela *Gartland?*"

"Yes."

"Who showed you a picture of me?"

"Detective Bricker. He asked if we recognized you, but wouldn't say why. You know how vague the police are. It's so frustrating."

The corridor closed around me a fraction, too barren to endure. Fluorescent lighting often had that effect on me: something about the glaring flatness of it. Under other lights, even subtle shadows offered the illusion of having a place to hide. In the hospital corridor, I felt exposed, as if my secrets were visible for everyone else to see.

"I'm sorry for your loss," I said. "What you must be going through. But right now, I'm on my way to … elsewhere."

"Please," Rose said. "Come and visit Angela. They expect to discharge her today, if her headache continues to subside."

Glimpses of Richard's wounds and staring eyes surfaced. How could I say why Bricker was asking about me? How did one break that kind of news? *I got to Richard too late. He died alone on the pavement.*

I felt gaunt, as if I'd been drained and probed by needles and scopes. A woman walking toward me held a sleeping child draped around her like a starfish. The woman's gaze was vacant, almost blank. Was that how I'd looked when I'd left with Dan yesterday?

"You are one of Angela's friends?" Rose persisted.

I focused on her. "I don't know how to say this. I'm the one who … I was on the road the night Richard died."

"*Oh*," Rose said with wide eyes. "We heard it was a woman who found him. I'm sure you were a comfort."

"I wasn't. He was already …"

"Please." Rose tugged my elbow. "Angela has agonized over the lack of information. If you can assure her at all—"

"I'm not able to. I arrived too late."

"I can see you need support as well, and no wonder, happening on a dreadful scene like that in the dark of night. Richard was the nicest man. He turned Angela's life around." Rose's eyes brimmed. "I'm not sure if she's awake. She's had to be sedated because of the shock. Won't you sit with me for a while? It's so lonely in the room."

I closed my eyes. "Maybe for a minute."

I followed her to Angela's room. Pulled to the bedside, I stared at the young woman's bruised cheek. She was a natural blonde, pale, and beautiful. Strength left my legs as I glimpsed what it must have been like to be attacked in the dark of night. Being grabbed by the shirt, and falling forward. Hitting her head. Struggling to break free.

Cloying, jarring, the image threatened to consume me.

"Here, you look about to faint," Rose said, taking my arm and steering me to a chair. "I'm no stranger to tragedy, I'm afraid. My husband passed away six years ago, then I lost a dear friend to cancer."

Slumped in an uncoordinated heap at first, I mustered my composure and sat bolt upright, clutching my bag. Rose fetched a half-knitted sweater and a canvas tote brimming with purple balls of yarn, sat down, and then busied herself with the project where she'd left off.

"How often do hospitals mix up records?" I said.

"Oh, it happens all the *time*," Rose said. "By the way, make sure you leave your phone number so I can alert you about the memorial service. I won't set a date until Angela can weigh in on it."

"That makes sense."

Rose began talking nonstop about Angela, saying she was too trusting of people for her own good. She worked in a high-end salon for a while, but the smell of hair dyes and depilatories bothered her allergies. Richard helped her get a job as an assistant at Beech and Grossman, where he worked. They had a lavish wedding and moved to Maine. By then, they were in their late twenties and had trouble conceiving.

"I hope the new evidence amounts to something," Rose said.

I emerged from the numbness. "New evidence …?"

"I'm sad to say it might have to do with Frank Winthrop," Rose said. "The man Angela was engaged to early on. Frank gave her a modest ring when he popped the question, but hardly a stone I would consider appropriate. One likes a nice, big diamond. Nothing showy, of course. But substantial enough to indicate the right level of love."

"Well … to each their own," I said.

Now that I was sitting down, the shock and disorientation started to fade. It helped to be in a confined, quiet room. No echoes, like out in the corridor. I was able to summon clarity from the knowledge that Rose and Angela needed support. I'd failed to help Richard. If I could assure his loved ones in any way, I felt compelled to do so.

"You can't imagine the shock of getting a knock on your door in the dark of night, and seeing police officers waiting there," Rose said. "I'd worried about Angela living in a rustic neighborhood. Richard installed a security system, but the awful burglar disabled it."

Rose described how Richard and Angela returned from a nice evening out, never imagining what was to come. Apparently, Richard managed to slip away while the intruder was sorting through a safe that he'd forced the couple to open. Enter Sonny, driving blindly along.

"I grew up nearby here in Maine," Rose confided. "After my husband died, I longed for a quieter life in the country. I parted with our home in Massachusetts and bought a house from a family who never *once* cleaned under the refrigerator. Can you imagine?"

"Everyone has their own way," I managed.

"Richard and Angela followed along afterward, wanting to raise a large family here. I was *so* hoping for grandchildren."

"How did they meet?"

"Richard grew up in Malden, Massachusetts, two doors down from my husband's family home." Rose smiled. "Came to our door with a lovely bouquet at the age of six and asked for Angela's hand. I took a picture of him standing there. It's on my bedroom dresser."

I'd come to the hospital seeking my records. Now I found myself wanting to see the picture of Richard in Rose's doorway, his hair neatly combed, and his shirt tucked in. I wanted to absorb every point he'd ever scored in sports, every test he'd ever aced. I wanted to know that he'd achieved his dreams before he'd met a terrible end.

"They were inseparable in grade school," Rose said. "Then *poof*, hormones kicked in, and suddenly Richard wasn't exciting enough. Angela's high school years were a blur. I warned her that boys with dashing good looks are trouble, but she had to learn the hard way. You have no idea what it's like to be the mother of a stubborn child. *No* idea."

"I'm sure it's a test of patience," I murmured.

"Here we go again." Rose flipped her hands. "That's what I said when Angela met Frank at the firm where Richard worked as a financial services attorney. Frank wowed her from the start. Once they were dating, he had her sign papers for a bank account under our name, Matthews, instead of his own last name. Can you imagine?"

"That is odd."

"Frank claimed it had to do with his mother's view of money. He said she had an aversion to wealth, but that makes no sense. He was laundering ill-gotten gains, no doubt. The whole thing tried my patience."

"I can imagine," I said.

"Then *poof*, Frank was arrested for bilking company clients," Rose said, her wide gaze indicating she was reliving the turbulent period in her daughter's life. "Frank insisted he was innocent, but said he might be away for a few years. Was he ever right about that."

"He went to prison, you mean."

Rose leaned in and whispered, "Long before that, Angela thought he'd been *murdered* during one of their phone calls."

This new thread riveted me to the seat.

"That was before Frank landed in legal trouble?"

"Yes," Rose said. "Am I mixing things up?"

"I understand. It sounds complicated."

"Let me see … right, they were on the phone. Angela said that Frank had just arrived home when he'd called her. All of a sudden, she heard him holler, 'Hey! What are you doing in here?' The next thing she knew, there was the sound of a terrible scuffle."

"And then?" I prompted.

"The line went dead. She confided in Richard. He was so worried for her safety. *Finally*, Angela realized he was the right man."

"Was Frank injured during the attack?"

"Oh, that. Who knows if it really happened." Rose waved one hand. "He has an alibi for the other night, but I have *zero* doubt the culprit was a crony of his. In the grocery store last week, a man smiled at Angela the way awful men do. I'm certain he was a mobster. Flashy clothes. Gold necklace. You know the sort."

"Frank was recently exonerated, right?"

"He pestered until he got an attorney at Beech and Grossman to take his case. Shamed them into it, I think."

"Frank was innocent after all."

"I suppose. Thank heaven Angela will have Apogee Antiques to focus on. Richard owns a share of the business, but Carl Woodlee opened the store to begin with, of course." Rose fussed with her hair as if thinking she wouldn't mind having dinner with Mr. Woodlee. "I'm certainly not about to run the business. Old fashioned, isn't it?"

"Not at all."

"Angela is an ace when it comes to business matters." Rose patted her daughter's arm. "It takes a keen eye and good bargaining skills to handle the fast dealings at auctions and estate sales."

I nodded, distracted by Angela's wedding ring. With my mother's knowledge of gems in mind, I couldn't help but notice that the diamond sparkled with the distinctive brilliance of a pricey stone.

Richard and Angela had gotten married, moved to Maine, invested in an antique store, and built a new house, the garage of which, according to Mr. Lurman, had been left unfinished. Maybe Theo's assessment of the situation was right: the couple had gotten in over their heads.

"You noticed it too," Rose said.

I paused. "What?"

"Angela's hands twitch now and then." Rose squeezed her daughter's fingers. "Imagine what she must be dreaming."

No need to. I had my own nightmares to dwell on.

But in the split second before Rose reached for her daughter's hand, I saw that Angela's fingers weren't twitching. She was gripping the bedsheet so hard that her knuckles were flexed and white. Richard's widow wasn't asleep after all. She'd been listening to her mother prattle on the entire time and quite possibly wanted to scream for her to stop.

If so, I could relate.

* * *

In the parking lot, I stopped and stared at the blood work results. It had to be a mistake. My name was on another patient's record.

Hearing the rasp of approaching shoes on the pavement, I turned as Nathan Kitteridge joined me under the flickering shade of the maple tree near my car. In a dark navy suit and classy tie, he paused and studied me with an air of disappointment instead of saying hello.

I sighed. "This isn't a good time."

"I'm glad if you're having a bad day," Nathan said. "It's good to know that casting suspicion on an innocent man has a downside."

"*Hey*," I said as I clapped eyes on Frank Winthrop petting Luke's nose through the open window of my car. "Step away."

"I was just checking him," Frank said. "Making sure he's ok."

This was the first time I'd seen Frank up close. His demeanor was dark and guarded, and it was clear from his wary gaze that he lived in a hard groove where he assumed the worst of people all hours of the day. I sensed he might be in his early thirties. He looked forty.

"I'm leaving, so we're all set," I said.

"I can walk him. Nathan has some questions."

"I have zero answers. I can't help you."

"I would appreciate a quick word," Nathan said. "In exchange, I have information that might benefit you. Meanwhile, Frank is willing to volunteer some training time with your animal. Working with dogs is how he survived on the inside. They have a program, and he excelled."

Frank glared at his attorney. "Nathan, I hate it when you talk about me like—" He closed his eyes, then he looked at me. "We're in the same boat, caught up in whatever went on the other night. Bricker is why you should give us five minutes. As for walking your dog, it's for me as well as for him. Dogs calm me. They're free of guile."

"I like that about them, too."

"Then how about it?" Frank said. "Let me walk him."

Luke did need a quick outing before we left.

I opened the door, feeling over my head, a little off the rails, but desperate to replace the whirling unknowns with some facts. I secured Luke's leash and handed it to Frank. Luke bounded out and sniffed him, then he sniffed Nathan's trousers, all the while wagging his tail. Poised to grab the leash back, I slowly eased out of my tense, watchful stance.

"Thank God," Nathan whispered under his breath.

I turned to him. "Seriously? You had doubts?"

"It's the animal I didn't trust," he said. "Frank is solid gold."

Frank walked away with Luke. My dog was trotting next to the ex-con as if he were born to step in line without pulling.

"Unbelievable," I said.

"Let's talk about the shock I got an hour ago, having thought we made a nice connection when we met the other day," Nathan said, "Why are the police asking if you partied with my client?"

I turned to him. "What …?"

"The past few nights, Frank was watching TV in his hotel room into the wee hours. News flash. You weren't there."

"I haven't accused Frank of anything."

Nathan paused. "Bricker is spinning a tall tale?"

"I think he's seeing what sticks to the wall."

"Well, that's perfect. They never learn."

I kept my eye on Frank. He had Luke lifting a paw for a shake, furthering my efforts to teach the trick.

"Can I ask why you're here?" Nathan said.

"To get my … never mind."

His wince said he'd prefer if I was straight with him. "If you visited a certain patient, I'm going to find out."

"Angela's mother recognized me in the corridor," I said. "I tried to put her off, but she seemed to need support."

"I bet Rose gave you a chopped salad of events."

"Kind of. It was hard to follow."

"I can be concise. Richard was not an angel."

"Look, I'm not comfortable speaking ill of him …"

"It's important you know the truth. Richard lands on the fast track at Beech and Grossman. Law degree and accounting chops. He's an asset. Recruits Frank when an opening comes along. Offers a signing bonus. All is well until Frank and Angela hit it off."

"Rose mentioned some of this," I said.

"Once Frank got tossed in the slammer, Richard won the tug of war over Angela's heart," Nathan said. "He was such a swell, upstanding guy, he took pity on his former rival. Kept tabs on Frank in prison. In fact, in the name of—" Nathan paused to make air quotes. "'Helping out,' Richard handled the estate sale when Frank's mother died. Guess what? Whoops! Stuff disappeared in the process. All kinds of valuables."

"That is troubling …"

Nathan paused. "Is that a bruise on your forehead?"

131

"I live on a farm. Things happen."

"Where was I? Right, I noticed the bruise because I was waiting to see you make the million-dollar connection." When I still looked blank, he sighed. "*Why* did Richard recruit Frank?"

"His qualifications, I assume."

"That's one theory. The way I see it now, he got wind of hidden wealth in the Winthrop family. He cultivates Frank. Brings him into the company, then sets him up for a fall. Boom, he's got Frank by the … I won't use off-color language, but you get my drift."

"If you're right, that would be awful."

"We're left to theorize that Richard had an accomplice. I can picture tension building between parties A and B once Frank got out of prison and started asking questions. That's where we stand."

"I sympathize, but …"

"I know, you want no part of it," Nathan said. "But there's a queue waiting to see you. Carl Woodlee is a friend, now?"

Seeing the shop owner nearby, admiring the clouds, I closed my eyes. I'd been having a nice, uncomplicated week. Now, from the alien environment of the hospital, I'd exited to the alien environment of the parking lot. Instead of fluorescent lights and lifeless floor tiles, I'd exited onto asphalt that was throwing heat around me in shimmering waves.

"You're a puzzle," Nathan said. "Tough to figure out."

"Trust me, it's best to not try."

"Let's put a hold on it for now. We have an appointment in the wings. Frank," Nathan called over. "Time to visit your ex."

"I don't think that's a good idea," I said.

"Angela texted him. Wants to talk."

I paused. "Really?"

"Frank, show Miss Littlefield the text. She's a skeptic."

Handing the leash back to me, with an entirely cooperative dog on the other end, Frank cast Nathan an impatient glance. He didn't appreciate his attorney's cavalier attitude on the subject of Angela.

As his phone dinged, Nathan heaved a tired sigh. "It's the office asking for another update," he said. "Hang tight, folks."

"Bottom line, I want no part of it," I called after him as he stepped away, then I turned to Frank. "Thanks for walking Luke."

"I saw you wrestle with the idea before agreeing to it," he said. "For an ex-con, a small gesture can mean a lot."

"I can imagine," I said. "Listen, I'm in a hurry—"

"I can shed light on why you're getting hassled," Frank persisted. "The way you switch gears doesn't add up. You got frisked because you were evasive. Today you're wide-eyed and rattled."

"Allow me to enlighten you in return," I countered. "You were at the roadblock. In town during the crime. If I were you, I'd focus on not adding to the rumors that you and Angela are involved."

"See? You've switched gears again," Frank said, studying me with his permanently cynical gaze. "What's with the rumors that you got high the other night? Folks think you were celebrating."

"You've got baggage from landing in prison. If you can't grasp that I'm struggling after finding a murdered stranger—"

"Easy, let's not be at odds. We're just talking."

"Not anymore." I tugged the leash to let Luke know we were leaving, then I found myself turning back. "You're right, let's end on a better note. I know a trooper who's a good guy. If you aren't behind Richard's death, do you have an alternate lead for my friend to check out?"

"Possibly," Frank said. "A long shot."

I hesitated. "Really?"

"A guy came at me one time," Frank said. "Smart, fast, and cold. Wore a mask. Took me by surprise on my own turf."

I stood stock still, feeling the air suck out of me and leave a note of recognition in my mind, though Rose had mentioned the incident a short while ago. Frank's description hit a nerve.

"Why did he come at you?" I managed.

"I have a complicated family history."

Studying me, possibly from noticing my reaction, Frank reached into his shirt pocket as if to snag a cigarette. Finding the slot empty, he folded his arms. Between his light tone and his absent-minded mannerism his pause had a lulling effect, as if he'd learned it as a trick, speaking softly and using his hands to captivate an audience with a goal in mind.

133

I shook it off. "Why is that relevant?"

"We had means of a sort, but I grew up on tight strings. A dirtbag was bound to target a big house in a nice neighborhood." Frank shrugged. "As far as a connection to here and now, I don't know. Unresolved events play with your mind when you get set up and land in prison."

"Was he ever tracked down?"

"The police didn't believe my account for all kinds of reasons," Frank said. "The guy got the upper hand fast. Used a chokehold. Left no trace. I could ID the guy in a heartbeat because of his tattoo. A snake, right here." Frank tapped his sleeve over his forearm. "You can't see it unless his cuff is pushed up. Other than that, he's a ghost."

Maybe I'm a ghost, a voice whispered in my head.

"Oh …" I felt dizzy. "Um …"

"Hey." Frank reached for my arm. "Steady, now."

"That last part … the description sort of …"

"Sort of *what?*" Frank prompted. When I blinked and floundered, he added, "The story hit a nerve. Tell me why."

"I don't know." I wrenched my arm away. "I was abducted by a man who wore a mask. That's why it rattled me."

"When?" Frank demanded.

"Back in May. The culprit … he's dead."

Frank paused. *"Dead?* You killed him?"

"No, and it's not relevant. It's long over with."

"Frank, what the hell?" Nathan said, gaping as he arrived. "I told you there's no need to push. I'll get answers."

"I wasn't pushing. We were just talking."

"You grabbed her. I saw it."

"It's ok," I managed. "He was, umm …"

"Helping you out of a bad spell," Frank pitched in, spreading his hands to emphasize that he hadn't meant any harm. "You wobbled and turned pale. I was afraid you were about to faint."

"Is that how you saw it?" Nathan prompted me.

"I guess," I managed. "I did wobble."

Nathan didn't look sold. "I'm not going to hear about this later? Some bogus addendum to Bricker's partying angle?"

"If anything, I could help you tank Bricker," I said.

"Tank him? I'm listening."

"Forget I said that. I need to head home."

"After your next meeting," Nathan said, indicating Carl Woodlee, who was admiring the clouds as he waited his turn. "I have a life in Boston to get back to. Let's see what Angela wants."

"*Wait*," I found myself saying.

Nathan and Frank swung back to me, startled by my sharp tone.

I hesitated, kicking myself, then plunged on, "Have you told the local police about the attacker you described? The one with the …" I indicated my forearm. "The tattoo? The snake?"

"Why would we?" Nathan said. "It never panned out."

"It can't hurt, right? No stone unturned."

The two men exchanged puzzled frowns.

"We can loop back," Frank said. "Angela is waiting."

"Ok," Nathan said. "You're the client."

Frank cast a parting frown my way, and I stared at him with wide eyes, torn between wanting to ask for a clearer picture of his attacker and following the impulse to dive into the nearest dark hole. Like the other fast-moving glimpses that had hit me, seemingly out of nowhere, the man he'd described blazed into focus. How could an attacker from Frank's past trigger a vivid scene in my head: a snake writhing around a man's wrist, and disappearing under his sleeve? I regretted reacting to it in front of Frank and quailed at the comment he'd tossed to Nathan before they'd stepped away, saying they could "loop back" to the subject.

He'd meant they could loop back to me.

"Miss Littlefield."

I jerked as a hand touched my arm, then sagged with relief to see it was Carl Woodlee in his beige attire.

"You're very pale," he said.

"I just maybe had … an awful thought."

"I come away from talking to him the same way. Rattled, and worried what kind of havoc he's going to bring."

"Frank?"

"No, his attorney. He's trying to freeze Richard's assets, and if he's successful, who knows how long it'll take Angela and I to extract ourselves. He's putting a lien on Apogee Antiques," Carl specified, seeing that I was not catching on. "The whole inventory."

"I'm sorry. That would be hard."

"If I heard correctly that Frank and Nathan are visiting Angela, I'll postpone my visit," Carl said. "But I can cheer you up in the meantime. I've found another item that belonged to Raymond."

I focused on him. "Oh?"

"It was Ken Babik who unearthed the piece after he met you the other day." Carl paused for dramatic effect. "What would you say about laying hands on a silver, embossed frame with a very special picture? Raymond and Ella on their wedding day."

I held my breath. "Are you saying …?"

"It's yours for the taking. An exquisite piece."

From his bland attire to his misguided combover, Carl was a calming influence after my brief unraveling. A feminine quality in his mannerisms had me thinking he might be gay. Once the dust settled, I'd make a point of getting to know him: a chance to get a male perspective on life without any worries about him making an unwanted pass.

"Why would Charlotte part with it?" I said.

"Well, Raymond left the farm to you instead of to her. That must have stung. Selling his personal effects is a way of acting out."

"Do you have the photo with you?"

"It's at Ken's house. If you follow me, we can fetch it."

"I was sort of heading home …"

"The problem is, there's overlap with Ken's things and the Gartland estate. If the attorney does succeed in freezing the assets—"

"I want the photo. Is Ken's house nearby?"

"Ten minutes."

I nodded. "That's doable."

16

I followed Carl Woodlee's sedan in a robotic state where my hands, legs, and other parts involved with operating a car performed tasks automatically as I pondered the drugs listed on my blood work, which I no longer disputed, given the extreme side effects I'd suffered. The muscle relaxants had never sparked that kind of a nightmarish high.

Benzodiazepine was enough of a shock. What on earth was zolpidem? With THC and psychedelic mushrooms in the mix, it was no wonder I'd been slammed with amnesia. Rubbing my brow, I tried to piece together who'd drugged me, and how they'd pulled it off the other night. I couldn't picture a dim bulb like Charlotte's son concocting a complex mix of medications. His involvement seemed less and less likely.

Which led me to the worst question of all. Why had Frank's account of being attacked brought on a moment of panic? The sense that I'd met the same "ghost" he was talking about? Smart, fast, and cold. A man wearing a mask, with a snake tattoo on his arm.

I yelped as knuckles rapped on my window.

We'd arrived at Mr. Babik's house. I'd parked in the shade of two stately oak trees flanking the driveway. Luke was wiggling in the back seat, whining softly in a bid to meet Mr. Woodlee.

I stepped out. "Sorry, I was lost in thought."

"It's an amazing house, isn't it?" Carl said.

With teal blue siding and white trim, bay windows, and decorative millwork on the railing that encompassed the expansive porch, the multi-story dwelling was a model of ornate uniqueness befitting its Victorian origins. The topiary and manicured yard were further indications that Ken had the means to keep the property in top condition.

"Miss Littlefield?" Carl prompted.

"Call me Sonny."

"What a lovely nickname."

"Tell my mother that. Give me a second?"

"Of course. No rush."

"I don't know if I did you any favors by rescuing you," I said to Luke, making sure the windows were open enough for him to enjoy a breeze. "You would have been better off in your pen today."

Luke grinned and wagged his tail.

The house was quiet as we stepped in. The dark, vintage wallpaper, exquisite furnishings, polished wainscoting, floor-to-ceiling bookshelves, rich drapery, and other signs of wealth brought me back to times during my youth when I'd endured visits with chilly Littlefield aunts and other relatives. Far from aspiring to copy the splendor of their homes, I knew it took an entire team of specialists to keep everything in top shape.

"While you're here, come and see this remarkable piece," Carl said, leading me into an office with more massive bookshelves. He stopped next to a large, highly ornate desk made of dark wood and scrimshaw details. "Solid mahogany. I can tell you appreciate history."

"I can't stay long …"

"Just hear this story. This desk belonged to the captain of a whaling vessel in the eighteen hundreds called the *Harriett Browne*. A tyrant, but it took a hard sort to keep a crew in line for long, dangerous voyages. The vessel stopped in ports. The captain had an eye for collectibles, which the crew tried to pilfer when he wasn't looking. *Hence,*" Carl said dramatically, "he had this beauty built with secret compartments."

"It's beautiful," I said, captivated by the scrimshaw details on the corners and drawers, from cherub faces to fanciful animals. Harpoons and other nautical patterns were carved into the wood.

"Some of the caches were easy to discover. The captain put cheap finds in those to let the crew imagine they'd won the game."

"He sounds crafty and smart," I said.

"Indeed." Carl chuckled. "Ken and Richard spent hours on end trying to find hidden compartments. They discovered a slot that could only be reached if Richard laid on his back, reached up, and figured out how to release the latch. A letter was tucked inside."

"From the 1800s?" I said in wonder.

"Penned with a goose quill and ink," Carl said, picking up a discolored page within a plastic sleeve. "Beautiful writing, isn't it? Imagine a whaling captain with this level of calligraphic skill. It was common in those days. By all appearances, this was a letter written to his niece, but Richard, Ken, and I wondered if it conveyed a message in code."

Frowning in concentration, I deciphered the calligraphy:

Darling Carina,
Your letters cheer me with bright chatter about Lupus and Lepus. I
can never recall who is who and which is which! It is nine plus ten,
and the moon bestows diamond glints on the sea. The rogues are
rowdy, roughnecking, and boasting when they think I'm fast asleep.
On the morrow, perhaps I will share my new ode with them:

There was a bold lad on a schooner;
Who wanted to be a harpooner.
The first mate would say, work hard for your lay;
But he got his deserts a lot sooner.

What do you think, Carina? Rogues they are, and ever shall be. My
good spirits depend on our family bonds.

Your adoring Uncle,
Samuel Brooks Winthrop, Perseus of the High Seas!

"I think Lupus and Lepus are constellations," I said.

"Carina and Perseus as well," Carl said. "Was he talking about the sea or actual diamonds? 'Bonds' could indicate paper currency, and 'deserts' is tricky. Linked to punishment, but it can also indicate a reward. I took it as a boast about his own career, the fact that he'd done well for himself. Richard saw it as a threat to keep the crew in check."

"Dare I ask what 'work hard for your lay' means?" I said.

"In this context 'lay' refers to the percentage of the profit sailors were allotted, though most of the poor lads ended up in debt to the ship owner. They had to borrow for food, necessities, clothing, and medicine. Whaling was a *ghastly* enterprise," Carl added, "the deck sloshing with oil and blood, with toxic smoke coming from the rendering fires. Fleas were rampant, disease a given. There are accounts of mutiny and treachery. Wrecks and horrific storms, with villains lurking in ports of call."

"How did they convince men to do it?"

"Family tradition. Once in, it was tough to get out."

"The scrimshaw details are from whale's teeth, aren't they?" I said with dismay. "The artistry is a marvel, but I've seen whales in the wild. They're intelligent and graceful. Awesome up close."

"As I said, the whaling enterprise was dark," Carl agreed. "The scrimshaw and other unique carvings are why we're careful in handling the desk. Ken got it for a bargain price, despite its uniqueness. As you can imagine, it would fetch quite a sum at auction."

"Is there a hidden cache you can show me that doesn't require lying on my back? I've had a rough couple of days."

"Let's see." With his forefinger, Carl tapped his chin. "Ah, yes. Some months ago, Richard noticed that each of the brass knobs has a different embossed design. See here?" He pointed. "This one has twelve marks, like a clock. He tried different things. This worked."

With a letter opener, Carl hit the knob with six careful, clockwise taps. A click announced a hidden release. Carl pulled out a hollow cylinder, a half-inch in diameter: the perfect hiding spot for gems.

"Clever," I said. "What was in the tube?"

"Nothing but air. Richard worked on the knob until the wee hours one night. He was downcast to have found it empty."

I had to admit, at any other point in my life, I would have committed myself to the challenge of finding secret compartments for however long it took. Today, I had too many pressing concerns, but to revisit the mystery when I had the time and energy to examine the letter, I pulled out my phone and took a photo of it.

"What are you doing?" Carl said.

"I'll ponder the letter when I get a chance."

"You won't show anyone else?"

"Not if it's a concern."

"That would be best. I'm sure you understand. For now, what does your gut say? You're an artist, trained to pick up on details ..."

"I'm sorry, but I really can't focus on it today," I said. "Is the photo of Raymond and Ella handy?"

Carl hesitated, then nodded. "Of course."

While he stepped into the next room, I picked up a magnifying glass from the desk and studied the letter, fascinated that it had survived, mostly intact, for hundreds of years. I admired the particularly elaborate swirls and loops the old seafarer had fashioned for the capital letters S, B, and W of his signature, Samuel Brooks Winthrop.

I studied the desk from different angles and zoomed in on a brass plate that would need polishing to see the maker's name.

"Here you go," Carl said, arriving from the other room.

With a flourish, he handed me the precious photo.

I gripped the silver frame, transfixed by the black and white image of Raymond dressed in a smart suit and tie, smiling at Ella as she grinned at him from within the froth of a veil. The neckline of her wedding gown was decorated with roses that I suspected she'd embroidered herself. The light in the image was gorgeous. The photographer had caught them in a mote of angled light with blossoms in the background.

"Amazing," I said tearfully. "This is wonderful."

"I'm so pleased for you." Carl dabbed the tears in his eyes. "It's moving, seeing your feelings for Raymond. If only you'd known him."

"What's the cost? I'll write a check."

"Oh, heavens. No cost."

"With the case in the background, I want to keep the purchase above board. And I want to thank Mr. Babik. Is he here?"

"Well, umm ..."

Seeing him falter, I frowned and listened for sounds that would indicate the old codger was on his way to the study to say hello. But no, Ken's wheelchair was parked in the next room, empty, and the house was silent. As Carl continued to stand there, struck mute by my seemingly innocuous question, my mind clicked back to the letter, and the elaborate signature that had caught my eye: Samuel Brooks Winthrop.

I swung around and stared at Carl. "The captain of the vessel and owner of the desk was Samuel Brooks *Winthrop?* As in Frank Winthrop, the ex-con who used to be Angela's old flame?"

"Yes, the captain was his ancestor."

"Good God, Carl! Frank's attorney said valuables are missing from the Winthrop estate. That means this desk is—is—"

"Hence, my desperate search for caches. I want to *fling* whatever we find at Nathan and say, 'Please don't close my shop.'"

"By 'we,' you had better not be talking about me," I said vehemently. "I've spent days trying to extract myself from this mess. I don't want to get involved." I paused and closed my eyes. "The wedding photo isn't the real reason you brought me here. You wanted my help."

"Two birds. It's a win-win."

"How much do I owe for the photo?" I demanded. "And since this is Mr. Babik's house, I'll need a receipt from him."

"This is the problem. He died."

I stepped back a few paces. "*What?* I just met him."

"It's the most awful thing."

"No—no—no—no—"

"I apologize for not telling you in advance," Carl persisted. "You're right. I wanted your help. You're so much like Richard, seeing angles and clues other people can't fathom. If we can spend a short while looking at the desk with the letter in mind—"

"Carl, how did Mr. Babik die?"

"Heart attack is the official cause."

I looked at him sideways. "But ..."

"It was awful," he said, wide-eyed. "I'm the one who found him. It was our pattern, me stopping in first thing in the morning to chat before his nurse arrived. I breezed in with a cheery hello and saw him already in his wheelchair. I was astonished. He always needed help getting from the bed to the chair. Then I saw his expression. My God ..."

"*Why?*" I demanded, then I thought better of the question and waved him off. "Never mind. I don't want to know."

Carl gripped my arm. "Ken's face was a picture of terror. That's the only way to describe it. His eyeballs had grown dry and looked appalling. It's the reason people try to close the lids. They were stuck open, his face blanched and his mouth agape, as if in mid-scream."

"Oh, shit," I managed. "*No.*"

"It's why I can't be here alone."

I backed away. "I can't hear this. How much is the photo of Raymond and Ella? Then I have to leave. Wait, oh no ... oh, crap ..."

My mind seized up as I realized I couldn't purchase the precious photo of Raymond and Ella. It belonged to Ken Babik.

And Ken Babik was dead.

Not just an ordinary kind of dead. Whatever the 'official cause,' I had a bad feeling the antique enthusiast had been questioned, threatened, and possibly tortured into disclosing the secrets of Captain Winthrop's desk, all of which meant that he'd been murdered.

"I can't buy the photo," I said. "The case ... it's impossible."

"Who would know?"

"It's *wrong*. I can't do it."

"Please, just wait a moment," Carl begged.

"I can't *be* here."

With a wrenching pain in my chest, I shoved the precious memento into Carl's hands, then I turned and all but staggered to the door. From a simple errand to fetch blood test results that were supposed to clear things up, I had amplified the nightmare a thousandfold.

I scarcely saw the road on the drive home. Almost there, I changed course. I *wasn't* alone. I knew where to turn for help.

17

A crime is like a dark living thing, my father had written on a sleepless, windy night. *It forms over the course of days, maybe even years, feeding on one want or another. Greed. Envy. Hatred. Then all of a sudden, something changes the course it was on. That's what I try to hone in on early in the figuring: why did this thing turn ugly now?*

I recalled the passage during my drive. What hidden string of events had led to Richard Gartland's murder? Had a specific spark set it off in recent days? And why did the crime insist on engulfing me in its horrifying aftermath? It was impossible to not dwell on my memory of Ken Babik sitting in his wheelchair in Apogee Antiques, looking pale and gaunt. I ached to go back in time and tell him that he was right to be worried. What kind of monster would menace an elderly man?

"It has to be a psychopath," Norris had said.

I turned down a tree-lined road of quaint yards, including Charlotte's property and notorious outbuilding of Raymond's possessions, and headed for "downtown" Gracious. Perched around the village green was a brick post office, a firehouse, a real estate office, and a B & B partially hidden by a picket fence. My destination was the Corner Pocket, a former pool hall that Sue Black and Kate McKenna had painted canary yellow and converted into a significant upgrade from the usual convenience store.

Vintage photographs of pool-playing locals lined the walls that framed gleaming oak aisles of necessities and baked goods.

I skidded to a halt out front and grabbed my dog, hoping Sue and Kate wouldn't mind if I brought him in with me. A bell jingled as I stepped in, and I was greeted by the aromas of apple pie and freshly brewed coffee. Haggard, beyond the capacity of putting two thoughts together, I stood there and waited to be rescued. It didn't take long.

"Sue!" Kate called out from behind the front counter and cash register. "Sonny is here, and it doesn't look good. Bring ice cream and brownies. Whiskey, too. The good stuff."

Soon they were voicing assurances as they sat me down at one of the oak tables set aside for customers to drink coffee and eat snacks. Kate gave Luke a dish of water and a chew toy. He turned in circles for a moment, plopped down, and started ruining their floor.

"He drools … I'm sorry …"

"It's easy to clean," Sue said, then tossed to their part-time clerk, "Mrs. Brooks, can you cover the register? We'll be a while."

I launched into a description of my past few days, starting with finding Richard in front of my car, getting frisked, reuniting with Dan, inspecting the contents of Charlotte's outbuilding, the night of mystery, fetching my test results, talking with Nathan and Frank, and Carl Woodlee duping me into going to Ken Babik's house. The story tumbled out in disconnected bursts, punctuated with the need to backtrack to make a point. Now and then I waved the sheet of test results in front of them, saying, "What is this about? Why would it be different? I mean, *why?*"

"Now Mr. Babik is dead," I plunged on. "He died of terror. Carl *tricked* me into going there. I had to leave the photo behind."

"It'll all be sorted out," Sue said in a calm, soothing tone.

Slowly, my mind started to spin down as I neared the end of the download. I was able to focus on their faces. Sue's Native American Passamaquoddy ancestry was evident in her features and her long, dark hair. On a cupboard along the far wall were the beautiful baskets she made, each with a bone or a piece of deer antler woven into its lid.

Red-haired and freckled, Kate alternately patted my hand and cut pieces of brownie with a fork. I obediently ate each one.

145

"What a story," she said softly. "Feeling better?"

I nodded and thanked them profusely for listening. I usually didn't enjoy being fussed over, but just then, the assurances of two strong, caring women helped restore some of my inner calm.

"We'd hoped you would stop in today," Sue said. "We have a plan worked out for tackling the amnesia issue. Tonight, we'll get someone to cover the store. Kate and I will come up to the farm. We'll light candles, and focus your mind with Reiki methods. I've had success hypnotizing people with memory issues in the past."

"Should we invite Dan?"

"My guess is you'll relax more with just the three of us," Kate said.

"You're right. You guys are the best."

I exhaled and focused on the wonderful ambiance of the store, feeling more and more grounded. As always, talking had helped. It was so simple. Like magic. The power of being heard and understood.

"I don't want people to think I'm popping pills," I said. "Especially Dan. We have to stop the cycle of him seeing me as a victim."

"We agree," Kate said.

"We were thrilled when you two hit it off back in May," Sue said. "You're both insightful and have a sense of humor. When he came in this morning and said you'd reconnected, it was obvious he was elated about it. You should have seen his smile."

I fiddled with my napkin. "Oh?"

"Some of those state troopers are on the macho side, but he's all right," Sue said. "Kate has known him forever, right honey?"

"I was in the same class as Connie," Kate said.

"His cousin?" I asked.

"No, his wife."

My mouth opened and closed a few times.

"His wife …?" Given that I was only just getting to know Dan again, this news should not affect me. "His *WIFE*?" I hollered.

The scene became a confusion of Sue and Kate attempting to hold me in place while I burst upward from the chair. I'm sure it was reminiscent of the times when bad weather rolls in during the Thanksgiving Parade in New York City, and one of the huge floats gets caught up by the wind, sparking the need for twenty people to haul on the ropes to keep the giant, airborne balloon from careening into the buildings.

"*Ex*-wife!" Kate hollered. "EX-wife!"

They finally held me down in the chair. I breathed in and out, trying to decide if this made a difference. I supposed it did. Sort of.

"It makes sense that he didn't get a chance to tell you," Sue said. "With all that happened to you in May, and whatever assignment took him out of town. Plus, it's not a story he likes talking about."

"I never liked Connie," Kate said. "She's a manipulator."

"When were they …?" I managed. "And how …?"

"We'll start with the basic elements and go from there," Kate said in a calming tone. "Connie's cousin mysteriously disappeared when they were ten. Her grandfather was a retired state trooper—"

"You've *got* to be kidding me." I clapped my hands over my eyes. "It's why Dan is a police officer. Their bond is deep."

"Will you just listen?" Kate said. "Connie was jealous of the attention her poor missing cousin kept getting. That's who she is."

"Why would Dan find her attractive?"

"He wasn't the only one," Kate said. "She had that dazzle effect high school guys go for, and she was geared to use her sway for all it was worth. Dan was the studious sort. The grandfather saw potential in him, but his endorsement had the opposite effect on Connie."

"She used boys like Dan to make her real heart's desire jealous," Sue added. "Fast forward. Dan gets back from his freshman year at UMaine, and Connie comes on strong. Says she missed him. All of a sudden, there's a test strip with a pink plus on it."

"He has a *child?*" I demanded.

"This will go faster if you don't interrupt," Sue said. "The grandfather was on his deathbed. Lung cancer. He implored Dan to do the right thing, saying it would be tough, but he could still attend college."

"I feel sick," I said. "My mind is about to snap."

"They tied the knot, shotgun style—"

"How old is the child now?" I said unhappily.

"There isn't a child," Sue said. "Connie used a positive test stick she'd gotten from a friend. Come to find out she'd hatched a plan to hock her grandmother's diamond ring so she could run off to Florida with her real beau. With her foolish ways in mind, the family kept the ring locked tight. Involving Dan got it out of storage lickety-split."

"Talk about an extreme plan," I said.

"Not for a girl whose fondest dream was to be a reality TV star," Kate said. "In the aftermath, Dan exploded. Norris and June exploded. Connie's grandfather exploded. It took a few months to get the deal annulled. She's married to a tycoon in Texas, now."

"An annulment," I said. "That's unusual."

"*Bingo.*" Sue touched her nose for emphasis. "Divorced people can say, 'It didn't work out.' No need for further details. Dan's parents insisted on an annulment. They meant well."

"But it's a word that invites lots of questions," I said.

"In legal terms, they weren't married," Kate said. "Dan made the giant mistake of saying to her, 'Don't *ever* call me your ex-husband.' Of course, she's done the opposite, practically making it a blood sport when she's in town. So, it's stuck that way. Even I fell into it today, calling her his wife. I'm sorry for the slip. I'll do better from now on."

"This is a lot to absorb," I said.

"It's a very big button for him," Sue warned.

"I get it. I'm glad you filled me in."

"What about tales from your past?" Kate said. "There's a rumor that you were living with a dentist before you moved to Maine."

"I had my own apartment, but for a while, we were sort of engaged."

"*What?*" they demanded in unison.

"You sound the way Arlene did when I broke the news. She knew he wasn't the right guy. Arlene had the perfect husband and three kids. I saw our dreams of raising families together fading away." I shrugged. "Charlie was a steady guy. Eager to settle down."

"You broke his heart in the end?" Kate said.

"Turns out he had a second prospect champing at the bit. Literally. She'd come to his office for braces to enhance her nearly perfect teeth."

"And now ...?"

"They're married, with a baby on the way."

"That was fast."

"I'm thrilled for them." Now that the subject of other women had been raised, I ventured, "So, has Dan dated recently, or …?"

"He wasn't geared for romance after his friend, Aaron, died," Sue said. "Then he met you. The timing is perfect."

"We agreed to a snail's pace back in May," I said.

Kate smiled. "When he invited you to handle his *gun*, you don't imagine he was talking about the practice range."

"He said *a* gun, not his gun."

"Look at her blush." Sue grinned. "Go easy on the trigger, Sonny."

"This kind of kidding has to stop," I said. "Before you know it, you'll say something in front of the wrong person, and—"

All three of us jumped when the door banged open as if blown by a supernatural force. Charlotte Bergley stood there: a fire plug in a dress, her navy pumps planted as if she were preparing to stop a train with her bare hands. The way she looked, lit from behind, in command of the doorway, I believed she could do it with a stare, alone. No wonder people said her husband resembled a greyhound: thin and wary, easily startled.

"People familiar with common courtesy know better than to block the gas pumps," Charlotte said. "It's only polite."

The habit of avoiding trouble had me yanking my keys out of my bag without any further back-and-forth. It went wrong. They sailed through the air and landed at her feet with a clank.

"What do you think I am, a valet?" she demanded.

"I'll move your car," Sue offered. The glare she shot at my cousin on her way out said, *Calm down, and be nice!*

Charlotte glared at me. "We're having déjà vu this week. Once again, you've acted like an imbecile, and blamed it on us."

Kate broke in, "Nobody believes that taking the lambs was a misunderstanding. You wanted the shock effect."

"How dare you say that," Charlotte said, turning crimson up to her hairline. "Of all the spiteful things I've had to endure—"

"Enough," I hollered. "Before you embarrass yourself, it's come to light that you've been selling Raymond's possessions."

Charlotte blinked as her air of indignation wavered. "People admired him. It's a sacrifice to offer his things."

"Baloney," I said. "It's a form of acting out."

"Who looked after Raymond when Ella died?" Charlotte demanded, regaining her head of steam. "Not you, certainly. It's thanks to me that his house is brightened with fresh coats of paint."

"*You're* the one who picked those colors?" I said.

Catching on that my tone indicated I'd slammed her taste Charlotte drew herself up to her full height of four-foot-eleven.

"Raymond would be heartsick to know you take after your mother," she said. "Speaking of whom, tell her to stop having flowers delivered to his grave. She's not family. It's outrageous."

"Trust me, if you insist on goading my mother, you'll end up stuck to the bottom of her shoe." I crossed to Charlotte and leaned in. "And guess what? She'll look classy when she scrapes you off."

"What kind of talk is that?" she demanded.

"It's city talk. Get used to it."

With a puff of indignation, Charlotte turned on her heel, stormed out to her Lincoln, slammed the door, and gunned the engine.

Sue came in with her eyebrows in her hairline.

"I guess Charlotte didn't want gas after all."

"Wait until Dan hears about this," Kate said as they gave each other a high five. "It's *city* talk! Get used to it!"

"Ladies," I cautioned. "Please don't make a fuss."

As we headed to the door, I realized my canine sidekick was fast asleep under the table. I'd no sooner started to prompt Luke when I clapped eyes on a man who'd been standing at the end of the nearest aisle, hidden from view. In the same tattered sweater that he'd worn to my farm, Ed Emery had his gaze trained on the items on the shelf in front of him, but it wasn't lost on me, Sue, or Kate that he'd been listening in.

"May I help you?" Kate said as she joined him. "Feminine products can be a bear to figure out. Which kind do you need?"

"I got turned around," he mumbled, casting about as if searching for the real section he'd been looking for. "I've got a situation with my ... that is to say, where are the batteries?"

"On the *whole* other side of the store," Kate said.

She tossed a wink my way as she accompanied him to ensure that he found the right aisle, and the exit sign as well.

"Do you know him?" I asked Sue, explaining my sense that he'd come to my farm at the behest of a local gossip.

"He's not a regular," she said. "I'll ask around."

I hugged her, and Kate as well as she rejoined us.

"Thanks for letting Luke come in. My watchdog trainee."

"Yeah, seeing him conked out gives me the shivers," Kate said.

"Don't make fun. He's all I've got."

"Uh huh," they both said at once and grinned.

18

I tossed my bag on the kitchen table when I arrived home, grateful for the motes of sunlight that stirred the scent of cinnamon through the room, though the disquieting bug-repellent smell also still lingered near the sink where my T-shirt was in the trash. I had a feeling I looked as pale as Ken Babik had appeared as he'd worried that "robbers were taking over the town," as Carl had put it. If only I'd asked more questions.

With my phone in hand, I looked up the coins Ken had mentioned and found examples for sale. Imperial Japanese coins, Tiger Tongues, bullet coins, and doubloons could be secured for what seemed a reasonable cost, but a few unique Greek coins had sold for millions of dollars.

I crossed to the shelf where I'd put Raymond's lucky coin and held it in my palm, unable to fathom how an object of a similar size could fetch such a staggering sum. What did make sense was how easily a coin could slip into a crack along the path Richard had taken.

I paced to the window, wishing I could kick-start my mind without involving Sue and Kate. But it was best to not be alone as I faced the notion that I was no longer able to deny. If the badgering voice was real, and my blood test results were real, then the monster was real.

There was a short, scary list of who it might be.

Until Sue and Kate arrived, I needed to keep busy.

I stepped outside and scanned the yard. A section of the fence was droopy. It looked far away. The flock's winter water tub had to be scrubbed out. Yuck. The barn was falling apart. A job only God could fix. Mowing the lawn would engage my mind like no other chore.

My father's old riding mower ran at only two speeds: painfully slow, and blazing fast. Painfully slow is not my style. On the plus side, there is nothing as exhilarating as taking hairpin turns on a vehicle that has the suspension and handling of a medieval oxcart.

Idling near the orchard gate, with the house behind me, I snugged on my ear protectors and slipped the mower into high gear. Soon, I was skidding around turns, speeding under branches, and becoming airborne over bumps on my way down the slope. My father's journals had forewarned the need to ease off the seat, jockey-style, to encourage the laboring engine on the steep climb back up the hill. It was tricky since the mower was designed to shut off if it sensed that the operator was suddenly missing — a feature to which I owed life and limb many times over.

All other thoughts fell away as I hung down low against the gearbox, with thorned plum branches sweeping by overhead in a blur. One, two, three rows down, and on I raced with my gaze fixed on the grass in front of the mower. Once in a while, my chin grazed the steering wheel, but overall, I felt powerful, downright unstoppable.

I glanced over my shoulder and was startled to see a grinning, ruggedly handsome man in a black Stetson near the orchard gate. I turned around, ready to apply the brakes, and *whump*, a low branch hit me across the sternum. I had a view of my sneakers flying against the sky, then darkness and vivid stars as my back hit the ground with a painful thud.

When the world brightened again, Jake "Brumby" Jones was kneeling next to me and fanning my face with his hat, stirring the scent of his hand-tooled leather boots into the air. Brumby had toughened up nicely from his thirty-odd years in the sun. The apricot color of his shirt sang against his tan and enhanced the glints of mischief in his eyes. Known for his skill with horses, he'd become a good friend, willing to help with chores from time to time and share his colorful insights on Raymond.

"Sorry for laughing," he said in his Australian accent. "Every time I stop in, there's a dance of disaster going on."

"I'm fine," I said. "Last I heard, you were in Vermont."

"A high-end barn hires me to do seminars over there from time to time," he said. "Horse intuition kind of stuff. I'm back because I'm called on a lot once the Meeting Fair starts."

"I'll be there all week for an assignment."

"I heard. That's partly why I'm here."

Knowing Brumby, the other part of "partly" was to see if I was ready to overlook the fact that he was one of the most hopeless skirt-chasing womanizers I'd ever met. My father had written of him: *Brumby is as smart and skilled as a man can get, but his attitude toward sex is appalling.*

Brumby helped me to my feet with his strong, callused grip, then he preceded me up the hill to put on his leather chaps and grab his tools to check Dodge's hooves, which were due for a trim.

With Luke watching attentively, I sat on a straw bale next to the pen where my father's old ram, Bubbah, lived a life of exile. My self-appointed job during the trimming was to hold the lead rope and stroke Dodge's whiskered muzzle and brow until he was all but asleep.

"He won't budge, you realize," Brumby said.

"You never know. I need to keep occupied."

Soon I was having to twist on the straw bale to pet Bubbah as well as he poked his nose through the rails of his pen.

According to Joan, Bubbah had been a splendid specimen of manhood early on. Now his elderly appearance and thinning, frizzy wool gave him a moth-eaten look, like a pair of slippers down in the heels.

"Poor fella," Brumby said. "He's starved for love."

"My flock is big enough. He gets lots of treats, and Effie the tabby sleeps in his pen. They're friends. It's really sweet."

"More like she's waiting for mice to go after his grain," Brumby said, cradling Dodge's left front fetlock as he worked.

Finished with that hoof, Brumby straightened.

"You know what's eating me about that scene you landed in?" he said. "Richard left his wife to fend for herself. Even in a seriously injured state, I would have stayed by her side no matter what."

I held my breath as the question I'd been asking grew in complexity all the more. Richard had not only frittered away his own life in his desperate bid to reach the road, he'd left his wife behind to cope on her own. Maybe he'd gotten Angela into a safe hiding place, in which case leaving might have been an attempt to draw the killer away.

"I saw Angela today," I said. "She's quite beautiful."

"Natural blonde, smoking hot," he agreed. "A lot of guys would sell their soul to be with Angela. That's an obvious angle if you ask me. Your father used to say clues are like smoke on the wind. A lot of the time, it ends up being from a plain old chimney fire."

"It's one thing for men to look. Was she faithful?"

"She didn't go for any guys around here," Brumby admitted. "But her and Richard? Talk about a mismatch. She goes to the post office in high heels, for crying out loud. Complains about Maine weather, the lack of a nightlife, the isolation." Brumby leaned in with an air of having saved the best tidbit for last. "This past year, she was making shopping trips to Boston, including a stretch after Frank was freed."

"You think they hooked up again?"

"Maybe. *But* here's another angle to chew on."

I watched as Brumby scrolled through videos on his phone, then I took the device and frowned at an unfolding scene.

"What's this?" I said. "It's too blurry to make out any—"

I stopped as the blur abruptly resolved into a movie of a flushed, angry Greg McDonnell shoving Richard against the brick wall of the firehouse, and drilling the startled man's chest with his forefinger.

"Those are his *grandma's* pearls. Admit it."

"You're insane," Richard sputtered. "We'd never do such a thing."

"This is not the way," Theo Lurman admonished, peeling Greg away with an easy flourish. "It's the wrong time and place."

"You want your pearls back, don't you?" Greg said.

"Leave it," Theo said. "Calm down and head home."

As Theo turned his frown toward whoever was taking the video, the feed abruptly ended. The whole thing left me breathless.

"Where did this happen?" I demanded.

"Bean supper last fall. Greg and Theo are out there wringing their hands, saying, 'Poor Richard, who would want him dead?' Come to find out there's all kinds of friction tucked away."

"Have the police seen this?"

"Well, yeah, I assume so," Brumby said slowly. "The friend who took the video is sort of married to a trooper."

I flipped my hands. "Back in May you said you hooked up with an officer's wife. I told you to show some sense."

"You should be thanking me. This is an inside scoop."

"You've only been back in town for a minute."

"She reached out to *me*. Said it was urgent."

With a disgusted roll of eyes, I dropped the subject and looked on as Brumby finished trimming Dodge's hooves. *Snap. Snap. Snap.*

Over and over again, I replayed in my mind what I'd seen in the video. Richard looking flustered and afraid as he'd weathered a round of bullying: a glimpse of what might have unfolded in his home the other night. And so much for Greg's claim outside Apogee Antiques, "It'll haunt me forever, the fact that I never got to help Richard like he helped us."

The physical demands of Brumby's work were evident as he stretched and walked off the soreness and back pain. Facing me, he rested a hand on Dodge's shoulder. The gelding was as steady as a building.

"You should've seen Raymond work this guy with Goldy, the other half of the team," he said. "Poetry in motion."

"He was heartbroken when Goldy died," I said.

"I was, too."

"Did he ever bring them to the fairgrounds?"

"Raymond didn't like contests, but he'd do demonstrations now and then. Think of the knack it takes to convince a pair of horses this size to start and stop on a dime. Raymond did it with quiet commands and clicks. Go, boy. Left. Whoa. The crowd silent so they could hear. The harness jingling. Eight hooves thudding in the dirt, the horses blowing as they pushed on. Then stillness, and Raymond murmuring praise. You could tell they were pouring their hearts out for that man. It was awesome."

I nodded, left to picture yet another special moment that was gone for good. I would never get to see it in person.

"How much for the trim?" I said. "And don't say a kiss."

"No charge. I'm staying for the séance," Brumby said. "The plan Sue and Kate have for bringing your memory back."

"With a *hypnosis* session. I'm surprised they told you."

"I wanted their take on people saying you're a drug addict. They exchanged a look. I demanded to be in on the plan."

As he gathered his tools, I decided the concept of a séance was fitting after all. A part of me had been crushed into silence. In that sense, Sue's plan of action amounted to making contact with the dead.

* * *

"Hey, sleepy head," a voice said. "Time to talk."

I inhaled sharply, trembling, with my eyes squeezed shut.

"He's awful," I whispered. "I can't do this."

Sue rested her hand on my brow, reminding me that I wasn't in any danger. I was with friends. It was eight p.m. With the stream burbling at the bottom of the hill, and the moon adding ghostly definition to the trees, Sue, Kate, and Brumby were kneeling in the darkness around me in the grass near my porch steps. We'd started in my bedroom, where the missing night had begun. Sue had lit candles and performed a Reiki technique to relax me, then she'd pulled me further inward with a hypnosis session. Warm, mystical vibrations had stirred from her hands as she'd rested one palm on my forehead and her other hand on my sternum.

There was a wobble in the process when I'd headed down the stairs, through the kitchen, and directly outside without stopping to take pills. Sue had shushed all questions and urged me on with whispers and encouragement. She helped me lay down on the grass.

Drifting, I'd reclaimed the early moments of the missing night, up to the point where I'd been taken by surprise and drugged. Fear threatened to encase the memory in clenched, inscrutable layers. With Sue's hand on my brow, I pushed the panic aside and let the night air connect my senses to the events unfolding in my mind. I allowed the missing night to happen again, and I kept talking my way through it …

* * *

A rushing sound swallowed me up after my head hit the woodwork near the broken door of Cat Town. I'd taken the subway through Boston many times. Knew the darkness and streaks of light, the roar of the train echoing against the tunnel walls as it careened on and on deep underground. That was how getting choked and drugged had sounded.

My arms had turned to rubber. I lifted my hands and was horrified to see my fingers melting like wax candles held too close to a fire.

Spitting to rid my mouth of a bitter taste, I squinted at a dreamlike scene of a black silhouette looming close against the night sky, part dragon, part ghost, its snout, tufted ears, and eye sockets outlined by blue neon bands that swam in circles when the creature moved.

"No yelling," the dragon whispered. "I pride myself on not leaving traces. Tomorrow, you'll think you had a bad dream."

I whimpered and tried to crawl away, but I felt dragged down by a cloying heaviness that tingled and seeped through my limbs as if I were encased in glue. A weight pressed down between my shoulder blades, anchoring my face and chest against the dewy grass.

"H-help," I moaned.

"*Shhh.*"

A thing clamped over my mouth, leaving me to make guttural sounds, my breath sawing in and out, drawing minimal air. It was the *dragon*. It had me pinned. Immobilized. My ankle was in a vice.

"Stop struggling," the dragon said in a near whisper. "Even a professional wrestler couldn't get out of this hold, so it's stupid to try. Answer my questions, and you'll be fine."

"*Mmm …*"

"Understand?" the dragon said. "I'm releasing your mouth."

I inhaled in a desperate gulp, feeling the dragon's bristled snout on my neck, as coarse as sandpaper. My feet were numb and cold, my back aching from the crushing weight pinning me down.

"You getting loopy? Nice and relaxed?" the dragon said softly. "You're doing great. Let's talk about last night."

My mind spun in erratic circles. *Last night …?*

"I heard what Richard hollered out on the road, so lies won't work with me. You know what I'm here for."

Trembling, staring at blades of grass that shone with drops of dew, I remembered the bloody wounds on a man's back. His lifeless, staring eyes. The awful sense that I'd gotten there too late.

"Start at the beginning. Why were you on the road?"

"Gave m' ... st'ment ..."

"You need to give it again. I'm in charge now." The dragon shifted his weight and tapped my face a few times. "Focus. You want this over with, right? Answer my questions, and you'll be fine."

Desperate to head home, I told him the story all over again. How I was lost from using the wrong map and trying to find the butcher's barn to save my lambs. There was a cornfield. A man was up ahead, looking drunk. He staggered toward me and dropped to the road.

"That was Richard. What did he say?"

I didn't hear him. I had the radio on.

The dragon was upset when I told him I didn't look inside the bag. I put it near the stranger's hand to comfort him.

"I don't buy it. Anyone would look and help themselves. Who would know? You decided to fill your little pockets—"

"*No* ..."

The dragon kept growling the same questions in my ear. I told him the truth over and over again. He refused to believe me and badgered me to start from the beginning. I started to cry.

"I want t' g'home," I sobbed. "Please let m' go."

"You're saying everything I've built my life around got dropped in the cornfield?" the dragon seethed. "That's just perfect."

"Dan ... c'n help ..."

The dragon snorted. "Sorry, babe. After I'm done here your boyfriend will rethink his options and see you as a problem. It was bound to happen anyway. Sit tight and behave, all right?"

The weight suddenly lifted. Moaning, miserable, I rolled and tried to hone in on the confusing scene coming in and out of focus.

A man-shaped silhouette pulled a hood from his head and rubbed his face. Hissing curses, checking his watch. I saw it gleaming in the night, with bright dials and readouts that swirled in captivating, circular patterns when his hand moved. Squinting, I reached out to warn him that a snake was on his arm where his dark cuff had gotten pushed up. The scaled coils appeared to writhe for a second, the snake's head pointing toward his hand, with its body extending under his sleeve.

Glancing at me, the man flipped me onto my stomach. The hard pressure returned to my back, the stubble to my neck.

"You're making me rethink the kind approach," he said.

"*Uhhh,*" I moaned.

"You're baked. I doubt you'll remember any details, but you never know. Are you listening?" He blew in my ear, a sharp blast of close-up noise. "Tell folks Bricker paid you a visit. I'm tired of the grind. I want my piece of the pie. How does it feel, me going this far to see if you were lying? Go ahead and come at me. See what happens."

"Can't ... breathe ..."

"Shut up and listen. Track two. I used to be a good man. Then I went to prison for something I didn't do. I got set up. Ripped off. I learned a lot when I was in prison. Made contacts. Picked up some skills."

My eyes closed, and the wet grass seemed rubbery.

"Maybe I'm one of those two. Maybe I'm a ghost, one step ahead of any *assholes* who think they can double-cross me," the dragon seethed. "Tell that to whoever comes around. William is back from the grave, and he's out for blood. You got all that?"

"Nnnn ..."

"Too wasted, huh? We're done with the main event, but there's one more seed to sow." He blew sharply in my ear. "Focus on my voice. I want you to repeat after me: 'I took pills.'"

"You ..."

"Not me. *You,*" he said softly. "Say it. Then I will leave."

"T'k ..."

"*Focus.* E-nun-ci-ate. Repeat after me: 'I took pills.'"

"I ... took ..."

"Pills. *Say* it. Then I'll leave."

"I ... took ... p-pills."

"Excellent. Say it again."

"I ... took ... pills."

"See how easy that is? Once you've mumbled it to whoever, nobody'll believe anything else that comes out of your mouth. You'll be thirsty. Bet I can figure out what you'll reach for once I'm in your house. Sorry to ruin your life, but business is business, and you weren't the brightest bulb, out there on your own last night."

I moaned, gasping, with tears streaming down my cheeks.

"You took pills," he said in my ear.

When I shut my eyes against his badgering, he blew in my ear hard. The feel of it drilled into my skull, loud and ferocious, a stabbing, horrid point that threatened to break me apart.

"Say—it—*again.*"

"T'k pills," I whispered. "I ... t'k ... pills."

"Say it again."

He wouldn't stop. Sobbing, I obeyed.

"The dog knocked you down. He's a bad dog."

"Nnn ... no ..."

"Bad boy! That's what you hollered when he broke the wood over there. He knocked you down. *Say* it."

"M'nster ... c't town ..."

"Whatever. The dog knocked you down."

"*Uhhh ...*"

The world narrowed and darkened.

My eyes closed.

I felt the weight lift from my back and cool air clamp around me. Shivering, I heard footfalls, and then the creak of wooden steps. A dog was whining. Muffled, but nearby. The footfalls returned. There was cursing, a man complaining that he'd wasted his time.

"Where's the vial? *Shit.* I dropped it."

There were scraping sounds, dragging rhythmically across the nearby grass. Forcing my eyes open, I glimpsed a man, nothing more than a shadow under the night sky. Raking, raking.

In a swimming, swirling void that made no sense.

* * *

161

"Sonny?" Hands gently hauled me from my stomach into a sitting position. "Wake up. It's time to end the session."

My eyes rolled. "Huh …?"

"Come back to the present," Sue said, pulling me from the memory that had felt so real a moment ago. Sue's hair spilled around her shoulders, framing her dark eyes. "You're safe. You were precise and clear about what he said. You stayed strong. You survived an awful ordeal."

"There's more," I said, remembering Joan changing me out of the damp T-shirt. The blurry ride to the hospital. A doctor prying my eyelids open. Bricker shaking my shoulder in the ER. He'd snapped his fingers in front of my face and demanded to know if I'd been partying because of an item I'd taken from Richard's jewelry bag. I recalled Dan bellowing, "*Out,*" when he'd arrived, then he'd blasted the detective.

When I opened my eyes. Brumby, Sue, and Kate were sitting around me in a semicircle, framed by the moonlit sky.

"Is anybody else shocked out of their minds?" Brumby said. "I thought we were here to help Sonny remember taking pills."

"We had an inkling of it after seeing Sonny's blood test results," Sue said with her phone glowing in her hand. "It's why we made a video of the session. Do you want a copy of it, Sonny?"

"Maybe later." I zipped myself into a warm polar fleece jacket Kate handed to me. "You'll keep the video under lock and key?"

"Of course."

As Sue and Kate pulled me to my feet and helped steady me, Brumby crossed to my car and opened the passenger side door.

"You figured Luke got scratched by a cat. I think the guy sprayed him in the face and put him in your car. Look here." He shined a flashlight on fresh claw marks on the panel under the window. "Probably spritzed another dose when he let Luke out so you'd buy the idea that you'd fallen on your own. The bastard had it all worked out."

"Did you see his face when he took off his mask?" Kate said.

"No, it was too dark, and he either hissed or talked in a rasp, I assume to disguise his voice. It could be anybody."

Phone in hand, Sue searched online and showed me a Halloween mask with neon markings similar to the one the attacker had used. The rest of the mysteries also fell into place: after he'd finished questioning me, he'd dumped three of the muscle relaxants he'd found in my medicine cabinet and put the bottle next to my bed with a glass of water.

He'd spiked my tea to spark confusion and self-doubt, and to convince even my most committed friends that I'd developed a problem with pills. Not everything had gone his way. He'd dropped the vial he'd used to store the drugs and failed to find it before he left.

"Dan noticed the area had been raked," I said, "He found the vial, and figured it was from a soil test kit. It's in my kitchen."

"The guy talked about getting double-crossed," Kate said. "What if that signaled a rift between partners in crime? He meant to befuddle things by implying that he was Bricker, and then Frank. If you accuse them and it goes wrong it would tear down your credibility. The trouble is, we can't rule them out. Alibis can be bought."

"Do either of them have a tattoo?" Sue said.

"I've only seen them in long sleeves, but I don't see how it could have been Frank," I said, explaining how Luke had instantly befriended the ex-con in the hospital parking lot. "If Frank was a threat, wouldn't Luke have bristled and growled instead of wagging his tail?"

"Dogs can be swayed with the right treat," Brumby said. "You'd left your car windows open in the hospital lot, right? Easy access."

"Ok, theory one," Kate said. "If it was Frank behind the mask, he'd worry that you'd seen him. Hence, he tossed you a story about a guy with a snake tattoo. Unfortunately, you reacted to it."

I gripped my head. "If only I'd kept my mouth shut."

"I think you covered it by telling him you were abducted by a similar scary guy," Kate said. "From now on, if Frank raises the subject, you can't let on that your memory is back."

I nodded. "Got it."

"Theory two. Frank was attacked years ago, and for whatever reason the perpetrator has surfaced here in Maine. For starters, Sue and I will ask our contacts if the name William rings any bells."

"Here's what's bugging me," Brumby said. "After he dropped Bricker's name, he encouraged you to go after him, right?"

"It sounded that way," I agreed.

"That's a classic setup," Brumby said. "If it was Bricker behind that mask, he came in with a plan to tank you as a witness."

"The fact that you saw his tattoo gives us an edge," Kate said. "All of us need to be on the lookout for a guy with that marking. Asking around is off the table. We can't tip him off."

"Agreed," I said.

"Ok, beyond that, we need to make some decisions," Sue said. "The culprit left you in one piece and grumbled about wasting his time. Logic says he's ruled you out as a source of information. If you report his visit, you won't be a false lead anymore. You'll be a threat."

"I think we need to delay reporting it," Kate said. "Even to Dan."

I paused. "You can't be serious."

"Just a brief delay," Kate said. "There's no proof that you didn't drug yourself. I'm sorry, but people already think that way."

"Ok," Sue said. "What are the pros and cons either way?"

As for reporting my account immediately:

Risk pitting Dan against Bricker. Battle with the detective myself. Get dragged deeper into the case. Endure official interviews and crime scene techs visiting my farm. End up with a target on my back. Submit my medical records to prove I didn't have a drug habit. Suffer the withering skeptics who would see the hypnosis session as nonsense.

On the side of keeping silent for now:

None of the above.

"You realize this means keeping Arlene and Joan in the dark for a bit longer as well," Sue said softly. "I'm sorry to saddle you with a secret like this, but it's best if we stick with a tight team."

I stared toward Joan's porch light flickering in the darkness past the pines at the bottom of my hill. Sue was right. Joan would reach out to one of my father's colleagues, and Arlene would buckle even faster. She would call Dan five seconds after promising to keep quiet.

"It's good that you'll be working at the fair," Brumby said. "Show all the suspects that you're focused, no sign of remembering an awful attack. I see it even now. You bounce back fast."

Kate rejoined us after stepping into my house.

"The shirt you wore that night is in the trash where Joan left it," she said. "It's evidence, so leave it in place. Put future trash in a separate bin. We'll toss any open food in case the assailant drugged it."

"I should call Dan," I said. "Not telling him feels wrong."

"Oh, I get it," Brumby said. "You cut him slack left and right, but it's a different deal with him. The trust only goes one way."

I glared at him.

"Don't listen to Brumby," Sue said. "Bottom line, Dan is an evidence-based guy in an evidence-based profession. Picture him having to say to his like-minded colleagues, 'My girlfriend found out via mystical arts that she was drugged by a guy with a snake tattoo.'"

"I guess that sounds kind of weird."

"We'll loop him in when we have solid evidence."

I nodded. "Hopefully, soon."

19

Sue and Kate spent the night to help me process my new level of jarring reality. Their departure at dawn was a flurry of hugging them and dashing to the orchard to fill baskets with pears, apples, and nectarines for them to take home. Luke and I sat together in the misty morning air as I hollered a tenth heartfelt thank you to them as they drove away.

As if fate couldn't wait to cause trouble, Dan called.

"It's not too early?" he said.

"Not at all. I'm heading to the fairgrounds today."

"That's what I figured. I love Maine fairs. There's history and great exhibits. Plus, there's *great* security. Dedicated patrols, cameras at strategic points, and off-duty cops making extra cash. Speaking of which, a retired trooper owns a cabin near the fairgrounds. To eliminate the heavy traffic factor, you could spend a night or two there."

"I'll think about it. Any other tips?"

"You'll love Bev's diner. It'll be packed during peak times, but it's a must. Excellent food. Listen, I talked to Roy Allen."

"If only he was in charge of the case," I said of the detective who'd handled the skeleton hand debacle last spring.

"Roy agrees that Bricker is off base," Dan said. "Plus, he's witnessed the Sonny effect. How you draw in people without meaning to, and end up in the middle of things. Hence, we're thinking it would be nice to have lunch, maybe starting today. An informal arrangement. That way, we'll be in the loop on the various people who approach you."

I closed my eyes and reviewed the list of reasons to keep Dan in the dark. Did I want to open the door to chaos? Pitch him against Detective Bricker? No, I did not, but there was no need to shut the door entirely. He was on the money about people approaching me.

"Sonny?" Dan said. "How does that sound?"

"It sounds too late."

I listed the people who'd landed in front of me during the past few days. Carl. Ken. Greg. Keith. Nathan. Frank. Rose. Angela. I didn't want to complicate the download by disclosing troubling hypotheticals like my suspicions about Ken's death, but I did confess that I'd gone to Charlotte's property to assess the contents of her outbuilding.

"Charlotte is to blame for most of it," I added. "When I heard she'd sold Raymond's fishing flies, I had to act fast."

"I can't claim to be shocked," Dan said in a way that suggested he was massaging his aching brow. "Why did you stop by the hospital?"

"To, umm, make sure they had my insurance information."

This was true. The clerk had made a copy of my card.

"So, the scratches on your legs were from Charlotte's roses," Dan said.

"You checked out my legs?"

"I figured you wouldn't mind, given how you strip off your clothes in front of me now and then. I'm not complaining."

I smiled. "Yes, the scratches are from the roses."

"I guess there's no need for a sit-down with Roy this afternoon," Dan said dryly. "Of course, the day is still young."

I assured him I was up to the challenge of being ruthless with people in the coming days. I was rested and razor-sharp.

"Please don't try to handle the pressure alone," Dan said softly. "We'll get everything sorted out. We'll get beyond it."

I felt ill as we signed off, fully aware it would be impossible to claim that the most glaring event of all had slipped my mind during our call: an attack that began with a chokehold and ended with a brainwashing session. I would calmly list the reasons I'd held back. After the shock wore off, he would understand, the same way I'd come to accept his reasons for not reaching out the minute he'd arrived back in town.

In between bites of the banana bread Joan had left, I started preparing my gear for covering the fair for *Coast & Candle* magazine.

It didn't go as planned. I paused for whole minutes at a time, seized by one element of the attack or another. Everything I touched got knocked over or ended up on the floor. Days had gone by since the man with the snake tattoo had upended my life. My memories were back, but he was still stealing from me. My focus. My confidence.

A text from Sue came in. *How are you holding up?*

Good moments, bad moments, I texted back.

Try yoga. Summon your power.

Those three words sent energy through my limbs.

Ten minutes later, in a blue unitard with spaghetti straps, I unrolled my exercise mat on a flat section of ground near the pasture fence, set down my portable speaker, then played the song list I'd created for practicing my favorite poses from yoga, tai chi, and Shaolin kung fu.

As the haunting notes of an Indian bansuri flute soared into the sky, I started on my stomach with the cobra pose, in defiance of the snake tattoo, and then I summoned the power of other animals.

Hawk. Coyote. Lion. Dolphin. Cat. Dog.

Pole dancing lessons had given me the strength to perform a whole new level of balance moves. I leaned down with my hands on the mat, focused my gaze on a spot in front of my fingertips, and rose into a tucked handstand. I stayed there for a moment, loving the sensation of being balanced against the force of gravity with the strength of my hands. I carefully shifted into a split handstand, and then a stag handstand. My eyes never strayed from the fixed point on the mat.

I smoothly returned my feet to planet Earth.

Whispering drew my gaze down the driveway. I was startled to see Harry and Jess huddled together with their backpacks set aside. Jess was holding up her phone as if they'd been recording my poses.

"Hey!" I said. "I don't want that online."

"I wanted to at least show some friends," Jess said, clambering to her feet. They raced up the hill to join me in the misty air, breathless, their freckles catching highlights from the rising sun. "We've only seen you do regular yoga and tai chi stuff before."

"Can you teach us to do handstands?" Harry said.

I pulled a doubtful face. "Well, I don't know ..."

"Come on, Sonny!"

I smiled. "Ok, I suppose. Isn't this a school day?"

"We were waiting for the bus."

"There it is," Jess said. "Bye, Sonny!"

They ran down the hill waving their arms to catch the driver's attention. As he stopped, he and a dozen children in the windows looked my way as if thinking, *What is that nutty woman up to now?*

"Getting ready to kick butt," I said.

* * *

The jumbled clouds above the fairgrounds looked like colossal sheets and scattered pillows as if a giant had slept in the sky overnight. They hovered overhead as I parked my car, and then the sun broke through with a burst of long rays, gilding wet leaves, and alighting in puddles. I took a few shots of the mist stirring upward from the heat of the sun's rays, dissipating into enchanted shapes, and glowing like a mirage.

A few other early risers were in sight when I shrugged my way into a quilted hoodie with front pockets for warming my hands. Next, I slipped on my father's fishing vest. With many zippered pockets, it was a handy place to stow filters, snacks, lens papers, and other essentials.

I locked my car and shouldered my camera bag, elated by the soft light as I walked through the radiant mist. Up ahead, one of the fairground's security guards was cursing at his cell phone.

"It was fully charged an hour ago," he complained.

"I hate it when batteries quit."

"Do you have a cable handy?"

"I can do better than that." From my camera bag I pulled out a battery pack with a cord. "Hopefully, it will get you through."

I waved off his vow to return the device to me at some point. "If you're helping to keep the fair safe, consider it a fair trade."

"Thanks," he said. "This is great."

I smiled. "My good deed for the day."

"Have we met somewhere?" he said curiously.

Possibly, at any number of crime scenes, but I said no and headed away before he put two and two together. Any back-and-forth would involve the need to spin evasions around my jarring week.

From the crest of a hill, I framed the wide expanse of grassy areas, dirt pathways, pavilions, giant tents, and rough-hewn barns nestled amongst trees scattered across the fairgrounds. I widened the shot and adjusted the view to include more of the dramatic clouds.

The fair wouldn't open for another few days, but there were plenty of farmers and employees preparing for the eight-day event. Exhibitors and judges from all over the country had been bringing their talents to the Meeting Fair since the 1800s. Printed flyers told me I would need to plan out my days with precision to cover as much ground as possible in between the events Mr. English had asked me to photograph.

I strolled through the indoor pavilions where artisans would be selling everything from toboggans and canoes to yarn, herbal teas, jams and jellies, candles, soaps, and endless other handmade goods.

The scent of freshly cut pine and the resonant thunder of hammering filled the air. In tents set up here and there in open spaces, I found potters, knitters, basket weavers, beekeepers, stone cutters, and quilters. While I photographed them at work, I took note of the general angle of the sun to determine times when the light would be best.

At noon, I paused to check incoming texts and concluded that my friends pictured me in a dark corner sucking my thumb.

Hooray! Sue texted. *You're awesome!*

Step back, bad guys, Kate added.

Call me ASAP! Arlene wrote.

From Dan came a simple, *Umm … wow.*

"I'm fine, everyone," I said. "Moving on, now."

On my way past the stalls offering stuffed animals for games of chance, I saw Frank talking to a man next to the Whack-a-Mole stand. He looked over and tossed me a nod in greeting. I gave a tepid wave and started to turn away, then I froze, mesmerized by the way he started carefully rolling up his left sleeve, turning the cuff once, then a second time. Still talking to the vendor, he repeated the process with his right sleeve.

Both of his arms were free of tattoos, snake or otherwise.

Relaxing out of my state of heightened attention, I pictured a future where I developed an aversion response when it came to looking at men's forearms. It promised to be a long week.

I texted Sue, Kate, and Brumby: *Re tattoo, Frank = 0.*

Turning to head away, I was dismayed to see the ex-con had rolled up his sleeves in order to play the Whack-a-Mole game with what could only be described as force and violence.

"I'm noticing it, too," a man said behind me. "Makes you wonder."

I turned and groaned. "Mr. Lurman …"

"He's the man to worry about," the butcher said, looking earnest and grave, but heavyset enough to be intimidating up close. "I've heard you're an ace at solving crimes. I could use your help."

"Remind me why they suspect you?" I said.

"After our farm burned down, I looked to the Gartlands for blame. They'd made a fuss over the hen manure I use on the cornfields near their house. Smelly stuff. The McDonnell boys felt they owed Richard after he helped with their tax fines. Wrongdoing is in their blood."

"You thought they started the fire?"

"Only at first. The police chalked it up to activists. We moved to the house I grew up in on the other end of town."

"You don't plan to rebuild?" I said.

"We weren't insured for this and that. You know how it goes." He waved this off. "Fast forward to now. My ATV and a knife were stolen from my farm. The culprit is trying to frame me."

"Umm, it might not just be that," I said carefully. "There's a video going around showing Greg hassling Richard …"

"And me pulling Greg off of him," Theo said hotly, wrenching his phone from his pocket and launching his photo app. "Look here. This is a picture of Angela from their web page. She's wearing pearls."

"I see that …"

"Next picture," he said, scrolling forward through his library. "That's my grandmother in her pearls. You're an expert on pictures, right? Isn't there a program for matching these necklaces?"

"You think Angela took your grandmother's pearls?"

"Right, you need to know the context," he said. "There was mold in the house I grew up in, so moving there was a rough haul. The Gartlands overheard our woes and offered to help, maybe to put the earlier friction over farm smells and everything to rest. A whole shed full of stuff was involved. I needed room for my tools. They sent an inventory of what they hauled off, but it was a general list. On the vague side."

"If you *agreed* to let them clean out the shed …"

"I did say they could take the contents," he admitted. "At the time, all I could see was dust and old junk in the way. But you get to watching these shows about storage units up for grabs, and people landing amazing finds. It doesn't seem fair or right if heirlooms are involved."

"Theo, this business with the necklace is not serving you well," I said. "And Greg is not the best ally to cultivate."

"Greg wasn't out to help me. He's always trying to muscle in."

"Theo!" a man shouted from one of the barns. "We're ready."

"Take care, Mr. Lurman," I said. "Hang in there."

As I started to turn away, Theo gripped my arm. "If you could put in a good word with that cop you're dating—"

"This is *also* not a good idea," I said, not liking the close-up look of sweat on his brow. "I'm not in a position to help."

"I'm sorry. I didn't mean any harm."

"Tell the police everything. That's my best advice."

As I stepped away, I stared at the dark stains on his overalls. Was it oil or dried blood? I all but collapsed as it hit me that Pinkie and Pablo were still in his barn. In desperation, I called Dan.

"I'm sorry to bother you," I said, breathless as I rushed to explain the encounter. "I don't think he meant to scare me—"

"Sonny, it's ok," Dan said. "We're aware of the situation with the pearls, and it's my fault that Theo hasn't returned your sheep. I didn't want him near your place. That's not to say he's guilty—"

"I get it. I understand."

"You did the right thing, calling me. I've had people checking the welfare of the lambs. They're happy, healthy, and well fed. They won't be harmed, Sonny. Don't worry on that account."

"Thank you," I breathed. "I owe you, big time."

"No worries. I'll check in later, ok?"

I stowed my phone with the understanding that I truly was in debt to Dan on a level that I couldn't let stand without a big gesture in return. A portrait of Norris, maybe. A gift that had meaning.

Looking up, I saw Frank watching me intently, and showing no effort to keep his scrutiny a secret. With a flash of anger, I shouldered my pack and cast him a look that instructed him to keep his distance.

By the time I reached the historical village on the east end of the fairgrounds, my pulse and breathing had calmed. I studied a plaque in front of the Morris House, a quaint family dwelling built in 1828 in a nearby town. It was moved to the fairgrounds to serve as part of a living history museum and village. Next door was a schoolhouse from the same period, and a barn of antique tools and other historical artifacts.

I stepped into the Morris House and smiled at the wide plank floors, the furniture stuffed with horsehair, the mirrors cloudy from age. I climbed a flight of narrow, creaking stairs to the second floor. On my right was an attic room with a single bed covered with a feed sack quilt and pine furnishings lined up along the plaster walls. Poised next to the room's small window was a mannequin in a calico dress and bonnet from the 1800s. Someone had positioned her next to the view of the village with her hand touching the curtain as if she'd seen someone outside.

The light coming in from the window was perfect, falling softly on the mannequin's face and dress. I checked my first shots, wanting flecks and bubbles in the old window glass to show. I liked how some of the highlights in the curtain were slightly blown out. The theme was looking back in time. I hoped for an image that inspired people to do a double take before they realized it wasn't a real woman in the photo.

Holding the curtain aside, I was not surprised to see Carl Woodlee heading toward the front door downstairs. I'd seen his name on the list of history buffs who were scheduled to sit in the house and answer questions once the gates opened to the public in a couple of days. I started to call out and say hello, then decided it was a fast track to trouble.

Carl crossed to the kitchen, where women costumed in period dresses would tend the fires of the cast iron stove and offer demonstrations during the fair, baking bread and other foods. Instead of exiting the building, Carl dragged a chair a couple of feet and sat down with a groan. I couldn't move an inch without the floor planks creaking underfoot.

"Let's see," he murmured. "Here we go, the *Harriett Browne* was a whaling schooner … S. B. Winthrop was at the helm …"

I held my breath as he mentioned Frank's ancestor. By the sound of it, Carl was flipping through the pages of a book.

"Blasted historian, doesn't know how to create a proper index." Humming, Carl flipped more pages. "Let's see … spars and sails. Cordage, rigging, and canvas. It's not even in alphabetical order." Carl sighed and clicked his tongue. "Whaling crafts, nautical instruments," he went on, "Cabin supplies and furniture. Cook's ladle, cook's fork, spittoons, a dozen corn brooms, a dozen birch brooms. I suppose there was a need to clean. Ah *ha*. My goodness, one ornate, mahogany captain's desk. Let's see …" Carl gasped audibly. "Handcrafted by Elijah Gartland!"

I straightened. Gartland, as in *Richard* Gartland?

I rushed through the doorway and thundered down the stairs, not pausing to consider how the sudden sound in an old house might affect a man who'd received a fright earlier in the week. I arrived in the kitchen a second too late. With a cross-eyed stare, Carl slumped backward into the old chair. I rushed to catch him before he fell to the floor.

"Carl." I shook his shoulder. "It's me, Sonny."

"What …?" He focused on my face. "Good heavens."

"I was upstairs taking photos. I recognized your voice."

"Why on *earth* did you burst down the stairs like that?" he demanded. "The reason I came here is because Frank and his attorney keep popping into Apogee Antiques unannounced," Carl went on. "I wanted to follow up on some hunches without letting on what I'm doing."

"Did I hear correctly that the desk was built by …?"

"Richard's ancestor," Carl agreed, indicating a book with a coil binder and a yellow cover featuring a nautical sketch. "It was self-published by a friend of the Gartlands. A man with no academic credentials, but his notes confirm what I'd discovered when I cleaned the label on the desk. The name Elijah Gartland is embossed in the brass."

Now that he'd revived out of his near faint, Carl shared what he read as he studied the footnotes included by the book's author. Historic records were cited showing that Captain Winthrop had commissioned Elijah, a renowned cabinetmaker, to build the desk with the secret compartments that Carl had shown me in Ken Babik's house.

"No surprise it took a year to finish the desk," Carl said. "When the work was completed, Elijah felt he'd done such an outstanding job that he doubled the price he'd originally quoted. Any dummy would know the purpose would be to hide valuables. Captain Winthrop said he first needed to complete another voyage to afford it."

"Please tell me he followed through," I said.

"It says here that Winthrop took possession of the desk, but never paid the updated price. So began a bitter, long-standing feud between the two families." Carl closed the book with a weary sigh. "According to the author, Captain Winthrop's heirs were afraid to reveal any signs of wealth. Instead of enjoying the level of affluence he'd secured, the family lived in fear lest the Gartlands noticed and demanded a share."

"Why not just compensate them for heaven's sake?"

Carl shrugged. "You know how these things go."

"How did the desk end up on dry land?"

"I could imagine the captain wanting to bring it home when he retired. Perhaps he saw it as a safe, preferable to a bank account."

"What are Richard's relatives like? Are his parents alive?"

"No, when the poor lad was in his late teens, their car went over a cliff on one of the Cape Verde Islands," Carl said. "Richard found it distressing and hurtful, being left with an elderly aunt while they traveled the world, but of course, if he'd been with them …"

"Their car went over a *cliff?*" I said.

"Richard hinted that he suspected foul play." Carl frowned, and then he wrenched open the book to check the footnotes. "The *Harriett Browne* stopped in the Cape Verde Islands for supplies. Perhaps his parents were tracing the path of the ship."

And somehow ended up dead. I closed my eyes. How far back did the unfolding nightmare go? My eyes flew open again as I recalled what Dan's father had said of Richard: "He was liquidating assets, and he had a plane ticket to the Cape Verde Islands. *One* ticket, if you catch my drift." Before I knew it, I was blurting the information to Carl.

"Richard was planning to *go* there," I said.

"He never mentioned a thing to me."

"This is frustrating beyond words."

"I'll call the author of this book," Carl said. "Perhaps Richard consulted him and mentioned what he had in mind."

While he stepped away, I reached for my camera, liking how the flaws in the old kitchen window cast patterns on the heavily scarred butcher block island in the center of the room. On the walls were corn brooms and garlic braids, with copper kettles and rustic crockery on the ancient floor. On the far wall was a hearth with bricks that were blackened from many decades of use. The scent of charred wood hung in the air.

Given the time period on display, Captain Winthrop and Elijah Gartland might have come home to kitchens very much like the room in front of me. I pictured them meeting to discuss the desk in top hats and flamboyant coats. Gentlemen on the outside, at least.

Carl looked blanched as he finished his call.

"I reached the author's widow," he said. "I'm not one to believe in curses, but he died during a boating accident last month."

"Last month? Good God …"

I paused for a long, sinking moment, then the attacker's cryptic comment about a past death and a vengeful ghost came to mind.

"I don't suppose his name was William?" I said carefully. "Or if you know of some other man with that name who died?"

Carl shook his head. "No, the name William isn't ringing a bell."

I sighed. "Frank's attorney offered a dark take on how Richard handled Mrs. Winthrop's estate. How did *she* die?"

"Cardiac arrest. I've gone down that dark line of thought as well, but I can't picture Richard plotting to murder a poor woman to secure treasure. There has to be someone else involved."

"The guy with the snake tattoo," I said gravely.

Carl paused. "The what?"

My eyes widened. Oops!

"I was comparing the situation to that old film," I said. "You know the one. A horror movie. There was a bad guy with a tattoo."

"I don't tend to watch horror movies."

Aware of the time, I conveyed my remaining questions, and Carl shot down my theories, one by one. The coins Ken had shown me in Apogee Antiques were not from the desk; most ranged from inexpensive to modest in value. As for the story the plumber had shared about Ken saying, "I cracked the code!" Carl was baffled and shocked.

"If Ken had a breakthrough in decoding the letter, he never shared it with me," Carl said. "The same with Richard. He was quite downcast in recent months. He and Angela had a little friction over—" Carl leaned in and whispered, "They had trouble conceiving."

I nodded, recalling Rose saying as much.

"One last thing," I said. "There's a story floating around about Richard and Angela helping a local farmer empty a shed …"

"The nonsense over the blasted pearls," Carl said with exasperation. "They helped the farmer out of kindness, and got zero thanks in the end. The shed was *packed* with rat droppings, junk, and dust."

"The farmer gave them permission to take the junk?"

"Exactly. His claims are preposterous."

I used my phone to take photos of the page in the book that said Elijah Gartland had built Captain Winthrop's desk.

"Have you shown this book to the police?" I said.

"Certainly not. With Frank's attorney threatening to sue me, I don't dare draw attention to myself."

I paused. "You can't expect *me* to do it."

"You're clever," Carl said. "I'm sure you'll find a way."

"Where would I say I discovered the book?"

"At the library?" Carl asked.

Mystified, I said, "Is that where you found it?"

"Rose finds it impossible to face the house, so she asked me to pick up some things. Richard's office door was open …"

I flipped my hands. "You stole it from the crime scene?"

"The house has been released by the police."

"Still, I'm not supposed to be involved."

"It's smart of you to be careful," Carl said. "Especially with the police wondering if you were dating Richard."

I gaped. "They're saying *what?*"

"It's that Bricker fellow. He and his team are checking Richard's social media accounts."

"Well, they won't find me on his platforms."

"Perhaps the book has no bearing on the case," Carl said.

We both looked away and assessed the room's 1800s furnishings. No dust bunnies came out to confirm or deny that the feud we'd unearthed had led to Richard's death. Even though Richard happened to have the book. Which meant he'd known all about the feud.

"You know," Carl said. "I doubt the police have a historian on staff. If I hang onto the book, perhaps I'll uncover more links."

"Exercise caution, of course," I said. "Stay careful and watchful."

"I absolutely will," Carl promised.

Heading through the door and across the yard, I told myself, *Ok that is it. No more talking to Carl or anyone else. I'm here to take photos.*

Period.

* * *

Following a map of the fairgrounds, I found Bev's Diner, the restaurant Dan had recommended. Covered in brown clapboards with quaint window boxes and a flag hanging outside the door, the diner was only open in September: a mere month out of the entire year.

Inside, the place smelled of bacon and eggs. From the booths to the walls, the diner was lined with tawny pine wood. The curtains and napkins featured a blueberry calico print. Beyond a counter extending the length of the diner, an open space showed the kitchen area.

I ordered coffee, a cheeseburger, coleslaw, and French fries.

"Pick anywhere, hon," the pretty thirtyish waitress said.

I'd no sooner settled into a booth when a bell over the door jingled. I groaned, seeing that Brumby had tracked me down.

He stopped short for a second, then he took off his Stetson and crossed to the counter. There was mysterious friction over his order.

"Big appetite, huh?" the waitress said.

Brumby's scowl turned into a grin as he strode toward me in his yellow cowboy shirt and slipped into the opposite side of the booth.

"We've got lots to talk about," he said, folding his callused hands on the table. "First, is that how you start every day?"

Seeing that I was not catching on, Brumby pulled out his phone and opened the photo app. As he hit the play button, unleashing the haunting notes of a flute, I was startled to see Jess's video of my yoga-plus routine. I had to admit, framed by morning light in my unitard, I looked fierce and focused: a testament to how well I'd landed on my feet.

"You didn't know Joan sent this out?" Brumby said.

"No, but it explains all the texts I got."

"So, listen. I saw a bunch of people near the barns, so I hollered at the top of my lungs if anyone had seen you."

I gaped. "*Why* would you do that?"

"It's a way to catch flies, and it worked. Three guys made a beeline for me. Theo Lurman, a security dude, and Richard's PI."

"You *met* the PI? What's his name?"

"Ed. Real piece of work. Slicked hair, tough-guy attitude. No tattoo. I shook his hand hard to see if he'd wince."

"Again, why?"

"To see if he'd been in a fight, maybe with Richard."

Just then, the waitress arrived. She set my meal and coffee on the table, then her face tightened as she plucked Brumby's plate from her tray and slammed it down in front of him. Some of the fries leaped off as if to escape the violence they'd just experienced. The waitress slammed down a plastic glass filled with soda, spilling the contents, and then she stood there regarding Brumby with her fist planted on her hip.

All the while, the rugged Aussie averted his gaze, his features feigning innocence, and his fingers drumming on the table.

The waitress turned to me. "Good luck. You'll need it."

"He's not getting anywhere with me," I assured her.

"You don't think I made the same pronouncement until I was blue in the face? Like I said, honey. Good luck."

As she flounced away, Brumby glanced at her over his shoulder, as if unable to resist recalling their private moments. When he turned back to me, I had my arms folded and one eyebrow arched.

"This would happen anywhere," I said. "Wouldn't it?"

"Not *every* place," he said.

"Back to the PI. I've been wondering about a guy who stopped by my farm and stalked me in the Corner Pocket. His name was Ed, but he was a shuffling bumpkin. It can't be the same man."

"Ed isn't exactly a rare name," Brumby said.

"What about the security guy?"

"No tattoo. Told me off for hollering your name. Called me a jerk."

"He's probably a friend of Dan's. What did Theo say?"

"Same deal. Told me to show some sense."

"Did you learn anything of interest?" I demanded.

"It's early days. I'll try again later."

"No more hollering my name."

"Somebody has to step in on your behalf," Brumby said. "You found Richard. Tangled with that nutjob who's probably the murderer. The police have mishandled you from the get-go."

"Never mind me. Don't take risks, ok?"

"I won't let what happened in May repeat itself," Brumby said with his mouth full. "If I get the chance, I'll show the attacker what mad as a cut snake means back home. No tattoo necessary."

"Brumby, *no.*"

"Save your breath. Raymond will be cheering me on."

I turned to my meal, but my appetite was ruined.

20

With my empowerment playlist blasting on my drive home, I reflected on the photos I'd taken that day. One of my favorites was a portrait of an Angora goat with long ringlets of silky wool. Having caught him during a nap, I came up with the caption: *It's so tiring being beautiful, with people wanting to take my picture and pet my fabulous curls all the time.*

I'd photographed a rooster who'd enjoyed my attention. He'd looked directly at my lens, preening and flashing his feathers.

I'd photographed a retired man who traveled the country with a mid-1800s chuck wagon that featured cookware, food, tack, and other gear that had been used on cattle drives. He was an energetic, non-stop font of lively stories about the hardships cowboys faced on the trail.

The impression of landing a successful day began unraveling when I arrived home at three o'clock and climbed out of my car to the din of my entire flock hollering for all they were worth in the pasture. My sheep had a team mentality when it came to signaling for help.

"Baahh! Bluuuh! Ba-a-a-h-h!" They hit every note imaginable.

I saw the reason for the hysteria. Two of the seven-month-old lambs had broken out of the pasture for the umpteenth time, and couldn't figure out how to get back in. As if to liven up her evolutionary plan, Nature had outfitted sheep with an insatiable sense of curiosity, and a complete inability to handle the consequences if their wanderlust went wrong.

I let Luke out of his pen, and then with my camera bag slung over my shoulder, I climbed the porch steps to fetch the tools I would need to fix the fence. My key slid from the lock hole. I regrouped and focused on the simple task. Insert key. I'd done it a billion times. It didn't fit.

I leaned down and was startled to see a different lock.

"What the heck?" I said.

Luke sat primly on my right with a look that said, *I know what went on, but you'd need to speak my doggie language to understand.*

I closed my eyes. Norris had changed the deadbolt. Not seeing a note or new keys in an obvious place, I texted Dan.

Not to complain, but I'm locked out of my house.

He texted, *Sorry. Check the sill above the door.*

I felt along the top, and there was a ring with four keys.

I texted, *Thank you!*

Practice range tomorrow at 8 a.m.? If so, I'll pick you up.

Works for me. See you then.

Inside the house, I grabbed a hammer and nails, slipped on my rubber boots, and headed for the sound of yelling.

Even without looking as I climbed the fence and walked down the hill, I knew it was Gracie and Jane who'd broken out. If they were human, they would be the naughty sort of twins who would trick people by switching their identities back and forth. They sported coats of silky white ringlets, like the other Corriedale-Finn cross ewes in the flock, but with brown facial markings and kneecaps that reflected a Shropshire ancestor.

"Ba-a-ah," they shouted from the other side of the fence.

"I'm coming," I said.

My first challenge was to ford the stream without getting wet. The rushing water lapped against my boots, bubbling over stones that were slick with algae. I wobbled my way along, ankles turning, arms swooping. I was midway across when Gracie and Jane sailed over the broken fence as neatly as a couple of equine show jumpers.

"You couldn't have done that before I came down?" I demanded.

They trotted insolently past me: *Got you good that time.*

Unless I wanted a repeat performance tomorrow, there was nothing to do but fix the hole in the fence they'd escaped through. A ten-foot section of the woven wire was sagging, and the electric tape that ran from one cedar post to the next around the pasture was broken. Chances were, a moose I'd seen the other day had caused the damage.

First, I straightened the sagging fence, and then I prepared to reattach it to the post. It was a good chance to practice my hammering skills. I'd been instructed to keep my eye on the nail, pull the hammer straight back without snagging my ear with the claw, then *pow*.

"Damn it!"

You would never know I was the same woman who'd performed hand-stands that morning. For every square hit, I either bent the nail in half or ineffectively dimpled the post two or three times. Hammering was one of the oldest arts in human history. Even cave people had hammered things. I pushed up my sleeves and concentrated harder.

Pow.

"Crap!"

Pow.

"Shit!"

Pow.

"Stupid nail!"

As I paused to confirm the wire was attached and straight, the air was eerily still in the sudden quiet. In the nearby forest, sixty-foot pines cast deep shadows over saplings and lichen-covered boulders, and maple trees were burnished with touches of autumn gold. I clutched the hammer, my heart in high gear as I realized the murderer could be out there. He was good at hiding. I should have thought of that before I came down.

In the dappled light, the forest was like an optical illusion that was meant to trick the eye. A sapling morphed into a man in hunting camou-flage. A knot on an old maple tree looked like a leering face. A forked root amidst fallen leaves could pass for a pair of legs.

I gripped the hammer, furious that in some ways, the attacker still had me in a wrestler's hold — locked in an aftermath that suited his goals, with most of my means of escape tied to potential pain.

In his journals, Raymond had written about investigations that had tumbled into chaos when a brash detective caused a witness to shut down. Here I was, forced to think twice for that very reason. Holding back felt wrong. I yearned to tell Dan the truth, but the second I pictured how the aftermath would unfold, I tripped over doubts.

I'd seen the concern in Dan's gaze when I'd theorized that my tea had been spiked. On patrol or elsewhere, he would surely have heard similar claims from addicts who didn't want to land in trouble.

I firmed my resolve. No more playing the victim. When the moment of truth arrived, I wanted to impress Dan with a tight case that meshed with his evidence-based world. I would knock his socks off.

Over the sound of the rushing stream came a sharp honk. I shaded my eyes and saw a car parked behind my station wagon near my house. Detective Bricker signaled for me to come.

"Talk about *excellent* timing," I said.

In an instant, the part of me who'd balanced on her hands that morning took control. Impatience carried me across the stream without a misstep. Even Gracie and Jane stepped back as I steamed past the flock up the hill. I pulled out my phone and started a video on the photo app, then I returned the phone to my front pocket with the lens facing forward. It might serve me well to let him think he was free to be a jerk.

Arriving near my porch, where he was waiting, I set down the hammer and nails, then I folded my arms and let him speak first.

"Miss Littlefield. Sorry to disturb you."

"I'd think you would be sorry in general."

"Why would that be?"

"You've been showing my photo to people connected to Richard. This has inspired them to confront me in parking lots."

Clearly, the detective didn't care. I studied his tough guy scowl, which nonstop irritation had etched around his mouth over the years. Even his ears looked tight, as if nature had decided he wouldn't be good at listening, so why bother with generous features.

"Why are you here?" I said.

"Frank Winthrop has tossed out a lead for us to look into," he said. "Apparently, you compelled him to report it."

I'd figured there was a chance Frank would follow through on the tip. I focused on assessing Bricker's folded arms: no tattoo.

"His attacker sounded scary," I said.

"Why were you talking to Frank?"

"I told you why. What did you think would happen when you showed my photo around? While we're setting things straight," I interrupted as he started to respond, "You do realize it was unethical for your wife to tell you I was in the ER. The hospital bigwigs knew enough to apologize. For you to question me while I was out of it—"

"You were *stoned*. Come on, Miss Littlefield."

Bricker paused as Luke bristled and softly growled. I was used to my self-appointed bodyguard trailing after me and sitting politely when company arrived. I'd forgotten he was by my side.

"Congratulations," I said. "This is the first time he's perceived a visitor as a threat. It's time to pack it in. We're done."

"We're not done. Step this way."

I folded my arms and stayed put.

Seeing that I hadn't followed him, as instructed, he looked irritated as he crossed back to me with a laptop he'd fetched from his car. He opened it and showed me a photo on the screen. I felt a flicker of shock. It was a bar scene of two people sitting in a booth, having a drink. The man was Richard Gartland. The woman was me.

Bricker looked pleased to have startled me.

"Well?" he prompted.

"You are not having a good day," I said.

"*I'm* not having a good day?"

"You didn't have this image vetted before you came. It's a fake."

"You're saying this isn't you?"

"Give me a digital copy. I'll prove it."

Bricker's jaw shifted as if he were rolling a piece of hard candy from one side of his mouth to the other. He'd barreled to my house with a narrow agenda, a notion of how our back-and-forth would play out after he knocked me off guard. No plan B. Now he was stuck.

I was the opposite, lasering in on a few nagging points.

"You told me Richard hired a PI," I said. "I was starting to think you made it up, but a PI named Ed approached a friend of mine. Is he a threat? Someone I need to worry about?"

"I'm not about to discuss the case with you."

"You're saying he's *not* a threat?"

"Steer clear of anyone involved. How about that?"

"Who is William?" I said calmly.

Bricker looked convincingly mystified. "You tell me."

"Are you aware of how Richard's parents died?" I said.

"How would I—? What are you playing at?" Bricker demanded.

I shook my head. "You don't know much, do you?"

"All right, settle down."

In my mind, Dan was signaling to me to not react.

"Here's the deal," I said. "When your investigators confirm the photo is bogus, I hope it sinks in how foolish it is to let a murderer use a trick like that to call the shots. If my father were here, he'd add his own opinion about not looking like a gullible mark."

"Now, *listen*—"

Luke softly growled. I stopped him with a sharp look.

"When you add this ill-advised visit to your lack of ethics in the ER," I went on, "We're talking about a pattern of harassment, a term you might want to look up. From here on out, don't approach me unannounced. Call in advance so I can have an attorney present."

Abruptly, I realized an officer was sitting in Bricker's car, rubbing his forehead as if he couldn't believe the spectacle he was witnessing.

"Hello there," I said loudly. "I'll be calling on you as a witness."

To speed their exit, I slipped my phone from my pocket to let Bricker know he'd stepped in ethical dog poo with the video rolling.

"Leave," I said. "*Now.*"

His shrewd gaze conveyed that I was bolder than he'd imagined, which I realized might cause him to suspect me all the more.

"I'll be in touch," he growled.

"Not without my attorney involved."

He retreated to his car and swerved down the driveway in reverse. I shook my head. His driving stunk, too. Only when the detective's car was surging away down the road did I end the video.

"Jackass," I hollered. "You ruined a great day."

Luke wagged his tail as if to say, "Are we a team, or what?"

"We are totally a team," I said, kneeling to pet him.

Seeing Dodge waiting on the other side of the fence, I climbed the gray rails and clicked my tongue. With a rumble of excited nickers and his hooves thudding on the grass, he maneuvered his muscled haunches into place. Once he was near enough, I gripped Dodge's mane and slipped my right leg over his wide back. His coat was dusty, in need of a session with the curry comb. I leaned forward to scratch his forelock.

Logic said the fake photo was meant to throw a wrench in the works, but it seemed a low-value, cheap trick to pull. Charlotte's delinquent son fit the bill when it came to low-value and cheap. I realized this was the second time in as many days that I didn't think twice before linking him with a bad turn in my life. He had himself to blame.

I texted Sue, Kate, and Brumby, *Re tattoo Bricker = 0.*

Kate texted, *Confirmed from our end. Checking arms of patrons nonstop with no hits. No viable leads named William. Still looking.*

Dodge nickered as he saw Joan walking toward us up the driveway. With tongue clicks and a gentle squeeze of my calves, I urged him forward along the fence. He understood the job at hand, thudding downhill until we reached Joan at the midway point. I reversed the onboarding process, climbing over the rails to join Joan near the driveway.

"Why were the police here just now?" she said.

"Routine stuff. No worries."

Joan folded her arms. "Let me rephrase. I saw Detective Bricker in the car. I know he's a pain. How can I help?"

"I suppose it would be good for you to see this," I said, handing her my phone and launching the video of the surprise visit.

Joan gaped as she listened to the exchange.

"How did you stay so calm?" she said. "You were right about the way your father would react. He would have put Bricker in an armlock and shoved his head into the water trough over there."

"That's why I don't plan to show the video to Dan."

"Why did you ask about a guy named William?" Joan said.

I shrugged. "Someone mentioned the name to me."

"I have some related intel to share," Joan said, pulling a familiar backup charger from her bag. "I stopped by the fairgrounds to drop off my entrance forms. I'm hoping to get a blue ribbon for my nectarine preserves.

Anyway, I heard a security guy named Cody asking if you were expected to stop in today. He asked me to give this back."

"I told him he could keep it."

"He fixed his phone, so he's all set," Joan said. "Listen to this. I asked him how the case was going. He's not looped in on the details, but from what he's overheard, an arrest might be imminent."

"I wish you'd started with that. It's the best news all week." I frowned. "You'd think Bricker would have mentioned it."

Joan gripped my arm with a look that said I was being dense. "Sonny, what if he'd planned to arrest *you* today?"

"Based on the bogus photo?"

"He clearly thought it was legit," Joan said. "I hate gossip, but after seeing this video … you know Bricker's wife works at the hospital. They were seen arguing, and she looked tearful."

"I bet she got into trouble for telling him I was in the ER."

"Possibly, but there's another angle. Bricker has been spending a lot of time at the hospital comforting Angela Gartland. It's sparked a rumor that they were involved. Having an affair."

I hesitated. "Bricker knew Richard's wife before …?"

"I don't know. Again, it's a rumor. But say they were involved. What better way to bury it than to accuse Richard of cheating?"

"Angela did accuse him of cheating. I heard Dan telling his father about it the other night. Bricker ran with it."

"Of course he did," Joan said.

"We're getting way, way ahead of ourselves," I cautioned. "Bricker was shocked when I told him the photo was a fake."

"Because he realized he'd been played," Joan said. "Somebody used his obsessive suspicion of you to their advantage."

I rubbed my brow, stunned by how quickly a power moment could reverse course and land me with more questions to sort out. Two seconds into picturing the scowling detective in love, I hit a brick wall. He didn't have a snake tattoo. That was all I knew for sure.

"I know we can't put stock in anything yet," Joan said. "But follow the logic. Richard is the one who hired a PI. That's standard procedure for outing a cheating spouse." With her eye on the lowering sun, Joan said, "I need to head home. Please tell me you're ok."

"I should be asking you that." I hugged her. "I meant to check in after you told me about your marital woes. How are you doing?"

"I've been agonizing over my marriage for so long it's like one of those knots you can't get out of a wet shoelace," Joan said, enacting the furious untying process. "You want to *pitch* it in the trash. But it's the only shoelace you have so you keep putting up with it."

"There are plenty of shoelaces in the world," I assured her.

"I think I want a divorce. There, I've finally said it. I think Harry and Jess will be fine. They probably see it coming."

"Let's have a pizza night," I said. "We'll get drunk."

Joan giggled. "We can't get *drunk*."

"Tipsy, then."

"Maybe next week," she said. "I have parent-teacher conferences in the wings. Has Dan gotten results on the tea?"

"Not yet. I'll be seeing him tomorrow."

Once she was heading down the hill, I distractedly tossed fresh hay into Bubbah's pen and refilled his bucket with fresh water.

Luke bounded ahead of me as I crossed to the house, squeaking his stuffed lobster toy to convince me to play. I picked it up and tossed it half-heartedly a few times, torn with guilt over my inability to be straight with Joan. Inside the house, I set down my camera bag, crossed to the couch, and dropped onto my back, numb from the widening array of tough questions to sort out as twilight began claiming the living room.

According to what I'd found online, the crash that had killed Richard's parents was ruled an accident. Were they visiting the Cape Verde Islands because the *Harriett Browne* had been known to dock there? Was Richard heading there thinking the crash wasn't an accident after all?

The attacker's harsh whispers had plagued me on and off all day. *Lies won't work with me. You know what I'm here for.*

If only that was true.

When I closed my eyes, I found it impossible to stave off the stark memory of Richard's fatal wounds. Had the murderer pinned him down? Hollered threats? Shot him at point blank range?

Why had I been spared from mortal wounds?

It was tough to ignore Nathan's dark take on Richard's efforts to hire Frank during their Boston days. Could the desperate man I'd briefly seen, his anguish seared into my mind's eye by the bright glare of my headlights, be capable of carrying out a cruel plot against Frank?

In the fading light, the scent of Raymond's pipe tobacco wafted upward from the couch cushions, and the maple floorboards softly ticked, as if in protest, as the last warm rays of the setting sun slipped downward along the east-facing windows, and then ebbed away.

With a sigh, I fetched the journal I'd hidden under the cushions and flipped to a passage from a little over a year ago.

Brumby took me to task last week, saying I was an idiot for not seeing Joan's awkward pauses and shy smiles as signs of a crush, Raymond had written. *I can't imagine why a pretty young woman would see me that way. Now she's got me looking twice when she smiles. I love her kids to pieces, but all this is pie-in-the-sky thinking while she's married. Joan has hinted of some kind of friction with her husband. A rift she won't talk about.*

"I'm worried this passage would tear Joan apart," I murmured.

Luke's head arrived on the couch cushion next to my arm.

"What's for dinner?" I said.

Luke grinned, a pushover for a joke, even if he'd heard it before.

21

Dan looked curious when he knocked on my door at 8:00 a.m. "Your car is casting heat out there. Did you go to the fairgrounds this morning?"

"I just got back. Dawn shots."

Plus a few other scenes. With a farmer's assurance that I wouldn't get gored, I'd climbed in amongst a line of white cattle with huge horns as they dozed in the misty morning light. With my 17-40mm lens attached, I framed shots with the horns of the nearest animal in the foreground to create a sense of actually being there in the shot.

Dan's expression said he was impressed by my dedication.

"Let's take a look at your father's firearms," he said.

"This way."

I led him down the first-floor hallway to my father's room, where rustic artwork lined the forest green walls, and Ella's needlework was on display on the quilt and bed pillows. In jeans and a blue shirt that I found myself admiring in the morning light, the way it set off his tan, Dan used the code I recited to open the gun safe. My father had left behind an assortment of weapons along with his service sidearm.

First came a lecture on the proper storage of firearms. The metal parts of guns can retain moisture, Dan said. It was important to store them dry and clean off fingerprints because natural salts on fingers could serve as an entry point for rust. A light coating of oil was sufficient to seal metal surfaces. The wooden gun stock of my father's old-style rifle needed to be waxed, and the bores also should be cleaned. Never overcrowd the gun case, Dan said. Put everything where it belonged, easy to find.

I widened my eyes and stared heavenward. I'd only keep one weapon in the end, maybe, and would strive to never, ever reach for it.

"I see you rolling your eyes," Dan said without looking up.

"People spend time on all this?"

"Sure, if they're enthusiasts."

I frowned. Was there a reason he sounded formal beyond the subject of handling firearms? He seemed extra contained that day.

Reaching for my father's hunting rifle, Dan checked to be sure it wasn't loaded: swivel, click, snap. In my hands, the gun was an ungainly length of metal and wood that accidentally banged into chairs and got stuck in doorways, which is why it definitely was not loaded. In Dan's confident hands, the rifle looked sleek and obedient.

"This gun is not appropriate for home protection," he said. "I know a guy who'd give you a good price if you're looking to sell."

"That would be great."

"Who else has the combination for the safe?"

"A few of Raymond's colleagues, Joan, Brumby."

This sparked a look of surprise. "*Brumby?*"

"He and Raymond were good friends."

"Yeah, Brumby's list of 'friends' is quite long," Dan muttered.

"You seem to have a certain concern in mind," I said.

"Nope." Dan closed the safe and glanced at me. "Ready?"

"Sure. Lead the way."

Sensing a slight level of friction, Luke appeared to be perfectly happy to be left behind. *It'll be more peaceful here*, his eyes said.

Dan stowed the rifle in the locked chest behind the extended cab, then we climbed into his truck. It truly was a climb for me. He more or less slipped in sideways. A couple of leather cases sat on the back seat, along with boxes of bullets. The smell of gun oil mingled with the scent of Dan's aftershave, soft and understated. He turned the truck around with a one-handed, circular move — of course not nicking the garden stones since he wasn't fallible like me — then he eased down the driveway, plucking a pair of sunglasses from the dashboard and slipping them on. Dark lenses. Expensive. Classy. I'd forgotten to bring mine.

Yesterday, he'd insisted he was in my corner. Now he was quiet, lost in his own thoughts. We held a silence contest for the first five minutes of the drive. I've never been one to win contests.

"What's going on?" I said. "You're acting strange and tense."

Dan took off his sunglasses and tossed them aside.

"I talk to Sue and Kate at the Corner Pocket from time to time," he said. "They're insightful and connected. They have their ear to the ground. When I brought up your bad couple of nights, they totally clammed up. I'm trying to understand why."

"Great. I'm sorry I asked."

"Benzodiazepine."

I froze and stared at him, and then realized I'd just lost the card game he'd devised to get me to talk. It was not to my liking at *all.*

"Why did you react?" he said.

"Careful, Dan. I've got ammo, too."

"Nothing on this level."

"All right. How's Connie?"

As he flinched in shock, I closed my eyes and condemned myself for letting my inner self-defensive jackass take control.

"I'm sorry," I said. "That was awful of me."

"I'm trying to understand a major element," Dan said with irritation. "You proved my point. Why did benzodiazepine hit a nerve?"

"You got the test results on the tea?"

"First thing this morning," he said. "Plus, I pieced together enough to know your cousins couldn't have spiked it."

"So, you're back to thinking I'm a drug addict."

"I don't know where to land. There were traces of zolpidem as well. That's a sleeping pill, which I guess makes sense, if not for the THC and psilocybin. Magic mushrooms? Seriously?"

"Please don't holler at me," I said.

"Why did you react, Sonny?"

"You can't just blast a person without warning."

"I'm sorry if I'm coming across the wrong way. It's from my level of concern. Mixing drugs is highly dangerous."

"I'm the one who experienced it," I pointed out.

"You were on board with testing the tea," Dan said softly. "That's what makes it confusing. Your cousins are ruled out, so how did it get spiked? Part of your pattern is to protect people."

"This is a disaster and a nightmare," I said, pinching the bridge of my nose as I whirled through the ins and outs of what would happen if I told Dan the awful secret. I pictured him hitting the brake so hard that the truck would leave tire marks on the pavement. He would swing around, drop me at my farm, and blaze off to battle with Bricker.

"Sonny, talk to me."

"I heard an arrest is imminent."

"If so, it's news to me," Dan said.

"How carefully did they search Richard's path to the road? My father wrote about the importance of using a grid approach."

"Bricker is conducting a second search."

"What's the latest? Have you heard anything?" I said desperately. "Do you know of anyone named William?"

"An officer or a suspect? The short answer is no, so—" Dan glared at me. "Unbelievable. You're dodging the subject."

"I don't like being played."

"I could say the same thing."

To my horror, the stress of being pulled in opposing directions took hold of my throat and had tears gathering in my eyes. I was protecting his reputation, his career. If only he knew.

Dan exhaled. "It was out of line to spring the drug name at you. My job can reinforce the wrong dynamic in my approach. I'm worried, Sonny. Desperate to know the truth so I can help."

Perfect. The more reasonable he became, the more miserable I felt. I should tell him. Just blurt the truth. I tested out a possible structure for the disclosure in the back of my mind: *I know it sounds outlandish, but the séance technique was really effective. The hypnosis session, I mean.*

"Sonny, I'm sorry," Dan said. "I don't see you as an addict. Dealing with trauma is complicated. I trust that you'll sort it out. I'm here if you want to share. End of discussion. Let's start over."

"From a point last year, maybe?" I used my fingers to stop the tears from spilling over. "Can we listen to music instead of talking?"

"That won't solve anything."

"It'll ease the headache I'm getting."

Dan's eyebrows twisted with concern. "You want some aspirin?"

"No."

"A soda?"

"No."

"Sonny—"

"Music, please."

Dan sighed, then reached for the stereo controls.

I folded my arms and prepared myself to hear a song that spelled out our lack of compatibility once and for all. Brumby spent all hours of the day listening to music that reflected his skirt-chasing, "*yeeha*" mindset far better than winks and words. I pegged Dan for an oldies guy. Not the soulful oldies I found appealing. He would like the monotonous, uninventive kind. No surprises. Strictly routine.

As a drum riff spilled into familiar guitar licks, a pint of blood left my head, and went south. Of all the songs Dan could have selected, he'd queued up *Texas Flood* by Stevie Ray Vaughan — slow and bluesy, relentlessly sexy, with the volume turned up enough to feel the bass through the truck's leather seat. It was the kind of song that points to the nearest horizontal surface and says, "Go at it, and take your time."

"Why this song?" I demanded.

Dan looked mystified by my tone. "Arlene said you like his music, so I checked him out. If you prefer, I've started a blues playlist—"

"Just leave it. Never mind."

It was clear that my best friend had decided to give Dan a subliminal helping hand. She knew I had a weakness for male vocalists. Guys whose voices were as smooth as whiskey, sliding here and there like a caress, while an electric guitar soared and peaked with wild abandon. I couldn't be the only one who pictured a multiple-orgasm scenario.

All kinds of flooding was going on in Texas as the truck bounced into a parking lot adjacent to a gray structure, beyond which targets were lined up in a row. The purr of the engine and the music stopped.

"Here we are," Dan said.

"So soon …?"

He leaned across the cupholder and took my hand.

"I wanted today to be a positive step," Dan said softly. "It kills me to see you struggling. I took the wrong approach."

Between his closeness and his warm gaze, a tingling awareness lifted through my body. The truck cab was roomy, the leather seats cushy and fully reclinable. We were alone. I managed a nod.

"We're about to handle weapons," Dan said. "We need to be calm and focused. We can talk, take a quick walk. It's on me to turn things around, so name the price." Looking soulful and intense, he kissed my hand and brushed a curl from my face. "Let me make it up to you."

"If you insist," I breathed.

* * *

"Relax," Dan said, close to my ear.

"I'm just a little …"

"Nervous? I don't want to push you into anything."

"I want this. I do."

"Then slow down. Yeah, just like that."

"I'm sorry I made all that noise the first time."

"Stop worrying, it's just you and me." Massaging my shoulders, Dan turned my muscles into putty. "Is that better?"

"Much, much better."

Dan's hands abruptly stopped. "Sonny, don't ever close your eyes when you have a firearm in your hands, even if it's empty."

I blinked. "Right. Sorry."

Dan stood close behind me under a long open roof that protected us from the bouts of drizzle and bursts of sunshine that had settled over the firing range. In front of an embankment some yards away was the expected row of targets, each with a bull's eye on the silhouette of a man. I didn't understand why the center was over the belly. If I were trying to stop the murderer, I would aim for his heart.

In front of us was a counter that ran the length of the open roof. Dan started my training with a .22 pistol. I focused on gripping the weapon correctly the moment I picked it up. Again and again, I went through the motions. In an emergency, fumbling was not an option.

As we moved on to loading the firearm, I maintained the same approach of repeating steps until my actions were smooth.

"Your dedication to technique is great," he said.

He'd stressed the need for strict rules: never leave a round in the chamber and always store the gun with no magazine. He drilled me with the sequence of installing the magazine, hollering a warning, and releasing the safety. My mind and hands absorbed the steps. If an intruder threatened me, I wanted my response to be seamless.

"Excellent," Dan said. "Proceed when you're ready."

I completed the loading sequence, hollered the warning, released the safety, exhaled, and pulled the trigger. Even with advanced knowledge of how the kick would affect my aim, I was off a bit.

"No worries," Dan said loud enough for me to hear. "I'm surprised you were off by that much. Your hands were steady."

I pulled off my earmuffs. "I was aiming for the heart."

"Not the X?" Dan paused. "Then that was pretty good."

"I think I'd do better with a heavier weapon."

"This is the right size for you to start with."

After demonstrating accuracy and speed with the lighter weapon, Dan gave me a look that said it was time for me to confess.

"Where did you train?" he said.

"Shooting a weapon? This is my first time."

"Come on." He studied my face. "You're serious?"

"Very."

He brought out a 9-millimeter Smith & Wesson. We repeated the routine of starting with the parts in front of me. Loading it. Shouting the warning. Releasing the safety. Firing it.

The kick was more of a surprise. I flexed my shoulders and focused all the harder. Playing out what to do in my mind's eye, I took a few more practice shots and found ways to fall into rhythm with the kick. I breathed. Focused. My accuracy got better and better.

Soon, I had the separate elements in front of me again.

"How many rounds does it carry?" I said.

"Seventeen."

"Golly. That sounds excessive."

"Just relax," Dan said. "If this is too much …"

"It's fine. Let me focus."

I pictured the night in May when both of us were fortunate to have walked out of the forest alive. What if Dan hadn't been there to dive in and save my life with a ballistic vest? Even worse, what if he'd been injured, and it was up to me to take down the horrid killer?

Swiftly, I loaded the magazine, completed the sequence, inhaled, exhaled, and drilled the target with five clean shots. Five seemed plenty. I couldn't imagine going for broke and emptying the magazine.

I engaged the safety, put the weapon on the counter, and took off my earmuffs with the feel of the shots still ringing in my hands.

"No way," Dan said. "Look what you did."

"Two were a little off."

"By an *inch*," he said.

"I pictured that night in May."

Dan shook his head. "I saw how you controlled your breathing. That's why I thought you had prior experience."

"Camera work requires breath control," I explained. "Plus, for a sharp image, you can't let the action of pressing the release translate to the rest of your hand. Arlene calls me the human tripod."

"Still, I'm blown away."

"I don't know how I'd do in a real situation," I said. "Guns should be barbed and ugly, with warning labels. Not shiny and sleek."

Dan nodded. "I never stopped to think about it that way."

I didn't admit that my powers of perception came and went in unpredictable bursts and often ended at my own doorstep.

"Let's stop for now," I said. "My assignment awaits."

"Sure." Looking distracted, he stowed the weapons, then he stopped and closed his eyes. "Who told you about Connie?"

"Sue and Kate. They thought I knew already."

Finished with the boxes, Dan blew out a breath and started pacing, rubbing his head and making odd growling sounds. Watching him, I felt a stab of anguish. Was he still hung up on Connie?

"If an alien is about to pop out of you, I'd like a fair shot at getting away," I said. "Maybe you'll allow me a head start?"

"I'm sorry." Dan collected himself. "When I got back from the border, Connie showed up in town, wanting to 'help' scatter Aaron's ashes in Vermont. His parents said no, flat out, which of course set her off. Her fondest dream is to be part of a reality show. Feuds and drama. I didn't want to risk having her get in your face, so …"

"Finally, the picture makes sense," I said.

"I did have the other issues. Insomnia, etcetera. The next thing I know I'm hearing your name over the scanner."

"I get it. No need to explain."

Dan rubbed his brow again, assembling his thoughts.

"Connie's grandfather was a trooper," he said. "Astute. Street-smart. He treated me like an adult when I was ten, eleven. It was a big deal for me, getting buy-in from a guy like that."

"I've seen instances where mentoring works," I said carefully. "And times when the adult has undue influence."

"You sound like my father," Dan said. "It's hard for a kid to see it, but I did grasp the problem over time. Wilson … that was his name. He developed a cough. Didn't get it checked. Lung cancer. He smoked. I felt helpless. Unable to sustain his mood swings. He'd push me away, then reel me back in. The one thing I could have done right, pull Connie out of the weeds, I let him down. A classic, idiot move."

"Dan, come on," I chided.

"You know the whole story with her? How stupid I was?"

"I've made plenty of wrong moves in my life."

"You go off the rails, it's charming," he said. "Even back then, I prided myself on being contained and rational, not …"

"Human?"

Dan frowned. "How did Sue and Kate convey the news?"

"Connie's name came up. They said she was your …"

"Exactly," Dan said tersely. "All day, every day, that word is out there, connected to me. An ideal that was supposed to be special in my life. I blew it and threw it all away." Dan gripped the counter like he wanted to shove it forward across the target range. "I can't believe Sue and Kate told you the details. Everybody knows to not talk about it."

I sighed. "I worried this might happen." Pulling my phone from my pocket, I opened a folder of photos I'd taken that morning and handed the device to Dan. "What do you see?"

"How is this relevant?"

"Humor me, ok?"

Dan scowled at the first photo. "A kid with a Holstein."

I motioned. "Keep going."

He scrolled and scrolled, then paused. "This one is familiar. It's Todd Aronson, I think. Why am I looking at these kids?"

"What do they have in common?"

"Farming background, local ties …"

"They're nineteen," I said.

"What does that have to do with—" Dan stopped and stared at the photo with a new level of attention. "They're …"

"*Nineteen*, the same age you were when Connie leveled your life for a short time. No lasting damage. Here you are."

"I know, but—"

"If this wide-eyed kid came to you with the same story, in turmoil after getting played, what would you tell him?"

With closed eyes and a tired sigh, Dan returned my phone. "I would tell him to get over it, and move on."

"Exactly."

Resting one elbow on the counter, Dan studied me with an assessing gaze, his turmoil drifting away, at least for now.

"You tracked down these kids and took photos of them to show me, knowing I'd been kicking myself for a decade," he said. "Handling it by shutting down any discussion of it."

I smiled. "Now who's the crack detective?"

"You're the boss, the bomb, the GOAT—"

"No thanks on that one. Goats are a little nutty, with spooky eyes that make you think they can read your mind."

"Then you're the BOAT," Dan said. "Best of all time."

"That's even worse."

"How about the COAT? Coolest of all time."

With irritation, I flipped my hands. "You've ruined the moment."

"Normally, you'd be laughing at this thread."

"Take me home. I have a busy day."

Truth be told, the turn of mood suited me, since it made the work of keeping him in the dark a piece of cake.

"You're not really angry?" he said.

"I'm a complicated woman."

Dan nodded. "That is for sure."

* * *

No surprise Dan lifted my mood by the time we reached my driveway, plotting a way to punk one of his colleagues. After acting a little ditzy on a joint trip to the practice range, I was to shock the colleague with the kind of precision one would see in competitive shooting.

"I can't pull that off," I said.

"Of course you can, with more practice."

"I *meant* I can't pull off being ditzy."

Dan devolved into a laughing fit, and then he tried to contain it when I glared. It took an effort. I could tell it hurt.

I smiled to let him off the hook.

"You punked *me* just now?" he demanded.

"You've had it coming for days."

Grazing near the fence on our left, Woolberry and Dot looked up with grass stems in their pink muzzles as we emerged from the shadows of the trees that bordered the road. I heard Luke barking, and the low growl of an engine. I sat forward and gaped. Across from my house, Norris was on his yellow backhoe, scooping the old septic tank out of the ground and dropping it into a dump truck while two other men looked on.

"Did you expect him to come today?" Dan said.

"No, it was left pretty vague."

"I'm sorry. He's out of control."

Getting a signal from his father, Dan parked in the lower space near the berry field so the dump truck could lumber down the hill with its load. After Norris hollered to us that the new tank was on the way, we parked my car next to Dan's truck so I wouldn't get blocked in. Norris was all business as I arrived, but I insisted on thanking and hugging him.

"I'm glad to help," he said, then resumed issuing commands.

Expressing apologies all the way, Dan accompanied me into the house. I assured him I didn't mind the surprise timing. Not if the clogged pipe debacle would be a thing of the past by the end of the day.

Luke greeted us at the door with zeal, then Dan offered to put him in his pen while I gathered my gear for a long day of shooting. Dan returned to the kitchen and closed the door with a look that told me I wasn't going anywhere until we said a proper goodbye.

He slipped his arms around me with a quiet smile. "I heard you called Bricker a gullible mark to his face."

"The colleague in his car told you?"

"It made my day," Dan said, pulling me into a kiss.

I closed my eyes and responded to his wonderful, expressive lips. Soft and gentle. Then playful and sexy, the same way our kissing sprees always unfolded. We melded together, moving, turning until we bumped into the table, his arms around me, and my hands savoring his flexed muscles. I felt his heart beating, and heat rising from his chest.

"J'ai raté ça pendant mon absence," he murmured, coming up for air.

"It's been a while since you've cursed at me in French."

"I was saying I've missed this. You vowed to be fluent by now."

"I got as far as downloading a language app. I'll get there." We kissed again, then I was the one coming up for air. "After hearing about Connie, I'm worried you have a type."

"You can't be serious," he protested. "Your energy is directed outward. You're thoughtful, generous, bent on taking care of others."

"That's nice to hear, but—"

Dan cut off my reply with a sexy kiss, his strong hands roaming all over the place, all the way down to my butt, snugging me close, then traveling upward again, past the small of my back, and then settling there, as if he wanted to release every bone in my spine.

"I get why you waffle," he said, planting soft kisses. "We've both been burned, so I want to be clear. I'm not into flings."

"Same here."

With his palm resting on my cheek, Dan studied me. "You look clear and focused. It's nice to have you back."

"I never left."

"You know what I mean."

I sighed, thinking, *Unfortunately, I do.*

We sank into another kiss, intense and warm, deliciously serious. I felt a heady mix of attraction and calm, of ties loosening in my soul. This one element of my nutty life had possibilities.

The sound of a truck laboring up the driveway was a reminder that we weren't alone. His father was outside in my yard.

We tried to evolve our way out of the spell of desire, then we crushed together again, breathing fast as we kissed, Dan's forward drive winning out at first, then me advancing and tugging at his shirt. With the clock ticking and the knowledge that we both had work in the wings, we finally stepped apart. Dan blew out a breath and walked in a circle for a moment. I caught my breath by gripping the sink.

It took a minute or two or five to cool off, then we walked out as if we'd been in there conducting a house inspection, or some other sober business. Reaching our vehicles, we paused.

"Thanks for showing me a thing or two," I said.

"At the range?"

I smiled. "There, as well."

22

The fairgrounds were bustling with activity, though the gates wouldn't be open to the public until the next morning. Hearing the distinctive *thwack* of an ax slamming into a target, I crossed to the arena where the Woodsmen's Contest would be held later in the week. With a high roof supported by arching metal beams, the arena was open-sided, with dark green bleachers on the two long sides, and a deep layer of fragrant sawdust that provided good footing for animals during shows, pulling competitions, and other events. The second I saw that it was Keith McDonnell wielding the ax, I stopped and ducked behind the rows of seats.

Appearing to be in a dark mood, Greg's younger brother was striding back and forth between a marked spot midway across the arena and a target with dozens of wounds. Over six feet tall, with a barrel chest, Keith yanked an ax from the target with a violent upward pull. I turned to leave, leery of tempting fate while he was handling one of the weapons favored by madmen with animalistic social skills. Then I heard him crying.

"It's the same darned thing every day," he said, snuffling audibly. "You hurt my *eye*, Greg," he hollered, though his brother was nowhere in sight. "All so you can win a stupid contest."

Keith threw the ax hard. *Thwack.*

I closed my eyes, feeling sorry for the poor giant lug.

"Miss Littlefield?" he said.

I straightened in alarm. Keith was turned toward me with the ax a safe distance away, with the blade stuck in the target. He squinted and leaned down to confirm that he'd gotten the identification right.

"Why are you hiding there?" he prompted.

"I'm scared of your brother," I said in a moment of genius.

Keith looked over his shoulder. "He's well away. It's all right."

"Whew." I stepped closer, then paused. "What are you doing?"

"Practicing. Greg'll win, though."

"Are you sure? You have great aim."

"It's better when I'm mad, which I kind of am." With a shy smile, he added, "I've heard you're real smart."

"I have my moments." I stepped closer with a concerned frown. "What happened to your eye? That's a bad bruise."

"Greg punched me."

"Why?"

"Doesn't need a reason. Do you have a tissue?" he said.

"As a matter of fact, I do." I felt the pockets of Raymond's fishing vest, plucked out a tissue, and offered it to Keith.

"One won't be enough," he said.

"Here, have the whole pack."

Keith blew his nose, then balled up the tissues and tossed them under the bleachers. I refrained from chiding him for littering.

"Did I see a granola bar in your pocket?" he said.

I sighed and handed him my afternoon snack.

"Gosh," he said, frowning at the single-serving packet. "It's tiny."

"Blame shrinkflation."

Keith looked dismayed. "I hate that word."

"Why?"

"It's made up. Greg says I'm too dumb to get it."

I took it upon myself to enlighten Keith, especially since it was a quick fix. I folded the wrapper in half and held it next to a dollar bill, saying the bar still cost a dollar but was now only half the size.

"It's a way companies handle higher operating costs," I said.

Keith's eyes were wide with astonishment.

"Miss Littlefield, I get it. Can you teach me other stuff?"

"Maybe later. I need to get back to work."

"It's not many folks who've been nice to me," he said with emotion. "You, Mr. Lurman … I guess that makes only two."

"You used to be neighbors, right?"

"He stopped my dad from hitting me," Keith said. "Always had a bible quote to explain things. Stuff about staying strong."

"I'm glad to hear he's in your corner," I said softly.

"He's helping me stay ahead of the law."

I hesitated. "Oh?"

"When we were moving Mr. Babik's desk, I heard a tiny thing drop. I no sooner picked it up when Greg hollered at me for losing my focus, so I put the subway token in my pocket. Days later, I went to Mr. Lurman in a panic. He said it wasn't theft. It was a mistake."

"Who told you it was a subway token?" I prompted.

"Mr. Lurman. He took care of bringing it to Mr. Babik to spare me any embarrassment." Seeing my eyes wide with interest, he pulled out his phone and showed me a photo of a gold doubloon. "Pretty, isn't it? I bet you have tokens like this, being from Boston."

"That is not a—" I closed my eyes. "Can I see your phone?"

"Sure, I guess."

I texted the photo to myself, deleted the thread from Keith's device, and then forced a smile as I handed his phone back.

"Well," I managed. "It's been nice catching up."

"*Hey*," Greg hollered as he arrived "What are you doing here?"

"I'm working," I said calmly. "I was checking to see if I'll need portable lights during the lumberjack events."

"You can't bring in *lights*. It'd be too distracting."

"She's not meaning no harm," Keith said.

"You shut up," Greg seethed. "I'll deal with you in a minute, talking to the enemy. You get stupider every day."

"Calm down," I said. "I'm going."

"Hang on," Greg said. "You went to Ken's house with Carl Woodlee. He's got you trying to figure out that desk."

Keith gave emphatic signals begging me to not mention the "subway token." No problem. I'd frozen in place.

"You don't fool me," Greg said. "I know what you're up to."

"I went to Ken's house to get a picture of Raymond."

"Bullshit."

Greg leaned closer, giving me a vantage point that offered a lesson on the perils of never brushing one's teeth. And of not shaving for days on end, or changing clothes, or washing one's hair.

"My sole focus is on my work here at the fair," I insisted. "In fact, do either of you compete in the modified chainsaw competition? *Coast & Candle* magazine needs photos of it."

"Gosh, that would be amazing," Keith said.

"Nobody asked you, moron," Greg said.

"I've heard you have talent, so I'll be counting on you to put on a good show. I don't know any other participants."

It was sad how quickly I'd neutralized Greg's inquiry. I was tempted to tell him that if he insisted on delving into the desk or any other element related to Richard Gartland's murder, he should keep his modified chainsaw handy at all times. The man who'd drugged me was a threat Greg would never see coming: smart, fast, and cold.

"You'll take pictures?" he said with a suspicious scowl. "Of us?"

"Of course. Take care, you two."

My escape path was clear. I walked away fast.

In need of a place where I could gather my wits, I found shelter in a gazebo with a gray floor and white pillars. I sat down on one of the benches tucked against each of the eight open walls.

I would delay asking Theo if he'd returned the doubloon to Ken. If he'd kept it, he might try to use Pinkie and Pablo as a means of threatening me into silence. I needed a solid plan.

Feeling distracted and overwhelmed, I assumed the worst when Hugh English called a week ahead of schedule. Given my luck, he was reaching out to say, "Forget the assignment, you're fired."

"Hello?" I said dismally.

"Miss Littlefield? Hugh English. I got your first folders."

"I know the fair hasn't started yet," I rushed on. "I wanted to give you some photos of the advance work going on."

"They're wonderful," he said.

I paused. "They're what …?"

"Fabulous, I should say. The powers that be have given the go-ahead for two articles," Hugh said of the magazine's founders, Jean Coast and Mike Candle. "We're thinking the February issue, then the May issue, in advance of next year's Maine fairs."

"Two articles. Wow."

"We'll double your fee. What do you think?"

I paused, trying to swallow away the emotion in my throat. I'd already nailed my assignment. I couldn't believe it.

"That's acceptable," I managed.

"The historical society might want to plan an exhibition around your focus. The specialized work involved with farms, and the rural traditions you've captured tend to be a fading way of life."

"Thank you, Hugh."

"I'll be in touch. And Miss Littlefield, I'd love to hire you for other assignments. Lobster fishermen, perhaps."

"Just send the details. Name the dates."

After we hung up, I marveled over the development, though I'd lost count of the times fate had delivered a hard kick in the pants, followed by a stroke of good fortune beyond words.

I left the gazebo and got back to work.

* * *

Nearing sunset, I was startled to see a truck parked near the berry field. Up ahead on the left, Norris was alternately throwing a toy for Luke to fetch, and raking fresh straw over a smooth stretch of ground where only days ago the plumbers had delivered their dire diagnosis.

In a blue sweater that set off his smile and tanned face, a glimpse of how well Dan would age, Norris smoothed his white, cropped hair and explained that the layer of straw would protect the grass seed he'd spread. Within a week or two, once the new grass took hold, it would be tough to tell where the new concrete tank had been installed.

"You were so kind to help," I said. "I'm grateful beyond words."

"Nonsense," he insisted. "It took no time at all."

During his previous visits, Norris had seemed amiable and upbeat. Just then, he looked distracted and worried.

"Norris," I said. "Did something happen?"

"No, nothing bad. At least not an *immediate* kind of bad. It's a nagging sort of thing. Let's forget I said anything."

"Come inside. I insist."

While I put my camera bag to one side, Luke slurped from his dish and then plopped down to reunite with his rope toy.

Norris sat at the kitchen table and folded his hands as if he intended to conduct high-level negotiations. It was impossible to not feel alarmed. Maybe he'd decided I was a pill-popping menace.

"Norris, if you're worried about Dan and I getting involved—"

"Heck, no." Norris blew out a breath. "He'd hit the roof if he knew I was here, but there are things you need to know. I might ramble a bit. It's hard to find the right words." Norris closed his eyes. "I'm sorry, Sonny. I hate to shock you, but it was Dan who found Aaron."

I shook my head. "Found him …?"

"Dan went to his house thinking he'd have to haul Aaron out of bed and tell him to quit being depressed. He looked through the rooms. It was silent. The garage is where Aaron made his last stand," Norris said. "The poor kid didn't want to mar the carpets."

I gaped. "Oh my God …"

Norris's eyes welled up. "June and I knew Aaron all his life. Had him for dinner all the time. We keep pictures of people in our minds. How they smile, how they carry themselves."

"Dan was alone when …?"

"He was alone. You can imagine the shock."

Shaking, I felt hollowed out as I crossed to the counter and brought a box of tissues to the table. Norris plucked out one. I pulled out a handful. Dan had *seen* that awful sight? Carried it in his mind ever since? My knees gave out. I landed in the seat with a thud.

"Aaron put on a false front about his marriage ending," Norris said. "Even cracked jokes. None of us saw it coming."

"I think it happens a lot," I said.

"Dan had bought an old house. Wanted to fix it up, but never had the time. The day after he found Aaron, he picked up a sledgehammer and started taking the interior apart. It's still in rough shape, but he insists on living there while he tries to tackle the upgrades."

"Grief comes out in crazy ways," I managed.

"Don't get the wrong idea. Dan is steady by nature. Reasonable. But after that day he got to arguing with us over nonsense. A case unfolding near the Canadian border was presented to him as a career move. He took it thinking he'd deal with his bad spell that way."

"I figured that out," I said. "Isolation is a stage of grief."

Norris gripped my hand. "We thought we'd lost him, Sonny. He'd come back from the border for a quick overnight stay now and then, darker than ever. If we expressed worry, that was that. He'd slam out and head back up north. June's birthday came up this past spring. We figured he'd drive down, then head straight back. Brooding all the way."

"I remember him mentioning her birthday."

Norris nodded. "There we are, thinking what a fine celebration it'll be, sitting at the table with our mouths shut, forcing smiles to keep the peace. He's there five minutes when a call comes in saying there's trouble up at Raymond French's farm. I pulled Dan aside and said, 'You're not on duty. Why are you involving yourself?'"

"Because the police knew the break-in was part of a harassment case," I said. "Aaron had been one of the targets."

"We didn't know that, and Dan didn't explain. He just left."

"He was in plain clothes. He kept me contained in the house."

Norris smiled. "I know. He told me all about it. This is the thing. We were about to reach out for professional help. We couldn't let the bright, shining star in our lives disappear on us."

I nodded. "He's so lucky to have you."

"We hear his truck pull into the driveway at the crack of dawn," Norris said. "We haul ourselves out of bed to ask if he wants a bite to eat before he heads out. Sure, Dan says. He's starving. Upbeat. Smiling. June was so startled she almost dropped her teacup."

"Because the case was reopened," I said.

"It wasn't the case, dummy," Norris said. "It was you."

"We barely spoke that night."

"Well, it was enough for Dan. You started to faint. He caught you and I guess you kind of leaned against him …"

"That did happen," I admitted, vividly recalling the moment, "but it was the case that pushed the cobwebs away. He saw a light at the end of the tunnel. New leads. Justice for Aaron."

"Maybe the case played a role, but that's not what came up every day he tempted fate and pushed the border gig to the limit. He took heat for it. Almost got fired. June and I had to make calls saying there was a family emergency. We helped hold the line."

"It was the *case*," I insisted.

Norris sighed. "I see the problem, now. My goodness."

"He would have told me."

"I think he did, by the sound of it. There was a day when he came back from having lunch with you all red in the face. Elated, smiling. I got the sense you must've shown real interest."

I didn't want to disclose the torrid details of how I'd taken Dan off guard and kissed him in the parking lot of a diner.

"Yes, but then I waffled."

With his tanned forehead and white eyebrows twisted with puzzlement, Norris was an endearingly older version of his son.

"Why it's like this with young folks, I can't imagine," he said. "June and I were high school sweethearts. My one true love."

"That's wonderful."

"Why the retreat?" Norris said.

"My family history is pretty bad."

"I'm sorry to hear it. Trust issues?"

"In buckets."

"So, there was misery in Dan again when it was time to go back to the border, given the night of horror you went through."

"Dan saved my life."

"I know. Couldn't have stopped him with a tank."

"We felt a separation would help us sort through the trauma. We decided we would implode if he stayed."

"How did that go?" Norris said wryly.

"Awful."

"Same with Dan. Plus, he'd never resolved his feelings around Aaron's death. He's bent on toughing it out on his own. There's this slant to his mind that darkness has to be kept under wraps."

"I am familiar with the concept," I said.

"We went with him to scatter Aaron's ashes. Another hard day. It's part of why Dan delayed reaching out to you."

"Plus, Connie was in town," I said.

Norris looked surprised. "Dan told you about her?"

"Sue and Kate filled me in," I said. "Dan and I talked about it today, in fact. I urged him to stop kicking himself."

Norris beamed. "I told him you'd take it well."

"As long as there's no lingering attraction between them."

"Leaping lords and ladies, Dan won't make that mistake again," Norris assured me. "Connie favors all the wrong things."

"That's not what you wanted to talk about?"

"No," Norris said. "What's got us worried is that Dan on edge again. It has to do with a new case in the works."

"What kind of case is it?"

Norris started to speak, then shook his head. "I came here to let you know, but it's not my place. Dan needs to tell you."

"The border situation is heating up again," I guessed.

"No, that chapter is closed for good, thank heaven." Norris patted my hand in a fatherly way. "Please talk to him."

"You don't think he should work on the new case?"

"His heart is in the right place in wanting to take the lead," Norris said. "But it's a bad idea. It'll eat him alive."

"Why? I don't understand."

"Ask Dan. I think he'll listen to you."

The Dan I'd come to know had been steady and calm, with an easygoing smile. There were flickers of turmoil, but not to the level Norris had described. Dan's air of stability was one of the reasons I'd hesitated when he'd flirted with me. Surely any attempt to enfold my turbulent path into his rule-abiding world would end in heartache. For me, at any rate. I figured he would learn fast and move on as a wiser man.

"Is he on patrol tonight?" I said.

"He's having dinner with Detective Allen. The new case is part of why Dan wanted to touch base with Roy."

"What time will he get home?"

"Not too late. He might even be home by now."

"Where is Dan's house?"

Norris paused. "You're not going *tonight?*"

"You've got me worried. I won't be able to sleep."

"Oh, boy. He's going to be so mad at me."

"Some day, I'll explain why I have trust issues. It makes me the perfect person for Dan to talk to about tough episodes. My coping skills have kept me going for twenty-eight years."

"Still …"

"Give me his address," I insisted.

It was time for me to rescue Dan for a change.

23

When I'd prepared to step out for a few hours, Luke had performed the trick he'd learned for sparking guilt, his brow deeply furrowed over his glistening brown eyes, as if to say, *How am I supposed to feel valued if you don't spend quality time with me? Is there another dog in your life?*

Hence, he was in the back seat with the windows rolled halfway down when I pulled into Dan's driveway. I liked the look of his old farmhouse, covered with cedar shakes that had weathered to a dark brown, with a spacious, well-maintained yard and attached garage. The door was solid wood, with a vintage knocker. Floodlights illuminated strategic points.

I didn't want to alarm Dan at 8:30 p.m., so I texted him.

Hi. I'm outside.

Dots appeared, and then he texted, *Meaning …?*

I'm outside your door. Right now.

Dan opened the door in jeans and a T-shirt with a towel draped over one shoulder. His wet hair said he'd just taken a shower. Looking stunned, he leaned out for a moment and glanced in all directions as if he expected the horsemen of the apocalypse to accompany my every move. Not seeing any sign of them, he stared at me sideways.

"Why are you …?"

"I wanted to see where you live."

He'd been eating a piece of chocolate. He put the rest in his mouth and slowly chewed during a brief pause.

"I just got home," Dan said. "I was …"

"Meeting Roy Allen. Your father told me. He stopped by."

Dan closed his eyes. "Oh no …"

"I'm sorry to drop by unannounced, but the way things sounded …" I paused and regrouped. "Can I come in?"

"Umm, sure."

I stepped through the threshold into the destroyed interior Norris had talked about. The living room showed signs of healing. Sheetrock with spackled nail holes lined the walls. Pushed to the center of the room, and loosely covered with clear plastic in an attempt to keep sawdust at bay, was a generously padded leather couch and two matching armchairs with a kind of stitching that reminded me of a baseball glove.

Along the far wall, an island separated the kitchen, where a gleaming new refrigerator and matching stove were a stark contrast to the roughed-in cabinets awaiting doors. The island top was covered with plywood. Here and there were toolboxes, sanders, saws, and wrapped piles of lumber that appeared to be hardwood flooring intended to cover the existing pine boards, which were old and scuffed from years of use.

A photo with a thin black frame caught my eye: an underwater scene of six butterflyfish shining amidst the blue waters of Hawaii.

I turned to Dan. "That's a photo I took."

"I bought it online from your website," he said.

I hadn't been paying attention to the stats. Money accumulated until it reached a threshold before I got an email alert.

"Your caption talked about how the fish slow down at dusk," Dan said. "They grow still and let the current carry them. I found it restful."

"It is restful. It's magical."

"Sonny, why are you here?"

I shook off my surprise. "Your father is worried about a new case in the wings. He urged me to ask about it."

Dan closed his eyes and turned away. "Perfect."

"Why would Norris be worried?"

"It's complicated. I'm not prepared to talk about it."

The word "prepared" created some waves in my resolve to be relaxed and supportive, even if he resisted my help. How much preparation was behind Dan's track record of unwavering calm? I tossed the concern aside. It was old news that men tended to compartmentalize.

"Norris told me about Aaron," I said. "You're the one who …"

"He shouldn't have done that."

"All this time there's been a perception that I'm the one with hidden turmoil. It turns out you're in the same boat."

With a groan, Dan sat down on the edge of the covered couch and rested his elbows on his knees, his hands rubbing his forehead. He was on his own turf. It was nighttime. He was bound to be tired. Having me ask personal questions was a new thing. Once again, I shook off my unease over encountering a version of him I'd never seen.

"Did you buy the photo after Canada?" I said. "Recently?"

"Fairly recently."

"Why didn't you tell me?"

"When would I have done that?"

"The minute you framed it."

Dan shrugged. "I guess that was an option."

"Look, I'm sorry if my approach is wrong," I said. "The editor of *Coast & Candle* magazine is hiring me to cover a second article, based on my early work. I've nailed the first part." I opened my hands. "So, I'm available. Unencumbered. I can be here for you."

"It's great about your photo work."

"Dan, I'm not a fragile vase," I said. "With my crazy early life, I'm the perfect person to talk to about trauma."

"That's good to know for when I'm ready."

"I hear you. What happened with Aaron can wait."

"Thank you."

Shot down on the problems I'd hoped to help him sort out I couldn't banish my worries anymore. "Your father was only there for a half hour, but golly, did he disclose a lot. Like the fact that you …"

"Which topic is this?" Dan said.

"The night you and I met. Your change in attitude gave them hope. It had to do with the case. You felt like it would get traction."

"Is that what my father told you?"

"Sort of."

Dan was fiddling with a scrap of wood he'd plucked from the floor. He was frowning, his mind working through options.

"Well?" I said.

"You haven't asked anything."

"Why do you seem like a trapped animal?"

"Because I am a trapped animal. You came here out of the blue—"

"When have you *not* come to my house out of the blue? I don't know why I didn't ask sooner. Where does the mystery man live?"

Dan flipped the scrap of wood into a pile of rubble.

"Ok, I know what you're asking," he said. "Sure, the crime scene at your farm back in May felt like a break in a stalled, cold case. But that's not what turned the lights back on. It was you."

If only he'd said this with passion. Instead, his tone was clipped and factual. Given the topic, it felt all wrong. His face was flushed, his shoulder muscles flexed as if he were ready to spring away, and his averted gaze was in danger of boring a hole in his own hands.

"That's not possible," I said. "We barely spoke."

Dan snorted. "You are so perceptive, until you're not. What did I see that night? A woman up against the wall on every front. Harassed, blind-sided by the news that she'd been lied to. Cut off from knowing her father. A lot of people would buckle. You launched in, full force. You can see how I handled a shocking event." Dan indicated the torn-up room. "You get singed and rattled, but you're unstoppable."

"Why didn't you …?"

"I was clear from the start. You balked a dozen times."

"Because you were a symbol of how steady a person could be if they made all the right choices, as opposed to me."

"Now you know better."

My patience gave out. "I'm an expert on stalling. However annoyed you feel about disclosing some of the background just now, I can tell you're using it to dodge the original topic," I said. "What new case has your father so worried? Are you going to tell me?"

Dan exhaled. "No."

"Why?"

"It's not an official matter, yet."

"When it is official, you'll say it's policy to not talk."

"Sonny, I'm begging you. Leave it alone."

"Dan, this morning in my kitchen—"

"I know, Sonny. I know."

"Apparently you don't. I haven't felt this way about a guy for a long time. Maybe forever. If you're about to pull a retreat on me—"

"I won't."

"Guaranteed?"

"My father was out of line. This is a nightmare."

"Sharing with me is a *nightmare?*" I blinked in shock. "Well, that spells things out clearly enough. At least I got to see your house."

"Sonny …"

"It's fine, Dan, but you should know your parents are worried sick. I guess I'm in the same boat because you're tipping back to being a zombie, and I'm not allowed to know why."

"Wait a minute—"

"I don't *have* a minute." I closed my eyes, forcing my tears to retreat. "There has to be balance between us. I thought we had a shot at a deep connection, but apparently, that's not in the cards from your end. I hope you get back on track. I really do."

"Sonny—"

"I have to go. I'm sorry I interrupted your routine."

I had the door half open when Dan stepped up behind me and shut it hard, rattling the windows and piles of boards.

"Don't block me," I warned. "Or I'll *really* get angry."

"I can't be the one to tell you. I can't."

"The one to tell me what?" I demanded.

Gripping his arm to release his weight from the door, I realized he was shaking, and tears were on his cheeks. My anger switched rails and hurtled down another track. To apprehension. Full-blown fear.

"Ok, this is freaking me out," I said.

"Let it go," he begged. "Please."

"Dan, *what* is going on? I can't think of a single reason …"

Tumbling through possibilities, I reversed through the past few days, desperate to recall any moments that struck me as odd. It had to be personal. A comment or an event or some other detail that had him holding back. I landed on seeing a flash go off in my bedroom while I was talking to Norris. Why had Dan taken photos of the ceiling?

"Sonny—"

"No, wait." I pushed his hand away.

My skin felt electrified as a sense of alarm tore through my mind. In my yard, he'd studied the place where Raymond had set up a ladder to break ice from the edge of the roof. "Nobody can figure out why he didn't wait until morning," Harry had said. The pan of water indicated a significant leak. Dan was right. Why *wasn't* there a stain on the ceiling?

"The pan of water," I said. "It would mean …"

Dan turned me to face him. "I *begged* you to leave it alone," he said roughly. "Why don't you ever listen?"

My heart clenched. "Are you saying …?"

"Don't go there."

"The pan of water was *staged?*"

"Let me make sure. It's not a hundred percent."

I searched Dan's intense brown eyes. We'd been through hell and back, and I'd rarely seen this level of emotion on his face. My guess was a hundred percent. Dan wanted to give me a chance to absorb the shock. My father hadn't died from an accidental fall.

He'd been murdered, alone, in the dark of night.

The room spun, and my legs gave out. I slumped against Dan's chest with a single emphatic word in mind. *No.* Over and over again. *No, no, no, no, no.* Dan held me in his arms, whispering curses under his breath. My mind collapsed into the dark hole of what was to come. Telling his friends and colleagues. Joan, Harry, and Jess. Sue and Kate. Brumby. Charlotte and her family. They would all have to be told.

"Why would anyone …?" I managed.

"I don't know," Dan said.

I'd learned a lot about killers, the lengths they would go to in order to snuff out a human life. Someone had trekked through the worst weather imaginable to kill my father. Sleet and snow, howling wind.

I couldn't begin to grasp why.

"Sonny, I'm so sorry."

"You warned me," I whispered. "You did."

Pulled back to the broken-up room by Dan's voice, I felt the rush of every other revelation. A few nights ago, I'd wondered if a day would come when a man tossed chairs aside in order to love me. Here he was holding me in his arms. I couldn't believe all the time we'd wasted. All the hints and openings I'd let slip by. I would mourn Raymond's death all over again in the days to come, but what I needed just then was to feel alive.

I gripped Dan's shirt and kissed him, desperate to convey the depth of my feelings in the surest possible way. His arms tightened around me, an assurance that he would upend the world to get answers. He wouldn't quit. His kiss was intense and soulful, his lips tasting of chocolate. My knees slackened, and doubt drained away through my heels.

Turning together, we bumped into a chair, our hearts slamming full tilt. Dan kept us upright, still kissing me, leisurely and warm, deliciously serious, and then he finally came up for air.

"You've just had a shock," he managed. "If you're not sure—"

"I want this. I want *you*."

He let out a moan as his lips returned to mine, showing effortless grace as he lifted me and held my thighs around his waist, moving in a relaxed orbit past the couch and chairs, a slow dance. *Talk about power,* this move said. *I've got stamina to burn. I can do this all night.*

Dan hit the power button on his stereo system as we floated by. Music poured down from hidden speakers, guitars wailing and drums pounding and a man singing about a woman he couldn't stop thinking about.

"My shoes," I breathed. "Let me get my shoes off."

Shirts were coming untucked. Jeans unzipped and tossed off.

"Watch out for nails," he managed.

I flinched. "Found one."

Dan lifted me and took whatever punishment was happening to his feet with zero hesitation until we crossed into a dark room and he hit a splinter or some other hazard. We pitched forward onto his bed and rolled in a tangle of arms and legs. He unhooked my bra and tossed it aside, and then we moaned in unison as our skin met for the first time. I shivered as his lips moved to my ear, igniting ripples of pleasure across my skin, and then I followed along as he rolled onto his back.

Dan smoothed the curls from my face, his gaze soulful, always asking if I was ok. I let a kiss do the talking for me. We'd waited and waited and waited, despite some rushed moments when we'd almost given into lust, possibly way too soon. Now came the payoff for our restraint, an intense, radiant connection that came from a sense of knowing him, trusting him. I dared to imagine that what I felt was love.

Unleashed at last, our united chemistry was like opening the door of a furnace. Loving. Intense. Barely contained. To my goal of feeling alive, his strong hands and smoldering caresses brought it about, my core humming, and my body singing a hallelujah chorus.

I drifted in a blur of sensations. His kiss. His stubbled jaw on my neck, moving downward. I moaned in breathy gasps, savoring the feel of his muscles flexing under my hands, the pleasure stirring, building.

He pulled me down and spoke French in my ear, sending the rumble of his voice through my skin. I gasped, eyes fluttering, and gripped his chest. Connection. Heat. Ecstasy. It tore through me in a long, delicious tremor that sent stars shooting through my head. I pitched forward, eyes rolling, and then draped over him, consumed by bliss.

Devoured by kisses, I had just enough wits to know he was giving me a second to savor the last flickers of rapture, then I followed along as he rolled me onto my back, unglued by our delicious, mind-blowing heat. My eyes fluttered, and the path to heaven began again. I heard the rush of his breath in my ear and inhaled his wonderful, freshly showered scent. Everything he did pulled drawn-out moans through me. Music poured down around us, and the delicious heat was building again. I flexed. He moaned. Connection. Ecstasy. My body twisted from the power of it, shivering, then all I could do was breathe in tiny gasps.

I lost track of the room, except for Dan's murmurs in my ear.

"I think I left the planet," he said, "I'm seeing stars ..."

"Totally," I breathed.

We settled in side by side, kissing, exploring each other with caresses, and smiling when our gazes met. As the song playing over the speakers switched to another, I caught up with space and time.

"Uh-oh," I said. "Luke is in my car. I didn't intend to stay long."

"I'll bring him in," Dan said. "Stay put."

"I barged in without warning. You probably need sleep."

Dan brushed curls from my face and looked me in the eyes.

"I almost forgot, even after an epic positive moment, you'll let worries take over," he said. "One, I'd like you to stay. Two, I'm planning to put a fish tank over there on the dresser. Restful, peaceful, the perfect backdrop for falling asleep. That's your influence in my life. Three ..."

Dan reached for a remote control by the bedside. As the song playing over the speakers was replaced by a ghastly, drippy, chewing and crunching sound, my confused gaze lifted to his face.

"It's Luke playing with his toy," Dan explained. "I snagged a recording of him the other day. Why, you ask? In college, my roommate and I made a movie together. I did the funky musical score and sound effects. These days, he's the head of a film production company in London."

I paused. "Is this the side hustle you mentioned?"

"An outlet for my creative side," Dan agreed. "I'll tell you all about it when I get back from bringing Luke in from your car. If you hear a beep, it's the brownies I'll be putting in the microwave."

I paused again. "I love brownies ..."

"Really?" Dan said. "I would never have guessed."

He tossed on gym trunks and was out the door before I could formulate any questions. Clearly, he thought that a few surprise disclosures, the promise of warm brownies, and further canoodling was enough to keep me firmly in place until he returned. I slowly smiled.

Dan wasn't just smart. He was a genius.

24

As we ate a cold quiche along the makeshift counter in the kitchen, Dan sat next to me in a relaxed slouch. Last night, he'd given calm instructions to Luke as he'd brought him inside and taken off the leash.

"No chewing up scraps of wood, understand?" I'd heard Luke thumping his tail. "All right. Here's a blanket to lie on."

Luke was a brilliant dog. Having entered the promised land of being invited along to someone else's house, he didn't bark or run around or chew on anything except his throw toy and had now stationed himself on his designated blanket. He watched us intently, his eyebrows shifting as he gazed toward Dan or me, depending on who was talking.

I indicated the last bite of quiche. "You made this?"

"All I could swing these days would be a sawdust omelet with a side of nails." With an embarrassed shrug, Dan added, "My mother has been dropping off food I can heat up a few times a week. It's a recent thing, ever since I got back from up north."

"You know that's how people tame stray cats."

"Exactly. I doubt it'll last." Dan looked serious as he swiveled my chair to face him. "This was a big leap. There will be rough patches. We will remain calm and optimistic. All will be well."

His eyes were keen in the soft light, earnest and soulful and everything my battle-weary inner pessimist needed to see. Our heated-up chemistry was undeniable now. We'd slept soundly together. He was playful and re-laxed in the shower. Now he was telling me all would be well. His easy-going take on our upgraded relationship was reassuring, but feeling a little less wary of getting burned was the best I could do.

"Got it," I said.

"I'm sorry about Raymond, Sonny," Dan said. "I really am."

"I still can't get my head around it."

"To avoid alerting guilty parties, Detective Allen wants to keep the truth about Raymond's death contained for now."

"Why didn't anybody else catch onto the lack of a ceiling stain?"

"It was icy and windy, very chaotic the night Raymond died. Accidents happen during storms, so once the idea took hold, nobody questioned it." Dan paused, looking pensive. "Did you ever make sense of Raymond's journal entry referencing a wolf?"

I'd pondered the passage many times: *I get sad when I look at The Wolf*, my father had written. *It brings me back to the day I found it. How Ella said it was the perfect guard for things we want to keep safe.*

"I've looked everywhere," I said. "Maybe you'll have better luck."

Reaching for an item he'd left to one side, Dan handed me an event lanyard with my name on it, with language stating that I had official access to all events at the Meeting Fair.

"I figured a gold pass would smooth your way as you dash from event to event," he said.

"This is awesome. Thank you."

"Best for last." Dan held up my keys and jangled them to show a new small item had been added to the ring. "I bought an electronic device that's linked to an app on my phone. It's a panic button. You will balk at the idea at first, then you'll see how pretty it is. A nice shade of red. You will use it in an extreme emergency."

"Will you have one on your keys?"

"If you refuse this sensible request, I'm back to drinking antacid from the bottle," Dan said with a wry twist of his eyebrows. "Think how that might affect someone's performance."

I sighed. "Ok, I'll keep it on my keys."

"And?"

"I will use it in an extreme emergency after I've sorted through escape plans and alternate means of resolving the situation." Under his cross glare, I took my key ring. "Ok, but I won't like it."

"My gut thanks you," he said with a light kiss.

"You have three scars to explain, now," I said.

His eyebrows twisted again. "You took advantage when I was naked?" Without waiting for a comeback, Dan knelt to roughhouse with Luke, who instantly came alive with excited yips and ridiculous wiggling, his dark eyes shining as Dan thanked him for being an ace.

"You're great with him," I said.

"He's got super potential. I want to bring him to a training facility and get him up to speed on protection skills."

"I'm not wearing a padded dummy suit."

"Rats," Dan said. "I had it all planned."

Tucked in the back of my mind was my revised sense of how stubborn, shut down, and unreasonable Dan could become when it came to his inner turmoil. Nevertheless, I'd launched a mission to rescue him for a change. Based on his smile, I'd succeeded a thousand percent.

* * *

I raced home, made sure none of my sheep had been abducted by cousins or aliens, replied to Arlene's annoyed texts with hearts instead of updates, put Luke in his pen with extra biscuits and toys to chew on, changed my clothes, and sped to the fairgrounds.

Forewarned by Dan that traffic would be fierce, I arrived in the nick of time. As I fetched my gear from my car at 7:15 a.m., cars were pulling into spaces at a good clip, with personnel at the end of every row to point the way and keep people from being too choosy or backing up traffic. The parking area I'd chosen offered shade from parallel rows of sixty-foot pines. Their needles softened the ground underfoot.

As I studied a sign showing a list of events, I assessed the options out loud: "Piglet Scramble. That's a must. Beano Building. That's next. No, the Blacksmith's shop sounds fun. Apple Queen Contest, Poultry Show,

Giant Pumpkin Contest. The Scarecrow Contest is at the same time? Are you kidding me? Oh, and the Skillet Throw is today!"

I easily dashed from place to place at first, then as more people arrived, I was hampered by a slow-moving sea of visitors. By ten o'clock, my way was blocked by processions of cattle and other animals moving from the barns to show arenas, and groups of people who hadn't seen each other since last year. Along the way, I photographed an old-fashioned popcorn wagon and a one-man band who carried a banjo, a drum, multiple horns with funny honks, cymbals, and a great sense of humor.

The air was awash with the din of voices and the squeals of children on the Tilt-A-Whirl ride. A thread of calliope music drew me through the midway to the Ferris wheel. I stood in line, and then as the bucket lifted me above the milling crowd, I updated Arlene via FaceTime. With my phone secured facing out in my vest pocket, she could glimpse the sweeping view of the fair while I honed in on occasional photographs.

"I'm getting seasick," she said. "But if this is what it takes to hear the latest, I'll put up with it. I'm thrilled things are great with Dan."

"He's still got Aaron's death stuffed way down."

"Give him time," Arlene said. "And you're one to talk."

From the swaying bucket, fifty feet in the air, I saw Charlotte Bergley below, pushing her way through the throng. She had her purse clutched under her arm as if it contained priceless jewels.

"I'll tell Dan some of my baggage," I said. "My main priority is figuring out—" Eyes wide, I chided myself for almost spilling my secret news. "Yes, I'll have a heart-to-heart with Dan soon," I corrected.

I smiled as Arlene texted a photo of Sarah, her four-year-old in a pink tutu performing a plié, and shots of her next in line, Sadie, clutching the stuffed giraffe I'd sent, and then baby Caleb swathed in the bunny blanket I'd helped wrap him in the day he was born.

"You're making me cry in public," I said. "I miss you guys."

"Hey, did you get your blood test results?"

I paused. "Umm, it was … I sort of …"

"Sort of what?" Arlene prompted.

"I'm good, now. Really good."

"I'm asking out of love," she said. "Honey, what's going on with the Ferris Wheel? Your bucket is stuck fifty feet in the air."

"That's the perfect tagline for my life these days," I said, having caught onto the lack of movement. "Let me check what's going on."

Once we signed off, I leaned over the bucket's edge and saw the operator banging the ride's engine with a wrench. I liked how the Ferris Wheel's metal framework cast a slanted, circular shadow over the pavement and fairgoers. I took a few shots, and then I caught sight of Greg McDonnell hassling Carl Woodlee near the Bingo tent.

Keith stood near them, looking dismayed. I was too far away to hear the discussion, but it was loud enough to draw Theo Lurman to Carl's aid. In typical bully fashion, Greg backed down with the look of a sullen child. Theo patted Carl's shoulder and waited for him to scuttle away, then he chided the McDonnell brothers for a prolonged moment.

Greg nodded, downcast and subservient, and then he flipped the bird at Theo once the larger man was heading away.

As the ride jerked into motion again, I saw another figure emerge from the shadows and stare after the retreating men: Ed Emery, the man who'd come to my farm and lurked in the Corner Pocket. His alert gaze had me recalling that Brumby had described Richard's PI as "a slick piece of work." If his old sweater was a costume he was using to blend in at the fair, there weren't two Eds in the picture. They were one and the same.

In turn, Ed Emery was followed by the security guard I'd helped out with a backup charger. If the safety detail had a list of troublemakers to keep an eye on, Greg and Keith would be on it. What about Ed? I made a note to get a solid description of Richard's PI.

And I would definitely revisit the Ferris Wheel, my new favorite place for observing parties of interest in secret.

By two o'clock, my camera lenses needed to be wiped clean, and my stomach was growling. I bought two large chicken pitas with spicy yogurt sauce. Seeing my camera, the grill master handed me extra wet wipes. I chose an empty picnic table. As often happened, the minute I sat down, someone else decided it was the perfect spot.

"You're very fast," the man said. "Hard to keep up with."

I turned and squinted against the sun to see who it was, and groaned. It was Frank's attorney, Nathan Kitteridge, looking out of place in a crisp striped shirt and creased light wool dress slacks. His attire was more casual than the suits he'd worn the other times we'd met, but still not the sort of clothes one wears to a country fair.

"I'm working, Nathan," I said. "Please back off."

Unfazed by my blunt plea, he sat beside me facing the opposite way on the bench. With his elbow on the tabletop, he turned toward me as a friend might do when they wanted a private word. I decided his choice of direction had to do with working on his tan while we chatted.

"I have a range of insider sources," he said. "Apparently, Bricker dug up a photo of you and Richard having a drink."

"The photo was faked. I could prove it if I had a digital copy."

"You seem pretty calm about it," he said.

"The police techs will confirm what I'm saying."

"I've left you messages," Nathan said. "No answer."

"Call blocking."

"You didn't add me to your contacts?"

I found myself enjoying his look of dismay over the messy nature of my pita sandwich. "Why are you here?" I said.

"For this." He motioned between us. "Catching up, exchanging news."

"The swine barn is nice," I said.

"Come on, I don't deserve that."

"Maybe not, but I'm working. I need to focus, and I'm tired of people coming at me because of the Gartland case."

As he stood up, I thought my cold shoulder effort had worked, but he crossed around the table to switch from sitting on the same side to facing me. He paused and scowled at his hand, having apparently set it down on gum or something disgusting on the table. Seeing the wet wipes next to my plate, he asked if he could "borrow" one.

"Get your own." I pointed. "Over there."

Nathan sighed. "I can help you with Bricker."

"Somebody's already helping."

"Your father's cop friends?"

I cast a warning glance at him.

"Your place has potential," he said. "Renovate the house. Bulldoze the barn from a horror movie. There's a nice view. Sell a few lots, and you'd have a decent … what?" Nathan said of my expression.

"You're not good at reading people."

"The hell I'm not. You can't want to live there as is."

"I love it. Wouldn't change a thing."

His widened eyes indicated I was nuts and beyond hope.

"All right, so much for small talk," Nathan said. "I assume you've asked yourself the obvious. Who would fake a photo of you and Richard? You want to move on. Somebody has other plans."

"Your big heart won't tolerate that," I said.

"If you've pegged me as a prick, you're halfway to knowing me. It's necessary in my line of work." Nathan studied me with his steely gray eyes. "Guess what was in the jewelry bag Richard carried out to the road? Nothing of value. What do you make of that?"

"He was dying and confused."

"You were alone. It must have been tough."

"Tough doesn't *begin* to cover it."

"That's clear enough." Nathan folded his arms, and I was slightly impressed that in between all the trips to the dry cleaner, he might work out a little. "Let's say Frank gets railroaded. Who knows if he's innocent. It's my *job* to represent him," Nathan pressed on as I shook my head. "There's a trial. Even though you have big puppy eyes, I'll grill you on a range of subjects, like why you reacted to the story Frank told."

"His attacker sounded scary. A potential lead."

"Look, Sonny," Nathan said with an air of wanting to wrap things up, "you've landed in the crosshairs for reasons I can't begin to grasp. Call me crazy for caring all of a sudden, but if Bricker keeps coming at you, I can shut him down. He's all kinds of wrong."

"Are you planning to sue the Maine state police?"

"That's where your mind goes?" Nathan said. "I know you've got local ties. This is the problem. You've got a bus coming at you, with jokers like Greg McDonnell possibly at the wheel. Can you rule him out? I sure as hell can't. You're looking the opposite way."

I closed my eyes. "I wish to God I'd never been on that road."

"Sorry, you can't unravel time." Nathan frowned as he searched the crowd. "Have you bumped into Frank, by any chance?"

"*That's* why you're here. He gave you the slip." Smiling at his irritated glare, I said, "Try the Whack-a-Mole game."

"You saw him there?"

"Talking to a guy the other day."

Nathan studied me as if figuring me out was his new favorite pastime. "You're changing your tune. You're tempted to sign on."

"I can't afford you."

"Come on," Nathan said. "You've got Littlefield kind of money."

"That's not even dimly true."

With a roll of eyes, he checked his watch. "I'm heading out of town by tomorrow, the next day. Time to wait in traffic amidst the shit trucks and animals staring at me from trailers," Nathan said, slipping from the bench. "Take care, Sonny. Thanks for your time."

As he stepped away, I reflected on his promise to shut Bricker down if the need arose. Who else could I enlist? Raymond's attorney was a kindly old man who blinked a lot when he was trying to recall details. With an internal groan, I added Nathan's numbers to my contacts. At the least, I could keep track of any time he tried to reach out.

I checked the time.

"*Crap*," I said.

He'd made me miss the beginning of the skillet-throwing contest.

25

I'd anticipated heavy traffic coming into the fairgrounds that morning. I hadn't anticipated heavy traffic leaving the fairgrounds at dusk, with the added complexity of incoming traffic thanks to a live band concert and the allure of food vendors and rides in the midway.

It was eight p.m. In the low light, I secured my camera on a tripod to photograph a team of oxen named "Bright" and "Early." I calculated the length of time to open the aperture with a pop of flash at the end, hoping for an image that showed the shifting motion of the oxen as a ghostly blur, with a moment frozen in time when the flash went off.

It was a peaceful time in the open-sided animal barns, with cool air drifting in from the darkened fairgrounds, and the rhythmic crunch of the oxen and cattle eating hay. Now and then one or more farmers crossed an adjacent area on their way to check their livestock.

Deciding the traffic must have thinned, I stowed my camera and broke down my tripod, then the glittering stars beyond the barn inspired me to open my photo app to ponder the constellations Captain Winthrop had mentioned in his letter. Carina was the Latin word for the keel of a ship. Perseus was a mythological hero. Lupus was a wolf, and Lepus indicated a rabbit. A predator and its prey. I didn't see a consistent theme.

Had Richard found a cache of gems or some other treasure and decided to keep the find to himself? If only I'd gotten to know him in person,

I might have a better sense of his character, though years of friendship didn't seem to be helping Carl sort out where to land.

While I had my phone in hand, I opened a folder of photos I'd collected of Raymond. As always, he looked frustratingly alive, with glints of sun on his face. Dan wanted to keep me out of the search for answers. He might as well try to talk me out of being a photographer. Carefully, quietly, I would unravel Dan's resistance. Whoever had murdered Raymond imagined they'd escaped justice. They were wrong.

A sound akin to rhinos crashing around in the nearby woods drew my gaze to the darkness beyond the open barn. Two men were cursing out there in the inky night, and then their altercation intensified into a frenzy of growling and unintelligible rage. I heard "son of a bitch," the f-word, groans indicating someone was getting punched, then a particularly sharp yelp seemed to indicate an added level of pain. Drinking and fist fights were a known factor of country life from time to time.

"Guys," I called out. "I'm calling security."

A tumult of snapping sticks and crunching leaves forewarned a man lurching from the shadows under the trees. He staggered to a grassy area just beyond the spotlights outside the open barn. A second man wearing a motorcycle helmet rushed after him, tripped him with a pole, and sent him into a tumbling heap. The man on the ground rolled and deftly lashed out at his attacker with savage kicks.

"Hey!" I hollered. "I have a camera!"

The attacker delivered a final blow and dashed away into the forest. Groaning, the victim rolled and lurched to his feet.

"Are you ok?" I said.

"Yeah … just *great* …"

I jogged to the other entrance and searched the misty fairgrounds for anyone who could alert a security guard. A farmer in overalls was sweeping pooled water from an area of stanchions set aside for washing sheep, cows, and other animals before showtime.

"Excuse me!" I hollered. "We need help over here."

"A veterinarian?" he said.

"No. It's over now, but two guys were fighting."

"Ok!" he hollered.

By then, the injured man was inside the barn, bent over next to one of the oxen stalls, breathing in gasps, and cursing under his breath. His black cargo pants and tactical vest with a range of extra pockets had me wondering if he was an off-duty police officer.

"The guy is gone now," I said. "Are you ok?"

With his head resting on his arm, he swiveled a fraction and squinted at me sideways. He snorted and swore under his breath as if my presence was a joke. I hesitated, realizing he was the security guard I'd met a few mornings ago. I'd given him a backup charger.

"Who were you fighting out there?" I said.

He snorted again. "Typical ... all wide-eyed ..."

"If you need an EMT—"

Abruptly, he hauled himself upright and launched toward me with his teeth bared, as if from rage. Too startled to duck or run, I tripped backward and found myself in his fierce grip with my back slamming into a stall door. Dust and hay chaff exploded around us, and one of the oxen bellowed, frightened by the explosive rattle of old wood. The man seemed huge and muscled, his eyes glaring at me from inches away.

"Were you ... in on the planning?" he snarled.

I grappled with his hands on my vest. "What is *wrong* with you?"

"What ... is wrong with me," he managed, gasping as he spoke as if he couldn't catch his breath. "Oh ... that's good ..."

"Help!"

Looking deranged, he gripped my vest by the open armholes, pulled forward, and slammed me against the stall door.

"Oh my God!" I gripped his arms and felt no evidence of living flesh. His muscles were flexed, as hard as iron. "Help!"

"*Shhh*," he admonished, swinging his arm around and pushing against my windpipe, shoving, shoving, cutting off my air.

I tried to knee him in the groin and missed.

"No ... you don't," he managed, grimacing, his teeth an appalling sight, coated with glistening blood.

A wall of angry brute force, he pitched his full weight against me and drove his knee against my thigh so I couldn't kick him again. Choking, winded, struggling, I looked down to find some form of leverage and glimpsed a snake's head tattoo on his forearm.

It was *him*. The man who'd drugged me. He'd hidden the mark under long sleeves the other day. A devious, hard-hearted killer.

With a burst of fury, I broke free and drove him back with an assault of elbows and knees. I'd drilled myself on strength and balance during Nadine's pole dancing lessons, landing on my feet for a split second and smoothly lifting upward again. Grace had been my original intent. Now all I wanted to summon was accuracy, power, and speed.

Assailed by backhand slaps and sneakers pummeling his crotch and legs, he tumbled backward and lay there, moaning.

"Jesus," the farmer from the stanchions said, arriving in a winded state. "I saw him come at you, and couldn't get here fast enough."

"He's the guy … he has a snake tattoo."

"Stand well away in case he gets up." Grabbing a pitchfork from an assortment of tools against a stall, he held the pointed teeth in a menacing position as he approached the man on the ground. "Come at me and I will stab the shit out of you. Don't move."

A security guard jogged in and joined us. He motioned for us to calm down, hesitated, then he knelt next to the prostrate man.

"Dude, are you ok?" Getting a cough for a response, he jumped back in alarm. "Damn! He sprayed me with blood."

"There's blood underneath him," the farmer said.

"I only kicked him," I said.

"I saw the whole thing from the get-go. Couldn't believe a man would lunge at a woman that way. He looked nuts."

"There was another man. They were fighting outside."

"What's your name?" the farmer said.

I told him, unable to tear my gaze from the attacker, then realized the farmer was giving my name to a 911 dispatcher.

"*Wait,*" I hollered, but it was too late.

With a trembling hand, I reached for my phone, and then I froze, paralyzed by the prospect of explaining the situation to Dan.

I called Sue Black instead.

"I can't think my way through this," I said. "What should I do?"

"You're safe? Unharmed?"

"Mostly."

I groaned as Dan rang my line. Sue walked me through what to say. Start simple. I was unharmed. Tell him the basics.

"Sonny?" he said. "Your name just came over the scanner."

"There was a fight between two men in the woods," I began, deciding it wouldn't help to tell him that I'd been assaulted and throttled. I tried to clarify things, including the snake tattoo, but the connection was not ideal, and Dan was shouting questions.

"Where is the guy now?" he demanded.

"It's all just ... a shock."

"Where *is* he, Sonny?" Dan hollered over the phone.

"On the ground. He's bleeding."

"Has anyone patted him down?"

"What ...? No, he's acting wild."

"Find shelter, Sonny. *Now.*"

With my phone in hand, I motioned for everyone to follow me, and then I clapped my eyes on the attacker, and the sidearm strapped to his waist, just visible below the edge of his vest.

"Oh my God. He has a gun."

"*Sonny,*" Dan prompted.

"Get away!" I hollered to everyone. "Look!"

Of all the times my voice had gotten lost in the shuffle of life, this had to be the moment when my urgent point was grasped by the wrong man. With a demented grin, the attacker reached for his sidearm and unclipped the fastener. The security guard saw it, too. We both dove forward at the same time to secure the weapon. The security guard caught a backhand strike across his temple. Clutching the wound, he groaned and rolled. This left me with the gun pointed in my face.

The attacker offered a bloody smile. "C'mere ..."

"You came to my farm," I whispered.

"Think so, huh?" he wheezed. "Guess you were drugged pretty ... pretty good ... except maybe ... you got it wrong ..."

"Got *what* wrong?"

He coughed and blinked in confusion, then his gaze shifted to a point over my shoulder. Afraid he was about to shoot someone I dove down and gripped his arm. I flinched, shocked by a gun blast so close to my ear I felt it in my bones. I clenched my teeth and maintained my grip, despite the guard and others jostling me as they helped pin his arm.

"I've got the sidearm!" the guard hollered. "Take it!"

Seeing that he was talking to me, I engaged the safety with shaking hands and figured out how to eject the magazine. Even after I emptied the chamber, I stared at the gun, breathless from terror.

I lost track of time as I stood there with the parts in my hands. Finally, the farmer stepped forward and gently took them from me. The security guard was now standing over the attacker.

"You're wounded," he hollered. "No more stunts, understand?"

"Need ... to listen," the attacker said, his eyes wide as if he'd finally realized he was in rough shape. "Don't ... let him ... win ..."

Minutes ago, he'd trained his gun on me. Now he was motioning for me to hear him as if I was his only hope.

"Who?" I said, grasping that his wide-eyed appearance was amplified by dilated pupils: a response to shock, or was he on drugs?

"S' your friend ... Fffffrr ... Frrankie ..."

"Frank Winthrop injured you?"

The man nodded. "He's coming for you ... he's worse ... than me ..."

"Save your strength. Help is on the way."

"Wait ... please listen ..." As the man reached out, I was so riveted by his imploring gaze, so much like Richard's, that I let him grip my hand. "Don't let him ... get her," he gasped.

"Don't let Frank get Angela?"

The man snorted. I couldn't tell if he was laughing or agreeing.

"She's out there ... almost found her ..." He closed his eyes, clearly in terrible pain. "What he said ... he used *my* trick ..."

"What are you talking about?" I demanded.

"It's *my* trick ... asshole ..."

"Don't let him get to you," the security guard said, taking my arm and trying to pull me away. "He's not in his right mind."

"He's trying to tell me something."

"What will you ... remember?" the attacker gurgled with wild eyes. "What will you forget? It's my trick ... *asshole* ... lying asshole ..."

Seeing people making calls, I said, "Where's my phone? I dropped it."

The guard cast about and then handed it to me.

"Do you know this guy?" I said. "Is he a colleague?"

"I've never seen him before. Why do you ask?"

"I saw him in a security shirt the other day."

"That camera is trained on this area." The guard indicated a lens aimed our way. "I'll head to the office and fetch the video."

"Can you make a copy for me?"

"Sure. I'll put it on a flash drive."

When he stepped away, I joined the farmer as he watched two EMTs assessing the attacker's condition with an array of equipment. My head whirled as I tried to reconcile how he'd behaved tonight with my previous encounter with him, a meeting so ordinary that it took a moment to recall specifics. He'd been clean-cut, maybe in his mid-thirties. A bit bulked out, in a long-sleeved shirt with "Security" written across the back. He must have intended to intercept me to see if I recognized him.

So much for checking men's arms for a snake tattoo. Even if he hadn't worn long sleeves, the task had escaped my mind.

I felt blood drain from my head. He'd approached Joan as well, using the backup drive I'd given him as an opening. He'd told her an arrest was imminent. A ploy to make me drop my guard? I could picture his constant need to stir, test, and hover in order to gauge the success of his covert activities. What was his goal tonight? Lurking in the shadows, watching to see who I met? Somebody had upended his plans.

"Justice," the wounded man moaned. "Need ... t' get justice ..."

"That's ironic as hell," the farmer said.

"You have no idea," I whispered.

* * *

With the remaining brain cells that were still able to make decisions, I called Nathan and explained why he needed to head to the fairgrounds and involve himself in my predicament: the man with the snake tattoo had surfaced, attacked me, and mentioned Frank's name.

"You promised to help me with Bricker," I said.

"You *clearly* haven't been straight with me," Nathan said crossly. "Ok, let me think. Here's the plan. You must be injured."

"I'm mostly just bruised."

"You are *injured* until I tell you otherwise," he instructed. "Ask for an EMT. You're too faint to answer questions. Got it?"

"Right. Got it."

Swathed in a blanket, hunched in a miserable heap, with blue lights flashing all around me, I found myself nodding when I was asked if I was up to the task of describing how the incident had unfolded. The heck with what Nathan had demanded of me. I wanted to go home, and I wanted to confront the problem of Bricker before Dan arrived.

The detective's scowl firmed my resolve to keep my prior contact with the attacker under wraps. I stuck to that night. I was photographing the oxen. Heard a fight. Hollered for help. Tried to help the injured man. He came at me. I defended myself. He fell. Help arrived.

"There's a video," I said. "Ask the security guard."

"I'll do that," Bricker growled. "Stay put."

I sagged, grateful that phase one was over. Searching the throng of onlookers, I saw the farmer talking to Theo Lurman. I'd delayed pressing the butcher to return Pinkie and Pablo, worried about getting pressured in return. As far as I knew, he had yet to be cleared by the police.

I looked away. My night was complicated enough.

After his conversation with Bricker, the security guard joined me with a disbelieving scowl. "What's up with that guy?" he said.

"Did you download the video?"

"Here's your copy." He handed me a travel drive, then continued his rant. "Never mind that we saved the day. The detective was like, 'Why didn't you frisk the perpetrator first thing?' I'm like, 'Did you not hear what I said? I tried and got sprayed with blood.'"

"Bricker has poor listening skills."

"He bled out, you know," the guard said. "The guy who attacked you."

I stared toward the barn. "He's dead …?"

"The guy coded. Nothing they could do."

The bleak news had scarcely begun to sink in when Dan arrived and swept into the oxen barn like a hurricane unleashed.

"Where is she?" he demanded.

"Calm down," Bricker said.

"Calm down? This is *your* doing."

"She's with the EMTs. Right over there."

In the split second that it took for Dan's wild gaze to land on me, I realized with a horrified jolt that he'd come in thinking I'd been shot. I lurched up and met him halfway as he rushed toward me, wishing I could unravel time and do things all over again.

"Sonny." He gripped my shoulders and looked me up and down.

"I told you I was ok."

"Then you dove for the gun," he said. "I heard it go off. What the hell, Sonny? You didn't think to call me back?"

"I'm sorry. It happened so fast."

"What's this garbled shit Sue left in a voicemail?" he demanded. "You got your memory back? This guy came to your farm?"

"The night I ended up in the ER."

Dan gaped. "That was *days* ago."

"There's a whole list of reasons—"

"Hang on," he said as Nathan arrived and launched into Bricker about endangering his client. "What's this about?"

"I called him," I said.

"You *what?*" Dan demanded. "*That* guy?"

"He told me he could shut Bricker down."

Dan fixed me with a scorching gaze that I'd hoped to never see on his face. "I'll need to weigh in," he said. "Are you injured?"

"Just bruised."

"Wait here," he said.

Dan spent one minute listening to Bricker growling at Nathan, and then he burst forth with a tirade of his own.

"Don't you dare," he hollered in Bricker's face. "You put a neon sign over her head, and this is the result."

"Take it down a notch."

"Your methods are *crap*. What is your problem?"

For a moment, I was terrified that Dan would punch the detective, but his colleagues began a campaign of pushing him away from the scene and telling him to calm down. Bales of straw were stacked next to the barn where the group of men ended up. Dan furiously kicked one, cursed, and then he vented his anger on it again.

"Leaping lords and ladies," Norris exclaimed, arriving in a flustered state. He hugged me and checked to make sure I was in one piece, then he jogged over to help reason with his son.

I closed my eyes for a while, a dizzy, miserable heap.

Footfalls approached. "I specifically told you to not talk to Bricker on your own," Nathan said crossly, as always in clean, ironed clothes. "Never mind, I got it sorted out thanks to that vocal cop over there. It's not often they turn on each other like that. Are you ok?"

"The security guard has a video of the attack."

"Excellent. Which guy is this?"

I pointed.

"I'll get a copy." Nathan closed his eyes. "Please tell me Bricker isn't right. The dead guy didn't blame his injuries on Frank."

"The attacker did say that."

"*Shit.*" Nathan paced and flipped his hands, ranting internally. "Why did I sign onto this? It's a form of hell."

"The guy was acting insane if that helps."

"Maybe. You mentioned he had a snake tattoo?"

"On his forearm."

"So that was for real. It's blowing my mind."

"I want to go home," I said.

"Yeah, I'm working on it."

26

At midnight I was lying on my couch, too numb and frazzled to sleep. I'd left the lights on to let Dan know he didn't need to worry about waking me up. Hearing tires on the driveway, I sat up and watched his headlights comb over the dark yard, and then the engine shut off.

Luke accompanied me to the door and milled uncertainly. Without pause, Dan walked in and pulled me into a kiss, his emotion palpable as his forward momentum backed me across the room. With tears in my eyes, I let his strength wrap around me and heal the whirling traumas of the night. We were there for each other. Whatever it took.

"You're ok?" he whispered.

"I am now."

Dan closed his eyes and hugged me for a moment. Tight. Intense. He was shaking a little, engaged in a battle over two crushing weights. Anger and relief. I tightened my hold on him, confident which side would win out once he understood that I'd walked away unscathed.

"I'm sorry," I murmured.

"Which part are we talking about?"

"The confusion during our call."

"Oh, that." Dan released me. "You mean, when I told you to take cover, and you dove for the weapon. Me hearing a blast."

"If I'd turned to run, I would have gotten shot in the back."

"I see." Dan nodded. "Good visual."

"I did my best, so …" I paused in confusion as he started putting on nitrile gloves. "What are you doing?"

"This is where you keep the trash?"

He opened the lower cupboard and pulled out the container, then he lifted the torn T-shirt I'd worn the night I'd landed in the ER. He tossed it on the kitchen table with the front facing up and studied it with a frown. He flipped the shirt and examined the back. Finally, he retrieved a new bag from the cabinet and secured the T-shirt inside.

I shook my head. "How did you know?"

"I remembered Joan saying she tossed it out," Dan said, wrenching off the gloves with an irritated snap and tucking them into his pocket. "Now that some of the blanks of that night are filled in, your T-shirt will need to be processed. I have to take this in."

I stared at him. "Right now?"

"You'll need to make a statement tomorrow. I can't do it for obvious reasons, so—" Dan frowned at the bag as if catching up with his thoughts, and then he looked at me with alarm.

I could tell the kind of assault he was picturing.

"It wasn't like that," I said.

"How did your shirt get torn?"

"Not the way you're thinking," I assured him. "You can put your mind to rest on that kind of assault."

"He didn't grope you, or …?"

"He only wanted information."

"He *only* wanted information." Dan snorted. "A prime suspect in a murder case, and you didn't think to loop me in."

"Sue and Kate felt it was best to—"

"Yeah, I heard the logic. The need to spare me from saying, 'Sonny's back in gear thanks to some Reiki methods.'"

"We didn't want to put you in a tough position."

"As opposed to where we landed tonight," Dan said, pacing to the bookshelf. He picked up a baseball that had been sitting there for who knew how long and started grinding it in his hands. "Sue and Kate talk about the dangers of enabling, yet here we are."

I stared at him. I'd been wrong about his mindset. Relief was there. It had to be. But anger with me had won out.

"Did you see the video?" I managed.

"What video?"

"Of tonight. There was a camera in the barn."

"I lost my temper, so communication broke down," he said. "But I got the gist. Guy gets in a fight with some mystery assailant. Staggers out of the woods. You step in to help for reasons nobody understands. He comes at you for a minute, then falls down—"

"He didn't just fall down."

"What else have you not bothered to mention?" Dan said. "In my bed, all night, kissing me. All the while …"

"We need to reset. What did Sue tell you?"

"The basics. The prior contact. It sickens me to say this, but it might have worked in your favor to be high. You didn't pose a threat as a reliable witness. Hence, he left you unscathed."

"That's what Sue said?"

"She wanted you to fill in the details, which is what people do when it comes to a friend's drug habit."

"Dan, oh my God—"

"You told me yourself. You took pills."

"You've got the situation all wrong," I said. "We were trying to protect you. And back to tonight. I fought him off."

"The guy was *mortally* wounded," Dan thundered. "If not for that, you would be dead right now. For God's sake, Sonny. What the hell kind of lane do you imagine for me in your life? What you did is blatant disrespect for who I am and what I do."

"This is a nightmare. Please stop pacing."

Dan crushed the ball in his hands until it squeaked. "You claim you don't want me in rescue mode, but that's the permanent gear. I shouldn't even be here. Your attack dog warned me off."

"My what …?"

"Kitteridge. You said you'd hired him."

"I said I'd called him. Out of panic."

"I think a pause would be a good idea at this point," Dan said. "Because do you know what I think? You were protecting yourself when you held back. For all I know, dragging Sue here for a hypnosis session is an effort to dodge the fact that you took pills."

Tearful, sobbing, I gripped his arm. "I'm sorry beyond words for not looping you in. I didn't take pills. Let me explain."

"You had *days* to explain."

"Dan, we're going to get angry now and then. Tomorrow. Next week. If you ask for a pause at this point—"

"The last time I felt this way I took my house apart."

"You didn't have anyone to lean on. Now you do."

"How can you help? Trust is out the window."

His words landed in my chest, a crushing weight. The conversation was getting incredibly worse, incredibly fast.

"What time frame are we talking about?"

"I don't know, Sonny."

"This is so unfair," I said tearfully. "When you first signaled your interest during the *original* nightmare, I told you over and over again that your sphere couldn't encompass me. Not for long. I'm an artist. Curious. Passionate. You said you liked that about me."

"Most of us go through nightmares and turmoil, it makes us careful," Dan said, caught up in his mind instead of looking at me. "You're the exact opposite. All I can think is that your former zip code is to blame. Tons of leeway, freedom to do as you pleased—"

"You did *not* just say that. Oh my God."

With a disgusted sigh, Dan returned the baseball to the shelf. "I can't do this when I'm angry. We can talk tomorrow."

"Why bother? You'll still be coming at me with half the picture, and I'll still be a pill-popping princess in your eyes."

Dan closed his eyes. "Sonny …"

As he attempted to fashion some other sentiment that would bridge the gap to an exit, I forcibly calmed myself and crossed to my bag to retrieve my keys. With trembling hands, I slipped off the panic button, planning to give it back and say it wasn't right for me to keep it during our so-called "pause," only to see him step out and close the door.

It was as if he'd hit a switch that sucked the air out of the room. I felt it in my ears. My chest. My lungs. I couldn't breathe.

Did that just happen? Did he just leave without another word? Imply that it wouldn't work? He couldn't handle who I was?

Desperate to get him back, I rushed to the door and gripped the knob, then I stopped and closed my eyes. I'd never begged a man to stay. I knew where it would land me. Nowhere. Hurting. Alone.

I flipped off the lights and locked the deadbolt, then I crossed to the table and slumped into the chair I'd sat in a few days ago when Dan had stopped by to say he'd turned down the chance to play an active role in the case. I remembered the moment so clearly, how he'd looked in the light. Clean-shaven, smiling. Handsome, his brown eyes showing no sign of his inner turmoil. It was the same day he'd realized my father's death wasn't an accident. Raymond had been murdered.

I felt numb. Cold from head to toe.

I yelped as Dan rattled the doorknob and knocked.

"Sonny," he said. "Let me in."

In the darkness, I sat with my elbows on the table and sobbed into my hands. Just hours ago, I'd fought off a militaristic killer in a desperate bid to survive. And here I was, surviving, but just barely. Dan continued to pound on the door and ask to come inside.

"Sonny, I'm sorry. You had to know I'd be angry."

I was tempted to open the door. We would kiss. Make love. Pour our feelings into the moment. Direct contact instead of getting mired in our heads. It would be intense and emotional. There would be a release. We'd melt together for a time. Then what? My mind stalled.

"Sonny, I'm not throwing in the towel," Dan said. "It's important that we work as a team. I need the facts so I can bury Bricker once and for all. And I need the T-shirt. I left it in there."

That was why he wanted to come back in?

I grabbed my bag and headed down the hall to my father's room, then closed the door behind me. In the corner, as far as I could get from the sound of Dan pacing and cursing on my porch, I sat on the floor in the darkness, picked up my phone, and called Norris. I figured he'd be up at that late hour, worried sick about Dan, and I was right.

"I'm sorry to bother you," I managed.

"Honey, don't apologize. Have you seen Dan?"

I filled him in, choking and gasping my way through the news that Dan's anger was to the point where he'd broken things off. I apologized for interrupting when Norris tried to get a word in edgewise, then I begged him to call Dan and tell him to leave.

"I don't understand," he said. "The way things sounded—"

"I'm not good for him, Norris," I pressed on. "He said as much. I don't think he grasped our differences. Not until now."

"Sonny, if he's wanting to come back in—"

"He forgot evidence. That's why he's still here."

"That's nonsense. You're not thinking straight."

"Norris, please. I'm barely holding on."

"I'll call him, but don't give up on him."

"Put me on hold. I'll wait until you're back."

I closed my eyes. Dan's phone rang. I heard him cursing and arguing. There was a moment of quiet, and then his truck door slammed. I heard him pull out, then there was appalling silence.

"Are you there?" Norris said.

"I'm here," I tearfully managed.

"Sonny, if you could've heard him—"

"I *did* hear him. That's the problem. He talked about my zip code in Newton as if it should have made me a better person. I was convinced it gave me strength, all the things I went through back then. Now I know better. My life is damaged beyond hope."

"Sonny, you're letting that awful attacker call the shots," Norris said. "You and Dan are in the same boat, dealing with the loss of a key person in your life. You can help each other heal if you give it a chance. I've seen it in Dan already. What you both need right now is to talk."

"I tried. He yelled at me."

"That was pain talking. Tomorrow morning, first thing—"

"It's not an easy fix, Norris. You're a fantastic father. I'm glad Dan has you. If only we didn't have to deal with murderers."

"That's for sure."

"Thank you again for helping. Send me the bill."

"Sonny—"

"Tell Dan … tell him I love him. I don't mind saying it at this point, but it doesn't mean that I'm going to cave in and change my mind. I can't be jerked around, even for good reasons, and to be honest, neither can he. One of us needs to be strong."

"This is nuts. Honestly, the two of you—"

"Goodbye Norris. I'm sorry."

I *was* sorry to cut Norris off by ending the call.

I texted Arlene, *Are you up?*

I have toddlers and my bladder isn't what it used to be. Five minutes?

Ok. I'm sending you a video.

I fetched my laptop and copied the footage the security guard had given to me, then I sent it to Arlene. I couldn't watch the attack. Not yet. Possibly not ever. What good would it do?

I brought Arlene up to speed but held back from disclosing the real reason I'd landed in the ER in case she went off script and called Dan. Sue, Kate, and Brumby knew the details. They could be trusted to keep it to themselves. I'd been stuffing secrets and burdens to the bottom of my soul my entire life. One more wouldn't break me.

"I can't believe it," Arlene said. "It's not fair to judge how Dan reacted if he hasn't seen the video. It's terrifying."

"For a spoiled rich girl, I have some moves."

"Tomorrow, you'll both see things differently. You know the kind of fights Lance and I have weathered. I almost left him. He almost left me. Blowups can bring you closer together."

"In my case, blowups only mean the end."

"Sonny, your huge feelings of loss are an indicator. I thought it was the same for him. I can't believe he walked out."

"Hang on," I managed, sobbing again.

From a locked place in my mind, tonight's ordeal careened out of the shadows. The attack in my yard as well. Shaking, crying, I couldn't fathom my terrible luck. Couldn't believe it had happened to me. The bitter taste of the drug. How it had felt as my awareness had faded into a haze. All the badgering I'd endured. *Say it. I took pills.*

All because I'd set out to save my lambs from a butcher.

Luke was curled in a heap by my side, softly whining and shivering in confusion. I pulled him into a hug to let him know the world hadn't come to an end. Only my world. His could go on, mostly as before.

"I bet Donald is relishing my downfall," I said.

"Donald is not coming at you from the grave," Arlene said. "Please tell me you're not going down that rabbit hole again."

I closed my eyes. "Sorry, old habits."

"Do you want me to call Dan?" Arlene said.

"I forbid you to call him. Leave it alone."

"I'm sorry, Sonny," she said softly. "I wish I could be there."

"It's ok," I managed. "I'll rally, like always."

"We need to find a counselor for you."

"When, exactly, would I have time for that?"

Arlene gave an exasperated sigh. "I saw online that Richard's memorial service is tomorrow. I assume you won't attend."

"Actually, I think I am."

"But all the potential bad guys might be there."

"Look where cooperation got me," I said. "I'm back to square one, and it's a relief. I'm my own investigator now."

"Uh-oh. I know where this is going," Arlene said.

"Don't worry, I'll be careful."

"Do you think Frank is the mastermind?"

"I don't know," I said. "But I'm going to find out."

In the silence after our call, I stared at the dark shapes of the clothes in Raymond's closet, his plaid shirts, and the jeans that were flecked with dirt from one of his last walks on planet Earth.

"How did you get yourself murdered?" I asked his boots.

27

A half-hour after I called, Nadine Gilbert greeted me at the door of her strip club. I was lucky she was in town. Her life had been a blur of activity after her blog had caught the attention of an agent with ties to the movie industry. Now an author was helping her write a book about her role in bringing down a stone-cold murderer in May. I'd conveyed to Nadine and her expanding entourage that I wanted my involvement in the story to be minimized. She was built for the limelight. I was not.

Dressed in her usual clingy leotard, with false lashes and vibrant blue shadow enhancing her eyes, Nadine offered sympathy and advice on the latest implosion of my life, saying my dire view of Dan's attitude might be premature. I didn't have time to argue. I was busy undressing, jumping into her shower, lathering my hair with her special, fragrant shampoo, and then plunking down on a bar stool that put us at eye level.

"Are you sure about this?" Nadine said. "A makeover is a big deal."

"You know my history. Donald's constant attacks made me feel like one of those Russian nesting dolls, trapped by imposed shells. Keep quiet. Lay low. In some ways, I've been missing in action for twenty-eight years." I fought back tears. "Now I've got Bricker coming at me, and Dan trashing how I've handled the stress. Last night I took a tally of how much slack I've given him. Apparently, it's a one-way road."

"A makeover will put you back in the power seat?"

"The driver's seat, at least."

"That's all I needed to know."

Nadine assessed my hair with her scissors in hand.

"You won't cut much, right?" I said.

"You want to be a knockout, don't you?"

A significant upgrade, at least. If people were going to treat me like an overindulged debutant, I might as well play the part.

"But my hair is wavy," I said. "Very tricky."

"Eyes forward. Let me focus."

I'd come to Nadine in desperation. I had to hope for the best.

While she worked, I spelled out the entire ordeal of getting drugged and landing in the ER. She paused now and then to cluck her tongue over my terrible luck, then started snipping again.

"A lot of hair is coming off," I said.

"Stop worrying. What happened next?"

As I described last night's attack, I thanked her for all her pole dancing lessons. The strength and speed she'd instilled in me had helped, though I wasn't sure I could call myself a badass.

"If you're not qualified, nobody is a badass," Nadine said. When Dan called a moment later, she motioned for me to pick up. "This is perfect. I want to hear what he has to say for himself."

I took a breath, and answered with, "What?"

"I saw a video of the attack," he said. "I didn't know how bad it was, Sonny. I should have been there for you."

"But golly, you found me out. Pill popper. Spoiled rich girl. All the perks of a Newton zip code. Never mind that I did everything you asked of me back in May. Where did it get me?"

"It's why you're still standing," Dan said.

"Yes, I lived to see another day. Only to get frisked, wrongly accused, attacked, hollered at, and best of all, I got canoodled and then put on pause the very next day. Wow, what a week."

"I'm sorry. I know you're angry—"

"Oh, I ran over 'angry' last night on my way to blazing mad. This is my confession. I heard *something* tumbling under the tires."

"Where are you? If you give me a chance—"

"Trust is out the window. You did say that, right?" I closed my eyes, hating how bitter I sounded. "Some of this is misdirected anger. I'm sorry for that. You helped me. I thanked you, and I meant it, but I've said from the start that it wouldn't work," I pushed on over Dan's protests. "A pause only delays the inevitable. We need to call it quits."

"*Sonny*—"

I hung up and shut my eyes for an agonized moment, pulling strength from nowhere, and then I tearfully blocked Dan's number.

When I turned to Nadine, she looked torn.

"Honey, I could tell you wanted to cave," she said, handing me a tissue. "You have to admit, he sounded remorseful."

"Don't start. I'm short on time, and I need a miracle."

Nadine continued clipping and filling the air with soothing chatter. "I've got you lined up to be in my movie."

"How would that be possible?"

"You can be a pole dancer in one of the club scenes."

"Nadine, I can't do that."

"I know, you're all concerned about getting naked in public. Honestly, I think you'd find it liberating. But we can put you in a cat mask."

"A cat mask … interesting."

"I wrangled the fee already. Ten grand."

I swiveled and almost got my ear taken off by her scissors. "What?"

"Think about it," Nadine said. "Dan is sitting there one day watching the movie about what happened—"

"It won't matter. He'll move on."

"Nonsense. You don't believe that?"

"Focus on my hair. It doesn't respond well to layering."

"Honey, you are too much, but I love you to pieces." Nadine kissed my cheek, a supportive mother hen through and through. "Now, we have a lot of choices to make. Eyeliner, shadow, shades of lipstick, and blush. Don't worry, I won't bring it to my level."

At 8:15, I was tottering out of her bathroom in her high heels, ensconced in the clingy black dress she'd handed me.

"Wouldn't my dress be better?" I said.

"I tossed it in the trash. It's a nun's outfit."

"Nadine! That cost me a fortune."

"I'll show you a fortune." She spun me around and pointed at my reflection in one of the mirrored walls. I straightened, scarcely believing the woman staring back at me. The dress was clingy, yet classy enough for the somber occasion. She'd nailed the makeover concept if I could manage to not wobble in her black stiletto heels.

"But this isn't me," I protested. "We overshot the mark."

"I work in one lane. It's called 'Wow.'"

"I do know that about you."

"Come on, toss your hair," Nadine said.

I moved my head and was astonished by the tamed body she'd added to my waves and curls, with wispy, angled bangs that framed my face. She'd used a silver eye shadow that enhanced my blue eyes, with mascara and a bold liner that boosted their color all the more and might possibly make them downright arresting from a distance.

"Practice your walk," she said, then immediately started sighing and indicating I was not getting it right. "Here, watch me."

Nadine flexed her shoulders. After a few languid forward steps, she paused and offered her hand to an imaginary stranger.

"I'm Sonny," she purred. "You look familiar. Have we met?"

"Why did you lean away like that?" I said.

"It's sexy. A subtle hint of hard to get."

"I can't pull that off."

"We don't have time for doubts. Come on."

As she always did during pole dancing lessons, Nadine began clapping her hands to get me moving. Scowling at my distraction, she crossed to her music controls and searched through her song list. Over the speakers came a strong beat and a female vocalist belting out an anthem for any fed-up woman who was not about to take any more guff.

"Cast off those lacquer shells people have imposed," Nadine said. "Implant the song in your mind. Walk. Stand tall. That's it. You clocked a killer last night. You walked out alive while Dan and his buddies stood there holding their you-know-whats."

"*Nadine*. Not helpful."

"It's telling me things. You just turned pink."

252

"I should get going."

"Hang on, I'll spritz a light fragrance in the air. Walk through the mist to get a subtle coating. Neither fast, nor slow. Got it?"

"Umm …"

"Stop stalling," she chided. "Nice. Perfect."

"Thank you, Nadine. Wish me luck."

"What you have is better than luck," Nadine said, holding me at arm's length and fiercely looking me in the eyes. "Strength, smarts, the biggest heart I've ever known. Plus, you do have luck, honey. Use it, and keep your guard up. Knock 'em dead."

I blanched at the old phrase. "Hopefully, it won't come to that."

* * *

During the drive to the chapel, I abruptly realized the Corner Pocket was on the way. I swerved into the parking lot, swung out my bare legs, and stood. Nadine had tossed my black pantyhose to one side with a roll of eyes. She'd applied bronzer expertly so I looked as if I'd just spent a few weeks in Saint-Tropez or some other exotic locale.

My high heels clicked on the pavement as I crossed to the door. The bell jingled as I stepped inside. In the midst of checking out a customer, Kate tossed me the routine smile she always offered patrons from out of town, and then she clapped eyes on me.

"Oh my—" Caught in mid-reach to hand change to the customer, Kate released the pennies and dimes into empty space. They clattered to the countertop. "—God."

The customer looked at me over his sunglasses and dropped his wallet. It had me flexing a little, and straightening my spine.

"Do you have any flowers?" I said.

"Sue!" Kate hollered toward the back of the store. "Bring the big bouquet of lilies!"

"She's famous, isn't she?" the man inquired.

"Very," Kate confirmed.

A moment later, Sue arrived with a bouquet of white lilies in a plastic sleeve and a sympathy card. She and Kate had prepared in advance for the memorial service. Nothing surprised them.

"Holy mackerel," Sue said, circling me. "Who pissed you off?"

"Dan, obviously," Kate said.

"He went nuts after last night's attack," Sue said.

"Sonny left him in the dark, blah blah," Kate agreed. "Not appreciating that keeping silent was a burden. She was protecting him."

"This level of heat is because they slept together," Sue said.

"Please put the flowers on my tab," I interrupted.

"Wait, one last touch, since crying is inevitable." Sue crossed to a display of sunglasses, searched for a classy pair, ripped off the price tag, and handed them to me. "Try these."

"Yes," Kate said. "Assess the room. When you decide who's going to get the blue-eyed stare, take them off. *Pow*."

"Sonny, be careful," Sue said. "Don't press it too much."

"Look where laying low landed me. Dan did me a favor by breaking things off. I'm free to move about the cabin."

"Until you hit turbulence."

"Are you sure Dan broke things off?" Kate said, frowning. "It's not making sense. What were his exact words?"

"Never mind, and I can handle turbulence."

At least, I would give it my best.

28

The chapel parking lot was packed. I arrived in time to slip into one of the last spaces. I slid my legs out of the car with a smooth, ladylike flourish, locked the door, straightened my hem, and stepped forward with a rhythm that was neither too fast nor too slow, my caboose swaying, and the purse Nadine had loaned me suspended on my arm.

She'd admonished, "You've got to stop it with the shoulder bag. One, it'll warp your posture. Two, it's a *sack*. I mean, come on."

My heart slammed as I saw a familiar extended cab truck parked close to the front. Of course, Dan would be extra punctual.

As Kate had predicted, gazes turned my way as I reached the doorway, people checking to see if they knew who'd arrived. I left on my sunglasses and assessed the room to see who was sitting where. Nathan helped me out by standing abruptly. He hesitated, not sure his impression of who'd stepped in was correct. Then he waved to me.

My gaze landed on Dan talking with a group of men along the far wall. He froze as he caught sight of me, sparking a rush of misgivings. I walked toward Angela at the front of the room and almost missed a step as the somber occasion hit home. What did I think I was doing, showing up like a reality star running amok? I'd let anger blast me out of my comfort zone and land me in a persona that literally hurt, my toes crammed into tight high heels for the first time in months.

I forged on with determination. By the time I reached the front seats and slipped off my sunglasses, tears had gathered in my eyes.

"Miss Littlefield," Rose said, hugging me. "How nice of you to come."

"I'm so sorry for your loss, Angela," I said.

Statuesque and lovely, even with a bruised cheek and grief-stricken eyes, Richard's widow smiled at the bouquet in my arms.

"Richard loved lilies. Keith, can you help with these?"

As Keith stepped forward to gather the flowers, I noted that the McDonnell brothers had donned jackets and ties that showed signs of the struggle that had gone into getting the knots right. Greg was alternately loosening his tie and then tightening it again.

"Thank you," I said as Keith gently secured the flowers. "You look very nice today. It's kind of you to help Angela."

He shyly shrugged. "We're, you know, neighbors."

"They've stepped up so much this week," Angela said. "I scarcely knew them before …" She dabbed her eyes. "We complained when their ATVs made too much noise. Now I can't believe we were on bad terms. Thank you for coming, Sonny. It's really sweet."

"I'm sorry we met under such circumstances."

"I think the service is starting," Rose said.

I hugged her in parting. "I'll find a seat."

Stepping past the seated mourners, I assessed my options. In a handsome jacket and a crisp shirt that set off his tan, Dan was standing at the end of a row of pews with a gaze that said I should knock it off and sit next to him. Stone-faced, I walked resolutely onward and stopped at the aisle where Nathan was leaning past Frank and signaling to me.

"You don't mind if I join you?" I said.

"I saved a seat in case you needed one."

Once I'd edged my way around Frank, who scowled and only vaguely shifted his knees to allow my passage, Nathan helped me settle in and appeared to be fascinated by my legs as I crossed them.

"How are you here?" he said. "You were attacked last night."

"One needs to take these things in stride," I said.

Following Brumby's method of seeing if anyone had been in a recent fight, I shook Nathan's hand the way an NFL linebacker might do. He seemed too agog over my breezy attitude to notice.

Frank startled me by reaching past Nathan and gripping my hand with an intense, perceptive gaze. "Why did that guy target you?"

"He didn't *target* me. It was …"

"Another fluke, huh?" he demanded.

"Frank, what are you doing?" Nathan prompted, irritated to have the ex-con's arm crowding his space. "Back off."

"She showed up, just like I predicted."

"Have some respect for the occasion," Nathan hissed, then he turned to me. "Sorry, he's on edge from the lack of answers."

"No need to explain," I managed. "We're all on edge. It's a shame the police here in Maine are so incompetent."

Fifteen feet away, Dan snapped open the printed memorial program and glared at the paper as if he hoped it would catch fire in response to my remark. When he turned and our eyes met, I made a sharp cutting motion that urged him to accept where we'd landed. Facing forward again, I instructed myself to resist any further appeals to engage.

Nathan was studying me with a concerned gaze, stirring the crisp scent of his suit in the air, a reminder of the life I'd ditched back home. I'd had dates with men like him, the sort who knew the best restaurants and nightclubs. I tumbled through memories of dancing to the beat of loud music under shifting colored lights: a hollow kind of enjoyment that never lasted long. I collected myself and mustered a tight smile.

"Are you free for dinner?" Nathan said.

"I'm booked. Maybe later in the week."

"The three of us should have a proper talk."

"Let me think about it."

"I saw the video from last night," Nathan whispered. "You decked the attacker. Laid him out like a sack of potatoes."

"He was already wounded. It's nothing to celebrate."

"You can rest easy about keeping the footage from going viral. For the short term, anyway. I made the security guard sign a contract."

"Thank you. I appreciate it."

"Listen, I was wondering—"

"*Shh*," I admonished, aware of Dan's glare heating up all the more as I leaned toward the attorney who was laying waste to police departments in two states. "Thank you again for helping me out," I went on.

"Please tell me this is the real you," Nathan whispered.

"*Shh*," I admonished again.

My slamming heart was a reminder that I was not just letting a flirt score points in front of Dan's smoldering brown eyes. I was flirting with trouble. I firmed my resolve. I'd been mistreated by the detective in charge of the murder investigation, despite other viable avenues to pursue. No element of my life would return to normal until the case was wrapped up. It would be tough on my own, but I would survive, like always, on scraps, if that's what it took to move forward.

Amidst the hushed, echoing cadence of people blowing their noses, a succession of friends and colleagues stepped to the podium to tell stories about Richard, or read poetry. Most of the mourners were from the Boston area. It hit me how little I'd found out about Richard's life, beyond what Rose and Carl had shared. My normal impulse to search for answers had gotten stifled by shock and turmoil, and Bricker's withering attitude. I'd focused on protecting Dan, for all the good it did. With a clenched jaw, I nodded tightly in thanks as Nathan handed me a tissue.

Once the service ended, I affirmed that I would think about meeting for dinner later on in the week, and slipped away.

Hovering to one side and pretending to check my phone, I waited until the mourners had settled into talkative clusters in the adjacent open room where a table of refreshments had been set up. In the doorway, I paused to shore up my strength, and then I crossed to Greg and Keith to complete my self-appointed mission as soon as possible.

"Greg, it's good to see you," I said, reaching for his hand and shaking it strongly. As the notorious bully winced in pain and flexed his hand afterward, I managed, "I hope we can bury the hatchet once and for all. Here you are, helping Angela in her time of turmoil."

"It's what neighbors do," he grumbled.

"Keith, the same goes for you."

As I shook his wide paw, he showed no sign of injury. Frozen, unsure of himself, he stared at my enhanced eyes and took a good long look at my chest, where my tight dress showed some cleavage.

"It's nice to know you," Keith said gallantly.

"Nice to know her," Greg sneered. "Listen to you."

"It's fine, Greg," I insisted. "He's being kind, as are you."

I clicked gracefully away before they invited themselves to the farm. If they did, I would bring in Brumby to push them back.

Exhausted from my false front, I crossed to the beverage table and asked the server for a small bottle of mineral water. Twisting the cap, I was relieved to feel the seal release with a sharp spritz indicating it hadn't been opened before. Was this a paranoia I would be saddled with for the rest of my life? Unable to trust what I drank ever again?

I turned and found Dan standing there with a tight expression. One word covered everything I needed to say.

"*No.*"

Dan snagged my arm. "Sonny, please. You're acting nuts."

"Thank you for being clear."

I pulled free and headed away.

Carl Woodley was the least likely person to have taken on and killed the attacker, but just then he looked burdened with secrets. As I neared him, I heard the ice in his glass tremulously clinking.

I touched his arm. "Carl …"

"Oh!" Startled, he swung toward me. "Sorry, I was lost in thought."

"Who are you afraid of?"

He blinked rapidly. "Excuse me?"

"Enough, Carl. You're scared out of your mind."

"*Shh.* Over here."

He guided me to a quiet spot next to a corkboard display of photos of Richard, then checked to be sure we were alone.

"A man threatened me since we last met," Carl whispered. "He said if I went to the police, he would kill everyone I know. My nephew, my secret lover. He knows I'm gay, somehow."

"Could you tell who it was?"

"He wore a dreadful mask."

"Did he drug you?"

"No, but—" Carl checked the crowd, then he used his forefinger to pull his collar down a fraction, revealing a faint bruise. He smoothed his shirt and appeared to regret showing me.

"Can you describe his build?"

"Athletic, dressed in military gear. He took me by surprise the same day you and I met at the Morris House. That night, rather."

"Did he have any distinctive markings?"

"It was dark. Impossible to see."

"What did he say? Anything specific?"

"Oh boy ..." Carl was hyperventilating. "Heavens ..."

"Calm down," I whispered. "You know you can trust me."

"He knew about Captain Winthrop's blasted desk and made it clear he hadn't found whatever he was looking for in Richard's safe. That means he was the one who—" Carl closed his eyes. "The way he grilled me was awful. I know why Ken died from fright."

"What did you tell him?"

"Everything. Richard came to me some months ago. He needed help handling a few items that didn't have proper documentation showing the chain of custody, or the provenance. It sounded fishy. Richard got testy when I told him no. He'd helped finance my shop, so ..."

"You buckled."

"Yes," Carl moaned. "Richard mentioned an old desk. I didn't see the harm in coming up with what I imagined was a fair price. Ken was eager to help as well. Of course, once I *saw* the desk ..."

"You realized it was worth a fortune."

"Exactly," Carl said with a wild look. "In time, I relaxed into thinking we'd rescued the desk from neglect. Now Frank is out for *revenge*," Carl desperately added. "Or whoever it was behind the mask. He ordered me to search for a hidden safe. I looked everywhere. Richard's office. The basement. No luck. I did find a letter Mrs. Winthrop wrote to Frank in the event of her death."

I frowned. "Why did Richard have it?"

"He handled her estate. I don't dare show it to Frank." Carl slipped a rumpled envelope from his pocket and handed it over. "She wrote about her husband's obsession with relics from the *Harriett Browne*. The whole family was troubled. Illness, sudden deaths, treachery, bickering amongst themselves. She saw Frank's inheritance as cursed."

"I've thought that for days."

"It might have been Frank in the mask, hissing to distort his voice," Carl said. "I've cautioned Angela to not trust him, but it's an uphill battle. He's been attentive and helpful. The sweet approach."

"Is Angela buying it?"

"He's her rock, all of a sudden. At least they sat apart here. Today is about honoring Richard. Those awful McDonnell boys are like jackals waiting to see if they can take advantage."

"Especially Greg," I agreed.

"I have to go," Carl said. "I need a stronger drink than this."

"Tell the police you were threatened."

"I can't. You have no idea what the goon was like."

It wasn't a safe place to admit that I *did* know.

"Thank you for your kind words," Carl said loudly as he reached for my hand. "Stop by the shop anytime, Miss Littlefield."

He'd forgotten the letter. I put it in my purse and assessed the room for people of interest. Theo Lurman looked startled as our eyes met as if my updated style was throwing him off. He guided a fiftyish woman in the opposite direction. His wife, I presumed. No sign of Bricker. I found that interesting. I hesitated, thinking I recognized one man.

Crossing to a table where a guest register was open to a list of names, I flipped through the pages. None of the entries jumped out at me.

All the while, I listened in on a boisterous conversation taking place amongst a nearby group of men. One of them was Ed Emery, who'd come to my farm after my night in the ER, and then eavesdropped at the Corner Pocket. Both times, he'd been a bumpkin. Now he looked at home in chinos and a sports jacket, one hand holding a drink, and the other in his pants pocket as he regaled his buddies with a tall tale.

I fumed, confirming my hunch that he was Richard's PI. He must have donned an old sweater and a bashful smile to see if he could learn a thing or two. In his natural state — a slick jerk spouting coarse jokes — I would never have given him the time of day.

"So, the guy unzips right there, and—" Ed stopped as his gaze met mine, and his surprise was so vivid that the other men looked in my direction. He murmured a comment that made them laugh, then he stepped toward me with a "don't-make-a-scene" gaze.

I bristled as he approached, all but bared my teeth, but didn't lose sight of the somber setting. I forcibly calmed myself.

"Miss Littlefield." Ed smiled and extended a hand.

I reached forward in return, following through on my mission of the day. He winced as I secured his palm in a furious, crushing grip. From an injury, or because he was a sissy? I couldn't tell. I flipped his hand over and studied his red, scraped-up knuckles.

"What are you doing?" Ed demanded.

"Checking to see if you beat a man to death."

Hearing a cough that sounded like an exhalation of disbelief, I caught sight of Dan standing on my right ten feet away, holding a beverage in one hand, and rubbing his forehead with the other.

I turned back to Ed Emery. "Where were you last night? Anywhere near the fairgrounds?"

"Why would I go there?"

"I just told you. To commit murder."

"Are you nuts?" he hissed, then in a normal tone he followed up with, "Hey, how about we grab some lunch?"

"Skip the fake civilities. Who are you?"

"Ed Emery. I didn't lie."

I glanced at the business card he handed me, then studied his insolent gaze and overly gelled hair. "You're a private investigator?"

Ed nodded. "Licensed and bonded."

"Richard hired you?"

"Correct again. You're on a winning streak."

"You claimed to know my father."

"Maybe I did know Raymond." Ed nodded to someone passing by as if he thought a show of cool would put him in the power seat. "You're in a jam, in over your head. I've got lots to share. Come on." He reached for my arm. "Let's find a place to chat."

"*Don't* touch me," I said with quiet heat.

"Look, a man I respect is dead—"

"Richard, you mean? How long have you known him?"

"A short while. He hired me to do some digging."

I waited to hear more. Information was going to flow one way, or he could hit the road. His gaze said I'd be waiting all day.

"Along what lines?" I prompted.

"You know a bit of it. You've talked to Carl and ended up in Ken's house. You saw the letter, I assume. Your turn."

"Who killed Richard? Do you know?"

"I can't say unless you ask *nice*," he quipped with a wink.

"A charmer. Wow."

"I'm saying, don't be a pain. What's the harm in teaming up?"

"You're a detective? For real?"

"You bet. Lots of experience."

"Well, Mr. Emery." I dropped his card into his drink. "You stink at it."

His jaw flexed and his ears turned red, but he summoned a tight smile. "Can't say I didn't try. Have fun figuring things out."

"Ice that hand," I said. "Plan better next time."

Ed Emery scowled at me for a heartbeat, and his expression as he stepped away was a silent warning, as clear as any I'd ever seen. Hot in the face, I watched him stroll away. His audience of men had dispersed. He did a good job of looking as if he belonged there, but he skirted around Angela and Rose. A weasel on the prowl.

I turned and collided into an implacable, suit-clad rock who'd stepped up behind me. Detective Roy Allen didn't move an inch, his face and head clean-shaven. His jacket smelled of nice cologne.

"It seems we're questioning the same sources," he said in a dry rumble. "I thought maybe our two agencies could work together."

I let out a nervous laugh.

Roy didn't join me. He just stood there looking utterly humorless and stern. During the horror show in May, he'd been fair and dependable. A man of integrity. Desperate to maintain his previous good opinion of me, I resorted to a burst of mindless small talk.

"I'm taking over the Gartland case," Roy cut in. "One question, if you don't mind. What in the *hell* are you doing here?"

"I can explain," I said, setting my hands into motion, my mind whirling like a hamster on a wheel. "I—I—I—"

"Want to cooperate any way you can," Roy suggested.

"No, I … *yes*, of course."

"And will follow me to the exit."

"Right. Sure."

I trailed out behind him.

Detective Allen stopped in the parking lot, where the sun reflected off cars, and heat shimmered upward from the pavement.

"We'll talk over lunch," he said.

"The thing is, I'm on my way to the—" I paused, abruptly aware that we were standing next to a dark sedan that I'd honked at and blown past on my way into town. "Is this yours?" I said meekly.

"It's an official police vehicle."

"You want me to get in?"

"Please." Detective Allen held the door.

The argument was over, my fate sealed. I cast a yearning glance toward the beautiful clouds that would be drifting over the fairgrounds within the next hour and then climbed into the law-smelling sedan.

29

The clatter of plates came from the kitchen of the old diner, and the air smelled of the lemon cleaner a waitress was using on the countertop. Sitting across from me in a booth next to the window, Detective Allen loosened his tie and tucked into a fruit plate, bran muffin, and black coffee. I'd ordered pancakes, bacon, home fries, and scrambled eggs.

Roy indicated my slender build. "Do you eat like this a lot?"

I nodded. "High metabolism."

He stabbed a grape, incensed by the unfairness of life. "Start talking. Who approached you. Where, when, etcetera."

"Can I call you Roy?"

"Why not? We have history."

As he opened his briefcase and pulled out a pad to jot down notes, I repeated the list I'd conveyed to Dan. I didn't complicate the download by disclosing details, theories, and hypotheticals that would compromise the need to convey my motivation from the start: to secure Raymond's possessions, which rightfully belonged to me.

"You've mucked things up in record time," Roy said. "You will cease and desist the nonsense I witnessed at the service."

I don't like lectures, the Boston Sonny from months ago railed.

The new me yearned to have known Raymond, sparking the need to examine my rebellion against a paternal influence. The new me could see both sides of an argument and knew when to hold her tongue.

"Fine."

The seasoned trooper narrowed his eyes. "Fine, meaning what?"

"I will endeavor to not muck things up."

Roy gave up trying to glare me into a cinder and stabbed a grape. For a minute we focused on eating. The pancakes were heavenly, the bacon crisp, the eggs cheesy. One day I would loop back to photograph the diner, with its ancient red booths, and its open window along the back wall where the cook's hands appeared with plates of food.

"It's puzzling that nothing of value was in Mr. Gartland's jewelry bag," Roy said. "Bricker is convinced you took something."

I sighed, exasperated. "I didn't even *look* inside the bag. I put it next to Richard's hand out of an irrational impulse to comfort him."

"All right, just verifying."

"Focus on the other leads. It's almost certain Richard was killed over the feud between the Gartlands and the Winthrops."

Roy looked baffled. "What feud?"

"*You* know," I prompted. "Over of the desk from the *Harriett Browne*. With the, umm … secret compartments."

With a disgusted sigh, Detective Allen slammed down his utensils and made a rolling motion to indicate that I should explain.

With a passionate reminder of why I'd gone to Ken Babik's house, I described what I knew about the desk, plus the backstory I'd learned from Carl in the Morris House at the fairgrounds. I texted Roy all the photos I'd taken of the various items of interest, including the ancient letter that was possibly written in code, and the list of provisions from the book that Carl had "borrowed" from Richard's office.

"Plus, I think Ken died from fright," I murmured, almost inaudible.

"Jesus Christ," Roy said as the photos uploaded to his phone. "Why didn't you bring this to our attention before?"

"You know how Bricker has treated me."

"I do, but still—"

"I thought you knew," I said, silently adding, *What do you people do all day at the barracks? I figured this out in five minutes.*

"This is a lot to unpack," Roy said. "Explain the feud concept again."

"The captain of the *Harriett Browne* was Samuel Brooks Winthrop, as in Frank Winthrop. To safeguard treasures he collected during voyages, Samuel hired a cabinetmaker to build this ornate desk. Elijah Gartland, as in Richard Gartland. You can imagine the effort it took to dream up and construct trick drawers and other hidden means of hiding things, but the captain never paid Elijah the full amount for his work. Hence, the two families were at odds with each other. It never got resolved."

"All these years later, it led to murder?"

"It makes more sense than coming after me."

"I apologize for the inconvenience you've been put through," Roy said diplomatically. "What's this photo of a gold coin?"

I explained the story Keith had told me.

"I don't want to land Mr. Lurman in trouble," I added.

"Theo gave us this doubloon," Roy reported. "Claimed to not recall where he'd found it. He must have a soft spot for Keith."

"That's great. A huge relief."

"Back to basics. What did you see and hear and do the night Richard died, step by step, moment by moment?" Roy prompted crossly. "Let's see if any other revelations pop out."

I sighed. "Richard staggered toward me, hollering. I had the radio on, so what he said was garbled, but how he looked is seared into my mind. I think at some point he might have said a word that began with an 'f.' Then maybe a 'th,' because I saw him do this." I demonstrated with my tongue. "Fffifth … No, it was more like fffaaathh …"

"Miss Littlefield," Roy said tiredly.

"You asked what I saw."

"What you *definitively* saw."

"I definitively saw Richard stagger toward me and drop to the road. He called for help, and then he died. Read my statement. There's nothing to add." I pointed to a sheet on which Ed Emery's name was highlighted in yellow. "Is that a printout of Richard's phone calls?"

Roy slammed his briefcase shut. His glaring powers were getting a workout.

"My turn," I said. "Who attacked me in the oxen barn?"

Roy squeaked open the briefcase enough to slip out a photo of a man with short hair, gray eyes, and chiseled features.

I hesitated, then pulled the photo closer. Did he have a family? A wife? Children? What had turned him into a monster?

"Jonathan Dorsett, known to some as JD," Roy said. "Spent time as a military contractor, hence his tactical chops. If he hadn't been wounded, and intended to neutralize you—"

"I would be dead, I know."

"You saw the tattoo on his arm?" Roy said.

"A snake. Does it mean something?"

"Possibly. It's the kind of tattoo that washes off."

I focused on Roy, feeling as if the news had been delivered to my mind through an electric shock. "It's not permanent?"

"We think it was a part of his tactics, his whole mentality," Roy said. "It would be the sort of detail a target remembered. Maybe he enjoyed that part. Used it to his advantage. Once it was washed off, he could stand right next to a victim without them knowing it."

"Imagine that," I said miserably.

I'd given Dorsett a backup charger. Talk about blind.

"Looks like you're sensing my next question," Roy said. "I've been told he came to your farm. I need a point-by-point."

I closed my eyes, suddenly wishing I hadn't eaten so much food. The masked assailant who'd drugged me and hissed every word to disguise his voice was supposed to be "neutralized." If the tattoo could be donned and discarded by whoever else knew about the trick, no one was in the clear. The way Frank had rolled up his sleeves near the Whack-a-Mole game now looked strategic. Had he staged that scene in the wake of my reaction to the story he'd tossed out in the hospital parking lot? If so, it had worked. Until now, I'd ruled him out as the man behind the mask.

Bricker was an even worse suspect to pull back into the mix. I couldn't break my silence until some other detail surfaced, allowing me to identify the man who'd questioned me beyond all doubt.

"Alison." Roy rapped on the table. "Tell me. Right now."

My eyes flew open, and I braced myself to get up fast and head for an open doorway. For a moment, it was as if I was sitting in front of Donald Littlefield in my childhood home. He'd used the same tone, and he'd rapped on his desk the same way if an important item had been misplaced, or any other problem required a patsy to accept blame.

"I'm sorry," Roy said in a softer tone. "How did his visit unfold?"

"He asked questions. Then he left."

"You still can't recall the details?"

Dan hadn't updated him? I rubbed my brow, too confounded by the entire jarring day to keep track of who knew what.

"Because you took pills?" Roy prompted.

"Those words did come out of my mouth."

"What *do* you remember?" he said.

"If I could offer a concise account with irrefutable evidence to back it up, I would tell you," I said. "For now, I can't."

"When you do sort it out—"

"Of course. If you'll excuse me for a moment?"

I slipped from the booth and crossed to the restroom, my feet aching with every step. My frustrated, emotional entrance startled a woman who was attempting to apply lipstick.

"*Hey,*" she said.

"I'm sorry."

I slipped into a stall and pulled out the letter Frank's mother had written for him to read in the event of her death.

In a tight hand, Mrs. Winthrop wrote at length about the ways Frank took after his "miserable, shortsighted" father. She wasn't the least bit surprised that Frank had landed in prison. In the hope of putting him on "a righteous path," she was selling items that had once belonged to Captain Winthrop. *You'll never know my pain and suffering*, she wrote. *How carefully the sales have to unfold lest one of the vultures takes notice. With God's help, I'm cleansing our lives of the sins of your father's family.*

Had her efforts to sell items on eBay attracted trouble directly to her door, and ultimately landed her in the grave?

Feeling jaded and spent, I stepped out of the stall, washed my hands, and confronted my glazed expression in the mirror. I looked drugged. Let Roy think that. What did it matter?

When I returned to the booth I didn't sit down or hand over the letter. I'd done plenty to help the police, with no gain in return.

"Are we finished? I have work to do."

Detective Allen eyed my plate. "You don't want that bacon?"

"Go ahead, help yourself."

At long last, he smiled. "Don't tell my wife."

When he dropped me off at the chapel, I stepped out to the dismal sight of Dan standing a short distance away.

"Perfect," I said under my breath.

Detective Allen held me back for a moment.

"As a friend of Raymond's, I feel compelled to take on a fatherly tone," he said. "At the service, I could see that something big had driven you into scorched earth mode. I have a feeling it's heartache."

"You're damned right it's heartache," I said with sudden fury. "I've had nothing but heartache since I grew up in the wrong house with the wrong last name. You want to help me? No more visits. No more lunches. Find out who murdered my father. *Then* we'll talk."

"Alison—"

"Don't." I pulled my arm away. "I'm glad you're on the case, but I'm sick of getting lectures from people who live in glass houses."

With my high heels creating sparks as I crossed to my car, I swung my bronzed legs into the sweltering interior, slammed the door, and gunned the engine. I swept on my sunglasses and swung out, fighting back tears that threatened to ruin my makeup. I didn't succeed.

I sobbed all the way home.

30

On my drive home, I realized there were advantages to spending nights at the fairgrounds. I could be on-site at dawn, and my animals would be spared the messy attacks, intrusive visits, and other forms of chaos they'd been witnessing for days. I texted Joan to ask if she'd mind having Luke as an overnight guest. I would repay her by hosting Harry and Jess when she needed to be out of town. Joan called right away.

"I'm stepping out of class to see if you're ok," she said. "Crazy stories are going around. You were attacked last night?"

"A guy was in a —" I closed my eyes, my heart clenching all over again as I pictured Dorsett approaching Joan the other day. "He was in a fight," I went on. "I tried to help. It went sideways."

"You sound stressed. You're ok?"

"I'm fine, but it's a reminder to stay vigilant."

"How about using the buddy system at the fair? Maybe Brumby can tag along with you if he's not too busy."

"I'll be fine, Joan. Can you mind Luke?"

"Of course. No need to ask."

Once we hung up, I let Luke out of his pen and indulged his need for love, stroking his ears and the knowledge knot on his head.

"Harry and Jess will be thrilled," I said. "They'll play with you after school. You won't even know I'm away."

When I straightened, I found Dodge and the sheep assembled in an attentive gathering along the pasture fence.

Magnolia and Dot pawed at the grass, conveying their desire for the apples that had fallen beyond their reach. I tossed them a few and stroked Dodge's soft, whiskered muzzle. He nickered as if to assure me that he would be in charge while I was away.

Once I was inside the house, I was like a machine as I undressed, setting Nadine's shoes near the door and her dress on the back of a kitchen chair. I scrubbed off the makeup until I was back to basic Sonny again. Unassuming. Happy to stay in the shadows.

With Luke milling in circles, sensing my gloom, I headed upstairs. First, I pulled out a lightweight backpack and tossed in underwear, three silky black T-shirts, plus an extra pair of jeans. In the interest of looking businesslike I selected a stylish black jeans jacket.

When Arlene called, my elation only lasted a heartbeat.

"I am so *steamed* at you," my best friend hollered. "Getting a makeover before going to the chapel? What were you thinking?"

I gaped. "Who told you?"

"They live-streamed the service. I watched the whole spectacle, how you handled being mad at Dan by confronting the suspects. I called him last night, by the way. I blasted him for letting you down. The next thing I knew, I was hearing his side. You didn't tell me that he came back two minutes after he lost his cool and stepped out."

"He hollered at me. He pushed major buttons."

"He thought you were dead. Imagine what he went through on his way to the fairgrounds. Things haven't added up for days, ever since you landed in the ER. I've never felt like you were lying, but lately … oh my God, Sarah, put that down right now!" Arlene hollered to her four-year-old. "Sonny, I have to go, but we are not done with this discussion. I love you," she added, sniffling. "I'll call later when I cool off."

Click.

I stared in shock. "Seriously? Unbelievable."

In the following silence, Luke softly whined, a reminder that he'd been traumatized as well. I knelt and hugged him. Whether I ever learned for certain if Jonathan Dorsett was the man who'd gone so far as to drug my dog, his gear and tactics on the night he'd died suggested that he'd perfected conducting business with harsh methods. Was he after riches? Revenge? Was he working alone, or as part of a team?

All he'd accomplished was ending up dead.

Hearing a truck pull in and park, I crossed to the window and groaned in frustration to see that Dan wasn't finished grinding me into a pulp. With a look of determination, he crossed to the porch. I heard him climb the steps, then he stepped inside without knocking.

"Sonny?" he called up.

"What are you doing?" I demanded.

"I'm here to apologize, and you're going to let me."

"I don't come with a simple shutoff valve."

"If it's helpful to know, I got schooled by Arlene, Sue and Kate, Roy Allen and my father. It's been like getting sucked into a Japanese restaurant with a hibachi grill. I started out as whole ingredients. The next thing I know, I'm sliced and diced with whirling kitchen knives, seared on an open flame, and dumped on a plate."

I closed my eyes, thinking, *Why does that make me feel awful?*

"Come down," Dan said. "Let's talk."

For a split second, I wanted to tumble down the stairs and get tangled up in one of our steamy kissing sprees. Holding him tight, apologizing for my performance at the service, crying from relief. Feeling the spark flame to life in my heart, and knowing it was the same for him.

Then my mind crumpled around the news that the snake tattoo was temporary. As always, the urge to confess tugged at me, but the same problems that had held me back from the start remained. I'd been brainwashed into saying that I'd taken pills. Without solid proof, it would be an uphill battle convincing skeptics that I was telling the truth.

"Sonny?" Dan prompted. "I wasn't complaining just now. When I'm an idiot, I'm happy to get my butt kicked."

"Give me a second," I said.

"We don't have much time to catch up. The Evidence Response Team is on the way. We need to process your yard."

I started to protest and forbid the intrusion, and then I realized the development was ideal. I could focus on my work at the fairgrounds while the technicians gathered evidence. Even if they found traces that backed up the extent of the question-and-answer session I'd endured, the supporting lab work might take weeks to complete.

As I came down the stairs with my slim pack slung over my shoulder, I found Dan leaning against the kitchen counter with an apologetic look on his face. He'd ditched his jacket but still wore the shirt that set off his tan and reflected light upward into his eyes. Dan's trousers were creased, a perfect fit, with a nice leather belt, and dress shoes.

"Going somewhere?" he said.

"I'm spending nights at the fair for the rest of the week."

"Sonny, I can't apologize enough for walking out, and for the things I said. The anger I felt got away from me."

"I'm sorry, too, but this isn't the right time for talking. I've lost half a day at the fair. I need to focus on packing."

"Sonny …"

"There's my T-shirt."

Indicating the bagged evidence that he'd forgotten to take last night, I remembered the glass vial Dan had found after my night in the ER. I crossed to the cabinet and eased the tube into a package of batteries. If I was right that the attacker had dropped it, the time to hand it over was after the Evidence Response Team completed their work.

"I avoided eye contact last night," Dan said. "It was because I got stuck in my head. You're doing the same right now."

"More criticism. Just what I need."

"Sonny." Dan gently steered me to a kitchen chair, swiveled a second chair to face it, and sat down. "Couples fight. We need to learn how to do it without trashing each other. If you look at the circumstances, our track record is unparalleled. How many people have to get to know each other during multiple murder investigations?"

"A lot. There are TV shows about true crimes."

"Sonny, listen. The guy was drugged. Crazed. Tactical. Super strong. You fought him off. You disarmed his weapon. That's from *one* trip to the range. You and me. We can build on it."

"It's getting late."

"Please *look* at me."

As Dan reached for my hand, I lurched up and stepped away, no idea why I'd tempted fate by letting him sit me down.

"Please wait here," I said. "I need to focus."

I crossed to my father's room down the hallway and paused to look at the forest green walls, the lampshades with pine cone designs, the patchwork quilts and rustic artwork. At some point, if fate allowed, I would need to spend time sifting through the boxes on the top shelf of the closet. Amidst the memorabilia and paperwork might be some clue that would prove relevant as I hunted down Raymond's murderer.

"Thanks for listening," I muttered as Dan stepped in.

He hovered by my side, smelling really nice, and radiating the invisible force field that dropped around a person like a makeshift shelter. I crossed to the closet and started searching for a clean fishing vest I could use at the fair. The one I'd been wearing the past few days was dusty. The hangers shrieked as I jerked them along the pole.

Behind me, Dan said softly, "Sonny, I was a shit at the worst possible time. I let anger and ego get in the way. I'm sorry."

"You don't need to be. I get it."

"Then look at the possibilities in this room, all the hobbies Raymond enjoyed. We can explore every one of them together, like camping under the stars." Dan pulled out the vest I'd been looking for and hung it on the doorknob. Irritating beyond words. "We can ski this winter. Think how great I'll look in racing gear. You'll look ok too, of course."

A few days ago, I would have laughed and delivered a comeback. Now I clenched my teeth, struck by the glaring imbalance of power between us. I'd begged him to hear me out last night. My explanations and desperate pleas had zero effect on the brick wall of his anger. Here I was, shaking from the effort to not cave and tell him the truth.

"Sonny, please talk to me."

I turned my head, hearing a vehicle growling up the driveway.

"Super," I said. "They've arrived."

"Ok, enough. Come here."

Calm and determined, Dan pulled me into a hug. I lifted my hands to push him away and paused with closed eyes, feeling the living warmth of him through his shirt, the muscles I'd draped myself across the other night, suffused with bliss. I'd imagined I could stop running. Stop searching. He was the kind of soulmate I'd dreamed of finding.

"We'll get through this," he murmured.

Trembling, unable to resist, I let him kiss me, thinking it might be my final taste of heaven. His lips were dreamy and persuasive, his arms crushing me against him with an air of relief.

I felt afraid. Conflicted. Tortured by dire possibilities. Our bond had almost gotten him killed last spring. Here I was again, confronted by turmoil and threats I didn't understand. A new mantra had been repeating itself for days. Keeping him in the dark meant keeping him safe. At last, my hands completed their task. I pushed him away.

"You were right," I said. "We need a pause."

As he searched my eyes, I retreated to the remote place where I'd been landing for twenty-eight years. He'd seen the opposite side of me the other night in his bed. Hooked-in and full of passion. He couldn't have imagined how securely the shutters could close against such warmth and light. I hadn't warned him. I hadn't been fair.

"You're pale and blank," Dan said. "What's going on?"

"I need to focus. I have an assignment."

"My father told me what you said."

"It's not fair to bring that up."

"It is if I feel the same way. I *love* you. I was like a wall that you leaned against the night we met. You didn't see me. From my side of the moment, the impact was immediate. It was like … déjà vu, almost. How can you be in the same room with me and not know?"

"Raymond wrote about how sentiments can get overblown in police work. Judgment takes a back seat. It happens all the time."

"You're shut down. Arlene described this, but seeing it in person—"

"It's what your parents saw after Aaron died. You wanted to sort it out on your own. You can't expect different from me."

I put on the fishing vest and crossed to the door.

"*Wait*," Dan said. "This all began on that missing night. You said you were protecting me. What in the hell went on here?"

"Follow the evidence, then you tell me."

"Sonny, don't walk away." In the kitchen, Dan stepped in front of me and held his hands to the side as if to indicate he would tackle me, if necessary. "If you don't take charge of the narrative, other people will fill in the blanks. You won't like the results."

"As opposed to my totally uplifting week."

"Please take a breath. Don't push me away."

"Choose better next time. A teacher, a nurse—"

"Sonny, for God's sake."

"I'm sorry, Dan. I really am."

I pushed past his look of shock and outstretched hands, then tossed back, "I *am* sorry. Please lock up on your way out."

Luke was sitting in tense silence near the kitchen door and responded instantly when I motioned for him to follow me out to the car. Whether it was a miracle or some trick he'd been taught by his previous owner, I couldn't say. My feet carried me forward, almost robotic. The huge lunch I'd eaten had burned away. I was shaking, on empty.

"Sonny, tell me what to do," Dan said behind me. "The risks you're taking are off the charts. I'm trying to understand."

The impulse to cave and turn to him pulled at me.

I shoved it back, ignoring the quick hellos of the technicians and their questions about where they should focus. They were on their own.

So was I until further notice.

31

I'd become an expert on driving while my mind was engaged elsewhere. Brumby added to my bleak mood by calling to tell me what I already knew: I'd missed the first half of the Horse and Carriage Show, a popular high point of the Meeting Fair. Brumby turned things around with a plan for landing me a prime parking space and getting me to the event at top speed. As promised, he was waiting in a golf cart with his Stetson tipped down for a quick snooze, and his boots crossed on the dashboard.

I tooted my horn. Brumby pulled out of the parking space, allowing me to slip in. I stowed my laptop under the back seat, planning to make trips to the car to upload my photos to my cloud account.

Smelling of sunshine and hay, Brumby secured my bag and draped one arm over my shoulders. "I heard Dan messed up. How bad?"

"We're on the skids. Don't gloat."

Brumby grabbed air and pulled down hard. "*Yes.*"

"You just firmed my resolve," I said. "I'm off men until further notice, but thank you for meeting me here. This is great."

"Any time." Brumby winked. "Day or night."

As we neared the arena for the horse show, I frowned at a man dressed in beige attire who closed in and ran alongside the golf cart, hollering and waving his hands. I realized it was Carl Woodlee.

"Stop," I said. "Hit the brake."

"You know that lunatic?" Brumby said.

"He owns Apogee Antiques."

I jumped out and gripped Carl's arm as he sagged to a halt.

"Sorry," he managed. "Winded … heart attack …"

"Just breathe. Calm down."

"Bag … the volume I showed you …"

Following Carl's breathless prompts, I opened the leather pouch he'd been carrying and pulled out the familiar book, with its plastic coil binder and a yellow cover featuring an 1800s engraved sketch of a whale breaching from the churning ocean.

"Page sixty-seven," Carl gasped. "The drawing of the crew."

I flipped to the tagged page, then seeing that it wasn't the best copy of an engraved ink sketch, dated circa 1888, I took out my phone and zoomed in on the details. I was about to ask what to look for when I was struck dumb by a tattoo on one of the men's forearms: a snake that began above his wrist and extended in coils under his sleeve.

Brumby had helped Carl sit down in the golf cart and was now fanning the winded man's face with his Stetson.

"Aren't you something," Carl said, staring in admiration at Brumby's muscles. "You're very helpful. My goodness."

I pushed Brumby aside. "Carl, what made you flag this?"

"In the Morris House, you mentioned a man with a snake tattoo," he said. "You looked worried and alarmed, so I wondered if it had to do with the case. I'm not sure I can take anymore, with Frank's attorney growling at me, and Greg McDonnell hanging about. You can't imagine what I've been through. Even the local butcher buttonholed me."

"Theodore Lurman," I said. "He's desperate to clear his name. Back to the drawing. Did you find any footnotes related to it?"

"I ran straight out to find you," Carl said. "The fellow with the tattoo is holding a harpoon, which brings Captain Winthrop's limerick to mind. Take the book. Do what you think is best. I'm leaving town."

I nodded. "If the police say it's ok, I think it would be a good idea. Go someplace unexpected. Don't leave a trail."

Carl paused, wide-eyed. "Am I hearing you correctly?"

I gave a rough recap of the events in the oxen barn. "The trouble is," I added, "other men might be using the same tattoo."

"Dear lord." Carl mopped his brow. "It keeps getting worse."

"Did your assailant ever come back?" I said.

"Not in person. He called from an unknown number when I got home from the service. I told him I hadn't found a safe. He cursed and growled and instructed me to keep my mouth shut."

"Who is this sailor in the drawing?" I said.

"That's for you to find out, my dear." Carl grasped Brumby's arm and implored, "I don't suppose you can bring me to my car?"

"Sonny?" Brumby prompted. "You're all set?"

"Yeah, I guess so."

Following a hunch as the golf cart whirred away, I flipped through the book and found a list of the schooner's crew: Daughty, Tardiff, Hilliard, Bradshaw, Crim, Dorsett, Abbott …

"Oh my God …"

I stared at the name William Dorsett. As in *Jonathan* Dorsett?

At last, I'd found a link that might explain the attacker saying, "William is back from the grave, and he's out for blood."

An asterisk led me to a footnote saying that William Dorsett was among several sailors who hadn't made it back to port. Two had died from smallpox. Dorsett had been washed overboard.

The book dropped from my hands as I launched my phone's photo app and scrolled to the captain's letter. His limerick was about a harpooner who "got his deserts," a tricky word that could refer to a punishment or a reward. What if the poem wasn't about hidden treasure? What if the captain was indulging a note of dark satisfaction after he'd tossed a thief into the churning sea? For all I knew, the sailor's death was an accident the captain had painted as retribution to instill fear in the rest of the crew. I flipped through the pages to see if there was any further mention of William's death, but the author hadn't seen it as relevant.

For a moment, I took the revelation as confirmation that Jonathan Dorsett was the man who'd drugged and questioned me, but the conflicting hints the masked attacker had growled were meant to throw me off. Doubts still plagued me. I was no better off than before.

As for alerting Detective Allen, I muttered, "The minute you put me on the payroll, I'll be happy to be a team player."

I jammed the volume into my bag, which made it a half-pound heavier to lug around. With a dark growl, I resumed my job.

* * *

Waiting in line to compete, teams of huge black Percherons, Belgian draft horses similar to Dodge, plus smaller breeds like Haflingers were a stunning sight, sporting braided manes and brushed tails as they stamped their hooves from within the elaborate leather harnesses attaching them to wagons of every color. Whether green, red, burgundy, or blue, most of the rigs had white wheels that promised to flash when they rolled.

Jammed into tight quarters behind a board fence that had been reinforced with chain-link, I was jostled by people pressing into me as they vied for a better view of the teams thundering by, buckles flashing, ribbons flying. The intricacies of the harnesses were a marvel, with complex reins and distinctive metal embellishments that I planned to study once I had time to zoom in on the details.

During the four-horse hitch event, I kept track of the approaching teams in my peripheral vision with my eye trained on the viewfinder. Zero fiddling translated to the sharpest photos possible. Pumped to the hilt as I pressed the shutter for multi-shot bursts, I was close enough to the action to feel every thud of the horses' plate-sized hooves landing in the dirt with a sound that I likened to Thor-level hammer blows. Next came the churning, jingling thunder of each wagon rolling past us.

Once the winning teams secured their prizes and took victory laps, I was able to take a breather and clean dust from my lens.

"Sonny!" Harry shouted, pushing his way through the throng with Jess behind him. "Brumby told us we'd find you here."

I hugged them. "Why aren't you in school?"

"We're done for the day, silly," Jess said. "Mom is over in the food pavilion. Her pickled asparagus *and* her nectarine preserves won first place. She used fruit from your trees, Sonny."

"Tell her I'll take pictures tomorrow."

"Charlotte's blueberry pie came in fourth," Jess added. "She's crying and wailing over there. Says the system is rigged."

"Dan was with the police techs at your farm," Harry reported.

"There were signs somebody prowled around the yard a bit," I said. "It's a reminder to stay alert. Be vigilant, ok?"

"Dan is teaming up with Harry for the golf cart race at the end of the week here at the fair," Jess enthused. "Sonny, let's you and I join forces. You can wear the blindfold while I sit next to you in the cart and holler directions. It's the most fun ever."

"When did Dan agree to this?" I said.

"Today," Harry said. "We fist bumped on it."

I fumed at the irritating news, then I caught sight of the time. "Can you save my spot here for when I get back?"

"Sure," Harry said.

With a groan, I dashed to another arena for the Volunteer Fireman's Muster. While opposing teams used hoses to shoot water at a suspended target in between, I tried to keep my camera dry and practiced my duck-and-roll skills at top speed. My phone dinged with increasing frequency. I checked my text feed and saw that Arlene was leaving sonnets of apology and voicemails imploring me to stop sulking and call her.

Not sulking, I texted. *Working hard.*

I took a shot with my phone and sent it to her.

Call me! Arlene texted. *This is frustrating.*

Can't now. Need to dash to another event.

Grrrrr!!!! she texted. *Love you. Stay safe.*

* * *

I'd learned from some of the farmers that their families slept in the straw lofts above the stalls in the barns from time to time. If allergies weren't a problem, a person could anticipate "a cozy night of rest."

At dusk, I decided it was time to choose my space. A farmer cleaning cow pies from the stanchion area added the shifting hiss of a hose to the evening air, bringing gooseflesh to my arms as I looked toward the barn where Jonathan Dorsett had uttered garbled threats.

He's coming for you. He's worse than me. It's my trick ... lying asshole.

Raymond had written about the lengthy process of assessing evidence and building a scenario that made sense— it often took weeks, rather than days. For DNA evidence, the frustration factor often extended into a few months. I wanted to help get justice for Richard, but from now on, I would conduct my pondering from the shadows.

One of the cow barns had a cozy vibe, and nobody was in sight. The black and white Holsteins were placid, munching on hay as I left the twinkling stars behind me. I cast wary glances in all directions on my way to a ladder that led to the straw loft. Looking behind me as I stepped forward, I felt my right foot connect with a strange, unstable object. There was a whooshing sound as if a long, thin pole were moving fast through the night air, then a rake handle struck my temple hard.

"*Crap*," I hollered, seeing stars and clutching my brow. "The tines are never supposed to be left facing up. It's common sense."

Squinting, I saw through two fingers that a security guard was huffing toward me past the stanchion area. Figuring he'd been prompted by my yelp, I inhaled to tell him I was fine, then he abruptly veered to the left with a quiet curse as if he'd hoped to not be seen.

Instinct kicked in. I dashed through the barn in the opposite direction, my heart pounding, and then I paused to get a bead on the man's whereabouts. It wasn't tough to figure out. His puffing breaths gave him away as he caught onto my sudden disappearance. I walked carefully, silently, and kept the barn between us. I halted abruptly when I heard him heave a frustrated growl and make a phone call.

"She vanished," he complained. "It's like she sprouted wings. I'm telling you, Dan, you'd better start pumping iron if you plan on keeping up with this one. She's here, she's there. I've had three coronaries trying to keep up with her today. I know, stop hollering. Meet me at the office. The security footage will tell us where she went."

As he puffed away, I glared at the nearest camera, which Dan would apparently be checking shortly. Sleep would have to wait.

Staying under the streetlights illuminating the fairgrounds, I crossed to the covered arena where I'd found Keith practicing his ax throw. It was well-lit, with security cameras in every corner. I could safely bide my time there until Dan showed up to get his butt kicked.

Midway across the arena, I pulled an implement from my pack that I'd grabbed from my car. To lift my spirits over the summer, Brumby had given me one of his broken-in bullwhips, with a weighted handle and properly braided leather with "bellies" that helped to create smooth action, and the all-important "cracker-popper" on the end.

I could wield it with enough accuracy to summon cracks with space in between to avoid landing an unintentional strike. I felt confident that I could convince any aggressors to not approach.

Unless they have a gun, I reminded myself.

While I worked, I whispered theories under my breath.

"Ok, there's Frank. I want to believe he learned his lesson, but Nathan doesn't know or care if he's guilty this time around."

Whooohhh, whooooohhh, SNAP.

"There's Ed Emery, dirtbag private investigator. He's working angles for sure. For a third party, or on his own?"

Whooohhh, whooohhh, SNAP.

"If not for Jonathan's death, he'd still be an unknown. What if other players are lurking in the shadows?"

Whooohhh, whooohhh, whooooohhh, SNAP.

About to begin my next windup, I saw Frank Winthrop standing next to the bleachers. His arms were folded as he watched.

"You don't want to be here right now," I said.

"What happened to the friendly vibe?"

"Step away. I mean it."

"I brought you a gift." Frank held up the silver frame with the photo of Raymond and Ella on their wedding day. "Carl confirmed it's why you went to Ken's house. You were heartsick to leave it behind."

"Stay back," I prompted. "I've resolved to live without it."

"It's your father and your stepmom."

"I saw their love in the image. It'll be with me forever, so I'm good to move on. Not everyone is obsessed with stuff."

Eyeing the whip in my hands, Frank crossed to the nearest bleachers and sat down with a tired groan. He set the photo aside and rested his elbows on his knees, rubbed his crew cut, and then steepled his fingers together as he figured out what to say or do next.

Scanning the misty night for other sources of menace, I saw Ed Emery skulking in the shadows behind the stand of bleachers. Had they come as a team, or was the PI playing his usual role, seeing if he might benefit from whatever he heard? For now, he stuck to lurking.

"Reconsider, Frank," I said. "You *don't* want to be here."

"It's great you're not obsessed with stuff," he said, sitting up to study me. "My upbringing involved doing without. My mother saying no to a new baseball glove, nice sneakers, electronics, a bike that wasn't a piece of shit. We're strapped for cash, she'd say. All the while—"

"Your troubles are not my concern."

Frank laughed without humor. "You keep insisting that, and then you inch along. A crime genius, for all I know."

"It's the opposite. From day one—"

"I do get that you're in over your head," he interrupted. "It takes one to know one. All I had to do day in and day out was stare at cell walls and wonder who in God's name set me up. I felt alone. Obsessed. Crazy mad. I never dreamed it was Richard—"

"I will not talk to you about this."

"Don't *play* with me," he growled. "You're working some scheme on the sly. Why else make the rounds at the memorial service?"

"That was a mistake. I was upset."

Frank stood and stretched a kink from his neck, then started pacing like the angry, caged animal he'd become during his prison years. My heart thudded all the harder. A security camera was in plain view, glaring down at us, though it amounted to a worthless piece of hardware if he'd come with a jamming device that could disable it.

"I regret how I came across today," I insisted.

"You're more readable than you know," he said, eyeing me. "Like the way you reacted to the guy I described."

"I told you why it hit a nerve."

"The incident in May. I looked it up online."

It was not lost on me that Frank appeared to be closing the gap between us by pacing sideways, as a determined, hungry wolf might do. So much for my plan of using the bullwhip to maintain a safe distance. I was afraid its lash would swing wildly and go wrong.

"So, you get it now," I managed.

"Fast forward to the shitstorm in the oxen barn. Wrong place, wrong time. Your favorite tune." Frank's gaze was piercing. "What did the guy whisper to you? It's not clear in the video."

"It's a police matter."

"You're not being straight with them, either."

"Stay away. I'll use this whip."

"No, you won't. I see you quaking. The path forward is simple. Quit lying, and tell me what the guy whispered."

"It was garbled nonsense. You're wasting your time."

"My specialized intuition says otherwise," Frank said softly, advancing straight on as I started backing up. "You see, I learned a lot when I was in prison. Made contacts. Picked up some skills—"

Flushed from shock, I stopped and braced myself with the bullwhip in hand, acting on instinct when he quoted what the tattooed attacker had said in my yard. Frank saw my swift change in demeanor and hesitated for a breathless moment, his gaze intense.

"Children, let's not lose our cool," Ed Emery said, emerging from the shadows and motioning for Frank to stay put. "Good thing Nathan hired me to keep an eye out while he's in Boston."

"Get lost," Frank said.

"No can do. I'm on the clock."

"I'm your boss. The money comes from me."

"Well, boss, if you don't get a clue pretty fast here, you're going to get your ass kicked really hard."

"You think you can take me, punk?" Frank said.

"Maybe. But I'm talking about *him*."

Frank and I turned in the direction Ed pointed. Lit from behind by a halogen light with moths swirling in the beam, Dan stood stock still as he stared our way with his palm on the butt of his sidearm. In jeans and a dark shirt, his chest in a ballistic vest, he approached Frank and projected his voice across the arena like an echoing hammer blow.

"I'm State Police." Dan flashed his badge. "Step *back*."

I caved and closed my eyes, unaware that I'd started shaking. My plans to holler at Dan were officially on the scrap heap.

"We were just talking," Frank said calmly.

"She asked you to step away," Dan said. "Time to go."

"I'll escort him to his car," Ed Emery said.

"You do that," Dan growled. Once they were well away, he crossed to me. "Are you ok? It's a miracle I heard your voice—"

"We'll catch up later. Frank will figure out what just happened, so we need to download the footage from the cameras in here." I pointed. "That one's the closest. Call Roy. I'm ready to talk."

Dan closed his eyes. "You stall for days. Now all of a sudden—"

"Frank's wording is proof of what happened to me. A direct quote that Sue and Kate can verify." When Dan didn't budge, I used both hands to bulldoze him toward the office where we could secure the video. "Focus! Chop-chop. It'll all be explained."

"Why not tell me now?"

"It's better to wait," I insisted.

Dan paused to slip the silver frame into an evidence bag he pulled from his tactical belt, assuring me that it would be returned to me in the end, but for now, he felt it best to go by the book.

Fifteen minutes later, I was gripping a travel drive with a copy of the video, in agony over how slowly Dan was driving down a pitted dirt lane. Up ahead was a cottage that belonged to a retired police officer who lived in Florida, but had an open-door policy for associates in law enforcement, especially during the Meeting Fair. Officers and security guards came and went to rest and grab a hot meal in between the long shifts involved with maintaining safety at the eight-day event. In Dan's eyes, it was a better place for me to spend the night than a straw loft.

"There's a reason people upgraded to beds after the Stone Age," he grumbled. "And it's best you're off the grid. Never mind that you told me to get lost. Here I am, come what may, for whatever that's worth."

"Big baby."

"I'm a *what?*"

"Dan, come on," I prompted as he braked for a gully.

"I don't want to destroy my undercarriage," he said crossly.

"I'll jog the rest of the way. I can walk faster than this."

"Stay in the truck. Seatbelt *on*."

"Good, Roy is already here."

Looking rumpled and irritated to be summoned on short notice, Roy squinted against the glare of Dan's headlights as we parked.

"This had better be worth it," he said.

We climbed the front steps and entered the cabin, where I was engulfed by the sweltering heat of a wood-burning stove. Roy and I sat down at the kitchen table, above which a fluorescent fixture from the ancient past beamed illumination to all corners of the room.

"Here." I offered the travel drive. "Cold, hard proof."

Dan tossed aside his ballistic vest and unbuckled his tactical belt, then he crossed to the kitchen counter to make coffee.

"All right," Roy prompted. "It's brave of you, Alison, admitting aspects of your life that you're not proud of."

"Roy, to do this, I need to be in a zone."

"There's no need for zones and embellishments. Just state the facts. Start from ten p.m. Your dog wakes you up."

"Correct."

"Get the hard part over with. You took pills."

I snorted without humor.

"What?" Roy said.

"You just quoted him."

32

Splashing water on my face in the cabin's cramped bathroom helped mask the hushed conversation going on in the kitchen after a group of technicians and officers had arrived in response to some sort of late-breaking development. I'd welcomed the pause, having found it difficult to arrive at the right tone as I'd told my story. My back-and-forth with the attacker had sounded outlandish, even to my own ears. Dan had sat next to me and slipped his hands around mine to offer support. Had he looked anguished because he believed me, or because he didn't?

In the soft lamplight of the bedroom, I pitched myself onto sheets that smelled freshly washed and pulled a pillow over my head. Things had been stable. Now I had the gnawing feelings that were known to silence female victims of crime. Fear of being judged. Shame for letting the attacker take me down so fast. The sense that in the end, it was my fault. Trepidation. Panic and turmoil over my life being out of control.

Breathing into the pillow helped. Exhaustion pulled at me the same way the attacker's drugs had dragged me down. I forced my eyes to stay open a few times, then drifted into a restless doze.

A while later, I was aware of the mattress shifting. Dan slipped the pillow from my face, stretched out beside me on the bed, and pulled me into a bear hug. Savoring the warmth of his presence, his steady heartbeats against my ear, I felt him inhale deeply, slowly. For a moment, his tight, supportive embrace was my entire world. Then reality sank in.

"Where's Roy?" I murmured against his chest.

"He left with the others," Dan said.

"So, they won't even hear me out."

"There's no need, Sonny. We—"

Hearing his voice hit a snag, I pulled away and rested my weight on my elbows. He looked gutted, at a loss for words.

"Tell me," I managed. "I can take it."

"Dorsett had a recording on his phone," Dan said softly. "The techs cracked the passcode this afternoon. We listened to the recording just now. The whole thing. His questions, your responses."

"He *recorded* attacking me?"

"From a point before you even stepped outside. We heard Luke break the door under your porch. Everything."

I stared in shock. I didn't need to prove I wasn't covering up a pill habit? My attacker, himself, had let me off the hook?

"I'm so sorry, Sonny," Dan said. "My gut told me it was off base, you taking pills. I should have connected the dots."

"Tricking us was the point, so—" I closed my eyes. "I don't understand how the recording could be on Jonathan Dorsett's phone. Tonight, Frank repeated what the attacker said, line for line."

"We'll get a solid ID on the voice in the recording," Dan said. "All we know for sure is that Dorsett had possession of the phone when he died. With all the signs of treachery going on, I could see him grabbing Frank's phone to use as leverage. I'm sorry you got cut off from describing what happened. If you want to continue tomorrow—"

"No, it's fine. This is much better."

"He used a chokehold," Dan said with emotion. "It's why you went dark so fast. No fighting, minimal bruising."

"I get the sense that he'd perfected the technique."

"Sonny, if he'd kept the hold for too long—"

"I came through it. Here I am."

Dan attempted to push a few curls from my brow, for all the good it did. They tumbled back to the place they wanted to be.

"I don't get it," he said. "How can you come out of that ok?"

"I was drugged. Even now that I remember the details, it's hazy. And there are issues from my past. You saw it today. How I go blank when the going gets really tough. It's not on purpose."

"I know. You were right that it happens to me, too." Dan's eyebrows twisted in a knot. "The other night …"

"With you? That was the opposite of going blank."

"Same for me." Dan leaned in and kissed me, testing the waters. He smiled when I stayed put. "You came in thinking it was Frank that night behind the mask. What does your gut say now?"

"Tonight, he used the same wording as the masked attacker. Let's say Jonathan did steal his phone. Maybe the fight outside the oxen barn was Frank's attempt to get it back. He lost his nerve and left."

"Let's assume you're right. It's safer that way."

I brushed my fingers over Dan's freshly shaved chin. "How is it that we're on a bed in a man cave, with clean sheets?"

"Good planning. The only surprise was that I didn't need to scoop you up, caveman style. You demanded to come with me."

"I was a little bossy," I admitted. "Your look of outrage at the memorial service is still with me. If you have things to say, go ahead."

"Maybe later."

"I insulted the police. I could tell it stung."

"You were talking about Bricker," Dan said.

I narrowed my eyes. "You're being way too mysterious and calm about this. You're plotting something. I can tell."

"*This* is when you decide to exercise paranoia and caution?" Dan said. "I want to focus on where we are now."

I slowly smiled. "I'm kicking off my shoes."

"It is kind of oppressive in here."

Once our shoes and jeans were on the floor, we faced each other on the pillows. There was a lot to discuss. No need to rush.

"Who is William?" Dan said.

"Right, you'll have heard that in the recording."

I grabbed my pack and pulled out the letter Mrs. Winthrop had written to Frank, and then I wrenched out the yellow book and flipped it open on one of the pillows. Dan mirrored my position, resting his upper weight on his elbows as he read Mrs. Winthrop's letter, and then studied the drawing of the harpooner with the tattoo.

While Dan combed through a succession of footnotes, I revisited my memory of how the attacker had sounded when he'd talked about William coming back from the grave, as if hell-bent on revenge. That pointed to Jonathan. On the other hand, the bitterness I'd heard in the dragon man's voice fit Frank's everyday vibe through and through.

I focused on Dan. "What's caught your eye?"

"If this account is correct, the *Harriett Browne* disappeared six months after Samuel, the original captain, handed control to his son. This footnote says the ship must have wrecked, but it was never found." Dan closed the book and looked at me. "In the oxen barn, Dorsett said, 'Don't let him get her.' You thought he meant Angela Gartland. What if he meant the *Harriett Browne?* Think of the value the ship would hold, either wrecked at the bottom of a bay or hidden in drydock somewhere."

"Plenty of gold has come out of shipwrecks," I agreed.

"Or, say the son balked at the grind of whaling. Instead, he tucked the vessel away to take his time finding where his father stowed any loot. The *Charles W. Morgan* down in Mystic Seaport is from the same period. In a tight family, Frank would know the ship's whereabouts, but his mother's letter indicates dysfunction. Infighting, mistrust. If whoever was guarding the secret ended up dead … it's a thought, anyway."

"Maybe that's why Richard planned a trip to the Cape Verde Islands," I said. "I thought it was because his parents died there."

"For all we know the captain hired cabinetmakers in every port. Which would mean more desks and more loot."

"I love sharing this lead with you directly," I said. "You'll never know how hard it was to keep you in the dark."

"Actually, I do." Dan reached for his phone, opened a folder of photos, and handed me the device. "What do you see?"

I studied the first photo. "A bearded guy with two black eyes."

Dan motioned. "Keep going."

"The same guy holding up his shirt to show bruises and stitches—" I looked up from the phone. "Oh my God … is this *you?*"

"This is where you ask if I took these photos months ago, knowing a day would come when you told me to start sharing details or hit the road," Dan said, looking pleased as he secured his phone and put it aside. "Then I say, 'Now who's the crack detective?'"

"You'll notice I'm not amused," I said.

"My Canadian counterpart, Antoine, got in a jam. It was a risk helping him out, but I couldn't say no." Dan squinted as he replayed events in his head. "Bar fight. Caught the wrong end of a broken bottle." He indicated the new scar I'd seen on his left side. "Car chase, bad guys in pursuit. I'm like, Antoine, step on the gas ..."

"*Then* what?" I demanded.

"It goes wrong, both cars roll a bit," Dan went on. "The airbag is a shock, hence the black eyes. We pry our way out. Shots fired. I dive over the guardrail and tumble down a hill. I can't keep track of Antoine. He's fine, so don't worry. I take shelter in a barn. Post and beam. Beautiful place. If you ever decide to upgrade—"

"*Dan.*"

"Sorry." He spread his hands. "I made it out."

"You talk about *me* taking risks."

"I know. Again, fair is fair."

With a groan, I rolled onto my back and rubbed my face.

"You're describing the worst possible trait for us to share," I said. "I'm not going to let things tumble along to the point where you end up running through a hail of bullets again."

"Pulling away won't prevent that," Dan said, relaxed and self-assured as he snugged me closer. "If you're in trouble, I'm in trouble. We step up communication. That's how we get through this."

"I don't know ..."

Dan cut off my protest with a soulful kiss. I explored his chest, aware of his heartbeats, and his muscles smoothly moving. His hands caressed my back, all the way down to my butt, where he discovered that my undies had shifted, leaving my cheeks mostly bare. With a low growl, he signaled that we might be done talking for a while.

"This is a hub," I murmured. "What if someone stops in?"

"I put the 'Do Not Disturb' sign on the door handle after everybody left," Dan said, pulling my shirt up over my head. Tossing it aside, he unhooked my bra, then he flipped his shirt off. "We need to communicate. This avenue worked pretty well."

"But … oh golly," I breathed, unable to resist the feel of his muscles against my bare skin. This way of resolving any confusion was a relief. No tortured back and forth. Let nakedness do the talking.

With an attentive gaze, Dan smoothed his fingers over my skin, as if to make sure I hadn't sustained any damage in the oxen barn, then he kissed me for a long, dreamy moment, his lips and hands taking me on a steamy, moan-inducing ride. Hungry and euphoric, we took up where we'd left off the other night, more certain and knowing this time, caressing each other and softly moaning amidst the heat of sensory overload.

I'd been hot and worked up, very emotional, and my body took charge. The pleasure was building. My breathing was getting loud.

"You were right," Dan murmured. "I need to say a few things."

"Now …?"

"For instance," he said softly, conducting nonstop caresses as he spoke, "If I lose my mind and storm out, and then come back five minutes later, it's not the end of the world. Understand?"

I shivered from his breath on my neck, the ripple of his voice traveling through my skin. He kissed me, knowing my response was a *yes*.

"I have your attention?" Dan said.

"Not fair … oh my God …"

"You swim with reef sharks and let tarantulas crawl up your arm," he rumbled in my ear, stirring moans and ripples of pleasure every which way. "It doesn't put me off. You run into a hail of bullets. I save your ass. You take risks. Tell fibs. It drives me nuts, but I'm not going anywhere. I'm in for keeps, understand?"

I couldn't answer anymore. Once the embers flame to life, they tend to take over. With a pleased smile, Dan invested himself in kissing me and all kinds of other sexy moves. After the turbulent day, there was bound to be an explosion. Sounds of pleasure ripped through me, and I wasn't the only one making noise. I was loud. He was loud. I pictured people miles away turning and saying, "What the heck was *that*?"

I floated on a cloud of bliss for a while, and then Dan's hand brushing my bangs away signaled that he had more to say.

"I'm sleepy," I protested.

"Sonny, I know the timing sucks, but things are in motion, and my gut says to press on. I'm sorry to bring up old wounds." With a determined expression, he picked up my left hand and selected my pinkie and ring fingers. "Tell me about these. What happened?"

"They got stuck in a desk drawer."

"Slammed in a desk drawer," Dan said. "Arlene is worried, Sonny. That's why she told me. Donald did this to you?"

"I tried to get my bear from his desk," I whispered. "Donald told me not to, knowing I'd disobey. I couldn't sleep without Mr. Bear."

"Jesus, Sonny. The comment I made about your zip code—"

"It's ok. You didn't know."

Dan's eyes glistened with emotion. The poor man should never have come to my house in May. He'd had no idea what he would be up against, and I'd still had a grip on my sense of hope. I'd imagined that if I tried hard enough, I would be able to achieve a normal life.

"Mostly, it was just hollering," I assured him. "Donald was fond of saying I would be the death of him. He died when I was ten. I thought it was my fault. You've seen the bizarre luck I tend to have. It felt like his negative influence stayed on."

"That's called magical thinking," Dan said gently. "It's causing you to make decisions on old, faulty information."

"During rough patches like this week, it feels real," I whispered. "Like Donald is coming at me from the grave."

Dan looked miserable. "Sonny ..."

"Raymond is up there trying to help," I went on. "I think it's why you were on duty when I made the 911 call. But Raymond is new at it, being up there in heaven and working the strings. He's a novice. Donald has been hounding me for decades."

"Look, we're going to pick up Luke. We'll get in my truck and keep driving until you feel safe. I don't care how long it takes."

"It won't work."

"Tell me what to do," Dan said. "I'm lost."

"Everything might be great for days, or months."

I paused, gripped by doubts as I dared to imagine a reprieve from chaos that extended into months. It was better to keep my guard up. To recall how I'd felt when Jonathan Dorsett's weapon was aimed in my face.

"What?" Dan prompted. "What did you leave out?"

"Nothing. It's leftover nerves."

"Arlene said you won't use the panic button I gave you."

"She's right. I'm sorry, I can't use it."

"There are two sides to this, Sonny," Dan said. "Back in May, I almost reached you too late. I have nightmares about it."

"I have nightmares, too. What I remember the most of that scene is you barely escaped getting shot. Please understand."

"Listen to me," Dan said fiercely. "Aaron's death hit me hard. If anything happens to you, exponentially worse. If you're not coming back, I'm not either. We're talking about *total* destruction."

"You're describing how I would feel if you were harmed."

"You will use the panic button. Promise me, right now."

"I can't. It would go wrong."

"Give me a shot," Dan insisted. "I'm a professional. I came through for you in the past. I'll do it again. If you say no, it's an insult."

"It's not an insult. Far from it."

"Promise!"

With gritted teeth and through tears, I turned my face away, hoping he would ratchet down the intensity. He didn't.

"*Sonny.*"

"Ok!" I tearfully hollered. "But if it goes wrong—"

"It won't. Jesus." Spent from the effort to break down my iron wall, Dan rested his head against mine, cursing under his breath.

"This sucks," I said. "Now I'm mad again."

"Tough."

Dan leaned in and kissed me, balancing his fierce effort with the gentle assurance of his lips, conveying how he felt without words—like a dance, steering me, loving me, which made me feel all the more torn. I couldn't put him in harm's way. He'd asked the impossible.

"Sonny," he said. "You've got coping skills beyond belief. You change minds from dark to light. Even bad people. If we combine our skills—" Dan exhaled as he attempted to boil down his message. "Other than asking you to use the panic button, I've come to understand that you don't need to change. I need to get up to speed."

I held my breath. "Say that again …?"

"You don't need to change," Dan said, playing with my curls, and then letting them settle in place. "I need to get up to speed."

No man had ever said this to me. I was amazed at how comfortable I felt lying next to him naked, our legs intertwined and our bodies fitting together as if they'd been made for each other.

"I suppose I could change a little," I said. "Take less risks."

"That would be merciful and awesome," Dan said.

"I'm still annoyed with you."

Dan smiled. "Speaking of annoying, I heard Brumby is spreading the news that he has a shot with you, which is puzzling. I saw him kissing a waitress outside Bev's diner. It looked intense."

"She buckled again after lecturing me?"

"You sound surprised."

"I'm stupefied and flabbergasted," I said, savoring the feel of his bare chest. "But not because of anything outside this cabin."

We finally slept so soundly that at one point, I heard rustling sounds in the other room, and it only stirred a flicker of alarm.

Footfalls approached. "Hey, Dan? Why is there a—holy crap!"

The officer chuckled and uttered commentary as he raided a snack bag in the kitchen, then retreated and left the cabin.

"I pulled the sheet over us," Dan murmured. "Mostly."

"Perfect. My reputation is ruined."

He cracked up. "As if that's possible."

33

All set? Dan texted me at 5:30 a.m.

We'd parted at dawn the previous day, right after I'd announced that I wanted to experience the "fun" of spending a night in one of the straw lofts in the animal barns. Dan had come close to waffling on his promise to let me call my own shots, but with security personnel lined up to keep track of me, he'd finally taken the news in stride.

I saw no advantage in confessing that he'd been right about the reasons people had upgraded to beds after the Stone Age. Straw was a prickly, dusty, unforgiving feature of Nature's plan that crackled with every move. A half-hour into my misguided venture I'd sat up in the darkness, sniffed the air, and wondered out loud, "Did somebody pee up here?"

Check this out, Dan texted.

The photo he sent showed Luke diving to catch a toy, a moment of fun during Dan's effort to assess my mutt's capabilities. The chance to cut loose was as good for Dan as it was for my dog.

Luke is awesome, he added. *Heading home tonight?*

Nope. Cow barn x 2, I texted.

Dawn was a prime time to shoot. I had to be strong.

Dan sent a twisted eyebrow emoji. I sent a smile back.

In the Agricultural Hall, I discovered that Joan had assembled all the people who'd won the prizes for pies, preserves, and other foods.

"You are the best," I enthused.

"And you are in *so* much trouble," Joan said as she hugged me for an extra moment. "We got Sue and Kate to confess."

I hesitated. "By we, you mean …?"

"Arlene did the heavy lifting. We're up to speed on the many, many instances where you left us in the dark this week." With a pointed gaze, Joan added, "You're lucky we love you."

"I'll explain later," I managed. "I promise."

Soon I was busy with the logistics of the indoor shoot. First up was a grandmother who'd won first prize for her blueberry pie. With her cheeks flushed from pride, she bubbled over with stories about pitting her skills against my stepmother, Ella, in the past.

"Ella would have won this prize for sure," Mrs. Maynard said. "How Raymond stayed so fit and trim, I never understood. What a handsome couple they were. I would *never* have imagined—" Mrs. Maynard looked abashed as the subject of my surprise existence came up. "But here we are. It's wonderful that you're keeping his farm."

Joan looked excited as she steered me to the side of the hall where long tables displayed stunning bouquets of flowers, from deeply fluted gladiolas to fragrant roses with marbled, pink petals.

Standing next to a dramatic vase of yellow, eight-inch "Dinnerplate Dahlias," Dan's father beamed and hugged me as I arrived.

"I won the blue ribbon," Norris said. "Can you believe it?"

"No wonder. They're beautiful."

"Dan told me the good news," Norris said. "You talked into the wee hours the other night and got everything sorted out."

"Yes, we … talked and talked."

"No need to take my photo. I don't want to be accused of nepotism."

"Nonsense. Straighten your sweater and stand here."

I assured all the prizewinners that *Coast & Candle* magazine would be in touch if their photos were chosen to appear in an article or an online gallery. Charlotte was noticeably absent from the hall. Her fourth-place pie looked sad and forlorn on a nearby table.

Finally, I photographed Joan with her pickled asparagus, and then her nectarine preserves, both of which had won first prize in their categories.

I took care to light her blonde hair and beautiful face to increase the odds of landing at least one photo of her in the article. As I packed up my gear, Joan fiddled with her phone and then held it out to me.

"Someone wants a word," she said.

"I'm kind of in a hurry …"

"Alison Evelyn Littlefield!" Arlene hollered. "Pick up *right* now!"

I gripped Joan's phone and stared at my best friend glaring back at me from the screen. Tearful and happy, I blew kisses, and then I looped my arm over Joan's shoulder so we could talk as a group.

"What the heck, Sonny?" Arlene said, devolving into tears as well. "I can't believe it. You've *never* shut me out."

"I know. I'm so sorry."

In a quick back-and-forth, I brought them up to speed as they grilled me with questions, and was relieved to hear that they knew how miserable I'd felt over keeping my best allies in the dark. Joan and Arlene grumbled that maybe Sue and Kate had made the right call.

"How are you still standing?" Joan said.

"Being busy has helped. Speaking of which …"

"Not so fast," Arlene said. "Sue and Kate left it to us to convey the latest thinking. I know you've spent the past day thinking Frank is the one behind the dragon mask, but there's wiggle room."

"He used the *exact* same wording," I insisted.

"How many times have you said, 'I guess so?'" Arlene asked.

"A lot. Dan laughs about it."

"Apparently, Frank fell into mental ruts, too," Arlene said. "There's news footage of him saying, 'I learned a lot when I was in prison' when reporters kept asking intrusive questions. If an enemy wanted to implicate him, he'd served up the exact wording to use."

"Don't cut him slack just yet," Joan prompted. "But it's important you know his involvement is less definite than you thought."

I groaned. "No wonder his attorney has left five voicemails."

"It's Frank's fault for confronting you."

Joan needed to head to work, and Arlene became consumed with getting breakfast ready for her toddlers. Once I was alone, I sat in the pavilion with my head in my hands. If Jonathan was the one who'd drugged me, he'd wound me up with hints about Frank. If Frank was the one who'd drugged me, he'd wound me up with hints about Jonathan.

Why fate insisted on dumping major crimes in my path, I couldn't imagine. My powers of reasoning stunk.

My day did not improve when I reached the arena where the Woodsmen's Contest was scheduled to begin at 8:00 a.m.

With a sly grin, Greg McDonnell stepped over to 'welcome' me to the event and deliver the latest round of awful news.

"I wouldn't be you for all the gold in Fort Leavenworth," he said.

"Gold is stored in Fort Knox," I said tiredly.

"Whatever. Kitteridge is a Doberman in a suit. He's mad that you double-crossed him after acting all nice at the memorial service. Says he's fixed on owning your farm in the end. Turn the place into condos and set up a kebab stand out front."

I closed my eyes. "Perfect."

"As in, it'll be curtains for your sheep."

"I understood the reference."

"But hey, that's life. We've got a business agreement." Greg reached out a grubby hand. "Truce for the day, picture-taking wise?"

"That is not a proper sentence."

"You *promised*. A deal's a deal."

"Greg, in what bizarro world would I be inclined to—never mind."

I sighed and shook his hand.

With that, Greg ushered me into the arena like I was a Hollywood agent who'd signed on to make him famous. I fell into my usual rhythm of checking the light and swapping lenses as the events unfolded. More than once I paused and grasped how surreal it was to find myself amidst burly lumberjacks and lumberjills wielding vicious-looking saws and axes. Every blade gleamed, so sharp it could probably sever a Tyrannosaurus Rex in half in the blink of an eye. Now and then I checked faces in the crowd, but saw no sign of Frank, Ed, or anyone else who might be lurking nearby with a nefarious agenda in mind. The impending dark turn of events I'd sensed was taking its time. It was wearing me down. Mostly, the demands of photographing all the fast-moving activity dominated my mind until my phone dinged at three o'clock in the afternoon.

All set? Dan texted.

I sighed and wrote, *Still alive and kicking.*

Let me know if Greg gives you any trouble.

I told you I would, I texted back with a roll of eyes.

When a handsome, witty man with no apparent commitment issues demonstrates added skills and dexterity in bedroom arts, you learn to look past any annoying habits. You make promises that you regret in the following days, and hope to heaven it all works out.

"Miss Littlefield," Keith prompted. "Are you ready?"

"Yeah, throw the ax."

"You're sort of in the line of fire."

"Whatever. Just do it. I'll duck if it goes wrong."

I raised my camera and caught the split second after his throw, his arms extended, and the whirling ax in focus on my left.

"Ok, next," I said tiredly.

A few hours later, the modified chainsaw contest brought me out of my dark inner world for a while. With a high-speed track of nasty teeth and an engine that makes ungodly noise, a regular chainsaw is a tool to be feared. The lethal force of the basic model was not enough for a range of men, from upstanding citizens who worked as firemen to less God-fearing guys like Greg and Keith. No two modifications were the same. Some had "direct fuel injection" stuff going on. Others had newfangled additions. The idea was to cut a fresh log in half with mind-blowing speed. Life continued to jab me with ironic twists: Greg won the modified chainsaw event with a dramatic, heart-stopping flourish.

"Did you get the picture?" he asked.

"Yeah, I'll send it to the magazine."

"Thank you, Sonny!"

"Whatever. Don't kill anyone with that."

"What's that?" he said, deaf from his machine.

"Never mind."

At 7:35 p.m., I retreated through the dark cattle barns on my way to my straw loft of horrors, where I would hopefully pass out from exhaustion. I paused near the stalls to listen for footfalls. Nothing. It was quiet, except for the sound of the cattle rhythmically munching on hay.

Looking behind me as I stepped forward, I felt my right foot connect with a strange, unstable object. There was a familiar whooshing sound as if a long, thin pole were moving fast through the night air, then a rake handle struck my temple hard.

"*Crap*," I said, seeing stars as I clutched the aching spot.

Looking down, I confirmed what had happened *again*.

"All right, that's it."

I retreated through the barns, past Bev's restaurant, and beyond the pavilions. I sighed with irritation when a farmer asked if I was the woman who'd clocked an attacker in the oxen barn the other night. Arriving at my car, I threw my gear into the cargo area.

In the driver's seat, I slammed my door and called Dan.

"What's up?" he said.

"I'm heading home."

"Sonny, we talked about not making sudden changes of plan."

"I'm in my car, and ready to roll."

I told him about the sociopath who was leaving rakes all over the place with the tines facing out so people got whacked in the head.

"Plus, I'm in the straw loft above the Holstein cows last night, and all of a sudden, I smell tinkle. I'm like, 'Who peed up here?' From somewhere in the barn this kid hollers out that his cousin pees there all the time. I had to switch barns and toss my jeans."

"That's awful, Sonny," Dan managed.

It was bad enough that he seemed to be laughing at my misfortune. I heard sniggering and hushed whispers in the background as well.

"Do you have me on *speaker?*" I demanded.

"We're gearing up for a joint venture. I had to multitask. Listen," Dan went on, "I need to let Brumby know there's been a change of plan. I told him to stay with you in the barn."

I gaped. "You asked a womanizer to spend the night with me?"

"I was desperate. He was available to keep an eye out."

"This is sad. A very low point."

"Text me when you get home."

"What are you gearing up for?"

"A stakeout. Don't worry, I'm with friends."

After I hung up, I sat there fuming over the fact that he got to go out and fight crime with geared-up colleagues, and I was where I'd begun: in my car in the dark of night, caught up with my own problems.

I started my car and turned on the headlights, and then I sat there and pictured Richard staggering toward me all over again. The last moments of his life were a tragic waste of his strength and vital energy. I would never forget how he'd collapsed to the road in front of my car. How he'd leaned on the fender, too weak to climb to his feet on his own.

I held my breath, then I opened the door and lurched out.

Kneeling in front of the fender, I squinted against the glare of the headlights and searched for a slip of paper tucked behind the license plate. Nothing. I dashed back and shut off the engine, not wanting car juice to drip on my face, then I pulled a flashlight from my glove compartment, returned to the front hood, and rolled onto my back, searching every nook of the wheel housings and undercarriage for a combination for a safe, or some other object that shouldn't be there.

All I discovered was that the engine and undercarriage were disgusting, coated with a thick layer of filth and road crud.

"Sonny?" Brumby said, his boots thudding toward me across the soft parking area. "What the hell are you doing?"

"Checking to see if I can find a … oh my God, there's feathers and goo under here. Apparently, I hit a bird at some point."

"I'm escorting you home. Dan called me."

"I know, I'm just—" I held my breath as a small object stuck in place for a second, then released. "Brumby! I found something!"

Shining the flashlight on the object, I realized it was a 4" x 2" magnetic holder. It was dirty, but overall had less road crud than the rest of the undercarriage. With a racing heart, I slid open the lid and found a key inside: the kind banks used for safe deposit boxes.

"I think this is it!"

"You realize I have no idea—"

A strange zapping sound accompanied his choked-off question, and then he thudded to the ground next to the front wheel, sprawled on his back and twitching as if having a seizure.

"Brumby?" I prompted.

I yelped as hands grasped my ankles and hauled me from under the fender, then I was looking up at a ghost from beyond the grave: muscled, in black clothes intended for combat, wearing a dragon mask that showed only his eyes. In the split second before he flipped me onto my stomach, I caught sight of a snake tattoo on his forearm.

Impossible! How many dragon men *were* there?

"*Uhh …*"

A bolt of pain struck my shoulder and my eyes crossed with a vision of exploding, careening stars. I convulsed from the power of it, too stunned to unclench and escape, my body quaking from what felt like a thousand hornets drilling into me, straight down to my bones.

Whirling in and out of view, the attacker dumped something into Brumby's mouth, then he snatched the keyholder from my stunned fingers and looped a thick plastic tie around my wrists.

Snap. Zip.

Working fast, he taped my mouth and flipped me over his shoulder, cursing from the effort of running, his shoulder driving into my ribcage with every stride. There was a sharp chirp, a car responding to a remote, then the release of a trunk opening. I was dumped inside, wide-eyed as the man with the snake tattoo looked to his left, then to his right, confirming that nobody else was in the grass parking area.

"*Impossible!*" I hollered through the tape on my mouth.

He leaned toward me. Even before he pulled off his mask, I could tell he was enjoying my confusion: smart, fast, and cold.

"Surprise," Nathan whispered.

He shut the trunk, plunging me into blackness.

34

Tossed around and jolted every time the car hit a pothole, I struggled to break free of the zip tie on my wrists and kicked upward at the trunk lid without a clear sense of the best spot to strike at in the darkness. Every kick resulted in a painful scrape or a new bruise.

"Settle down," Nathan hollered. "You don't want to injure yourself."

"*Mmm*," I screamed through the tape.

"You should have seen your face," he said. "JD had lots of tattoos in his kit. I planned to approach you tonight. Mess with your mind. See how you reacted afterward. Then a miracle happened. You got the brainstorm of the century, and I was there to grab the prize."

I closed my eyes and moaned unhappily.

"Get this. I faked going to Boston and put Ed Emery in charge, half hoping he and Frank would kill each other. Instead, Frank ditches my advice and approaches you. It goes sideways right in front of Ed Emery and your cop friend. The timing is perfect. I can make it look like Frank nabbed you. You're my lucky charm!"

I growled out a shriek at the top of my lungs.

"There's another option," Nathan said. "Which Alison is the real deal? I thought I had you pegged, then you sat next to me and crossed those legs. I wasn't sure you *had* legs, wearing jeans all the time. You'll need to explain yourself so it adds up. Jonathan could tell you weren't the usual target. He was the one who drugged you and mixed you up. I'm not off the charts. I'm not like him. You saw I left your friend alive back there. It's warfare. Only take out the big threats."

I kicked at the trunk lid.

"Hey, stop it, all right? This is an expensive rental."

I aimed for the latch and kicked hard.

"I left the JAG Corps under a slight cloud," Nathan said. "Jonathan helped me cover up a thing or two. Once he left the paramilitary realm, I returned the favor by tossing him freelance investigative work. There's big money in estates. A lot of people think they'll live forever. When they die, there's things you can do to capitalize."

"*Mmm,*" I screamed through the tape.

"Your nickname makes you sound fluffy," Nathan said. "But you have fighting skills. If you're willing, we'd be an unbeatable team. I can picture you crossing those legs while I pick some guy's pocket. I fell for Angela for a while, but she'll bat her eyes at anyone. Now that I have the bank key, there's no need to string along that potential fiasco."

"*Rrrr.*" I kicked the lid with both feet.

"It was Jonathan who got wind of the Winthrop-Gartland feud three or four years ago," Nathan said. "The rumor of big riches hidden away. I was skeptical at first, but was he ever right. It was tough to keep him in line. JD wasn't the brightest bulb when it came to business affairs, and he had a weird thing about Frank from the start. A vendetta, almost. He said the whole Winthrop clan were crooks and cheats."

I closed my eyes in despair, wondering how Nathan would react if I told him his "dim bulb" friend had tricked and used him for years, bent on a personal mission involving an ancestor named William, whose death at sea was looking more and more like a murder.

"Given the feud element, you probably guessed that Richard didn't hire Frank," Nathan said. "I was the one working the strings. I got us all cozy at Beech and Grossman. Gave advice. Made steady progress. Then Jonathan set up Frank so he'd land in prison. I'm like, we need to groom these people, asshole. Our first big argument. I was close to getting the conviction overturned when Frank's mother ended up dead. I was so steamed. I knew it was JD, but he covered his tracks."

I kicked the trunk lid. "*Mmm …*"

"Meanwhile, Richard worms his way into handling Frank's mother's estate. I'm like, are you kidding me? But I don't complain, and guess what? If not for Richard, we'd never have known the desk was the key to the lion's share of riches. Fast forward. I get a breaking news alert that Richard was murdered. I texted JD, and he basically says to me, 'oops.' I didn't know he'd gone totally rogue until you reacted to his description. After all I did for him, looking the other way while he murdered people left and right, he decided to grab the prize for himself."

I struggled to break the wrist tie, to no avail.

"JD had to be taken down," Nathan said. "It took some doing to plant suspicions in his mind. If he escaped my plan, he had to think Frank was the one who attacked him. I drugged JD's food, but the bastard still came at me full tilt outside that oxen barn. He almost got the upper hand."

I gave up kicking, disgusted by his self-involved rant.

"Ok, here we go," Nathan said.

The car slowed to a stop. The tires crunched over gravel, then I heard a garage door opening. After a moment the tires rolled onto a smooth surface. The garage door closed behind the trunk where I was trapped, and then the drone of the engine shut off.

I gathered my legs into a tight coil, ready to deliver a blow. Nathan crossed around to the trunk and knocked a couple of times.

"You know what'll happen if you fight me," he said. "You're either a victim I pin on Frank, or my coworker as we open that bank box."

I waited in silence.

"All right, here we go."

The trunk unlatched, and then the lid slowly lifted. Once the space was wide enough and I saw his shadow looming toward me, I lashed out. With a quick move, he swung his shoulders away, snagged my right ankle with a noose, and pulled hard.

"*Mmm.*" I kicked with the other leg.

He looped the rope around that ankle too.

"Now you're in a pickle," he said. "I learned Jonathan's tricks and trained with another guy. It's why I'm the last one standing."

Nathan flipped me, grabbed the back of my pants, then swung me out and dumped me onto the concrete floor of the garage. Stepping on the rope, he hauled me to my feet by my pants, having tied the ankle loops in such a way that I could walk as he pushed me along. When I kicked out, he pulled on the rope and it tightened. I nearly fell.

"Almost there," he said in my ear. "It's your fault I acted on impulse and grabbed you. Those big puppy eyes—"

"*Nnnn*," I furiously hollered.

Desperate to escape before we reached his notion of "almost there," I ducked forward and pitched him to one side. Our struggle was loud in the dark room, my feet milling too fast for him to grab. With a curse, he rolled and secured the rope, regaining control of my legs.

"See, fighting skills," he managed. "Luckily, I'm into it."

Eyes wide, I was hauled past the floor-to-ceiling bookshelves in Ken Babik's well-appointed rooms. Arriving at a rough wooden door at the end of a hallway, I braced one foot against the frame. Nathan used the awkward angle to shove me into a dark, musty basement.

"*Shit*," he hollered as I started tumbling down the stairs.

The rope jerked me to a halt, and then he fed out slack, which had me bumping down at a painful, but steady pace. At the bottom, chill air and dank smells and the feel of cold dirt consumed me.

"You haven't done yourself any favors," he said, twelve steps above me. "Thanks to you, I need to take a shower."

"*Mmm*."

"Sorry, babe, I'm late for a meeting."

He slammed the cellar door, plunging me into darkness.

I closed my eyes and hoped Brumby was receiving medical aid at the fairgrounds. Dan would be waiting for my text saying I'd arrived home, no idea how easily I could be separated from the panic button he'd begged me to use. It was in my car, out of my reach.

Above me, Nathan splashed in the shower, whistling.

I couldn't recall a time when I'd felt so stupid and ashamed. If only I'd had the sense to not attend the memorial service. Every second of tonight's horror show was my fault. But I'd promised Dan that I would never give in to the agents of hell. I had to free myself.

After my eyes adjusted to the darkness, I saw objects gleaming in the faint light coming in through a small ground-level window. It took less than a minute to find a box cutter. I freed my hands and pulled the tape from my mouth, then I cut the rope in multiple places so Nathan couldn't use it to bind me if he got the upper hand again.

Brushing the damp basement dirt from my pants, I paused, feeling a hard object in my front pocket. My heart raced as I pulled it out and crossed to the window to verify that it was an extra panic button Dan had slipped into my jeans. I don't know why I was surprised. The button shone green in my hand. I hesitated, wanting to press it. And then resisting. What if Dan rushed to the house and things went wrong?

He'd been gearing up for a stakeout when I'd called. My heart raced all over again as I wondered if his team was outside already. My presence in the house would change their approach.

Upstairs, Nathan was taking his time in the shower.

I closed my eyes, and then I followed through on my promise, turning the upper disk of the button in the direction two arrows pointed. There was a click. I pressed the button hard.

The light within the device turned red.

I was surprised to feel elated. If I was wrong and Dan's team wasn't outside, a SWAT response would soon be in motion. I needed options, a way to free myself on my own if all else failed. The window was just big enough for me to fit through. I pulled a wooden stepstool to the ancient fieldstone wall and tested it to be sure it would hold my weight. Wobbling slightly, I gripped the window latch and tried to loosen it.

Just then, the door in the room above me opened with a whine of hinges. I held my breath as the floor creaked under a footstep.

My heart thudded so hard I felt it in my ears. Nathan had finished his shower. I heard wire hangers sliding along a closet pole, then muffled sounds. He was putting on a change of clothes. If I called out, he would stop and listen. He would know someone had arrived.

Casting about, I rejected multiple objects to employ as a weapon if the need arose. Not a hatchet or a hammer. Too apt to be used against me. Finally, I found an old rake handle without the row of metal teeth attached. My nemesis would now come to my aid.

I crossed to the bottom of the stairs.

The newcomer shifted, causing a board to creak. Footfalls thundered from the direction of the bedroom and then the room above me exploded with noise. Furniture was knocked around. I heard two men cursing as they hit the floorboards so hard dust rained down into my eyes. I gripped the pole, rendered mute by indecision.

I jerked as a gun went off. A body slumped to one side.

"Dan?" I called out, then louder, "Answer me!"

Greeted by appalling silence, I tumbled up the stairs and savagely attacked the door with the pole. I slipped and lost my footing.

"Answer me!" I shrieked. "What *happened?*"

I hammered the door, focusing on the old knob. It broke, but there was a latch holding it shut from the other side. Crying and hollering curses, I applied my shoulder to the door, using the pole to help me gain leverage. All of a sudden, the door gave way and I tumbled into the hallway, breathless, trembling, tears streaming down my face.

A man loomed above me. It was Keith McDonnell.

"What's happening?" I managed. "Where is Nathan?"

"He's dead. I'm sorry."

Crawling forward toward a huddled shape on the floor, I was shaking so hard I didn't think I had the strength to stand and walk. I reached Nathan and confirmed that his eyes were staring upward into the dark room with a permanently shocked expression.

"Oh my God," I breathed. "I can't believe it."

"I'm in so much trouble," Keith said.

However much I wanted to continue crawling until I reached the door, I saw that Nathan had left his dirty clothes in a pile nearby. With shaking hands, I searched through his black pants until I found the vital piece of evidence Richard had put under my car. I tucked the key holder into the same pocket where I'd put the activated panic button.

"Miss Littlefield?" Keith said. "What do I do now?"

"Help me up. It's all right."

Pulled to my feet by his big hands, I gripped his arms with gratitude. "You're a hero, Keith. How did you know I was here?"

"I saw him drive in. I heard you kind of screaming."

"The police will be here shortly."

"What?" he said, looking alarmed.

"It's fine. You saved me."

"We need to leave."

"Keith, there's nothing to worry about." I pointed around the room at a few glowing lights. "I think those are security cameras. If so, there will be a record of you coming in and—"

I yelped as Keith gripped my arms and secured my wrists with a zip tie. He ushered me forward, weeping and cursing under his breath.

"What are you doing?" I demanded.

"Following orders. Sort of."

"Whose orders?"

As big as a linebacker, he propelled me forward. I tripped and stumbled, my legs windmilling in space as I was lifted through the front doorway and then clumsily put on the ground again.

"Is it Greg?" I demanded. "Ed? Frank? Who *is* it?"

Keith stopped behind a car, swung open the trunk, and pushed me inside amongst filthy rags and chainsaw parts that smelled of gasoline and oil. I gasped in the darkness, unable to fathom how I could have won freedom, only to end up in another trunk.

"Keith!" I shrieked. "Listen to me!"

"I'm sorry, Miss Littlefield. I really am."

He gripped my head and taped my mouth shut. It was soft painter's tape, easier on my skin than the duct tape Nathan had used.

We jolted down the road at top speed.

35

Winded from hollering, I groaned as Keith hauled me out of the trunk like a sack of potatoes. Landing in yet another garage, I saw labels on shelving that told me he'd brought me to Richard Gartland's house, where the entire nightmare had begun. Keith flipped me over his shoulder, then assaulted my ribcage with every stride. The world brightened as we entered the home. We passed modern furniture arranged on polished maple floors, fancy floor lamps, and display cases of antiques. As Keith paused, out of breath, I saw a woman's shapely legs curving down to feet that were ensconced in high-heeled pumps.

"What the hell, Keith?" Angela Gartland demanded.

"I had no choice."

"Have you seen Nathan?"

"Well—"

I kicked and struggled to keep Keith from blurting a truth that most likely would not help matters. Not for him. Not for me. I had a feeling Angela would not react well to Nathan's death. Emotion might blast the situation into an even worse danger zone. My struggling kept Keith occupied. Containing my legs with one arm, he tipped forward and dumped me onto a softly cushioned beige leather couch.

I blinked against the bright light. Frank was standing nearby, looking shocked as he gazed at my bound wrists and taped mouth.

"Keith, have you lost your mind?" Frank demanded.

Angela motioned for him to stay calm. "He probably caught Sonny snooping around," she said pointedly to Keith, mirroring my air of wanting to control the situation. "You've told me yourself that she can't be trusted. Let's keep her in restraints until Nathan gets here."

"I repeat, have you lost your mind?" Frank hollered. "Nothing justifies kidnapping. Nathan will lead the charge on that point."

"Where is Nathan?" Angela demanded.

As Keith opened his mouth, I kicked the back of his thighs to get his attention. When he turned toward me, I shook my head with wide eyes to reinforce the message that he should not tell her that he'd killed Nathan. Keith frowned for a long moment, then he started to speak.

I kicked him again and shook my head.

I couldn't articulate words through the tape, but I needed to control what happened next. I had a range of possible treasures to toss out in hopes of gaining leverage. Angela struck me as simplistic, her grasp of the stakes uninformed, so I started with the obvious.

"Jewels!" I hollered through the tape.

"Did she say jewels?"

I nodded vigorously.

"Take off the tape," Angela said.

Keith obeyed. The painter's tape came off easily, without ripping my skin. I closed my eyes and attempted to catch my breath.

"Well?" Angela demanded. "Where are they?"

"Can't ... I have bad circulation ... the bindings ..."

"*Where* did Richard put the diamonds?"

"The bindings ... too tight ..."

I feigned passing out and forced myself to not flinch when she tapped my face. She roughly shook my shoulder. I was a rag doll.

"Just undo the bindings," Frank hollered.

"She can't be trusted," Angela said.

The staccato rhythm of her high heels crossing the room ended with the sound of a cabinet door banging open. Her footfalls returned.

"Jesus," Frank hollered. "A weapon, Angela?"

"My husband was murdered. What if she did it?"

"This is a nightmare," Frank said. "I'll land in prison again."

"I'll make sure that doesn't happen," Angela said. "We're a team now. A united front. Keith, take the bindings off."

"Are you sure?" he said. "She's really feisty."

"Just *do* it, would you please?" Angela said.

Soon my wrists were free. I continued pretending I was passed out, not just to buy a few minutes to formulate a plan, but also in the hope of selling the idea that I was too slow and injured to be considered a threat. It was true. After days of attacks, my entire body ached.

"Miss Littlefield?" Keith's sour nervous breath washed over me as he leaned closer, took my hand in his big paw, and rubbed it vigorously. "Miss Littlefield? Come on, now. Wake up."

My eyes fluttered. "Where ...?"

"You're here with us," he said brightly. "Are you ok?"

"My medication ..."

"You didn't have any on you."

"I'm really dizzy. Help me up ..." As he leaned down to slip his arm under my shoulders, I gripped his collar and furiously whispered in his ear, "You killed Nathan and kidnapped me. You need to trust me, or Richard's death will be blamed on you as well."

"What?" Keith said.

"Don't say *anything*," I hissed.

"What is she whispering?" Angela demanded.

"I'm thanking him for helping me up," I managed, rubbing my brow and squinting at her. "You know Nathan is helping me as well. Is it true you two are involved? If that's the case—"

"Shut up or I'll put the tape back on." Angela leveled the weapon at me, hopefully with the safety still on. "You've been lying from the start. Richard told you where he hid the diamonds."

Winded, trembling I stared at the weapon's ghastly opening.

"That's not true," I managed. "What little I know ... it wasn't until today that ... umm, Ed Emery filled me in."

"That jerk private investigator?"

"Yes. He's ... he's blackmailing me," I desperately lied.

"*Enough* with waving the weapon around," Frank hollered. "Is she right, Angela? You and Nathan are involved?"

"Of course not. She's lying."

"I want to look Nathan in the eye and ask," Frank growled. "He's an hour late. Does anybody know where he is?"

"Nathan is not coming," Keith moaned. "He's—"

"He's probably dealing with Ed!" I hollered. "It's why I'm ... Richard warned me about Ed. He's a lying, conniving—"

"I *knew* it," Angela seethed. "What did Richard say?"

I shut my eyes. "I can't focus with that pointed at me."

"Angela, put the gun down," Frank ordered. "You can see she's not a threat. Let's talk about why you look devious right now."

"*Devious*? I'm trying to protect us."

Worried by the misery on Keith's face, I touched his arm. "Let me lean on you. I need to move around, or I'll pass out."

"Sure, I guess."

With him shepherding me in a circle, I hissed another warning for him to keep quiet, and then I peeled away from him.

"Thank you, Keith. I'm all set now."

"This is an act," Angela said.

"For once, I think we can take Sonny at her word," Frank said. "She was attacked the other night, now Keith took her by force and brought her in like a sack. I'm surprised she's still standing."

"Plus, you know I landed in the ER," I agreed, trembling. "They put me on medication. I have side effects, memory loss—"

I paused and nearly dropped to the floor from the shock of knowing I'd just blurted a story that Frank might not buy if he'd been the attacker behind the dragon mask. Then I remembered Nathan confirming that Jonathan was the one who'd drugged and questioned me.

"It's out of control," I said tearfully. "It's too much."

"Angela, give her some space," Frank said. "It's high time somebody called Nathan. In the meantime, stay calm."

As he stepped away with his phone in hand, Angela didn't look calm. Keith didn't look calm. I was the opposite of calm. Shaking, hopeless, confused. Unable to recall details I might be able to use.

Panic-stricken, no idea how to escape the nightmare, I froze as a flick of movement outside the floor-to-ceiling windows drew my gaze to a figure crouching behind a large urn on the dimly lit patio. My eyes widened as Dan leaned into the light a fraction and held my gaze. He was in camouflage and a ballistic vest and did not look happy to see me there.

I burst into tears, sobbing, desperate to run to him.

He'd shown up too late. I'd escaped the basement and landed in worse trouble. Dan needed to turn away. Spare himself from the trauma of seeing me gunned down. He would never recover from it.

Behind me, a miracle was unfolding. Frank was hollering questions at Angela again, having not reached Nathan, and Keith had joined me in crying. I had a few seconds to regroup.

Dan signaled to me in ASL. *Stay calm. Focus.*

I nodded and wiped my tears.

Weapons? he signaled.

I nodded, and said, "Two."

His face exploded with shock as I spoke out loud.

Careful, he signaled.

I turned away from the window, desperate to not give his presence away. Thinking, thinking. With Keith holding one weapon, and Angela in possession of another, there would be no safe way for Dan or anyone else to storm the house. I needed a plan.

I turned to Dan and signaled, *Best exit?*

He signaled, *North.*

In exasperation, I flipped my hands. How was I supposed to know north from south?

Dan hitched his thumb over his shoulder.

"Hey, what are you doing?" Angela demanded, stepping closer.

"It's the medication they gave me in the ER," I said. "You can't believe what I've been through. My hands … they shake a lot."

"She was looking out the window," Keith said.

"Yes, I was checking the yard," I said. "Because I'm clearly the only one who is wondering if that two-timing, lying investigator Ed Emery is out there, ready to ambush us. For all we know, he's the one who killed Richard, and … his next target would be Nathan."

Angela blanched. "No way. Oh my God."

"And *there* it is," Frank said. "You two are involved."

"Nathan is our attorney. That's why I'm upset."

"This is not the time for arguing," I said. "If I'm right, we need to be smart. Keith, you should head out and check the yard."

"She's right," Angela said. "I never understood why Richard hired that jerk. I bet he's been pulling the strings all week."

"Wait!" I hollered. "Keith, don't hold your gun out, for heaven's sake! Eject the magazine and empty the chamber."

"But then it won't work."

"Do you want to accidentally shoot Nathan?"

"I'll be careful."

"You are the opposite of careful," Angela said. "Do it. Empty the gun, and don't break anything on your way out."

Sweating, afraid the tide would turn against me any moment, I made sure Keith rendered the weapon inoperable.

"Tuck the gun in the back of your waistband," I said. "That way, if you startle Nathan on his way in, he won't be confused and shoot you."

Keith groaned unhappily. "But Nathan is—"

"Keith, you need to trust me!" I hollered.

"Just do it," Angela prompted him.

"And go that way," I said loudly, pointing in the direction Dan had indicated. "To avoid confusion, keep your hands visible at all times." I held mine straight out so he understood what I wanted. "Crouch. Walk slowly. Pause a lot. I'll bet you're strong enough to sustain a stun gun jolt without going down! So be careful! Really careful!"

"Why are you yelling?" Angela demanded.

"How many times do I have to say I'm on medication? The ringing in my ears is horrible. I'm sorry if I'm loud."

"Keith," she said. "Get going."

"Can I have some water?" I said. "I'm feeling ill."

"I'll get some," Frank said.

I closed my eyes. My mouth truly was parched and my heart was thudding unevenly, as if on the verge of giving out.

When Frank returned and handed me the glass of water, I couldn't grip it. With a look of sympathy, he cupped my fingers against the glass, his hands warm and human, his gaze searching and concerned.

I was stunned. Frank was a flawed man. Bitter and prone to losing his head from pent-up frustration, but in that moment I felt I was glimpsing who'd he'd been before his life was upended by Jonathan. My whole sense of him reversed. Frank wasn't capable of murder.

"Where is Nathan?" Angela demanded. "This is a nightmare."

As Frank inhaled to respond, I held his gaze and conveyed the desperate message that he needed to stop feeling jilted and wounded and read the freaking room. Angela was back to pacing with the weapon in hand. Frank was not the right person to reason with her.

It had to be me.

Just then, Angela wheeled toward the window as grunts and struggling sounds erupted outside. Dan had pulled back into the shadows.

"What was that?" she said.

"I bet it's raccoons!" I said loudly to cover the tumult of Keith being taken down in the yard. "They're active this time of year."

"It sounded like Keith yelping."

"I bet he tripped over something," I said. "He is the clumsiest man I've ever met. At the fairgrounds today—"

"Shut *up*," Angela said. "Frank, go check on Keith."

Frank stared at me, looking conflicted.

"Check on Keith," I said pointedly. "Show some sense, like you did when my friend showed up. You remember *Dan?*"

Grasping what I was trying to convey, that I'd managed to summon specialized backup to the Gartland residence, the misguided, unlucky ex-con looked doomed and pessimistic about not landing in prison again, but he nodded, braced himself, and headed down the hallway.

I froze as Angela stepped to the window to watch him exit, but once again Dan stayed in the shadows out of view.

"All right," I said, switching gears on the fly. "We don't have much time. I hate to break it to you, but Nathan is dead."

Angela stared at me. "*What?* You're lying."

"I'm not lying. He brought me to Ken Babik's house ten minutes away and threw me into a basement. He said he planned to pin everything on Frank. You as well, maybe. I know it's hard, but—"

"You're making this up."

"Nathan had clothes at Ken's house," I desperately went on. "Like he's been living there … Angela, stop waving the gun around," I said, guessing that her erratic behavior would factor into the decision to hold back or storm the house. "You're safe now. The threats are gone."

Instead of calming down, she rushed to the window and hit a control panel, sending the motorized blind into motion.

"No … *no*," I hollered, as the view of the night disappeared, foot by foot. "You can't do that! Hit the stop control!"

"What if Richard's PI is out there?" Angela said.

"It was a fleeting worry. I doubt he's involved."

"For the last time, shut *up*. I need to think."

Once the blind stopped unfurling, I rested my hands against the gray folds, plunged into despair. Now what? I'd depended on having back-and-forth visual access with Dan. When I turned to Angela, her weapon was trained on me, her hands trembling, and her grip was entirely wrong. Nobody had shown her the proper technique.

"You're being very reckless with that weapon," I said loudly. "There's no need for it. We're alone. We're fellow victims—"

"We are totally Richard's victims. This is all his fault."

"Please, Angela—"

"He stood right where you are now and told me it was over," she tearfully seethed. "He knew I was seeing Nathan. Waved a plane ticket in my face. Talked about leaving me with nothing. Insufferably calm. Then he headed for the door. He walked *out* on me."

I hovered, vibrating. "This was … the other night?"

"He'd been weird for weeks, but didn't bother to give me the slightest heads-up on his plans. So, I got out one of his guns and went after him," Angela said, shaking with a look of rage in her eyes. "He'd reached his car. I shot him. He tried to run. So, I shot him again."

"Good God," I whispered.

"Don't stand there looking shocked," she said. "I heard about your break-up with that cop. I bet you wanted him dead."

"Never," I tearfully managed.

I'd been gripped by the opposite frame of mind.

"All of a sudden this commando guy rushed in," she said. "He taped my mouth. Bound my hands. He questioned Richard. Hit him. Cut him. But Richard was too far gone. That's what we assumed," she added, wide-eyed as she recalled that part of the horrific night. "The guy dragged me into the house. Made me open the safe, but it was empty. The guy was like, 'we're partners in crime, now.' He barked orders. Made me change and wash my hands to get rid of the gunshot stuff. He took the weapon. He *blackmailed* me. I couldn't even tell Nathan. You can't imagine what that guy put me through. I don't even know his name."

"His name was Jonathan," I said. "Jonathan Dorsett."

I chided myself for drawing her attention back to me. Angela's gaze went from rattled to cunning in seconds flat.

"Keith brought you here tonight," she said. "He killed Nathan, am I right? You were afraid to admit it in front of him."

"Keith did kill Nathan," I said.

"Perfect. We can pin everything on him. Nobody will doubt it. He's a lowlife. A pothead. That leaves you and me to cut a deal. I'll make it worth your while. So, where are the gems?"

"They're, umm, here in the house. Richard told me before he died."

"Just show me," she said with a wild light in her eyes.

I assessed the furniture in the room, committing to a plan of action on the fly. My gaze landed on a cabinet and hutch.

"There." I pointed. "Richard talked about a secret safe on the *east* side of this room," I said loudly for the benefit of the police in the yard. "Along the wall. He mentioned a cabinet."

"Impossible. I looked through it."

"Did you look behind it?" I said.

"Of course not. It's fixed to the wall."

"No, it's not. There's a trick latch."

"Get to it," she hollered. "Show me how it works."

Angela looked on as I gripped the cabinet with both hands. I gritted my teeth and pretended to growl in frustration.

"It's too heavy," I said. "And I just remembered, there are two latches, one on each side. Grab the other end. Find the latch."

"Talk about a nightmare." With the gun aimed my way, she ran her hand along the left side of the hutch. "There's nothing here."

"It's subtle. A small lever, and you're using only one hand." Abruptly, I let go of my end. "Let me go get Frank—"

"*No.* He'll say the gems belong to him."

"He loves you. I'm sure he'll be happy to share."

"No more men, all right? I'm sick of all of them. Now get moving before they come back, or I swear to God—"

"I'll try again, but I need your help."

Finally, Angela put the gun down, but very close to her hand.

"You're sure there's a lever back here?" she demanded.

"I found the one on this side. Keep checking."

I gripped the cabinet with my free hand close to a bowl that looked to be made out of marble, or some other stone.

"Any time now!" I hollered. "I'm fading fast!"

"I can't find the latch," Angela said.

"I found it!" I hollered, trying to mask any entrances going on behind me. "For Pete's sake, focus! Any time now!"

"Police!" multiple voices shouted behind us. "Show your hands!"

With a curse, Angela reached for the gun a split second after I grabbed the bowl and swung it down on her manicured fingers.

"*Ahh,*" she shrieked. "Horrible bitch!"

I grabbed the weapon and ejected the magazine with shaking hands and then I set it down. If I had a sledgehammer, I would pulverize the gun into oblivion. Render it inoperable for all time to come.

"You broke my fingers," Angela wailed.

"How do you think it felt to be shot in the back?" I hollered, stepping forward to vent my anger. "That's what you did to Richard, the man you were supposed to love. What is *wrong* with you?"

"Easy," Dan said, pulling me away. "Let them finish putting her in cuffs. Come on. You did great. You're all right."

Trembling, I allowed myself to be turned around.

I looked up at Dan's face. His brown eyes assessed my scraped chin and bruised forehead with a look of dismay. My eyes brimmed.

"Nathan is dead," I whispered.

"I know."

"He used a stun gun. He … he locked me in Ken's basement."

"Sonny …"

"You made me use the panic button. *Never* again. I heard someone come in. I thought it was you. Then a gun went off."

"It's ok. We're both safe."

Trembling, I sank against Dan's chest. He gathered me in his arms and gripped me tightly. In my mind's eye the night rocketed through my head all over again. This time I allowed myself to feel the terror. To grasp how close I'd come to meeting Raymond face to face, but only as a ghost. All the while Dan whispered assurances that everything was ok. I'd shown my strength. My grit. My speed. I'd made it out alive.

Again.

* * *

There was a flurry of explanations around the delay in getting to the scene. Ed Emery was to blame. Nathan had fed him bogus information on Frank. The stakeout Dan had mentioned earlier in the evening had unfolded at the wrong location. I nodded when Detective Allen paused, dimly aware it would be helpful information once I recovered from shock.

Roy studied me. "Ok, step by step—"

"Did you find Brumby?" I said. "Is he ok?"

"He's fine. Focus on your account."

"I want to go home," I said, staring at the scene of officers without really seeing them. "I can't do this. I want to go home."

"Take a breath, and tell us what happened," Detective Allen said.

How was this possible, when the night had compressed into a jarring, confusing nightmare? I curled inward and shut my eyes.

"Roy," Dan prompted. "We can't do this now."

"She refused a trip to the ER."

"Because that's a worse option," Dan said.

They stepped away, arguing, leaving me sitting in a folding chair in the darkness. Nearby, the EMTs were assessing Angela's hand. I'd broken her manicured nails, but her fingers were only bruised. You'd think I'd severed them, the way she kept hollering.

My gaze landed on an arresting sight beyond the flashing blue lights and moving figures: an opening of broken stalks cutting through the cornfield. Richard had made that path on the night of his death.

I hesitated, and then I left the lights behind me, staggering forward as he had done. I'd had no role at his memorial service. No stories to tell about what kind of man he'd been. Selfish and misguided? Honorable in the end? Somewhere in between? All I cared about was that he'd spent his last breaths on a mission that led through the cornfield up to the road. He'd reached out to me for help. I'd failed him. Until now.

I reached out and pushed past the first stalks with both hands. They rustled with ghostly noise, bending as I walked through them, then springing back upright behind me.

"Sonny!"

Catching up with me, Dan tried to grasp my shoulders. I pushed him away, crying, desperate to escape the horror of telling him what I'd gone through. He spoke softly into his radio. There was a reply in police code. Dan shut off his mic and continued walking behind me, probably scared out of his mind. What was I doing, stepping away from the crime scene through the cornfield? Had I lost my mind?

Yes.

Nearing the road, I saw headlights approaching.

It was *me*. That's what Richard had seen.

I reached toward the car, just as Richard had done.

It slowed to a stop, cold and unhelpful, expelling exhaust, and casting twin beams of painfully bright light into my face.

I pictured Richard's spirit hovering there, watching, waiting, hoping, agonizing. Hollering at me, desperate to be heard.

"I'm sorry," I sobbed, staggering forward. "I didn't know you'd been wounded. It was shocking, seeing you yelling. You were desperate, but you looked scary. I'm so sorry. I was afraid of you."

"Sonny, please …"

I pushed Dan's hands away.

It was not my car, I realized. It was a police car.

I staggered forward and dropped to my knees, gripping the fender. Richard hadn't merely tried to stand, as I'd assumed on that awful night. He'd hidden a treasure under my car. A bank box key that he didn't want his unfaithful wife and her malevolent lover to get.

"Sonny …"

"This is what Richard did," I whispered. "I figured it out."

Swaying, kneeling on the pavement, I reached into my pocket, pulled out the keyholder, and pressed it into Dan's hand.

Finally, I'd helped Richard complete his mission.

"Sonny …"

"Richard hid it under my car," I said. "The missing piece. I found it tonight. Brumby was there. I felt a lightning bolt on my shoulder, and then I saw … it was *him*. I saw a *ghost* …"

"Sonny." Dan hugged me tightly, shaking the same way I was shaking, and needing to know I'd come out of it alive.

"That's my statement," I whispered. "I'm not saying more."

"You don't need to. Not for now."

"Not ever …"

I closed my eyes.

Not ever.

36

Check your email, Carl Woodlee texted.

I'd discovered it was pointless to insist that he and Frank not involve me in their efforts to learn the fate of the *Harriett Browne*. I'd clicked on their first salvo of maps, letters, riddles, and property deeds, revealing that my protests were false. I was my father's daughter through and through when it came to maps, especially ancient maps with cryptic markings and exotic ports of call. It was impossible not to become obsessed.

No time now, I texted him. *But do you know if there was an actual person named Harriett Browne? A family friend or maybe a mistress?*

Dots appeared, and then Carl texted, *We'll look into it*.

"You're out of control," I told myself, hoping to heaven they were abiding by their vow to keep the search a secret, lest they spark another murder spree over the potentially landmark find. Jonathan Dorsett's relatives were filing lawsuits claiming rights to a portion of the treasure that had come out of Richard's bank box; Jonathan had left behind compelling evidence that Captain Winthrop had murdered William.

I returned to the task of preparing myself for attending the "Fall Fest" underway at the local Grange Hall, my first public appearance since I'd crawled out of the latest ordeal. Dan had assured me it would go well, likening this method of rejoining the world to, "grazing the atmosphere." After a quick visit, he would craft a smooth exit and bring me to the coast for our long-overdue dinner date. I'd planned to look resilient, strong, and comprehensively clothed for comfort, but Nadine had urged me to make an effort. She'd left a box with a pink bow on my bed.

Braced for an over-the-top option, I relaxed when I opened the box and pulled out a charcoal dress with a matching jacket: a workhorse sort of outfit that would serve me well in the Grange Hall. Without the jacket, bathed in the flickering warmth of a romantic fireplace, it would morph into a sexy number once we arrived at the restaurant.

I pulled out another item Nadine had tucked into the box: a flimsy assemblage of black silk and lacy cups that would help sculpt me into the proper form underneath the clingy dress.

"It *can't* be the right size," I said.

In the back of my mind, Nadine told me to quit the nonsense.

Hoping for the best, I started shimmying my way into the slip, pulling it over my head and unrolling the fabric downward until the hem reached my thighs. I gave a little shake, and voila, I had an hourglass figure, with my peaches transformed into cantaloupes.

"Nadine, you're a genius," I said.

I applied mascara, then with a scrunchie and a few pins, I arranged my waves and curls — neat and contained, yet with an air of abandon, though I felt the opposite of carefree as my sheep demanded apples with a grating din that I didn't want my handsome date to overhear.

Crossing to the window to tell them to pipe down, I gripped the sill, confused to see one of the youngsters chasing Gracie. It was odd, how the lamb was behaving, almost as if it were …

"Pinkie!" I shouted.

Mr. Lurman had warned me that it wasn't a good idea to keep a young, unneutered ram. I should have listened. I ran down the stairs, pulled on my Wellies, hiked up the slip, and then dashed down the porch steps with the loose boots slapping against my calves.

I grabbed a halter from the gate on my way into the pasture. Pinkie darted away with cunning moves, then swerved back to Gracie. I used the halter like a lasso to snag his head. Once I brought his eighty pounds to a halt, I was able to slip the nose band into place.

"Shame on you," I hollered, backing through the gate with him in tow. "Some of these girls are your aunts and cousins."

Pinkie fought against the rope all the way to Bubbah's pen.

"I am not in the mood for any nonsense," I growled at the old ram as I shoved Pinkie inside. "No more escaping."

Bubbah paid no attention to me. His gaze was trained on the driveway.

"*Bluuuh,*" he hollered.

Panting, with my pulse pounding through my limbs, I knew with blazing certainty that Dan had arrived. I turned, and there he was standing next to my porch steps in a dark blazer and a classy tie, doing his utmost to act as if he'd just witnessed a normal event. When I just stood there, breathing and staring, he slipped off his jacket on his way over and draped the contained warmth of it around my shoulders.

"I guess our heart-to-heart talk will have to happen now," I said. "I'm glad you get along with Arlene. It's thanks to you they drove straight here to comfort me that night, but I overheard some things."

"Come on," Dan said. "Let's get inside."

"Denial doesn't work with me," I continued, dimly aware that we'd reached the kitchen, where Dan was lifting my legs and removing my boots with his warm hands. "It's time to face the truth."

"Sonny ..."

"Admit it. You've pulled back."

"You were traumatized. The counselor said—"

"I predicted it from the start," I reminded him. "Our slim chances of making it work. We've been together in person a few dozen times, at most. Two of those instances involved a SWAT response—"

"*Sonny,*" Dan interrupted. "Arlene found the Wolf."

I paused. "What ...?"

"Come on."

Dan led me down the hallway to my father's forest green room. Next to the bed, he knelt and flipped the braided rug away to reveal a large knot in one of the Pumpkin Pine floorboards. As I slowly knelt and focused on it, the knot became a canine face, wrought by the mysteries of a living tree reacting to one element or another long ago.

"When Arlene and Lance brought in their luggage, this rug got displaced," Dan said. "She saw the knot right away."

I touched the long snout reminiscent of Luke's nose, and the two dark swirls that appeared to be looking back at me.

"I wanted to delay telling you," Dan said. "Arlene insisted you needed to find it on your own. *That* was the intense conversation you overheard. I planned to drop hints. Nudge you in this direction."

"The board lifts?" I said.

Dan nodded. "Based on the wear along the edges."

"I want to wait. I need to prepare myself."

"Of course," Dan said.

I trailed out of my father's room, headed for the couch, and sat down to assess how I felt. Luke was sleeping nonstop after days of playtime with Arlene's children. He lifted his head to see if anything of interest was going on, then he stretched out again and resumed snoring.

Dan stepped around the coffee table, scooped me up, and then with a deft turn, he settled onto the couch with me draped across his lap. Once again, his jacket was applied over my shoulders for warmth.

"I suppose the panic button did work," I said.

"I told you it would. Here we are, safe and sound."

"Tell my mind that in the dark of night."

"Same here." Dan's muscles flexed as he held me close. "This is how we handle it. Holding each other. Letting it sink in."

"Just so you know, my bruises are healed now."

"If what I witnessed out there in the pasture is any indication, you're in peak form," Dan agreed, tracing the workings of my spaghetti straps. "This is all one piece? No zippers or clasps?"

I melted under the feel of his warm palms sliding over my bare shoulders, but distracting questions intruded again.

"Why haven't you updated me on the case?" I said.

Dan smoothed my hair. "You know why."

"I'm sorry if my account comes across as a list, but it's impossible to feel open when I get zero answers in return."

"Roy is still piecing things together."

"I heard Ed Emery has been cleared of wrongdoing."

"In legal terms," Dan agreed.

I waited expectantly.

With a roll of eyes, Dan said, "I'll tell you the basics. Somehow, Ed didn't foresee trouble when he confirmed Richard's worry that Angela was having an affair. Ed suspected that Frank had been set up, but had no clue Dorsett was involved. Richard updated his will, naming Frank and Carl as his beneficiaries, and stored it in a bank box with the diamonds he'd found. Dorsett apparently had the Gartlands under surveillance. My guess is he could have stopped Angela from shooting Richard, but he used the crime to blackmail her. Things spun out of control."

"I couldn't believe it when Angela told me what she'd done," I said. "Her lack of remorse. I was theorizing that if she or Nathan knew about Richard's updated will, Carl would be dead."

"It's within the realm of possibilities."

"So, maybe Richard's trek to the road wasn't about treasure. He feared for Carl's life." I closed my eyes. "If so, it's a weight lifted. I'd seen his last moments as misguided. Now there's a noble aspect to it."

"I'm glad if it helps," Dan said.

With a groan, I indicated my phone dinging every other second as my friends texted to ask for our ETA at the Grange Hall.

"Remind me why I promised to go to the Fall Fest?" I said.

"To avoid getting peppered with questions every day for however long. This way, the curiosity factor will be handled all at once."

"You conveyed the rules of engagement to everyone?" I said.

"Let's see …no questions about what you went through."

"That's a start. What else?"

"No clapping, maintain a safe distance, no eye contact." Dan paused. "This is familiar. It's how to handle a wild bear."

I cracked up. "No more of that if you have any sense."

"I will never stop trying to make you smile."

Dan looked pleased with himself as he caressed my thigh, which was readily available for caressing because my slip had sprung up to the border of wonderland. He kissed me, slow and dreamy, signaling enjoyment with a low growl when I slid my hand under his shirt to explore his flexed muscles, but then his sexy activities abruptly stopped.

"I'm not fazed by many things," Dan said, "But the trophy buck on the wall is scowling at me. I think it's an effect of the orange walls."

"*Or*, reading Raymond's journals has his voice stuck in your head," I said. "Come to think of it, further canoodling would involve showing up in town with a serious case of bed hair."

"We'll stick to the plan," Dan said. "Fall Fest. Dinner. Lots of talking. Home again. More talking. Then … we'll see."

It was almost as if he knew I was still a little off kilter.

A half hour later, when we arrived at the Fall Fest, my friends broke the rules every which way, hugging me and asking questions. Brumby took me off guard and planted a heated kiss on my lips in front of Dan. Norris pulled him away by the ear and gave him a stiff talking-to.

My *mother* showed up. Surprise!

She and Charlotte circled each other like gladiators.

"Save me," I whispered.

"Stay calm," Dan said.

I didn't recognize half of the assembled townsfolk. Some stepped up to say hello for the first time out of respect for Raymond. I knew he wouldn't mind if I rode his coattails. He was my father, and from my blue eyes to my stubborn streak, I was his daughter through and through.

About the Author

Night Shot picks up the action shortly after a string of cold cases are solved in *Kiss Your Strawberries Goodbye,* the first novel in the Sonny Littlefield mystery series. This second fast-paced book was made possible by encouragement and positive feedback from readers.

Nina's Sonny Littlefield novels are based on her own experiences as a photographer, and the years she and her husband raised sheep and horses on a small organic farm in rural Maine. During her travels to jungles, coral reefs, and other destinations, Nina is always on the lookout for ways to incorporate interesting characters and realism into her fiction. In writing the series, she draws heavily on her own brushes with disaster, moments when she pressed her luck too far, even the time she brought a tip to the police and ended up helping them solve a crime.

Nina's albums of nature audio tracks are available through Spotify, Apple Music, and other streaming services. Examples of her photos and videos are on her website, www.ninadegraff.com. Her Etsy shop is open when time allows. Her fabric designs, some of which are created with her mystery novels in mind, are available through Spoonflower.

If you enjoyed reading "Night Shot," please consider putting your review on my Amazon book page. To stay in the loop about future books you can follow me on my Facebook page, "Nina DeGraff Books."

Made in the USA
Columbia, SC
21 December 2024